WILDE STORIES 2013

WILDE STORIES 2013

The Year's Best Gay Speculative Fiction

edited by
STEVE BERMAN

LETHE PRESS
MAPLE SHADE, NEW JERSEY

Wilde Stories 2013
Copyright © 2013 Steve Berman. ALL RIGHTS RESERVED. No part of this work may be reproduced or utilized in any form or by any means, electronic or mechanical, including photocopying, microfilm, and recording, or by any information storage and retrieval system, without permission in writing from the publisher.

Published in 2013 by Lethe Press, Inc.
118 Heritage Avenue ◆ Maple Shade, NJ 08052-3018 USA
www.lethepressbooks.com ◆ lethepress@aol.com
ISBN: 978-1-59021-071-0 / 1-59021-071-9 (library binding)
ISBN: 978-1-59021-131-1 / 1-59021-131-6 (paperback)
ISBN: 978-1-59021-186-1 / 1-59021-186-3 (e-book)

These stories are works of fiction. Names, characters, places, and incidents are products of the authors' imaginations or are used fictitiously.

Set in Jenson, LemonChicken, Bookman Old Style, and Courier New.
Interior and cover design: Alex Jeffers.
Cover photo: Rob Lorino.

"Breakwater in the Summer Dark" copyright © 2012 L. Lark, first appeared in *Boys of Summer* (ed. by Steve Berman, Bold Strokes Books) / "The Keats Variation" copyright © 2012 K. M. Ferebee, first appeared in *Strange Horizons*, June 4 & 11, 2012 / "Tattooed Love Boys" copyright © 2012 Alex Jeffers, first appeared in the March 2012 issue of *GigaNotoSaurus* / "Grierson at the Pain Clinic" copyright © 2012 Richard Bowes, first appeared in *Icarus* 15 / "Wave Boys" copyright © 2012 Vincent Kovar, first appeared in *The Touch of the Sea* (ed. by Steve Berman, Lethe Press) / "Renfrew's Course" copyright © 2012 John Langan, first appeared in *Lightspeed*, June 2012 / "Wetside Story" copyright © 2012 Steve Vernon, first appeared in *Bad Valentines* (Crossroad Press) / "Next Door" copyright © 2012 Rahul Kanakia, first appeared in *Diverse Energies* (ed. Tobias S. Buckell & Joe Monti, Lee & Low Books) / "A Strange Form of Life" copyright © 2012 Laird Barron, first appeared in *Dark Faiths: Invocations* (ed. Maurice Broaddus & Jerry Gordon, Apex Publications) / "Night Fishing" copyright © 2012 Ray Cluley, first appeared in *Shadows and Tall Trees 3* (ed. by Michael Kelly, Undertow Publications) / "Sic Him, Hellhound! Kill! Kill!" copyright © 2012 Hal Duncan, first appeared in *Subterranean*, Spring 2012 / "Keep the Aspidochelone Floating" copyright © 2012 Chaz Brenchley, first appeared in *The Touch of the Sea* (ed. by Steve Berman, Lethe Press)

TABLE OF CONTENTS

INTRODUCTION—Steve Berman	ix
BREAKWATER IN THE SUMMER DARK—L Lark	3
THE KEATS VARIATION—K. M. Ferebee	29
TATTOOED LOVE BOYS—Alex Jeffers	51
GRIERSON AT THE PAIN CLINIC—Richard Bowes	83
WAVE BOYS—Vincent Kovar	97
RENFREW'S COURSE—John Langan	119
WETSIDE STORY—Steve Vernon	139
NEXT DOOR—Rahul Kanakia	157
A STRANGE FORM OF LIFE—Laird Barron	175
NIGHT FISHING—Ray Cluley	189
SIC HIM, HELLHOUND! KILL! KILL!—Hal Duncan	207
KEEP THE ASPIDOCHELONE FLOATING—Chaz Brenchley	227

Introduction

A glance at the table of contents for this edition of Wilde Stories may offer puzzlement as to the number of tales involving fisherman, oceans, and submersion. I did not intend a theme (and readers do remain on dry land for several stories). But I did conduct some research to discover the synchronism:

There are 1,968 male gods, demigods, eidolons and spirits of the sea. Or so some website informed me the other day. Some of them are quite bearish (Poseidon is so much froth and foam though why he bothers to wax, I am not sure), others more slender like the sweating Celtic divinity Grannus, who was the first male to ever seduce a hero in a spa. Idliragijenget is fortunate that the Inuits did not develop cell-phone technology, as texting his name would be so burdensome and Idli is not a very grand nickname. And Agwé is smart to wear a naval uniform and probably trolls a different American port every Fleet Week.

So perhaps the call of the sea is justifying in its temptation to gay men, after all. No reason we should not enjoy the attention of pirates and anthropomorphic squids.

Not that every story in this anthology is so whimsical, so safe. As an orientation, the attraction of men to men has never been wholly embraced. There are caveats, shibboleths, and rules. Even in 2012, when it is far easier for two men to meet, to dine out, to hold hands, to dare kiss in public, to announce to open public their love or their parting (within seconds the status on social networking sites can reflect the Sturm und Drang of ardor), there are dangers. Men are still silenced. Men perish.

But not always. There is a (sea) change in speculative fiction with the emergence of writers (no matter what their gender and identity) who purposefully choose to write stories of gay men confronting the fantastical as much as the horrific but without trapping the storyline within the confines of the characters' sexuality. So, whether that man or beast is queer is irrelevant. Books take precedence here over other media, trumping video; it is through stories, print on page, ink or bytes, where gay men can happen upon stories that speak to them without being pedantic.

Turn a page. Welcome to strange evenings. The men—be they student or inmate, vagabond or tortured soul—who inhabit them, well, they might well reveal all that is on heaven and earth and sea before the end of the tale.

STEVE BERMAN
SPRING 2013

Cody has the feeling that he shouldn't turn around. He has the feeling that if he turns around, that will be the end of everything he thought he knew about Camp Oxwater and the world, and he's not ready for that.

Breakwater in the Summer Dark
L Lark

Part I

Though Cody Simmer does not believe in the monster of Oxwater Lake, he is the fifth to see it and the first to photograph it—an out-of-focus cell phone shot that shows the beast's back breaking through a layer of summer-thick algae. This happens during his morning row with the kids from Blue Bear cabin. Afterwards they clutch each other on the lake's bank, pink-faced and screaming, "Did you see it, Cody? Did you see it? Did you see it?"

"No," he replies, pocketing the phone, and tying the rowboat to the dock without another word.

Cody Simmer is nineteen years old and he is afraid of the dark. He is also afraid of large dogs, old elevators, and the noises that ricochet through his apartment's stairwell at night.

But darkness is the worst. This is why his heart does not slow until well into the afternoon, when he forces himself to gather his laundry and drag it across the camp to the employee facilities. He is not scared of the lake because of the monster, he tells himself. He is scared because the water is deep and black.

Lark

Cody has been away from Oxwater for too long to be able to cope with mysteries.

Harris Webb is sitting cross-legged on top of the camp's only washing machine, reading a paperback copy of *The Phantom Tollbooth*. With his teeth buried in the skin of his lower lip, Harris's expression is ambiguous. He does not move when Cody drags his laundry basket into the room, and shoves three loads worth of clothes into the empty machine. Harris licks his finger, turns a page, and stares at the text as if it were revealing some devastating secret about the universe.

Cody starts a rinse cycle. The stillness of the room is put to rest by the tidal whirr of the water pumps and the sound of a quarter tumbling against the machine's walls. Only then does Harris acknowledge Cody with a nod and an impassive smile.

Cody hates when people smile at him, hates the obligation to smile back. He hopes Harris has finally given up trying to talk about what happened last summer.

"My parents said they're not letting anyone swim or go boating in the lake until the monster is dead," Harris says. The vibration of the washing machine makes his voice sound as if he is speaking through spinning fan blades.

"That's crazy. There's no monster."

"Heather Cromley says you saw it this morning."

"Heather Cromley is eight years old."

"She said you took a picture."

Cody's phone remains silent in his pocket. There is no reception at Oxwater, but occasionally he manages to pick up Wi-Fi from the general store two miles down the road. He's avoided even that indulgence for some time now, unable to cope with the reminder that his friends are enjoying their last summer before college in places where buildings have a thirteenth floor and no one carries acorns in their pocket to ward off ghosts.

Harris unfolds his legs, and drops one down against the face of the washing machine. He is composed of more protruding angles and lines than he had been last year.

"I don't know what I saw," Cody says. "And it happened too fast. I didn't get a picture."

BREAKWATER IN THE SUMMER DARK

Harris dog-ears his page, and tilts his head. The light slanting in from the window casts his face in silhouette, and Cody has to draw it from memory. Harris has a mouth like a frog, wide and jutting, and eyes that approach every object with the same tremulous concern. Harris is eighteen, one year younger than Cody, but his frame is slight and Cody often confuses him for a camper if he has his back turned.

"Well," Harris says, turning his eyes down to examine his hands. Cody had once felt one of Harris's hangnails snag in the hairs at the base of his neck, but he hasn't thought about that for ninth months, and he is not going to start dwelling on that now. "Maybe next time."

There's not going to be a next time, Cody thinks, *because there is no monster,* but feels his throat constrict because he is not entirely sure can believe the lie.

Camp Oxwater has been nestled between the base of the Pocono Mountains and the dark expanse of Oxwater Lake for thirty years. The air is thick with the scent of pinesap. Cody can feel it coating his lungs. At night, mosquitoes hum outside his cabin. He imagines breathing them in and the way they would become trapped inside his body, struggling against the muck.

Darcy Webb, Harris's mother, had been the maid of honor at his parent's wedding. As a result of this, Cody has spent every summer at Camp Oxwater since the age of eight.

As for Harris, Cody has begun to suspect that he has never left these grounds, even for school. The gulfs in his practical knowledge are frighteningly wide, and three months of each year in Cody's childhood have been spent chasing after Harris to keep him from wedging knives into electrical sockets or tossing rocks at wasp's nests.

This is why Cody does not understand Harris' statement, when the boy approaches him the following day.

"*Elasmosaurus platyurus,*" said Harris.

"God bless you."

Cody is the leader of Blue Bear cabin, Harris, Red Rabbit. These children are between eight and ten, Oxwater's youngest campers. Cody knows he has been burdened with this responsibility because of his outward projection of unending patience. Harris—well, he suspects Harris might have trouble communicating with anyone who walked the path of puberty.

Today, Blue Bear and Red Rabbit are scheduled for an arts and crafts activity together. This means that Cody and Harris will proceed to make eighteen macaroni pictures, while the campers chase each other throughout the cafeteria, yelping and belching and killing insects in staggering numbers.

"No, *Elasmosaurus platyurus*," Harris repeats, adding the last bit of dried pasta to what appears to be a giant alien scaling the side of the Empire State Building. "Otherwise known as a plesiosaurus. Estimated to have gone extinct over sixty-five million years ago. It's the same dinosaur they suspect the Loch Ness monster to be."

"You're joking."

"You've claimed many times I have no sense of humor."

Cody closes his eyes and thinks of eating Italian Ice in Central Park… and of Cynthia Harper, who might finally hook up with him now that she is moving to Boston in the fall. He thinks of how wonderful it will be to sleep in his parent's eighth floor apartment, where the risk of being eaten by a coyote in the night is negligible enough to ignore.

"Cody…"

"I heard you. I've just chosen not to let this conversation proceed."

Harris stares at him for a long moment, his expression unreadable. Cody tries and tries not to think of the way Harris's mouth had been dry and warm, the way their teeth had clicked together, and the way Harris's neck had smelled of pine and insect repellent and campfire smoke.

That week the monster is sighted for the sixth, seventh, and eighth time, though never more than a curved spine breaching the water's surface or the glimpse of an elongated neck in the distance. At night, Cody stares at the mass of grey skin captured by his cell phone camera with his finger hovering over the delete button.

It could have been anything, really, he tells himself. *Anything.*

But the campers are no longer allowed within a forty-foot radius of Oxwater Lake, and yesterday a news van arrived at the camp's entrance. Harris met them at the gate, waving violently, and gave the reporter an enthusiastic tour, ending at Oxwater Lake. Cody had been there when they'd arrived, surrounded by Blue Bear kids who'd begged to go watch the newscast.

"My research has led me to believe that the monster may in fact be the last living species of dinosaur, making it a discovery of great scientific importance," Harris says to the cameras. Both the children and reporters stare at him as if he were the sole source of stability in a rapidly tipping world.

"If I am correct, we have little to worry about. They have never been known to consume human prey, and exist primarily on small fish and cephalopods."

Later, Harris flops unto the ground next to him uninvited, hair green from the reflection of sunlight on the grass. Cody expects him to speak, but Harris presses his cheek against the soil and inhales. Cody watches his ribs expand and contract, but he's not looking anywhere else, not ever again. Around them, the babble of the children is constant and steady.

Cody misses his early summers at Oxwater—wading shin-deep in the frog ponds, and plucking bees from Harris's shoulders. Those days are gone now and must remain gone. Maybe he should write a letter to his parents, complain about the prehistoric animal rearing up out of the black water, ask to go back to New York, and then maybe Cynthia will let him fuck her, and that will forever dispel the memory of wanting to reach across his sleeping bag and move Harris's hair out of his ears.

"I'm so happy," Harris said finally, and knowing Cody will not respond adds, "About the monster."

"You're crazy."

"No," Harris says, into the earth. "I'm just not afraid."

Cody cannot trust his own memories of The Incident last year. They are uncomfortable but not unpleasant. He wants so badly to wince and cringe and retch dryly into the camp's portable toilets, but he can't.

It had happened like this: Harris was chopping vegetables in the mess hall, Cody watching over him. Harris's cooking privileges had recently been reinstated, after a two-year period of forced abstinence following an incident known as The Great Oxwater Kitchen Fire. Now they were alone and Cody was eyeing the knife, because Harris's fingers seemed too relaxed to hold a pencil. The knife tipped and wobbled over the cutting board, but it was impossible to tell the moment Harris actually cut himself.

"Cody," Harris said. He was holding the wrist of his right hand. There was a slim cut on his index finger, but his expression seemed to register no pain. He eyed the wound skeptically, as if he had never considered this issue to be within the realm of possibility.

"Idiot," Cody said, but didn't mean it. He fetched the first aid kit from the Blue Bear cabin, and bandaged Harris's finger. Blood did not bother him. Next year, he would graduate high school and study biology at Columbia, then medical school, and then he would never see Harris or his bleeding finger again.

"This next year is my last," he said, without being sure why.

"Yes," Harris continued, watching Cody's hands over his own.

"What are you going to do, Harris? You can't stay here forever."

Harris blinked. Cody watched the words DOES NOT COMPUTE flash across Harris's eyes.

"This is my home."

Cody taped the gauze in place and drew back, but Harris's eyes did not leave the place where their hands had been joined.

"Why don't you go to school? You're smart, sometimes. You can get a job. You can do anything you want."

"Anything I want," Harris repeated, his voice flat. His attention shifted to the half-sliced tomato on the countertop. "I like it here."

Cody sighed, picked up the discarded knife and began slicing.

"I do too, but this isn't real life."

By now, Cody knew that he was Harris's only link to the world beyond. Every year Cody brought pictures and playbills, Japanese candy, American comic books, cell phones, and MP3 players, and loved the way Harris's eyes widened in dumbfounded amazement.

"I like it when you're here," Harris said, disregarding Cody's second statement. He reached out and dabbed up an eyelash from Cody's cheek.

Cody's hand froze mid-motion.

"I like you," Harris said again, his bandaged finger scratching Cody's forearm. After a moment, he pressed the digit into the soft crook of Cody's elbow and left it there. Cody watched his arm lean into Harris's touch, until the pressure of his finger on Cody's veins was too much and his fingertips went slack.

BREAKWATER IN THE SUMMER DARK

The knife clattered to the countertop. Harris moved closer, and their knees knocked together. It was painful. Cody wanted to move away, but didn't. A group of older campers approached the mess hall and then continued along the path towards Oxwater Lake. When their voices faded, Harris took another step forward.

"Harris," Cody said. "I don't know…what—"

Perhaps it was because Harris had never had any friends aside from Cody, or that he'd never experienced the awkward humiliation of grade school. Maybe he was just so socially crippled that he didn't know to be nervous. Harris reached out, took Cody by the collar and pulled him in. In the end, Cody could not know who closed the distance between them, only that Harris tasted like honey graham crackers.

It was nothing like kissing Cynthia Harper…or any of the girls from high school, drunk and eager and sloppy. It was not pleasant at first. In fact, it hurt. Harris's teeth scraped across the dry skin of his lower lip, and Cody was sure the sharp edge of the bandage had nicked his cheek.

Harris drew back, as if he had only just realized what was happening, but this time Cody was sure he was the one who lurched forward, recapturing Harris's mouth mid-word. He'd never thought about Harris like this, never, even when they'd spent hours a day swimming naked in the canals that lead to Oxwater Lake, but now that it was happening, it seemed natural.

Cody and Harris, together. Like they'd always been.

"No," Cody said, although he wasn't sure why, since this felt good, and Harris's fingers had moved to his lower back and were pressing in with a force that was more than enough to remind Cody that he was *not* making out with a girl. "Stop."

Harris did, and pulled back, his mouth wet and down-turned. He did not speak, but inhaled as if about to begin a sentence. Cody waited, realizing his hands were still bobbing in the air where he had once been clutching Harris's ribs, but he couldn't drop them now without breaking the terrible stillness that stood between what had just happened and its backlash, crouched and ready in the future.

He was unable to suppress the sigh of relief that escaped his mouth when Harris turned away.

"I should have figured," the other boy muttered, "Sorry."

Lark

He did not have the chance to respond and three days later, he was on a train to Manhattan, where he could forget about Harris's warmth beneath the cold shadows of 5th Avenue.

The next day the newscasters are back because the remains of an eight-foot gar washed up on the shore of Lake Oxwater, and the wounds on its side look exactly like they were made by row after row of giant teeth. Cody only gets to see the fish because Harris wakes him up by tapping frantically on the glass of his cabin at six in the morning.

Cody hates waking up before sunrise. Pre-morning darkness is the worst; in the city, they have gurgling late night buses, and sirens, and taxis vying for parking space, but here, there is nothing but Harris's arrhythmic breathing.

"You have to see—I just want you to see, so that you—," Harris says, beckoning Cody along. "I want you to believe me."

Cody is struck with a rush of misplaced sympathy, but he's not about to let Harris know that, especially not when he's running on four hours of sleep, and he's supposed to take Blue Bear hiking up Mount Oxwater in two hours. The thought of the altitude makes him dizzy. Cody is not entirely afraid of heights, but he used to dream of the mountains, bending forward towards the camp, impossibly large.

Cody smells the fish before he sees it. He feels his stomach seize, but Harris seems unperturbed, so he is too embarrassed to voice his discomfort.

The fish is tipped on its side, mouth open. The rising sun hits its scales at an angle, and Cody is temporarily blinded. He stumbles, and reaches out to grasp Harris by the forearm. Harris does not pull away, but continues walking, oblivious.

"Anything could have done that," Cody whispers. He hasn't yet let go of Harris's arm, but the movement would be too obvious now. They remain connected, watching two men in lab coats haul the fish unto a hospital stretcher. The mattress sags under its weight; Cody had not seen the chunk missing from its torso until now.

"They say it was bitten by something much bigger than it is," Harris says, and bends his elbow so that Cody's finger slides into the crook and stays there. Harris does not seem to notice. His eyes are exuberant. "It's amazing."

Breakwater in the Summer Dark

This time, Cody does not argue.

Cody masturbates unenthusiastically, thighs sore from the day's earlier hike up the mountain. Then he sleeps. Next to him, his uncharged cell phone sits on the nightstand.

He dreams. At first, about New York City, feeling claustrophobic beneath the shadows that fall on his back and shoulders. He dreams about Cynthia Harper's tits, and the frozen lemonade kiosks in Central Park, and then about Lake Oxwater.

In the dream, he is stumbling down the fishing pier with Harris's hand clutching the back of his shirt. He dreams about Harris pressing into him over the black water, Harris's breath warm on the skin behind Cody's ear. The other boy's face is dark. The shadows beneath his brow and chin seem too heavy. Cody leans in, searching for a hint of reflected light in Harris's eyes, but finds none. It's so unsettling that it makes the moment Harris lurches forward and pushes his mouth against Cody's seem mundane in comparison.

It doesn't hurt, like it did in the real world. In fact, Cody feels nothing, aside from the cold wetness of Harris's tongue, and curls of water vapor rising into his clothing and hair.

After a moment, Harris draws back. "You shouldn't be afraid," he says. It's a dreamvoice, bouncing joyfully between Cody's ears.

"The monster isn't real."

"I'm not talking about the monster," Harris says, but that doesn't matter, because a shape has unfurled out of the water behind him. He does not seem to notice, although the water running off the animal's muzzle showers down onto his hair.

Cody wants to run, take off down the old fishing pier, back to Blue Bear Cabin, where he can fall asleep listening to the long sleep-breaths of the children in the next room. He gains the courage to test his legs, feels his calves tighten in preparation, but Harris's grip on his arms does not falter.

Harris kisses him again. This time it is soft and brief, and over before Cody has a chance to react. The monster tilts its head down to watch, but makes no other motion.

"Don't be afraid," Harris says again.

Cody, for a moment, believes him.

Lark

Cody hears the steady tone of the generators in the distance, and a series of intermittent thumps that are too loud to come from the raccoons that come to steal sequins and glitter glue from the storage cabins.

He has been lying in bed, staring at an empty patch of sky through the window. Cody hooks his fingers over the window ledge and pulls himself up. Outside in silhouette is the hunched figure of Harris, dragging behind him the rowboat that had recently been placed into storage.

Cody indulges in a long moment of hesitation. There is no reason to try to stop him, he figures, even though he is already searching beneath his bed for a pair of flip-flops.

There is nothing in the lake, he knows, though an hour of every evening has been spent staring at a grainy photograph on his cellphone screen. Harris will ride around all night, and maybe that will finally quell his obsession with the monster, and life around Oxwater can return to normal.

"I hate you so much," Cody whispers, shutting the cabin door behind him.

Harris doesn't notice him until he is pulling the boat up to the edge of the lake.

"Hello," he says, unexcited, as if he'd known Cody would be there all along.

"Hello," Cody says. Harris's skin is ruddy from too much sun, but the whites of his eyes are like beacons in the darkness. "I thought you might need help."

"I don't." Harris lifts a cord that's been dangling from his neck. On the other end is the rusted key that Cody knows opens the lock to the storage shed where the boat is kept. "I've been doing this every night, all summer."

Cody helps him to push the boat out regardless. Harris settles into his seat, pulling a paperback book from the waistband of his jeans. It's too dark to read the title, but Cody recognizes the cover. It's *A Wrinkle in Time*—Cody read it in elementary school, but he can't remember anything about it.

Harris makes Cody row, of course, and remains silent until they travel far into the lake. He reaches down, flounders about along the boat's bottom, and emerges with a can of anchovies. Cody watches him drop them one by one into the lake. The cradle of mountains around them amplifies the sound they make as they hit the water.

Cody doesn't bother to ask. He knows he can't grapple with Harris's logic.

"Aren't you my friend anymore?" Harris asks, propping his head against the palm of his hand.

"Of course I am. Don't be ridiculous."

Harris is silent for a long time, staring out at the water's surface. "I was glad about the monster. I thought it would give me an excuse to talk to you again."

"You don't need an excuse."

"Yes, I do," Harris says, with such authority that Cody doesn't bother to question him.

He leans back into the boat, and feels it rock as he shifts his weight. He wants to tell Harris to move his foot, to turn the boat around, to crack a genuine smile for the first time all summer, but he *can't*, physically can't. He feels like he's swallowed a mouthful of lake water and now there is algae coating his throat and lungs, and if he tries to speak, it'll just pitter out of his mouth ineffectually.

"Cody," Harris says and leans forward. Cody feels his body respond involuntarily before realizing that Harris's eyes are not fixed on him but on a spot just over his left shoulder. Harris attempts to repeat his name, but it comes out as a mess of vowels.

Cody has the feeling that he shouldn't turn around. He has the feeling that if he turns around, that will be the end of everything he thought he knew about Camp Oxwater and the world, and he's not ready for that.

Across the boat, Harris is grappling with the oar. Cody reaches out for his own, but his grip falters when the boat rises and tips to the side. It takes him a moment to steady himself, and give the boat one powerful heave, but by that time, the water has stilled.

It doesn't matter. They row until the boat lurches against the banks of Lake Oxwater, and then they keep rowing until they realize they've hit the shore, and stumble out of the boat, holding each other by the elbows. Their run is directionless until one of them locks onto a faint sodium light in the distance, and they tumble towards it together, finally collapsing into the grass, muscles spasming in odd syncopation.

Lark

"I didn't actually see it," Cody says, once he's evened his breathing. His leg is still wedged beneath Harris's, and he can feel the other boy's calves tense. The sound in his ears reminds him of driving too fast with the windows down.

"I didn't see anything."

For a long time, Harris does not speak. His skin looks sallow in the yellow light, and there is a moth sifting through his hair. Cody wants to take back what he's said, wants to erase the look of betrayal from Harris's eyes, but he's been hurtling down this path for so long, he'd not sure he can turn around.

Harris never replies. Instead, he stands, brushes the dirt from his jeans, and disappears into the unearthly darkness of the camp.

The fear—which he has lived with for so long now, that is seems powerful and alive—crawls back to settle in Cody's throat.

The following morning, Kimberly Stout goes missing.

She is a ten year old from Green Goose. Cody can't recall her face—by their second week at Oxwater, every kid resembles the same greasy, devastatingly sunburned creature—but he knows she kept her hair in a braid. She wore pink shoelaces, and refused to use a fork.

Peter Bentley is her cabin leader. Cody finds Peter lingering in front of the mess hall, holding a lit flashlight, despite the fact that the sun has fully risen. He looks like he's just witnessed a car accident.

"One of the other girls said she saw Kimberly heading for the lake. You don't think—?" he begins, but interrupts himself to listen to a twig snapping in the distance. Cody knows Darcy Webb led a search party into the woods three hours ago, but the counselors have been ordered to stay at the camp and watch over the children.

"No," Cody says. "That's impossible."

He is lying, but as it turns out, he's right.

Kimberly Stout strolls into the mess hall that evening, interrupting a solemn dinner shared by the campers, parents, and volunteer rescue workers from the town below. She is soaking wet, barefoot, and there is a mint green tendril of duckweed in her bangs. Her skin is faintly blue, but she is smiling.

"That was awesome!" she says, oblivious to the dumbfounded stares of everyone around her. Cody finds Harris's face in the crowd, and sees that he has hooked his index finger over his bottom lip and is also grinningly wildly.

The girl is not given the chance to speak again, because her parents descend on her at that moment. They are weary and smell of liquor and the cheap detergent they use on airline blankets. Cody has met them before. Kimberly's father is in politics. Her mother writes religious novels. Cody does not think they are going to be very happy that their daughter was kidnapped by a monster.

"I saw—" Kimberly begins, but her mother clamps a hand over her mouth.

"Not until we speak to a lawyer," she says, picking a mayfly out of Kimberly's ear. "When we enrolled our daughter into this camp, no one felt the need to mention there was a *creature* living in the lake."

The entire Webb family is visibly rattled, except for Harris. The threat of legal action has done nothing to smother the delight in his eyes. He is staring at Kimberly with what Cody might misinterpret as romantic love, if he did not know Harris so well.

"Kimberly," Harris calls, as her parents begin to usher her out of the cafeteria.

"It was amazing!" she yells back.

Cody does not understand, but Harris obviously does.

He turns to Cody and raises a fist in victory.

At night, there are noises.
Or wails, more properly.

Oxwater has always had its fair share of strange sounds, but none like this—long and deep and lonely, like a voice from a dream in the moment before waking.

Cody has one of those moments we have all had. It goes like this: Something bad happens and you move on, because you don't have a choice but to keep on waking up and brushing your teeth and walking out into the sunlight with your hand pulled over your eyes. Something bad happens, and you think you'll feel something, but you don't.

Then one day, you're standing beneath the showerhead, and you feel as though your heart is struggling to restart after years of deep stillness, but by now, the period in which you had to react has come and gone. It's

Lark

too late to scream and cry and beg, so you just stand there with the water heavy on your hair and shoulders, unable to move.

Somehow, you step out of the shower and into the bathroom. Somehow, you wipe away the steam on the mirror and comb your hair, and then put on a shirt, pants, and a matching pair of shoes. You stumble out into the world, and life proceeds as usual.

But you're not the same, and you can't say why or how.

You might not even be there at all.

As Cody reaches for the doorknob of Red Rabbit Cabin, he is unsure as to whether or not his palm will actually grip the metal or if it will pass through it, useless and intangible. But it's cool and firm beneath his hand.

Cody turns the knob and pushes.

The room seems empty. Cody knows the campers are out on horseback riding lesson, but Harris is not immediately visible. Cody catches the other boy's reflection first, shirtless and barefoot, hair damp from the shower. His spine looks knobby and prehistoric beneath his skin.

"Hey," Cody says before Harris turns around. He knows Harris may be thin, but he's strong. "I think we should go out on the water again," Cody goes on, when Harris refuses to fill the silence. "I want to look for the monster. I lied. I did take a picture of it."

Harris moves out of the bathroom, silently gathering his shirt and shoes. There is an open book on the nightstand, facedown and pressed flat, tension across the wear on the spine. It's *The Lion, the Witch, and the Wardrobe*, which Cody has never read.

"Are you even listening to me?"

Harris bends down to tie his shoes, his hair brushing against Cody's shin.

"I'm confused."

"So am I," Cody mutters, because Harris's forehead is resting on the side of his knee, and neither one of them seems to be making an attempt to move.

Harris stands, his body freckled with rusty water. Cody stares at the mosquitos trapped in the window screen.

"I'm sorry," he gasps, suddenly forgetting why he came. This is stupid, but Harris's breath is audible and comforting, like rain sliding down an aluminum roof. Cody wonders what it'd be like to press his ear against

BREAKWATER IN THE SUMMER DARK

Harris's chest—wonders if he would hear Harris's heart bellowing against his ear like the monster does in the night, deep and filled with strange longing.

"S'okay," Harris mutters, tugging self-consciously at the towel on his waist. Above them, the cabin's ceiling fan spins on high and Harris's arms are covered in gooseflesh.

"I just wanted to tell you that we should look for the monster again."

Harris takes another step forward. He is close enough to touch Cody's face and so he does. His eyes remain flat, as if his hand has acted autonomously and his brain has not had the chance to react. Cody imagines he can still feel the scar on Harris's finger; a slice of sunken skin that will stay with him forever.

He's unsure whether he's about to start sobbing or laughing, so instead he leans forward and presses his mouth against Harris's. It is not a kiss, not really. They remain close-mouthed and awkward, but he can feel Harris's pulse against his bottom lip.

"I thought," Harris begins, without moving. It's good to feel Harris speak against his mouth. He tastes like mint toothpaste.

"Yeah," Cody says.

"So?"

"So."

Harris kisses him properly. Or at least, he attempts to.

"Not so hard."

"Sorry." Harris pulls away.

Cody is left standing with his mouth open, listening to insects slapping against the windowpane.

Harris is still sunburned. There is a strip of skin on his nose, curling back like a white snail, and for a moment, Cody is afraid that this is rejection. That he will never get the satisfaction of peeling away the dried skin from Harris's shoulders.

But Harris's eyes are warm, like they were the first time Cody met him. Back when they'd just been campers and Cody had spent the first week homesick and terrified of the nighttime bear rumbles from the forest. Harris slept on the top bunk, and at night he would let his upper body dangle down and tell Cody that bears mostly ate plants anyway, and there were no monsters out there.

At least, there hadn't been at the time.

"Why now?" Harris mutters.

"I don't know," Cody says, which is the truth. "It's the monster, maybe. Possibly. I want to go look for it again, and we might both get eaten."

"Not eaten. Drowned, potentially and accidentally," Harris clarifies.

Cody kisses him. This time, it feels good.

Harris's chest is damp and bony, and Cody presses his palms flat against it, feeling Harris's heart flit against his skin like a wounded sparrow. He is vaguely aware that Harris's penis is half-hard beneath his towel, but his brain is not entirely certain what to do with this information. It's one thing to kiss another boy, but he hasn't thought beyond that.

He's fooled around with girls before. Sorta. In theory, this should be easier, but he can't seem to make his hands slide any lower. Harris is still kissing him, sloppy and enthusiastic, but his shoulders are stiff and Cody can practically feel the muscles in his back, locked and rigid against his spine.

He hadn't expected Harris to be the reticent one, but now it seems obvious. Of course, Harris would force him to take the next step. Harris is a bastard, but Cody is tired of being afraid.

He reaches down to cup Harris's erection in his palm.

"Ah," Harris gasps and jumps back, which was not exactly the reaction Cody had been hoping for. The towel has slipped low on his waist, and Cody's brain settles uselessly on the muscles of Harris's too-narrow hips.

"Sorry, I'm sorry," Cody says, as he watches a swell of terror rise in Harris's face. His stance is hunched and unassertive, water dripping from his bangs to his eyebrows. Cody struggles with a moment of ground-tilting vertigo.

"Let's, uh, let's plan for tonight," Harris says.

Cody feels the world around him creak and moan, sagging under pressure.

Heather Cromley appears an hour later, beating on the door of Red Rabbit cabin with a pink fist. Cody curses into Harris's shoulder, because he's finally coaxed the other boy unto the sheets with him, and they're studying a map of Lake Oxwater with their heads leaning against the same bedpost, the smell of oak rubbing off on their hair.

Heather Cromley stumbles into the room, and folds over, hands balanced on her knees. Her breath sounds like a door being ripped from its hinges, and her jeans are covered with stinkweed. Heather Cromley's mother sends her to Oxwater with expensive madras shorts and white sunglasses, but by the second week, she's always managed to compile a closet full of clothing borrowed from the boys in the next cabin.

"Mr. Cody," she says, "We've been looking for—did you hear? It's here!"

"What's here?" Cody says, hoping an eight-year-old can't interpret the pink streak across his cheeks and nose. Thankfully, Harris has dressed, but his lips are bruised like he's been eating grape popsicles.

"The monster! It's here, it's dead, and it's here!"

The muscles in Cody's thighs give out, but he scrambles after Harris, barefoot and blinded by the sunlight.

Cody smells the monster before he sees it.

It is not what he expects, a mixture of brine and rubbery fat, but rather a bitter smell like a blood orange and not entirely unpleasant. By the time he finally catches up to Harris, Cody is scratched and bleeding from the overgrown hedges on the path to Oxwater Lake, and the bottoms of his feet ache from the burning soil.

Harris looks worse for wear. There are grass shavings in his toenails, and he is blinking down at them, rubbing two fingers along his left brow. He does not look up as Cody approaches, and drops a hand on his shoulder, which he does more to steady himself than to comfort Harris.

"It's dead," Harris mutters, but Cody can already see that.

The creature alternately heaves and shrivels. There must be bacteria multiplying in its stomach. It is massive and purple, neck spiraled counterclockwise against its back. Cody does not want to look into its exposed eye; it is circular and lidless, the color of watered-down lemonade.

He turns back to Harris to say, "I think I owe you an apology," but the boy is already gone, lumbering uphill with his hands in his pockets.

Part II

Harris does not return to the lake, not even to watch a group of graduate students haul the monster onto a giant blue tarp and then drag it into a U-Haul truck. In the sun, the monster has pruned and turned a speckled pink. The skies have blackened with crows and vultures, screeching and clobbering each other in mid-air, while a student waits with a long-handled broom to shoo them off the carcass when they get too close.

Cody, on the other hand, cannot seem to pull himself away from the lake. This is all well and good for the kids in Blue Bear Cabin, who have eschewed all their other activities in favor of a daily vigil around the monster. Cody has never seen them so quiet. They stand shoulder-to-shoulder, forming a long row, still and silent.

"What is it?" Heather Cromley asks him, her eyes hidden beneath the shadow of a baseball cap. She sounds older, as if witnessing this spectacle has unleashed some adult understanding that had been cocooned inside of her all along.

"I don't know," Cody says, which is the truth.

They fall quiet again, listening to the asthmatic gasps of gasses shifting inside the animal's stomach.

No one knows, and tomorrow, the monster will be gone from Lake Oxwater forever.

Harris does not say anything when Cody follows him into the woods, the light of their campfire trembling in the distance. Harris has never missed a campfire; Cody used to like watching him handle roasted marshmallows with the tips of his fingers.

"Where are you going?" Cody calls out. The woods are dark, and full of bears and snakes and other terrible life forms. All around him, he hears branches creak and snap. "Hey, man! Stop!"

Since the monster's death, Harris has been content enough to offer his mouth up for kissing, but he's refused to speak about Oxwater Lake, and shies away whenever Cody's hands wander below his waist. *I really should have figured,* Cody thinks. With his narrow shoulders, and children's books, and the way his eyes wobbled in the sunlight, Harris has always seemed entirely asexual.

Ahead of him, Harris finally comes to a stop and slumps against a tree trunk, pushing his sneakers beneath a pile of last year's fallen leaves. He does not look up when Cody approaches, swinging a branch ahead of him to tear down the cobwebs.

Harris's face is hidden by turquoise shadow.

"I'm sorry," he mutters. His voice does not sound human. Cody thinks of a wounded dog, grunting and struggling in the dirt. Cody is afraid of big dogs. Cody is afraid of darkness, and car accidents, and earthquakes, but he thinks of the monster now, bloated and bruised on the shoreline, and only feels sad.

"Don't be."

"I just...I think..." Harris begins, but can't finish.

Cody drops his hand down on Harris's neck, cradling the base of his skull. "Don't be," he repeats. "I understand."

It's because he loves the darkness, Cody realizes. This happens late in the night, as his pulse finally falls in line with the rhythm of the croaking frogs outside. Harris loves the mystery. It is why he won't leave this place, with its bottomless lakes and its nightmarish forests, and the monsters that whip and churn beneath the water. He regards the civilization outside in the same way he watches a storm collecting along the horizon—a rush of electricity and light that will cast away the hidden places of the world.

Harris never actually wanted to see the monster, Cody knows. Harris just wanted to know it was there, to feel his heart overflow with desperate happiness, because it meant Camp Oxwater still kept secrets from him.

For the first time in Cody's memory, the campers beg and whine until someone drives into town and picks up a dozen newspapers from the general store. Everyone is desperate for news on the monster—the palm-sized articles that appear on the third page of the local section, detailing the latest scientific findings from the university.

Only the Red Rabbit kids are forbidden to handle this literature. Harris performs regular raids on their cabin when they disappear for archery or horseback riding, scooping them up in one shot and waddling to the dumpsters. Cody catches him there, standing in repose, as if awaiting instructions.

"What are you doing?" Cody snaps, and watches Harris's spine tilt slowly to the left.

Harris refuses to answer him.

Lark

That evening, the monster is spotted for the twelfth time. Cody has to ask Harris's mother to confirm the story three times before he begins to make sense of it. This is what happened:

Peter Bentley and Bree Watts, leaders of Green Goose and Purple Porcupine respectively, had snuck down to the edge of Lake Oxwater to engage in what Darcy Web had insisted were the most heinous of activities.

"He had his hand on her breasts," she hisses, and Cody decides not to mention that he's been trying to get into her son's pants for the last two weeks. "The thing rears up out of the water behind them in one swoop. Bree had my husband's camera with her, and she managed to snap a photo. Here."

Cody takes the Polaroid. He does not mention that this is not the first photograph of the monster in existence. It is better than his, showing the long neck of the monster parallel to the tree line. Harris will be so pleased.

"You know what I think?" Darcy says, reaching out to take Cody's wrist in her hand. Her hands are callused from years of gardening gloves, and firewood, and glue.

"I think there's a lot of monsters out there in the lake. I never told anyone this, not even Harris, but—I swear, sometimes, I hear them call out to each other in the night. They are lonely sounds, and lately louder and more desperate. I think they know one of them is missing. I think they're looking for him."

Cody pushes the Polaroid back into Darcy's hand, and folds her fingers over it. Cody can remember when Darcy Webb looked like a supermodel from the sixties, tanning topless on the dock in a pair of over-sized white-rimmed sunglasses. Now, her clothes are bleached from insect repellent and Cody is certain that she has forgotten how to apply mascara, but he wishes he could keep his hands suspended over hers for just a moment longer.

"Oh, Cody," she says. Her breath is cold against his cheek. "Please make sure Harris doesn't go out on the lake at night. You're the only one he'll listen to."

Cody thinks of the bronze key, still dangling from Harris's throat. "Sure thing," he lies.

BREAKWATER IN THE SUMMER DARK

"We're breaking out of here," Cody whispers through the screen. Harris is staring up at him from beneath the comforter, a cloth mask pushed up on his forehead. When they'd shared a cabin, Harris couldn't sleep with the lights on, but Cody was too terrified to leave them off. Harris had worn the mask in compromise.

"Grab your shoes."

Cody watches Harris stumble out of his bed and feel for his sandals in the dark. The camp has been in chaos since the latest monster sighting, and they have not spoken all day. From outside the cabin, Cody cannot tell whether or not the curve to Harris's lips is a grin or a scowl. It doesn't matter. By the time he appears outside, shrugging on a white t-shirt, Cody has covered Harris's mouth with his own.

"You seem optimistic," Harris mutters.

Cody doesn't quite understand, but he's enjoying the kissing and the way Harris's eyes seem to retain the reflection of his lantern, even after he's turned away. "I thought you'd be happy." Cody's hand travels down Harris's breastplate. The key is there, heart-warmed and heavy. "You were so upset when you thought it had died."

"It *did* die," Harris says, which Cody supposes is true. "Of course there are more out there. They must mate, Cody. They must reproduce in some way."

Cody knows this. He's going to study biology at Columbia. He wouldn't even believe in monsters if he had not seen them for himself.

"Then, what—?"

Harris kisses him to shut him up. It's not fair play, but Cody lets it happen. He takes Harris by the wrist and tugs him in the direction of the storage cabinet. Together, they pull the boat down towards Oxwater Lake, switching off at intervals.

It is an unusually cool night. The scent of pine, crisp and antiseptic, fills Cody with complete gratification. Even the sky is winter-clear. He has to squint against the stars whenever he looks up.

The lake is flat. Harris rolls his jeans to the knee and drags the boat in. For a moment, watching water creep up the fraying strands of Harris's pants, Cody thinks he will never be able to leave this place. Not if this boy is here, reading and dreaming and sneaking out in the middle of the night to search for monsters he has always known were there.

"Let's go," Harris says, and they do.

Lark

The sky is reflected perfectly on the surface of the lake. Cody has to fight a wave of vertigo, hand heavy on Harris's knee. It feels like they are encased in a shell of stars and infinite nothingness.

"Don't be afraid," Harris says, not for the first time.

"I'm not," Cody says and means it.

They do not spot the monster that night or the next. It doesn't matter. After their third excursion, they haul the boat back into the storage shed, and Harris takes Cody's hands. For a long time, he does nothing, staring down at the places where their calluses rub together and flake off into the soil below.

"Do you hear that?" Harris says quietly. Cody's nose brushes against his cheek.

"It takes him a moment, and he feels it first—a low-frequency vibration in his jaw and eardrums. Cody thinks of the electrical wiring outside his window in New York, or the potential energy suspended in the air a moment before lightning hits.

"Is it them?" he whispers. The sound burrows into the valves of his heart, deep and lonely. Darcy Webb was right. This is a mourning call, an expression of grief. He has never heard it before, but it must be embedded deeply into his genetic code, his most primitive of memories.

Harris says instead, "I'm not ready to leave this place," and punctuates the sentence by kissing the crook of Cody's mouth. "But I may be, one day."

Cody understands. He doesn't think he's quite interested in summer courses, anyway.

They walk without speaking, stepping carefully over luminescent white stones and crickets and candy bar wrappers. Owls watch from overhead, faces flat and cruel and beautiful. Harris's hair is damp beneath Cody's fingers.

They come to the edge of the forest, and then Harris kisses him in earnest, placing his palms on Cody's stomach. After a moment, Harris tugs the shirt off him and flattens it against the ground. He allows himself to be guided down, feeling dried grass crackle beneath them. Harris's mouth finds the untouched places behind his ears, along his jawline, his Adam's apple.

BREAKWATER IN THE SUMMER DARK

Cody Simmer and Harris Webb are not afraid because they are together, clinging to one another in the darkness, while the voice of a lonely monster winds its way through the woods around them.

The hospital to which the dormitory was attached was called after a saint with such a crook: St. Crix, who had been martyred among the fields by Roman soldiers. The method of his martyrdom had not been told to Keats; it was thought to be too gruesome. He dreamed of the saint naked, with his stomach stitched, like a surgical patient. The stitches were neat and perfect, done in black thread. St. Crix smiled at Keats and raised his curving staff. He said, Little lamb, I will shepherd thee when thou art dead and buried. What about now? Keats wanted to ask, but he could not speak in his dreams.

THE KEATS VARIATION
K. M. Ferebee

There was a ghost in the hospital. They had told Keats this. "They" were the other boys, the older boys, who lived like him in the apprentices' dormitory attached to the hospital, but higher up, on the second floor. Bish, Taylor, and Barrie: larger boys who came and went clattering loudly on the dormitory's wooden stairs. They had served, each of them, as an apprentice under the surgeons for two years already, and told stories of malformed infants, amputations, massive wounds that emptied all a man's blood from his body across the floor, so that you must needs wade through it to reach the exit and it lingered, black and sticky, on your boots and under your fingernails. You would not believe, Barrie said, you would not believe how much blood is in a man.

Keats was quite ready to believe it. He believed most things at this time. He had come, at the credulous age of thirteen, from the country, where men did not tell so many lies, or they were a different sort of lies, not fat distended fancies like soap bubbles that rise from a washer-man's wand and swell and swell the expanse of their shining hollow bodies till they burst and you are left with just a thin wet sour residue. Country lies were smaller, harder. They had substance, which you sometimes had to fight to figure. They might be a truth about some other thing. A fairy man in the lane taught the miller's wife to dig, she said, for buried treasure, which she found on his instruction but which come the morning was not lapis and diamonds but a felt hat filled with mouldy leaves. Mrs. Hayscomb saw the Devil out walking; she said he wore the fine black coat of a merchant and smiled as he passed and had a white crown round his head like a saint. Keats had seen the mouldy leaves; he had touched and smelt them. They had left damp flecks on his fingers. They had reminded him of well water pulled from far, far down in the clammy pit where moss fronded wild in silent darkness and, one suspected, old things lived. Those leaves had brought the miller luck. His wife had cooked them in a pot-au-feu and eaten them and given birth to three children, white-skinned infants with flat solemn eyes like coins, who never cried. Everyone said in Eastsake that these were fairy children and the fairies would be back for them; and that the miller, if he'd drive a hard bargain, could do well out of it. He could get a cartload of gold, or a saucepan that never emptied, or a shuttle that threw itself through the shed, to do the weaving. There was no limit to what he might expect, in exchange for these children. So there had been treasure in the leaves; that was a truth.

And as for the Devil—Keats himself had seen him, or something of his nature, or not quite seen. That had been in the purple part of the night, in summer, when heat bowed the high barley in submission and the earth was an ember into the evening, when the glassy sun had gone and night birds called throughout the cooler air. Keats, coming homewards, had cut through the barley. The stalks were higher than him. They had a sweet white woody scent. The long leaves had a language, snaps and whispers, over his head. He held his hands crossed on his chest and whispered a song, a song about the Apostles, a song to summon angels to your bedside. He was careful to tread only where he knew the path. But he took not care enough, for soon he was lost and he heard a footfall behind him. A step. A stop. A hard dry cough. A hesitation. His heart crawled and stuttered. He did not turn to see. Slowly, slowly, he walked forwards. The listless barley shed long shadows. The shallow dark seemed living. In back of him the sound again commenced. Something striking earth, a slow and laboured step, like one leg dragging. A ragged, monstrous breath. He ran, then; his nerve broke, and he raced ahead. Still he could hear it following him: its long strides, its effortful gasps, the air in its unseen lungs rattling, till he was free of the fields and could see the lamplight leaching towards him from his aunt's front window. He reached it. This was the radius of

THE KEATS VARIATION

his safety. When he told the story to his aunt, she did not disbelieve him. So now you've seen the Devil, is what she said. As the days progressed he came to accept this explanation. His unknowingness diminished. To his school friends he said, I saw the Devil. The statement assumed a quality of truth: of definition, which, after all, was truth's right hand.

So the idea of how much blood was in a man did not overmuch stretch his imagination. Nor the stories Bish told about babies born back to front, or with fins instead of hands, or the woman whom, he said, they had cut open—he clearly relished the cutting-open; when he reached this part of the story his eyes lit up and he rubbed, one against the other, his thin white hands—only to see that there was inside of her a number of strange objects: Roman coins, and the stump of a candle, and a soap-stone figure in the shape of a lamb. They had sewed her up, but she died later—not from sepsis, but from starvation. She would not eat meat, milk, potatoes; she could not be sustained. She wanted only to swallow down these certain odd antiques. But the doctors would not let her. Her wanting killed her, Bish said; she wanted it to end.

It? Keats asked.

Bish spread his hands, bored, expressive. It, all of this.

I don't understand.

No, you wouldn't yet, you're just a squeaker. A little country rat of a thing.

Barrie joined in. Hallo, country rat. Said your catechism yet today?

Catechism sounded like cachexia, the kind of slow sickness that Bish's woman had died of, the wasting disease. Keats practiced his catechism daily. He had promised his aunt when he left Eastsake. Besides, he had a fear of the Devil. You had to do certain things, say certain things, and this kept the Devil at a distance. A distance greater than six or seven paces, a distance that the saints maintained, so that you would not hear the Devil's hacking cough or heavy footsteps, so that you would not hear him drag his leg.

I don't know why you make fun, Keats said.

No, Bish said, you wouldn't yet. Squeaker.

And so on and on this game went.

There were no other apprentices of Keats's age; he was quite the youngest. It amused Bish and Barrie and Taylor to call him names, to make fun of his country faith, his country way of speaking, to keep sometimes in the dark at the side of a hallway, at night when he had thought them all in bed, and reach out suddenly to grab hold of his wrist or a fistful of hair at the side of his head. This they called a mousetrap. I've caught a country mouse, Barrie had said triumphantly, the first time it happened; a country mouse in a trap. The coinage had stayed.

Keats had learned to keep still, not to fight his capture, though the shock of it turned his heart to a struck church bell. The leaden echoes of its reverberating could be felt throughout his tired body. His response was to clench the muscles round his mouth and think hard about large bright things. He pictured saints the size of houses, huge towering men who shed a soft, tawny light from their hands and robes and heads. He pictured angels, white entities without faces who, suspended on their opalescent feathers, hung in the cramped space of the hallway. And when he had scampered off, often after an indifferent beating, and was safe inside his room again, he would say the song he had been taught in the country, asking these saints and angels to stand round his bed. He never saw them, but sometimes he suspected their presence: when he woke up warm on winter mornings and saw scratch-marks on the floorboards where perhaps some saint's hard shoe or shepherd's crook had scuffed them. The hospital to which the dormitory was attached was called after a saint with such a crook: St. Crix, who had been martyred among the fields by Roman soldiers. The method of his martyrdom had not been told to Keats; it was thought to be too gruesome. He dreamed of the saint naked, with his stomach stitched, like a surgical patient. The stitches were neat and perfect, done in black thread. St. Crix smiled at Keats and raised his curving staff. He said, Little lamb, I will shepherd thee when thou art dead and buried. What about now? Keats wanted to ask, but he could not speak in his dreams. He was too transfixed, always, his tongue silenced by dread.

There had long been some legends, part of the city of Ludminster's general lore, of St. Crix lingering in the halls of his hospital: to heal the sick, to dispense mercy, to direct the souls of the dead. But the ghost about which Bish, Barrie, and Taylor had begun to tell stories was an innovation. Keats perceived that it might not exist. It was the sort of thing that these other boys might do—seize upon his fear of the darkness and invent for it a bespoke creature, a demon cut whole-cloth to suit. He did not like to think so badly of them, despite their lies; and anyways

THE KEATS VARIATION

he believed that there was in all people something tending to be true. There was this magnetic force; you could not resist it; it warped your stories northwards, in spite of you. So he listened at night, when they were all gathered in the dormitory kitchen round a candle, as Barrie and Taylor and Bish related tales that grew ever more extravagant. Barrie, a solidly built boy with auburn ringlets and an India-ink gaze, cupped his hands over the candle. Light leaked through his fingers from the flame, casting seaside shadows on the wall, wandering underwater shapes.

Theatrically he said, In the dead of winter, there rode into St. Crix Hospital—

Rode? Keats questioned.

Yes, it was in those days.

All right.

There rode a soldier. His horse was black; it smoked with hellfire.

A bit rich, Bish muttered under his breath.

I heard that. Shut it.

I was only saying.

Barrie cleared his throat. It smoked with hellfire, he said again. Its rider slid to the snowy ground. His blood turned it red. Blood-red, from the gash in his belly where a bayonet had been. The soldier's guts spilled out—

But they didn't really, Keats reasoned. Or else he'd be dead.

He held them in. Like, thus. Barrie demonstrated.

Anyway, Bish said, he'll be dead in a minute. Wait and see. That's the best bit.

Barrie let Bish tell that part of the story. Spectacular deaths were Bish's talent. Pale hair sparked by firelight, light eyes gleaming, he leant in. By this point in the tale, the soldier had reached the operating theatre, where a noble surgeon tried to save him. And then, Bish said, he saw the soldier's immortal soul rise from his body. It was a bloody thing, all blackened and hideous, naught but bones, no flesh on it.

No flesh on it, Taylor echoed. He was not, of the three, the most inventive. But he embellished the description: And gaping sockets, where the eyes had been.

Staring out, Bish said, towards their damnation. Bish was alive with pleasure at the image; his small lithe body shuddered. He said, The surgeon's sight grew dim! He thought he would faint, for standing before him was—*death!* The darkest angel! A horrible figure, scythed and grim!

Barrie added, And behind him followed all of hell. An awful scene. Seas made of the bloody hearts of men, still beating. Heaps of bones that writhed and clattered, the howling of the damned calling out—

What did they call out? Keats asked, curious.

They called out: James Keats, we're coming for you… Barrie drew out the vowels, darkened his voice to a wail, grabbed at Keats's shoulders. Keats, ineffectual, tried to shove him off.

That is not what they called out. I was not there. That is not true.

Oh, well, they might have done. Had you been there.

Bish and Taylor were laughing soundlessly behind their hands. Keats was angry, but he did not show it. He said, So what happened then?

Barrie shrugged. The soldier would not go with him. The soldier said, Death, I will not go with you, to get my heart sucked out in hell, to suffer forever and ever in pain and blood and so forth, in endless burning. Instead I will stay and give a taste of hell to mortal souls who remain, that they might fear your eternal horrible approach and repent of their sins.

How about you, Keats? Taylor asked, grabbing onto Keats's arm and twisting it round so that it hurt. Do you repent your sins? You will; you will repent them.

That story ended with Keats's hand held above the candle till tears streamed down his face and the skin on his palm swelled into white hilltops: a new, painful, penitent landscape. He choked out sins, some real and some imagined, writhing like a hooked fish while Barrie said, No, I think he is a sinner, I think that he has further sins.

Keats confessed that he hated God, that he had impure thoughts about women and about men, that he disbelieved in the Devil and in hell, that he had often wished their tutor—Dr. Haylebury—to damnation, that he thought wickedly of others as well.

Bish said, This is what hell is like, now he will believe in hell.

It was unfair, Keats reflected later, bitterly, for almost certainly they did not believe in hell; not a one of them did. They thought it a source of fun. They laughed at him for saying prayers, for practising his catechism; they thought him primitive. They had irreligious convictions. They were not afraid of the dark. They did not experience the world as he did. He lay

THE KEATS VARIATION

in the dark, in bed, and fingered his forming blisters. They had a wormy feel to them. Morbid flesh, like maggots under his skin. He did not mind the pain; it was the weakness that turned to white worms and gnawed at him. When he pierced the blisters with a pain, weak water welled out. It turned his stomach. He thought, From now, I will never be weak again.

And to the Devil in the darkness, he recanted his confession. He whispered, I do believe in him. Not daring to speak directly to the Devil, and risk his gravel cough, his livid, unseen stare. He did not want to believe, but there it was: the thing he clung to, this small dark truth, the reality.

During lectures he considered the ghost. It would not be a soldier; that much he knew. Barrie and Bish favoured soldiers for their stories. They invented wars for the Continent, conflicts, bloody and endless, from which no hale man withdrew. Their heroes and ghosts were always horribly maimed, most often by bayonet thrusts—though sometimes blackened by gunpowder, from musket fire, for a change. But Keats thought, Perhaps a knight. A knight from ancient times, a knight in armour like a carapace that creaked and rattled. A very sad knight, ponderous and solemn, who went about the corridors in tears. Keats could see him: sighing in the light from the yellowed windows that lined the lecture hall, dust congregating in curious motes about his broadsword's hilt and blade. The knight had white hair, which Keats had not expected. He wore no helmet. He had a young, elfin face.

After the lecture had finished and the last students had departed, taking their anatomical notes, their sketches, their tenuous understandings of skeletal structure and phthisic symptoms, Keats crept back into the hall. The knight still lingered. Like a night watchman he held his posture, sorrowful and alert, nobly standing.

Hello, Keats said. I wondered how you did.

The knight did not turn his eyes to Keats, but rather lowered them. Ah, woe and alas, he said. Ah, woe the day.

Keats was taken aback by this gloomy assessment. Following narrowly on it he realized, however, a number of things: for instance, that the knight's armour must be heavy, which accounted for a part of his poor temper, and, too, that he was, after all, dead. The wound that had caused his death could not be seen, but blood pooled at his feet, dripping out from under the greaves of his armour in a slow black viscous seep. What is it that's wrong with you? Keats asked.

Ferebee

The knight looked at him piteously. He tried to raise an armoured hand, but stopped and dropped it, coughing. Blood came from his mouth and stained his lips. He could not speak. Keats offered him a handkerchief. The knight held it to his mouth. His eyes mouthed mute gratitude. All at once the truth came to Keats.

You've got a terrible wound, he said. It can't be healed. No one knows what to do. That's why you're a ghost; you were a great knight, but a sinner in life and so you were afflicted. Now you haunt the hospital because you are waiting for a surgeon who can heal you.

The knight bent his head. He said, Ah, woe the day. He handed the handkerchief back to Keats. Arterial blood was on it, the brightest shade of red.

Keats said, I am a surgeon. Well, a surgeon's apprentice. Someday I shall be a surgeon. I can change a dressing, and mix a compound. I can say when a man is dead. Perhaps I can help.

Despite this declaration, he was not quite sure what to do. He removed the knight's armour piece by piece, stacking it in a corner carefully. It was heavy, as he had suspected: made of iron plate, and faintly tarnished. It felt hot, as though the knights' body still held some incalescence, as though the cold of the grave were incomplete and some memory of fever had got through. When he reached the knight's under-linen he could smell the stench of the grave, a green and efflorescent smell like water stagnating, and see the stains that hinted at decay. He said, I do not know that I can fix this. But he placed his hands on the knight's abdomen anyway. He probed for a deep gash or some contusion. He knew how to sink the swelling of the latter, and sew the former up with careful stitches. But the source of the knight's suffering remained at bay.

At last he sat back on his heels and said in frustration, I can't find a wound. And your heart does not beat, anyway, so how is it that you are bleeding?

The knight directed at him a steady gaze. His eyes were limpid, like marbles, light grey. He lifted his hand and closed it around Keats's. Keats felt the shock of contact: his own little hand subsumed by the lack of heat, the dead cold of the grave. He thought, Perhaps his armour is heated by hellfire. Then was ashamed of the thought, and afraid. The knight's fingers locked around his wrist, icy, starved, insistent. Keats smelled his foul breath. The fragrance of rot, of cease. He saw what it was the knight

THE KEATS VARIATION

desired, but he would not give it. He wrenched his hand out of that grasp. He pulled away.

You would eat my soul out, he said. You do not want a surgeon. The hurt you have no surgeon can assuage. You want to live, and I can understand it. But if you took my soul, I would die in despair. The Devil would have me.

The knight's mouth moved. Keats leant forward, to hear him speak. But he merely coughed, misting the air with his arterial breath. Keats wiped the red from the knight's white lips.

I'm sorry, he said. I will not give my soul away. If you come back tomorrow I will make you a cup of tea, though, for the cough, and tell you a story.

This was clearly not sufficient. The knight closed his eyes in dismay. His face grew slack and lost; an aura of sorrow came off him. It was tangible, that aura. It had a dank smell. It made Keats nauseated and homesick, with the sharp bitter homesickness that was his hardest pain. He tasted at the back of his throat the air of Eastsake: its raw pollen; its ripened grain; the rays of sun that skimmed the river, fomenting dark weeds down in its shallow waters; the light that shocked a rich hot life from orchard branch and undersoil, from loam and summer tree.

He wrapped his arms around himself. He said miserably, I'm sorry. I understand. I would like to. Can we not be friends anyway?

He had thought that the knight might cease his grieving and be a companion. But the doors to the lecture hall burst open; laughing, Barrie and Bish came in. They had been looking for him; Bish said, Oh, run tell Taylor we've found the country mouse at last, we've mousetrapped him.

Keats felt trapped indeed. He glanced over his shoulder. The knight had gone: his body and armour, as though he had never been. The faint scent of brimstone remained, and something sweeter, stronger—a thicket of jasmine, growing on the wall beside the window. Colourless flowers tart and star-shaped amid flat leaves. The odour was everywhere. He inhaled, and felt lonely. Bish grabbed his arm. What's this, what've you been up to in here?

He looked scared, Bish: his face imprinted with astonishment. As though he thought Keats might have made the flowers on purpose, to impose fear.

Talking to the ghost, Keats said.

Ferebee

I suppose you think you're funny.

No. He did not feel funny. He was tired; he could not comprehend why Bish punched him in the stomach upon hearing him say this. He doubled over. He pictured himself safe, curled in a tiny knot upon his bed, like a leaf that had not budded. Dense and hidden, its forms obscure still, its structure still unwrit.

In the weeks that followed, he went back to his studies. He did not see the knight again, and he was glad. Exams were approaching; he was required to pass them if he wished his apprenticeship to continue, if he were to be awarded qualifications. He bent over his books. The bad light strained his eyes. He learned to palpate the vital parts to determine liver or kidney size and function; he looked at diagrams of dead lungs, showing where phthisis had ravened them. With his eyes closed he could draw the human body, stripped down to skeleton or muscle, reduced to what anatomy he knew. This much he understood about that body: what made it up, what composed it. He looked at his own fist clenched about the pen as he drew. It seemed very small, full of frailty. He could feel the flat scars of blisters lining his hand.

Sometimes at night, when he was sat alone by lamplight, he would see a shadow in the corner start to stretch its arms and legs. Or a casement clatter open and let enter the unpleasant wind, wet and urban, one-note, nosing the hair at the back of his head. Fear stuck its needles in him then. He was happy when Barrie, Bish, or Taylor found him, so that he had something to flee from. And when he fled and still they found him, he thought, But while they are here, nothing else will be here; nothing else will get in.

It was not the ghost he was afraid of. It was the other things, the large and small incidents that started to trouble him. For instance: Barrie bought a hand off one of the resurrection men who slunk about the hospital's back doorway, selling corpses. Whole corpses, three days from the grave, ran sixty pounds each—quite costly, on a surgeon's salary—but you could buy them piecemeal, as students did, to practice your dissection. Barrie had bought his hand for a prank. He put it into Keats's bedclothes in the evening, tucked up under the flat folds of the duvet. So that Keats, climbing into bed, later found it: the bone protruding slightly from the wrist, the flesh plastic and sickening. He picked it, barely pla-

THE KEATS VARIATION

cating his nausea, from the sheet by one of its dead fingers, and flung it doorwards as the other boys burst in.

Did it touch you, Keatsie? Did it feel you up?

You stink now, you smell of the dead.

Barrie brought the hand back to the bed, waggling its white fingers. Ooh, it's come for you Keats. It's come to haunt you. That's what happens when you talk to dead men.

I bet you're scared, Bish said. Look at him, he is, he's petrified. Like a little trembling mouse, a country infant.

I'm not scared, Keats said.

The other boys were laughing, and so did not hear him. Look at him! He thought a dead man had come to get him! I shouldn't wonder if he wet his bed.

I'm not scared, he said again.

This time Barrie took notice. No, you're not, are you, he said. He looked at Keats from up to down, from side to side, considering. Keats understood that what he had said had been an error, that he should have feigned being frightened, that this would in some way have soured the game. He stood with a sinking feeling and saw Barrie toss the flaccid hand from fist to fist like a juggler's object, jaunty and sharp, like a sword that would pierce your skin.

I am rather scared, Keats said. Now I think of it.

Hold him down, Barrie told Taylor and Bish.

They did as they were told. They pinned him to the bed, kneeling upon his shoulders with their hard patellas digging into him. Keats twisted the tendons of his arms. He struggled. He did not want the dead hand touching him. But Barrie brought it close, brushing Keats's face with its fingers. Keats closed his eyes. A smooth cool nail traced his lip. He thought, I will not be sick, I will not give them the satisfaction.

Do you know how St. Crix was martyred? Barrie asked.

I do, Bish said.

Quiet, Bish.

The Roman soldiers ate him.

To think that we still study Classics, Taylor said with a smirk. Civilisation.

They cut him up, all into little pieces, because he would not give his sheep to them. We're told there is a Christian message. I think he must have tasted good. The Romans knew what they were about. What do you think, Bish?

Bish said, Filthy savages. Not like Englishmen.

Very educated, is our Bish. But I meant about eating saints and so forth, eating dead men.

Oh. Bish's face expressed revulsion. Really? Even for you, that is excessive.

Keats could smell Barrie's breath, hot and excited. He thought, He is not bluffing; he will do it, he enjoys it. Barrie pressed the limp hand hard into Keats's lips. Keats tensed all the musculature that he possessed, his whole small body, in a bid to throw off Bish and Taylor. He felt something in his chest crack: not a bone, but larger and more solid, farther down inside of him. The taste of darkness filled his mouth, He drowsed. He said to himself, as he said always before sleep, Blessed guardian-angel, keep me safe from danger.... The small room scented itself with a sweet wild fragrance, as of torn herbs and river weeds. A lightness came over him and he laughed. He was, he thought for a moment, still asleep, lost in that bright pastoral; that was why the air turned sweet. But no, the anchor of his soul was wedged still in his body; he felt Bish and Taylor both back from him; he felt his release, and he rubbed his shoulders, blinking. In Barrie's fist, still outstretched, inches from Keats's face, where the hand had been, was now a small bird of a dun indifferent colour, with a large beak and an outsized head. He recognized it as a nightingale. It was a plain bird, unpretty. Barrie's hands around it were trembling.

Let it go, Keats said.

He's a witch, said Bish.

Barrie said, I can't, I can't move, I can't do anything. He looked around wildly.

Are you frightened? Keats asked him. He was curious. He could not see why Barrie would be frightened. It was such a little bird, so enchanting, and, even as he watched it, it opened up its mouth and sang. An ordinary song, a sudden warble, sourceless as night, its notes water-coloured and sweet.

Yes, Barrie said, and in a sharp motion dropped it. The bird took to its wings and flew. It bore itself out of the open window, into the city air. Keats could see the pale line of its body pass upwards, crossing the silhouette of St. Lachrymose Cathedral; then it soared beyond his field of view.

THE KEATS VARIATION

Back in the narrow, candle-lit room, Barrie rubbed his hands together. He stared at Keats. He said, There's no such thing as witches.

No, Keats said. I know that you don't think so.

So what is it then, how did you do that, what are you.

It was not apparent what answer Barrie wanted. This being the case, Keats withdrew into himself: hunching his thin shoulders. It occurred to him that he did not have to speak, that the other boys would not now pull his hair and pinch his skin if he stayed silent. Indeed, Bish and Taylor were backed against the far wall of the room as though Keats displayed some symptoms of disease, something leprous that might infect them. They looked likely to bolt if he so much as sneezed. He tested this theory: he coughed, and they jumped. The power itched at him. He did not understand it. Surely they had seen before some bit of this power, some piece of the world that stalked behind them. This was not its sole manifestation. His own life was so full of such things. He said, It is good to believe, it offers some protection.

Believe in what? Barrie asked, still dazed.

In ghosts. In angels. In saints. Saints will save us, I think, from the Devil.

He was being earnest. He was anxious that they should understand; in some sense he wanted them dead and gone, yes, but in another he felt he could not leave him to those footsteps, to the black drag and the Devil's limp. Not even they should be left to it.

But Bish and Taylor laughed, after a moment. Time restored complacency to them. Perhaps they were saying already, No, I did not see that, there was no truth in it, it was a trick. Tomorrow they would wake more sure. They would forget the fear, its hard and bitter kernel. Keats, with a sinking feeling, predicted it. When he looked at Barrie, though, his mouth still slack and angry, he thought, But you, you will not forget. You will feel it on your hands. The little feathers. The bones, the little twitching bones, still moving. You will not be rid of this.

Keats slept that night by the open window, in a thatch of blankets pulled from his bed. He awoke damp and sticky, as though from a fever, his hair stirred uneasily by the stifling wind. Hello, he said, who's there? He had heard footsteps. A creak, as of someone sitting down upon a chair. But the sole chair in the room was empty. He could see the light upon its straw bottom, the wan dilute light of the moon. Something

Ferebee

skidded on the floor. He caught at it; it was a feather. Furled and insubstantial. It might easily have been from the nightingale, but he thought not; he thought it had come in while he slept; it was the night's debris and harbinger of a new bird in the darkness, something larger, spreading its wings. He shuddered. This was the feeling that the feather gave him. He wondered where St. Crix now was, who had promised to protect him—or no, that was not it: to shepherd. What was the distinction? A shepherd's task, surely, was to intercede wolves and other predatory creatures. To disperse his own flesh foremostly amongst the starving Roman men.

It is true, said the chaplain to whom he went for clarification of the story; we are told that St. Crix died in such a way. He was a very noble shepherd. but you are too young; who has been saying to you such things?

Never mind, Father. Can you tell me what was the miracle of St. Crix? For Keats knew that there would be a miracle at the centre of the thing. It was in the nature of martyrs and their narratives. To twist with truth a death into a mystery.

The chaplain hemmed, resisted. Subject to Keats's cool, light-eyed stare, he surrendered finally. He said, I believe that there was about his flesh a certain aspect, a holy and indwelling quality, that called its eaters unto grace. They gave up their soldiering, and spoke in tongues, and became ascetics. They were exiled from society. They ate no more the meat of animals, nor any other thing, and then they died in starvation. As you would expect.

Keats considered this. He said, I see.

Do you, though? You are very young.

That is what everyone keeps telling me.

The chaplain said, You are a worry. He regarded Keats: the worry. Through his eyes, Keats saw himself: small, tired, and far too devout; a fragile, put-upon thing. He saw the burns on his hands and the shadows on his face. I could be, he thought, a figure in your windows; you could ornament a chapel out of me. Sometimes he felt like stained glass. The light shone through him. His skin and bones were coloured bright, were melting.

Thank you, Father, Keats said. And please don't worry about me.

THE KEATS VARIATION

That night in his dreams he saw St. Crix again. The saint was not now stitched together. He wounds could bleed, and they did; the blood ran down his body like rain that streaks a window, from the butchering cuts on his arms, abdomen, and legs. The raw muscle gaped. The blood kept welling smoothly. You would not believe, Keats remembered Barrie saying, you would not believe how much blood is in a man. The saint seemed not bothered. He raised a hand in benediction. Keats squirmed away; he could not stand that cold and hallowed touch. St. Crix turned sad eyes on him. He opened the same hand: imploring.

Keats said, What do you want, I don't understand—and woke. His window casement was clattering in the rain. He went to check the storm, to see that it was in fact clear water, that warped but did not stain. He tasted it: that sour, guttered taste. Water. He closed the window. Outside, an hourless night clung to the pane. When he lit a candle, the light welled up. He set the candle at his bedside so he would not be afraid. But he was, anyway; the radiance did not diminish his discomfort. Raindrops tapped against the window, or else unseen things, black and winged. Oh blessed guardian-angel, keep me safe from danger whilst I sleep.... But he was not sleeping. He hauled the duvet over his head. Sleep, he thought, sleep. His own breath came back to him in the closed alcove of the blankets. It smelled of fear, mephitic. He was glad the candlelight was filtered. He did not want to see direct its raw source, undiffused by the duvet's weave. A long shadow passed his body. He said to himself, It is the flame, flickering. But it was not. A hand clamped down upon his shoulder. Or something hand-shaped, with weight and heat. It rested there. It did not shake him. He did not move. He did not breathe. The hand tightened, just for an instant, as though measuring out his anatomy: feeling the clavicle ridge, the edge of muscle as fine and slack as glassine. It dug into him with long and circling fingers. Go away, he thought, please leave me be. The hand did not lift, nor the shadow alter its position. For a long time they stayed that way: Keats and this other entity, this formless thing in the dark that had no pulse, or none that he could feel beat. Perhaps, Keats thought, perhaps it is the knight. He had not a heart; perhaps it is him, come at last to speak with me. But he did not think it was the knight. This figure was a new nocturnal shape. The knight had not imposed the sudden sense of terror, subjugation, shame, as though his soul were unspooling from his chest and he could not force a cessation; as though all the brightness and fear within him were pulled out for display. He drew a breath and then another breath, at least, feeling them shudder through him like a sickness. There were tears on his face. He trembled like that through the night, till he was sleeping, and then he was not sleeping, but sitting, blinking, in his wilderness of blankets, and dawn was forming around him into flesh-coloured day. On the floor, ringed round his bed, were feathers: the largest feathers that he had seen. He picked one up: it was smooth and sharp, not white, but a burnished ivory. An aged colour. He curled his palm around it. It pricked him with unease.

In spite of these incidents, he passed his exams; or thought he did. For some weeks the results would not be posted, but he sensed achievement: predictable and rigid. A surgeon, one of the scorers, stopped him in the hall to congratulate him on the diagram he had submitted showing the progress of a phthisic lung. The other boys got wind of this. For the next week they carried on about it: Keats the teacher's pet country mouse, the country animal the masters keep in a cage. He did not mind it; at this stage, still cowed, they mostly kept their distance. And he was scheduled to soon visit his home in Eastsake. He thought, If I can make it till then, if I can board the diligence, I will hear the driver tut and the wheels rattle onwards, the snap of the whip; I will have escaped.

Resolutely he fixed himself on this destiny. He turned himself to an arrow, fletched and narrow. It was the target at which he aimed. When Bish taunted him by loosing live mice in his bedroom, little white mice with febrile eyes that fed on the edges of his papers and fled from him, he said to himself, I can stand this. When Taylor left pinned to his door a dead pigeon, its wings shedding feathers, its feet curled into crescent moon-shapes, he shuddered but knew that this, too, he could stand. Seeing the pattern, he awaited Barrie's contribution: perhaps a bleating goat, he thought, a sacrificial beast, or a country lamb. But no animal appeared, and as the date of his departure approached he became nervous. He began skipping dinner and breakfast, to avoid the dining hall; when he walked through the corridors he kept his back to the stone siding. He stayed out of doorways. He started when he heard noises. He could not stand the voices he heard in other rooms, shouting and laughing. They came through the dormitory walls undifferentiated, the damned roaring, a raucous din. It was distant, but not so distant as he might have liked from him. Sometimes in the street outside his window he heard a new

THE KEATS VARIATION

sound: someone coughing, a cold hard bark. Keats clenched his hand into a fist. There are in this city, he thought, many thousands of men: men from the mines, with miners' lungs, men with incurable phthisis—consumptives. There are even women, turned frail by the factory, who cough up woolstuff and cotton threads. Why shouldn't one of them idle for an odd moment outside my window? But he knew that this was not it, that he who coughed beneath the casement unseen was not a stranger. He would not wander onwards, out into the city; Keats would see him again: his face. He had a presentiment, a foreign feeling. He would see him soon, someday.

At night he packed his precious items into a travelling case. His saint's medal and his little inkstand, his surgical books and all his papers. His serge coat, though it would be nigh on summer in Eastsake, once he passed the boundaries of the city, where seasons never seemed to take. When he had quite finished, he lay atop the sheets of his bed and studied the shapes on the ceiling: dark clouds where the plaster threatened decay. The candlelight controlled them: its sharp relief or shade limiting, then exposing their outlines. Yet somewhere behind them a force, a slow drip of water from damaged pipes or rain, was real: not subject to light's inconstancy, not likely to change. Keats considered this original point. He imagined the water: a cool and tawny wealth pouring over him, a true source, a wellspring. He took measured breaths. He could taste mouldy leaves. It was not a bad taste; he was not displeased; it tasted of mulch, the rich spring soil, the rot that leads to growing things. Sometimes he thought he could eat that earth, with all its embers of half-ripe seedlings, of cedar bark and stalks and weeds. He could eat it now: he had been subsisting on dry toast snatched from the dining hall between sittings and cups of tea. A certain lightheadedness sometimes took him, as now. He felt his body lift from his bed, become weightless; it was an airy, wondrous feeling, and he thought, This is what it's like to be dead.

There was a knock at his door: the sad downcoming. He opened his eyes. Yes, who is it.

George Barrie.

Hesitation. Keats said, I suppose you'd better come in.

He sat up on the bed, cross-legged and wary. His body tensed. He had no weapons prepared. He watched the door swing open; Barrie came in. He looked worn. He had lost weight. His cinnamon hair was limp, the curls flattened. His shirt looked as though it had been slept in. He said, after a moment's discomfort: I must apologize for Bish. The mice showed no imagination.

And the pigeon? Keats asked coolly.

Well, that is Taylor.

Was it dead? Or did he kill it?

Barrie said, Am I my brother's keeper?

We are told, yes.

Even so. Barrie stopped speaking. Then he said, I believe he found it dead.

I'm glad, Keats said.

Barrie offered no response.

Keats said, Are you trying to put me off my guard, is this some new strategy?

No.

What then?

Again Barrie faltered. Then said with sudden fury, Whatever witchcraft you are at, you must stop working.

You don't believe in witches.

I cannot eat. When I eat, it turns to ashes. Bread, meat. And I dream— he broke off.

Keats, curious, asked him, What do you dream?

You know.

I don't.

You have made me so I can't rid myself of it. The dream. I am walking, and behind me is a figure whose face I cannot see. It coughs, a bad cough, phthisic. I can smell where its lungs bleed. And it is slow, and limps with dying. I want to turn and see its face; I know it will be—he fumbled for the foremost word. Radiant. No, that is not right, but I desire it. Desire to look at it. And then I wake from the dream.

Keats considered Barrie's pale face: in earnest. He was numbed by the account. He could not imagine wanting to turn towards the Devil. All his life he had stumbled from that dark pursuer, the dread in the darkness, stalked, had become a pursuee. He said, That is not my dream.

You have sent it.

It is not from me.

THE KEATS VARIATION

Barrie stepped forward. His black eyes glittered feverishly. I cannot eat or sleep, he said, you are haunting me. Is it you, Keats? Is it you in the dream? Sometimes I think it is. You or your demon. Your God-damned bird. Your ghost. Your country lungs that bleed. You have a sickness.

Keats found himself in retreat. He backed against his bed. He said uneasily, I don't know why you think that. At the same time he sensed it beginning to open, in the earth's inebriate darkness: the embryo of truth, the sprouting like seed. It split his heart like a husk. It spread its roots down through him. He resisted. He said, You're wrong. You invent things.

There was a tapping at the window, steady and insistent.

Barrie said, Why are you starving me?

He was stood close by now. He touched Keats's face. His hand was hot and greedy. It groped the long line of jawbone, the high arch of the cheek. Keats tried to pull away. Barrie's grasp would leave bruises. But harder and more brutal was the hungry way he looked at Keats.

Please, Keats said. Don't. Please.

He felt the pressure of those eyes. Stripping, as you would strip the bark from a tree, the wings from a beetle, as cruel boys did in the country, so that it writhed and died in the sunshine, its inner workings exposed for all to see. It is not me, he thought, it is not me you want; it is the ghost, the bird, the Devil; it is not me.

A bright wind touched the back of his head and he closed his eyes in sorrow or relief. The casement clattered against the wall beside the window. He heard, out in the unceasing darkness, the sound of wings. He had hoped for some other entity to save him, for a saint. With resignation he saw the angel sweep into the room, enraged, resplendent. It spilled glory. It spooled forth from Keats. He felt it pull his soul out from his body. The air turned molten, and then the floor. His lungs ached. His feet seared and blistered. He said, in agony, Stop, please, no more, no more. The angel did not hear him. Or had its own speech, beyond the human repertoire. It advanced on Barrie. Its eyes were blank and harsh; they showed no kindness. Keats staggered. He was weak. He felt the weakness in him. He choked on the new, hot, raw, thin air. He began to cough. He coughed up darkness. The radiance filled him up. He filled with despair.

Before she allowed Raf to tend her wound, Emmanuel rose to her feet and regarded herself in the mirror, pleased by what she saw. Wide shoulders, expansive chest, trim, defined midsection, narrow hips. The logoed elastic of her boxers cut straight across her belly below the hips, cutting short the furry trail that led the gaze toward the meaty lump behind the fly of khaki shorts. It shifted, all by itself, buckling the fabric of the fly to reveal a flash of copper zipper, and Emmanuel grinned at her reflection.

TATTOOED LOVE BOYS
Alex Jeffers

The second week, Emma discovered a tattoo parlor down an alley off the main square. The young man behind the counter took one look at her and said, in careful English, "You are too young for a tattoo."

"I don't want a tattoo. I don't think I do. My brother does."

The guy (his name sounded like *Raf*) asked how old Theo was—seventeen—and suggested she bring him in. Raf looked only a few years older than Theo. Emma liked the little blue-black glyph inked on the concave bone of his left temple between hairline and eyebrow. She thought it was meant to evoke a bird's wing. But then Raf turned to change the CD and the tattoos on his shoulder and back, what wasn't covered by his wifebeater, disappointed her. Koi fish, lotus blossoms, a whiskered Asian dragon—boring. As cliché as the horned skulls and flames and roses Theo dreamed about.

But when Raf returned his attention to her Emma decided he was good looking so she asked how he'd known to speak English. "You speak it very well," she added. She wanted a moment to contemplate the image that had just come to her of Raf kissing her big brother, caressing Theo's shoulder and arm. Raf's long fingers left strokes of color on Theo's skin, fire-breathing skulls, schools of glistening koi.

"You have the American look," Raf said.

Emma didn't believe he meant to sound condescending.

Jeffers

They'd come on vacation, Emma, Theo, Mom, Dad, but it promised to be a dreary sort of vacation because Mom and Dad had responsibilities—for them it was a working vacation. Every morning they took a train to the bigger town thirty kilometers away to do research in the university library, leaving their children to entertain themselves.

Theo wasn't much entertainment even back home. In a foreign country where he didn't know the language, he spent hours hunched over his laptop (he had terrible posture). Complaining to friends on Facebook, playing World of Warcraft, piecing together angsty doom-metal loops on GarageBand though he never seemed to paste the loops together into actual songs. Now and then he took a break to reach for his sketchbook, struck by another vision for the sleeve of tattoos he intended for his left arm as soon as he turned eighteen. If he wasn't on the internet, he was usually in the home gym at the top of the house.

They'd traded houses with a professional couple, a dentist and a professor, who were abnormally fit for men in their forties: there were photos of them without shirts on all over the house. Theo made fake gross-out noises over the photos but he attacked their exercise machines with fervor and learned the metric system right away so he could keep track. When he didn't smell of sweat, he smelled of the rank bodyspray TV commercials back home had told him would attract girls. Not if they had functioning olfactory organs, Emma often almost told him. Emma thought her older brother might be more interesting if he were gay. Emma thought she'd make a better boy than Theo.

She had the guts to go out with her phrasebook and wander the town. Village—it was barely a town, surrounded by fields and pastures. Her guidebook to the country said the village had once been known for its livestock fair, but now the market ground had become a park and the abattoir municipal offices. She didn't carry the guidebook with her because the village rated only half a page.

Emma walked through the park, noting the public pool for a future occasion, but she saw a cluster of girls her age who she could tell thought themselves too pretty to get wet. She had exactly as much use for girls like that as they would for her.

Walking the towpath beside the canal east of town, she imagined boarding a barge that would carry her upstream to the university or downstream a hundred twenty-five kilometers to the capital and the sea. On the far side of the water, a fence prevented golden-brown cattle from blundering into the deep canal. Approaching the fourteenth-century bridge, she startled a gang of teenage boys. They scuttled down the bank into the water. She saw several white butts before brown water hid them, before she noticed heaps of clothing by the towpath. Crouching in the shallows, the boys glowered up at her, and she wondered whether she found the notion of skinnydipping with a bunch of girlfriends appealing.

Not really. She couldn't imagine any of the girls she knew being up for it. She wasn't certain she would be. Public nudity was different for boys, she thought, though she still couldn't imagine any of the boys she knew, American boys, willingly hanging out bareass with other bareass boys (certainly never Theo). But the image was oddly attractive. If she'd known these boys she might have gathered up their clothes and run off with them.

She didn't know anybody in town yet. Raf at the tattoo shop wasn't the only person to speak to her in English but he was the only one who knew right off his native language wouldn't serve.

Walking on, leaving the boys to their fun, she recalled the dream she used to have of waking one morning to find herself a boy. Emma had read about gender dysphoria—she knew she didn't suffer that. She had never felt any conviction that really she was a boy trapped in the wrong body, but if she played World of Warcraft she would choose a male avatar. All the best adventure stories, the heroes were boys who got to slay dragons or be apprenticed to wizards, embark on voyages of discovery or quests to rescue magical talismans (or tiresome princesses). Girls *were* tiresome, generally, the ones she knew. Although it was entirely likely, if she could penetrate the secret world of boys, incognita, she'd find they were also tiresome, consumed by trivial concerns she wouldn't even comprehend because she lacked the context.

Theo was tiresome in just about every way—he smelled bad—but she had to admit he was pretty to look at when he forgot to look sullen. It was easy to place her brother's face on the untried heroes of fantasy adventure novels, to populate the sweet fumblings of slash fanfic with Theo's lithe body.

It would revolt him utterly to know that about her, the uses her imagination put him to.

Besides, Raf at the tattoo parlor was prettier, really, though she didn't usually find blonds appealing. He didn't give her that look, that startled, hungry, *boy* look, as if he'd just noticed you weren't hideous and were a girl, so she thought probably he was gay.

The second time she visited the tattoo shop, she asked Raf if he'd like a soda or coffee from the café on the square. "You didn't bring your brother," he said.

Emma was used to boys being disappointed. She hadn't even told Theo about Raf and the shop. "He's afraid—" she thought he was—"to get inked while he still lives at home. Mom and Dad might get angry."

"It's not their affair, surely, what he does to his own body."

Emma saw the hole. "Then it shouldn't be anybody's affair if *I* wanted a tattoo. I'm only two years younger than Theo."

"But you don't want one." Cheery, Raf grinned. "I don't even know why you're here."

"To talk to somebody friendly. To fetch you a cup of coffee or a Coca-Cola from the café."

Raf went wide eyed in a charming, fake way. He glanced around the empty shop. The stop-start buzzing of an electric needle came from somewhere in back, behind the life-sized ventral and dorsal photos of a Japanese man vividly inked over every square centimeter of skin below the neck. "As you can see," Raf said, "I have no customers presently clamoring for my artistry. I will walk with you to the café."

When he turned to call in his own language to the invisible co-worker, Emma saw his ventral tattoos weren't what she remembered. Glossy black spikes and blades pierced his pale skin and showed through the thin fabric of his shirt, looking like the crazy weapons of *Star Trek* Klingons, clashing. *Tribal*, she thought the aesthetic was called, just as clichéd as the dragon and fishes she must have imagined. She was relieved, when he came around the counter, that the wing glyph at his temple hadn't changed, and startled by how short he was. The floor behind the counter must be raised. Theo would be a full head taller.

"Shall we?" Raf asked. "We'll bring our treats back here, if you don't mind. Better for Hender not to be interrupted."

He walked beside her, asking how she and her brother came to be visiting this tiny, unimportant town. He knew the professor and the dentist—the dentist was his dentist, he'd done some of the professor's ink. Emma found herself telling him more than she meant to, if she'd meant to tell him anything, on the short walk to the square. He was easy to talk to, dropping all the right hints to lead her on. Theo interested him but that was to be expected: Theo might be persuaded to drop a couple hundred euro on ink. If Raf was gay, he might find Theo attractive. Theo *was* attractive. Once again, the two boys were making out in the back of Emma's mind, beautiful, almost innocent, so she was surprised when Raf opened the café door for her. Going in, she noticed a porcelainized plaque fixed to the wall beside the door, Delft-blue letters spelling words she couldn't read.

Inside, it was noisy and cheerful, smelled of coffee, warm milk—spices and baking bread, hot sugar, mustard, salted meats. The odors were comforting, though Emma imagined they could also be nauseating as she realized she'd forgotten lunch. "Are you hungry?" she asked Raf.

"Are you?"

"Famished. I only noticed now."

He smiled in a way she liked for a moment, then didn't like so much as he walked right to the counter and spoke to the man behind it too fast for Emma to have any chance of understanding. She stepped up beside him. He was barely taller than she, still smiling, but the fellow behind the counter was taller than Theo and quite nice looking. "Perhaps ten minutes," Raf said.

"I'm paying."

"Not this time. You may dislike what I chose for you."

"What?"

"A traditional hot sandwich and our traditional way of serving coffee. Hot milk and a taste of bitter chocolate."

Coffee Guy (so she christened him) blinked, encouraging.

"Yummy." Emma held out the ten-euro note in such a way that Coffee Guy would have to fold it back into her hand or take it. Raf made falsely remonstrative noises but Coffee Guy took the bill with a smile.

Moving aside, Emma asked, "What does the sign by the door say?"

"Hmm?" Raf was still pretending pique. "It notes that this is an historic building, dating to the early sixteenth century, and that it was built over the site of the witch's house. Excuse me." Returning to Coffee Guy, he accepted a white paper bag and a cardboard caddy carrying three tall paper cups with plastic sippy lids.

"Witch's house?"

Raf was leading her back to the door. Outside, he indicated two words on the plaque that Emma could now interpret—the languages were not so distantly related. "Another tradition," Raf said, "older than the coffee or the sandwich." He seemed in a hurry, brisk and brusque.

As he strode away and Emma hesitated, puzzled, it appeared to her the inky spikes and blades and flourishes on his back were writhing, contorting, blushing with blots of clear color, but when she blinked and looked again, hurrying after him, they had resolved into intricate flowers tangled in wreaths and garlands on his shoulder and upper arm. Scarlet poppies, indigo cornflowers, peonies, Japanese chrysanthemums—she didn't recognize half of them.

"I become anxious about Hender," Raf said when she caught up. "I'm sorry. He is not always good with people."

"Your tattoos—"

"Yes? I like the flowers better as well."

From across the street, through the plate-glass window of the shop Emma saw a customer waiting, back turned, peering at the display of photocopied flash as if each sheet were a painting on a museum's wall. "An American," said Raf.

"How can you tell?"

"I can tell. Perhaps your brother."

"Theo has long hair. Halfway down his back." She didn't have to see him close up to see the *American* customer had little more than the shadow of stubble on his skull.

Raf leapt the step to the door, pushed it open, and said in ringing English as the bell tinkled, "I'm sorry there was no-one here to welcome you."

"He said you'd be right back, the other—" Turning from the wall of skulls and dragons, magickal symbols and WWII pinups, Theo froze when he saw his sister behind Raf. "Emma?"

"What happened to your hair?"

Triumphant, Raf grinned.

"What are you doing here? You're too young for ink."

TATTOOED LOVE BOYS

Startled into petulance, Emma blurted, "So are you!"

"My friend Emma bought me coffee," Raf said equably, placing cup caddy and sandwich bag on the counter. "That is why I wasn't here to greet you. Let me just give Hender his and then we can discuss your plans and wishes."

When he took one of the paper cups behind the curtain, Emma asked Theo again, "What happened to your hair?" It had been beautiful hair, wavy and lustrous—much prettier than hers.

"His *friend?*" Self conscious, Theo shifted his sketchpad from one hand to the other, then back. "Since when?"

First surprise passed, Emma imagined Theo was maybe even handsomer without long hair to distract from the fineness of his features, the shocking paleness of his eyes. A queasy-making thought to have about her brother when he stood in front of her big as life, so she turned away. Incomprehensible voices sounded behind Hender's curtain, three of them (she hadn't seen Hender yet), and the thrumming of his needle. "How'd you find the place?"

"Google," Theo said, but not as if she was stupid.

Distracted by annoyance, Emma didn't often remember how shy he was. She took her cup from the counter and sipped through the vent in the plastic lid. The coffee wasn't very sweet, not like cocoa—she tasted milk and coffee more than chocolate. "Why?"

"You know I want them."

"Why now?"

When she looked over her shoulder, Theo was sitting on the bench below the display of flash. Staring at his clasped hands, he looked miserable. For an instant she felt sorry for him. "Why now?" she asked again.

"Simon got one. Bragging about it on Facebook."

Simon and Theo were barely friends, back home. Simon had a guitar and people to jam with, not just GarageBand on his laptop. They were World of Warcraft rivals, though Emma didn't really understand how that worked.

"*Your friend got one* isn't a good excuse for a tattoo," Raf said, pushing through the curtain. He went straight for his coffee. "It's a permanent alteration to your body—" Emma wondered about his, Raf's, though— "you need to really want it."

Theo raised his head. "I do!" His face was tragic.

"What did Simon get?" asked Emma, mildly curious.

"Line of kanji down his spine. Really hurt, he said."

Emma snorted. "Bragged, you mean."

"Close to the bone hurts more," Raf said in the tone of a master craftsman imparting lessons to his apprentice. "I do not recommend it for your first experience. I won't do kanji, either, by the way. It's not my language—I don't like to trust the published interpretations or the designs themselves. They're often inaccurate."

"Simon's probably says *happiness puppies*," Emma said, uncomfortably sympathetic, "instead of what he wanted."

Theo looked down at his hands again. "*Fight fierce, fight strong*," he mumbled.

"That's possibly stupider than *happiness puppies*."

"Your sandwich, Emma." Somehow Raf had got it out of the bag and wrappings without her noticing, arranged nicely in little wedges on a pretty plate.

Emma's hunger asserted itself. Ravenous, she stuffed a wedge into her mouth. It was still hot. Crunchy and buttery toasted bread enfolded molten cheese and shavings of something like prosciutto. Feeling guilty after bolting two, she looked up to offer a taste to Raf and Theo.

They sat side by side on the bench, knees nearly touching, Theo's sketchbook between them. "Any of these might be executed to fine effect," Raf said, flipping through the pages again. "But you can't decide, am I correct?"

Emma edged closer. The uppermost page showed a disembodied arm (thicker, brawnier than Theo's) encrusted with patterned lozenges like Turkish tiles, but Raf flipped it and the next arm was decorated with a menagerie of vivid zoo animals.

"I keep changing my mind," Theo admitted, his voice mournful.

"Then I'm sorry to say you are not ready."

Theo lifted his eyes, stared into Raf's for a long moment. He looked ready to cry before he moved his gaze to Raf's upper arm and shoulder. "Yours are…" he began.

Beautiful, Emma thought he meant to say, but beauty wasn't a quality Theo could ascribe to another man. They were beautiful, Raf's garlands of inked flowers. Theo raised one hand as if to caress them, another gesture halted as he abruptly rose to his feet. The sketchbook clattered to the floor. Raf looked up mildly.

"You're right." Theo crouched to retrieve his drawings. "I need to decide what I really want." Without another word, he bolted out of the shop. The bell over the door tinkled gaily. Emma sat beside Raf and they shared the rest of her sandwich, except one sliver saved for Hender.

After the first bitter bite, Emma didn't mind the needle chewing at her skin. She'd had to assume an awkward position on the settee to give Raf access to the fleshy inner surface of her upper arm, and the moment of removing her shirt had been disorienting. She'd never done it for a boy who wasn't interested in what was inside her bra.

She had determined Raf wasn't. He was interested in what was in her brother's undershorts, but not in any urgent way—when Emma confessed her fantasy of Raf and Theo necking, Raf just laughed, delighted, and wondered aloud why it was so many women loved those images. When she decided, quite abruptly, she *did* want a tattoo, just a small one in an inconspicuous place, he wasn't difficult to argue around after she told him what she wanted. He sketched the symbol for her, fast and decisive in colored inks, and Emma became even more determined to have it. He ushered her behind the curtain at the back of the shop. She got only a glimpse into one small room where a man in a white undershirt like Raf's leaned over the serpent on the back of another man, before Raf waved her into the second. He gave her a moment to settle herself, ducking into the other room to give Hender his wodge of sandwich.

It didn't actually take much time for Raf to inscribe the design on Emma's arm three inches below where she shaved. She liked his hands on her, swabbing the skin with alcohol, then transferring the design, finally going to work, though she wished it was skin to skin uninhibited by his latex gloves. After a while, the rhythm of the stinging needle and regular pauses to wipe off blood and ink relaxed her into a kind of trance that blundered into memory.

Unfamiliar memory. Half-familiar memories. They were old, well worn, blurred around the edges as they bubbled up from among quite different memories she knew to be hers but that faded even as she reached after them. When her little brother Theo was small he couldn't get his mouth around the four syllables of his big brother's name. *Emma*, he called her, and had to be taught that Emma was a girl's name. Theo's brother's name was Emmanuel, which didn't admit of a convenient shortening like Theo for Theodore. (Theo had been *Teddy* until he turned ten.) What had their parents been thinking?

She remembered throwing a football for Theo, who was miserable at catching it—she remembered wrestling with him when they were nearer the same size—she remembered helping him with his algebra homework, impatient when he didn't get it.

She remembered the first boy to kiss her (not the first she wanted to kiss), Steve, a nerdier nerd than her brother, who refused (at first) to suck her cock though he was extremely happy when she went to town on his. How old had she been? Fourteen. Almost nineteen now, lying still under Raf's calm hands and the sting of his electric needle, she felt her dick plump up a bit in her boxers at the memory, felt her balls shift around.

She remembered the expression Theo got when she told him his big brother was gay. Liked other boys instead of girls. Liked their muscles (some of the boys she liked didn't possess much muscle), their scratchy beards, their odor. Liked touching them, kissing them, sexing them up.

Theo didn't so much recoil as subtly withdraw, bending his head so dark hair obscured his transparent eyes. "I'm still your brother," Emma had said. "Nothing's changed, except that little bit of dishonesty between us. You want me to be honest with you, right?"

Now Raf set the silent needle aside and swabbed her arm again. The evaporating film of alcohol tingled, its fumes fizzy in her nostrils. Raf stood, stretched, clenching and flexing the fingers of his right hand, and gazed down at her, his expression neutral, thoughtful. She wasn't the type of boy he was attracted to.

Annoyed, Emma said, "Done?" The depth and richness of her voice distracted and pleased her.

"Yes. Do you wish to see?"

A big mirror hung on the wall but Raf reached for a hand mirror and held it for her. First, momentarily disconcerted, she noticed the aggressive growth of hair in her armpit that thinned only a little where it fanned out to mesh with the hair on her chest. The kind of boy *she* was attracted to would never shave his body hair. Raf shifted the mirror a fraction.

It was reversed in the glass, the symbol incised on the pale flesh of her inner arm, arrowheads pointing off past eleven o'clock instead of one.

TATTOOED LOVE BOYS

Inflammation blurred the outlines, seeping blood obscured careful gradation of tint and shading. It was probably stupid, overly obvious, but she liked it: paired Mars glyphs, unbroken circles interlinked, arrowheads parallel. Within indigo outlining, the rings and arrows were tinted like anodized aluminum. She liked it.

"I like it," Emma said.

"Nice work, Raf," said a new voice, more heavily accented speaking English than Raf's.

Emma blinked away from the gleaming oval of the mirror as Raf said, "Hender—my new American friend Emmanuel, who bought your coffee."

"And my tasty bit of sandwich? Thank you, Emmanuel. They were much appreciated."

Hender appeared older than Raf, ten, fifteen years. Emmanuel didn't find him especially handsome or his ear and facial piercings enticing, but his eyes, a brown so pale it was nearly gold, were compelling. The glyph on his left temple was larger and more complex than Raf's, foliated, tendrils looping and extending into his hairline, onto his cheekbone, as if Raf's were merely a preliminary sign, incomplete. Both stepped back when Emmanuel sat up and swung her legs over the edge of the settee. Hender placed a proprietary hand on Raf's shoulder—his fingernails were unpleasantly long, lacquered black, and he wore too many gold rings—and smiled, exposing teeth that looked inhumanly sharp. Under his hand, the flowers on Raf's shoulder appeared to catch fire.

Emmanuel blinked. Flickering flames resolved into stylized scrolls, yellow, orange, red, like the decals on an ancient muscle car's fender, and she blinked again, disappointed.

"Show Emmanuel how to care for his new art while it heals," Hender said, squeezed Raf's shoulder again, and went away.

Before she allowed Raf to tend her wound, Emmanuel rose to her feet and regarded herself in the mirror, pleased by what she saw. Wide shoulders, expansive chest, trim, defined midsection, narrow hips. The logoed elastic of her boxers cut straight across her belly below the hips, cutting short the furry trail that led the gaze toward the meaty lump behind the fly of khaki shorts. It shifted, all by itself, buckling the fabric of the fly to reveal a flash of copper zipper, and Emmanuel grinned at her reflection.

Raf swabbed the tattoo with stinging alcohol again, smeared it with greasy antibiotic ointment—he gave her the tube, opened fresh, to slip in her pocket—taped over it a square of plastic film, explaining as he went along how to care for it so it would heal quickly and cleanly. Because she wanted him to, he kissed her, but it was an uninvolved, almost chilly kiss—he was more attracted to Theo—and he wouldn't go further even after she groped his crotch and found him stiff. She didn't have enough cash on her to pay the full price of the tattoo but he said it didn't matter, she could cover the rest next time she dropped by.

Emmanuel liked being a boy. A man, really. Her voice was deeper and she was taller than her dad, outweighed him by twenty or thirty pounds. Nor was her hair thinning, though she kept it short and butch. Now and then she caught him staring at her, bemused by his big gorilla son or almost (she didn't really think so) remembering his daughter.

She liked being a big brother. She half remembered watching out for Theo when he was a geeky high-school freshman with no friends and girly long hair—remembered intimidating the bullies who wanted to intimidate Theo. Those memories gradually became more vivid, washing out bleached memories of growing up a girl, Theo's little sister. She remembered encouraging him to work out, get bigger and stronger so the bullies wouldn't bother him. She had moved bench and free weights to the basement because she knew he was uncomfortable *invading* her bedroom to use them. What really made Theo uncomfortable in her room, she knew, was the home-made screensaver on her desktop monitor, endlessly cycling raw beefcake. The nerdling needed just to deal: his big brother—bigger in every way, not just a year and a half older—was gay and pretty happy about it.

Well, not so happy maybe about not having done much recently. She regretted not pushing harder with Raf. God, the blue balls when he finished with her and sent her home to the dentist's and professor's house. That night she'd had to beat off twice before she could sleep. The first *experienced* (she recalled earlier but it wasn't clear they'd really happened) boy orgasm almost disappointed her. She kind of remembered girl orgasms being more profound, less localized and fleeting, if more effort to achieve. But she liked spunk. Splooge. Cum. Even the names were fun. As a girl, she'd thought it gross without much acquaintance—as a boy,

TATTOOED LOVE BOYS

she licked it off her hand, savoring the slimy texture, the salty-bitter taste, and rubbed it gummily into the hair on her belly and chest.

When she woke, early, she was delighted by the morning wood in her boxer shorts but needed to piss so she left it alone. She stumbled to the bathroom and remembered she could do it standing up, lifted the seat, fumbled her dick out. Unused to pissing while half hard (or maybe she just didn't care), she made a mess. After brushing her teeth, washing hands and face, replacing the dressing under her arm, she went back to the bedroom and fired up the laptop. She pointed the browser to her favorite slashfic site. After only a few paragraphs she found the story insipid. The boys were insipid, dreamy and yearny, barely out of adolescence—big eyed and delicate like the figures in yaoi manga, for which she used to have more patience. When she was a girl. Without much trouble, she found a site more to her liking and, reading badly spelled, pedestrian porn, rubbed out another. She smeared the splooge over her abs, sucked the remnants off fingers and palm.

She pulled on a pair of b-ball shorts, stuffed her big feet into shoes, and climbed the stairs to the professor's and dentist's gym. She preferred free weights, which required more finesse and, by way of their instability, worked peripheral muscles as well as those directly involved, but the machines were all she had till they returned home.

She was benching, legs splayed wide while her arms pressed the bar up, when she heard her brother's feet on the steps. She finished the set before looking toward the door. Theo gaped at her. "What?" Her shorts were too long for anything to be hanging out in public and perturbing his masculinity.

"What did you do to your arm?"

"Got Raf to give me a tattoo." She sat up. "Wanna see it?"

"*Raf?* That's his name? He didn't talk you out of it?"

"It was a sudden thing but I only had one idea, one small design, not dozens."

"Just nine."

Emmanuel peered at her brother. He was unhappy. "I'm going back today, if you'd like to come with me. Didn't have enough cash to pay him yesterday."

Aimless, Theo turned away. Running his hand along the white plaster wall, he paced until the descent of the peaked attic roof prevented further progress. "There's no point if I can't decide what I want."

"I should have let you get yours first." But then she'd still be a girl, and younger than Theo. It seemed likely, anyway.

"For once," he agreed without turning, his voice thin with unsuppressed bitterness. It was hard for Theo, being younger, smaller, less. "Is he gay, Raf? Your summer-in-Europe boyfriend? He shouldn't ask you to pay."

"I'm not his type, as it turns out." *You are*, Emmanuel didn't say. "You should come with me anyway. Get out of the house. Maybe we'd meet a girl for you."

Theo still didn't turn. "Are you done? I want to work out."

"Fine." Irritated, Emmanuel got to her feet. She was done. Her brother smelled worse than usual, as if the bodyspray had rotted his skin overnight. "Have at it."

"Wait," Theo said when she was almost out the door. "When are you leaving?"

They walked along the towpath in hot sun, brother and brother. Strangely, after his shower Theo hadn't fragranced himself to hell and back: he smelled of boy, soon of sweat. He smelled good. Emmanuel wanted to rub his head where pale scalp gleamed through dark stubble but figured it wasn't a liberty she ought to take. She wanted to ask again why he'd cut it. Probably some fallout from his on-line rivalry with Simon, like the disappointing first visit to Raf's shop.

"When I came along this way yesterday," she said, "there was a bunch of kids skinnydipping in the canal."

"Girls and boys? Or just boys?"

"Just boys."

"Musta been a treat for you."

Startled, Emmanuel laughed. She liked the sound of her own laughter nearly as much as the evidence that her brother had a sense of humor. "Not much to see—they were in a hurry not to be seen. You ever done that?"

"Not really my thing."

Theo didn't like even just taking off his shirt in public. He was shy about it even with her, though she had her suspicions about that.

"You?" Theo asked, startling her again.

"Sure," she said, not really sure. "Not here. Yet."

"Wouldn't try it *here*," Theo muttered. "That water looks nasty."

"Wanna find out?"

Before he could react, Emmanuel had him in a mild chokehold, lifting him against her chest. The stubble on her cheek rasped on the stubble of his skull.

"Fuck!" Theo grunted—she hadn't cut off his air—grabbing at her arm with both hands. Somehow he twisted and heaved in her grasp. As she went off balance, unlikely pain ripped through her shoulder and then the ground came up and knocked the breath out of her lungs. In an instant, coughing, she was tumbling down the grassy bank. The water pounded her with a crash. She went under.

She came up spitting. When water cleared her eyes, she saw her brother down the bank, teetering on the verge. "Stupid!" he hollered. "You've got an open wound!"

"What—" The new tattoo.

When she struggled upright, the warm silty water only came to midthigh, dragging at her shorts as she floundered back to the bank. Theo wasn't going to plunge in and help but he stood waiting, looking worried. "Jesus, Emmanuel, don't surprise me like that."

Emmanuel couldn't help herself: she guffawed. "How'd you do that, anyway? Been sneaking out to some dojo, little bro, learning super-secret martial arts moves?"

"You surprised me." He shook his head, extended his hand for her. "Are you okay?"

"Sodden," she said, letting him help her onto the embankment. "Fine. Maybe more surprised than you. Who knew that was even possible? Let me sit for a minute."

When she sank down onto the grass and pulled off one bucket of a shoe, Theo crouched at her side. "I'm not the whiny kid who gets beaten up at school anymore, you know. Are you sure you're okay?"

She worked the other shoe off, turned them both upside down and set them aside. She didn't expect further explanation for Theo's mysterious super-powers. "Yeah, sure." Testing the rotation of her shoulder, she felt the twinge but it wasn't bad. "Prolly some bruises and a bit of stiffening up tomorrow."

"I'm sorry."

"Don't be. Glad to know you can defend yourself. And like you said, I shouldn't have surprised you—my own fault."

"Pick on someone your own size next time."

Astonished again, Emmanuel choked on a laugh. Recovering, she said, "Excuse me, Theo, when did you turn into a human being?"

Regarding her gravely, her brother said, "Occasionally one has lapses." Then he sat down properly by her side. "At the moment I'm worried about your tattoo. You don't know what kind of bacteria were swimming in that water."

Reminded of it, she felt the clammy suction of the tape and plastic on her inner arm. Except for her shorts and what was in them, the rest of her, exposed to sun and air, was practically dry already. Peeling at the tape, wincing when it ripped hairs from their follicles, she said, "I doctored it up pretty thick with hi-test antibiotic stuff. It's greasy. Probably the germs couldn't even get through the grease."

"Still. I would be happier if you got it properly cleaned and tended. Soon."

Looking up, Emmanuel caught him staring at her fingers picking at the dressing, at her hairy underarm—her hairy chest. She didn't understand his expression.

"We're closer to your friend's shop than the house," Theo went on. "He'll know what to do. As soon as you're ready."

Raf was calm, undismayed—pleased to see them, Emmanuel thought. Pleased to see them both. With little fuss, he cleaned Emmanuel's tattoo—the alcohol stung, weirdly worse than the first times, fizzes and pinpricks more irritating than her memory of the needle—anointed it with a dose of antibiotic, dressed it anew. He advised her to keep a close eye on it as it healed although he had never heard that the canal bred flesh-eating microbes. Indifferent, he accepted the damp euro notes she pressed on him and rang them into the register. And then they were at a loss.

While Raf tended Emmanuel, Theo had been leafing through a thick album of photos of the shop's work, absorbed, intent—beautiful, really, as a studious child. He had failed to remark on Raf's transformed tattoos but now that Emmanuel noticed the cheap stylized flames were gone, the garlands of flowers returned. The same flowers? Possibly not but near enough. Had Raf changed them back on Theo's account?

He stepped away from Emmanuel to peer over Theo's shoulder and point something out. The smile her brother turned up at him made her heart contract and then thump uncomfortably. They were too pretty together—like manga boys, they looked too alike. Theo was quite a bit taller and their coloring was different but it was the difference between African-American Barbie and the standard model.

Her tastes had changed, it seemed, since she became a boy herself. The thought of them getting it on was still attractive (the inevitability of it, it almost looked like) but what she wanted for herself was a bigger man, a big, hairy, muscly guy. Like her.

"Anybody want coffee?" she said, loud. "I'll go get it."

Theo started but Raf only glanced at her, his expression mild. "That would be very pleasant, Emmanuel."

She half turned toward the door, then turned back. "Will somebody speak English?"

"Probably, but I'll write it down for you, shall I?" Raf did that, his printing precise and legible, and coached her through the pronunciation.

For some reason that reminded her and she asked, "What was that about the witch's house?"

"Witch?" asked Theo.

"Town legend," Raf said. He appeared slightly put out. "Perhaps *wizard* would be the better term, in English. A learned man back in the fourteen hundreds, more learned than he had need or right to be, not being in holy orders, lived in the house where the café stands now. There were suspicions about him, rumors, but they came to nothing until it was noticed there were strangers, foreigners, living in the house whom nobody recalled arriving. He called them nephews, or sometimes visitors from the Holy Land." Reciting, Raf's voice was thin, precise, almost pained. "The scholar was abruptly wealthier than he had been. Some claimed to have seen peculiar lights and other manifestations about the house in the depths of night. A child died raving, inexplicably. Another, older child murdered her father some days after being seen conversing with the scholar and the foreigners. A youth claimed one of the strangers had bespelled him to perform an unnatural act. Signs, portents—there were others: stillborn or deformed livestock, blights, comets. The mob chose him and his guests as their scapegoats but the guests had vanished. Under torture, he called them, the three of them, angels or sometimes devils whom Lucifer had sent to tempt and aid him. Naturally, he was killed, burned alive. His house was demolished, the soil under it sown with salt. The town's misfortunes eased. A hundred years later a new building was raised on the spot and eventually, say ten years ago, the café opened."

"Whoa," said Theo, fascinated. "We don't have history like that back home."

Raf regarded him soberly. "So you're privileged to think. The stories weren't written down, the storytellers died of smallpox and their languages disappeared, somebody built a Starbucks just like every other Starbucks on the salt-sown foundations of the forgotten wizard's house. Here we do too much remembering. You Americans are fortunate to live in the present as it happens." Turning away, he seemed to mutter, "I too prefer the now."

Emmanuel left them to argue that out—or not. At the café, Coffee Guy behind the counter didn't seem to recognize her (how could he?), but was charming, friendly, flirtatious, and spoke sufficient English that she didn't have to wrestle with Raf's language lesson. Taking her money, he touched her hand with his own in a way he didn't need to and looked into her eyes with great promise. When he turned to prepare her coffee, it seemed he fumbled his white shirt open two buttons more so she could be sure of the interesting knotted tattoo on his chest, just below the left clavicle, its flourishes glowing through curly brown hair. Flowers twined through the knots, poppies and cornflowers—she wondered if it was Raf's work. Surely it was, or Hender's. The town was too small to support more than one tattoo shop. Handing over the three tall coffees, he said, "See you around," as if he'd memorized the phrase but in a tone that made it both a question and a promise.

Walking back, Emmanuel pondered how to encounter him again without a counter and a transaction between them—how to discover his name. He was as tall as she, as substantial. She somehow didn't wish to ask Raf, who would probably know. Spend an afternoon at the public pool swimming and tanning—he had a nice tan, perhaps that was where he'd acquired it. Loiter around the café until he went off shift. Google for the places gay guys congregated. For a few steps they were making out in the back of her mind, Coffee Guy and Emmanuel, necking and grop-

TATTOOED LOVE BOYS

ing—chest hair caught in her teeth when she nibbled his nipple—but then the vision became Theo and Raf again, similarly pleasing in a voyeuristic way but interestingly different.

They weren't necking when she stepped back into the shop, not that she'd really expected them to be. The front room was public space, windowed to the street. Theo was shy…wasn't gay

They were, however, too preoccupied to acknowledge her entrance after making sure it was her. Raf leaned over a large sheet of paper, delicately maneuvering his pencil. Theo watched—watched Raf's hand but glanced up often at his face. Theo's expression was dopey with intent, and something else.

Emmanuel set a cup before each. Raf offered her a distracted nod but Theo nothing. The drawing taking shape was a spidery branch of cherry blossoms. Emmanuel could imagine it spiralling up somebody's arm, twining over biceps and triceps to spray blooms across the upper back, then up and over to deposit more on the round ball of the shoulder and a final profusion on the gentle swell of one pec. Raf paused, sketched in a butterfly alighting.

It was subtle, pretty. She wouldn't have expected *pretty* of Theo. The designs he'd drawn were aggressive, mannered. "I thought you wanted a full sleeve," she said, too loud and abrupt.

He glanced at her but didn't seem to see her. "So did I." He reached for his coffee.

"It's just an idea," murmured Raf, concentrating.

Emmanuel no longer had to imagine the tattoo: the spindly branch climbed Raf's arm, looped onto his shoulder and back, under the translucent white strap of his wifebeater onto his chest. Blossoms blushed rose over the paler pink of his skin. Faint blue shadows made them stand out. Unopened buds and baby leaves were tender spring green. The butterfly was black, blue, purple, with shards of clear, bright yellow. Bruise colors, except it was precise and fine within its outlines, not blurred and sore. She could never manage a seduction so well. She didn't have his talents.

She'd finished her coffee in fifteen, twenty minutes, and Theo and Raf hadn't become any more entertaining. "See you around," she said, echoing the object of her interest. Raf glanced up with a faint smile, Theo nodded absently. She left.

In the square, she waited a while on a bench across from the café, hoping Coffee Guy might emerge, but that would be too easy. Other people did come out. One of them she recognized as Hender. He recognized her as well, raised his paper cup in a salute, but didn't come over. She wondered if he was going back to the shop—if he would be annoyed or jealous at the sudden rapport between his protégé and her brother. She wondered if she'd ever see Coffee Guy again. She went into the café but he was no longer there. Disappointed, she blundered out again without buying anything.

The *Gay Guide to Labassecour* Google found for her directed Emmanuel to a pub that, while not strictly a gay bar, was the next closest thing in this small town. Another site suggested a grove in the park where sordid things might occur, and another told her to try the same café after midnight, when it was the only place still open. Overall, though, she'd be better off making a trip to the university town where her parents did their research. She filed all the information away for later.

It was Theo's night to make dinner, something he was usually pretty responsible (if resentful) about, but he didn't get home till twenty minutes before she expected their parents. He looked a little bruised around the eyes and—was she imagining it?—chafed around the lips. He looked halfway to exaltation and moved his left arm gingerly. "Did he do the whole thing in one go?" Emmanuel asked.

Theo grinned, open, delighted. "Just the outlines. Filling in and coloring later, couple of days." Then he winced and looked a little worried. "Don't tell the 'rents?"

"As if I would. They're going to wonder about long sleeves, though."

"Let them wonder."

"I want to see it but I won't ask you to get all unwrapped right now."

Theo shook his head. "After dinner, maybe. Oh, hey, help me make dinner? I'm kinda running late."

"You'll owe me."

He shook his head again. "Well, you know, I already owe you so what's a little more."

In the kitchen he got busy fast, pointing her at things he needed cleaned or peeled or chopped. It was going to be some kind of stir-fry, apparently. Slicing beef into thin strips, Theo ignored his brother, but when he had it marinating in soy sauce and the ginger she'd chopped he took a moment and just looked at her.

"What?"

"I'm, umm, going out after dinner. You want to come with so the parents don't freak?"

Emmanuel set her knife down. "Out? Out where? You never go out."

Looking away, he smiled. "Raf invited me to join him for a drink. He said you'd be welcome."

"You're underage."

"Not here. Civilized country. I'm not planning to get drunk or anything. I'll buy you a beer."

"Raf? Huh." Emmanuel snorted, keeping her delight to herself. "Am I to understand you're not as straight as I've always been led to believe? Or is this not a date?"

Startled, Theo squeaked, "Date? It's not—" He blushed, blinked a few times. "I guess maybe you could call it that. Hah. That's a shocker." Blush fading, he shook his head. "And I don't quite know what I am because I still think girls are all kinds of sexy but kissing him was hella sexy too."

"Well, good for you," said Emmanuel in jovial, big-brother tones. "Sure, I'll chaperone you, Teddy—" she hadn't called her brother Teddy since he was a little kid—"if you promise not to put on any of that noxious bodyspray."

"Lend me your big-boy cologne?" he suggested with a cock of his head both flirtatious and naïvely mocking.

After his shower, Teddy knocked on her door to show off his ink— get Emmanuel's help doctoring it. She was less surprised by the delicate tracery of branches and shoots and bruises on his arm and shoulder than the unprecedented act of his coming to her room wearing only a towel hitched around his hips. The temptation to make it fall, discover what he had in the downstairs department to offer Raf, tested her resolve. He smelled of her cologne (he'd used too much), which she really felt smelled better on her.

With a kind of brusque tenderness, she swabbed the twigs and branches and uncolored blossoms with a pad steeped in alcohol. The softness of Teddy's skin perturbed her. The hair on his forearms was translucent and there was none on his chest, just a faint glowy fuzz. Glancing at his legs, she noticed that shins and calves appeared only as downy as his arms. He noticed her noticing. "You got all the wild man of Borneo genes from Dad's side. I take after Mom's family. So I'll never go bald."

"Except on purpose." Emmanuel seemed to remember her little brother being more hirsute. Not like her, maybe, but not like a girl either. Under her hand, the muscles of his arm and shoulder felt different than as recently as the morning, when he tossed her in the canal. Not flabbier, but less purposeful than simply useful. Perhaps it was just that he was at rest. She smeared on the greasy ointment. When he stood up to have her apply the dressings, he looked willowy standing before her, not lean and wiry. "What's up?" he asked.

"Nothing." She went back to work, taping squares of plastic like patchwork to his skin.

When that was finished, she told him to go get dressed if they were going out. At the door, he turned back fast and had to grab for the slipping towel. "You didn't say what you think of your friend's work."

"It's—" Emmanuel hesitated. "It's not what I'd have expected for you. Not to say it isn't very nicely done. When Raf completes it and it's all healed up, it'll be...lovely."

Clutching the towel, Teddy frowned, but then he visibly let what he didn't want to hear go and opened the door. Fifteen minutes later he was back, dressed, black shirt severely buttoned and tucked into black jeans, buzzed head making him look an ikon of severity. It was momentarily impossible to imagine him necking with Raf. In her mind Emmanuel stripped off the shirt, finished off the tattoos, and then all was well. She followed him downstairs happily enough, out. She had dressed equally thoughtfully if with different calculation: tight t-shirt was meant to showboat her build, low-slung shorts make it evident she'd chosen to go commando. She hoped to meet Coffee Guy, though another guy might do almost as handily.

Teddy knew the way. He had memorized Google's map, she imagined. They walked through long summer twilight, bucolic suburb to mediaeval town alleys, not saying much until Teddy asked, "What's it like? What guys do with guys, after the kissing?" So he had taken note of her outfit.

She peered at him. He had his head down, looking away. "It's sex," she said. "It's big fun. I mean—" She turned her own head, not really embar-

TATTOOED LOVE BOYS

rassed. "I mean, I've never done it with a girl so it's not like I can compare and contrast." She could, but not in a way that would be helpful.

"Me neither," Teddy muttered, voice small but defiant.

"Really?" It was almost not a surprise.

Teddy half stumbled, recovered. "Not all the way."

Brotherly, Emmanuel put her arm around his neck, holding him up. "It'll be okay, Teddy. You don't have to go through with it—you don't have to do anything you don't want to do. Say *no*, easy as that." Teddy was bigger than Raf.

"But I *do* want. I want to do everything. Will it hurt?"

Emmanuel released him, stepped away. "If you do that? For a moment or two, yeah. Not as much as tattoo needles."

Her brother hurried to catch up, passed her, remained a few steps ahead until they reached the pub, where he held the door open for her as if she were a girl. They saw Raf right away, pale as an exotic orchid in the gloom. Strangely, he was talking with Coffee Guy, who beamed when he saw Emmanuel. His name was Thijs—he spelled it for her. He wasn't wearing the collared white dress shirt and black slacks from the café but a dark green hoodie unzipped nearly to the waist so she could admire the furry expanse of his chest, his tattoo, the steel pin through his left nipple, and jeans worn so low she could make out his swimsuit tanline and be sure he, too, had foregone undershorts. It was all thrilling. By the time he'd bought her a beer that had so much flavor it astonished her she was entirely smitten and Raf and Teddy had vanished.

When the fact penetrated, she said, "Where'd they go? I have to look out for Teddy."

"See over there," said Thijs, soothing and calm. "Teddy is quite safe."

Looking where he indicated, Emmanuel saw a line of private booths and the backs of the two heads, one buzzed to blue shadow, the other blond. "I should—"

"Teddy is quite safe," Thijs said again. "Now and then Raf discovers an interest in women, *particular* women, an impulse that startles him so much he is extremely careful, gentle, easily dissuaded. Your sister will come to no harm."

"Teddy—" But Emmanuel knew her sister would be furious, if it was something he really wanted, if Emmanuel barged in like a clumsy knight in shining armor to protect the damsel's virtue. Still, she watched a moment longer, unsure, saw Raf's fine long fingers caress Teddy's skull and saw her sister turn his head for the kiss. He was beautiful, her little sister—the shorn scalp made his face at once stronger and more vulnerable. When he did it, their father, oddly pleased, said his daughter was prettier than Sinéad O'Connor and ran a Google Image search to show them how Teddy compared to the pop-star crush of his youth.

Thijs attracted her attention back to him by lifting her hand to his chest. One point of the steel pin, not quite sharp, poked her finger. Leaning to her ear, he said, "I also have a, what do you call it in English, a Prince Albert. Would you like to see?"

The sex was good. Not great. Perhaps they were nervous of each other, being so newly acquainted. Perhaps Thijs depended on the novelty of his PA in lieu of technique. She'd had a moment or two of wanting one for herself—he became inarticulate trying to express the sensations it gave him—but the desire passed. Rolling a condom over her own stiff dick, she'd felt a pang, thinking she ought to have said something to Teddy about the importance of birth control (she didn't know if he was on the pill) but Thijs distracted her before the pang could bloom into panic, and she didn't think of her sister again. Anyway, Thijs and Raf were housemates, it had turned out, sharing the big apartment two floors above the café on the square. Teddy was just down the hall. If he got scared, needed his big brother, he knew where she was.

But afterward, dozing on Thijs's bed with Thijs spooned up against her back (his chest hair tickled her when he breathed, the metal in his nipple scraped), Emmanuel had what felt like a dream. She remembered growing up with, not an annoying little tomboy sister, but a nerdy, differently tiresome little brother. Theo. Not Teddy. Then her breath strangled in her throat as she recalled that Theo was Emma's *big* brother and she, Emma, for almost sixteen years had been a girl.

She sat up abruptly. Thijs grumbled in his sleep. "Thirsty," Emmanuel said, though she didn't think he could hear her, and clambered off the bed. Still naked, she stumbled out of the room.

She thought she knew where she was going but ended up in the kitchen, where a low candle in a glass jar guttered on the breakfast table and somebody sat beyond it, face shadowed. "Thirsty," she said again because she didn't know who it was.

"Hard or soft?" The voice with its distinct accent was Hender's. He leaned forward and candlelight caught his stark features, gilded the piercings at eyebrow, ear, cheek, lower lip. The baroque ink at his temple looked purple, like wine in a glass.

"Water."

He stood. Emmanuel flinched back. "Sparkling or still?" Hender asked, stepping away from the table but not toward her. He was as nude as she. Thankfully, she couldn't make out details in uncertain, wavery light.

Unthinking, she took another step toward the table. "Just water."

"Sit, then. A moment."

She was afraid he'd turn on an electric light or just open the refrigerator and she would have to look at him, but he rummaged through the cabinet for a glass without hesitation, filled it at the sink. Emmanuel sat. The polished wooden seat felt unpleasantly slick and cool under her bare flesh. Hender set the glass before her, stepped back. "Thanks," she said. lifting it to her lips. As he turned to round the table, she caught a glint of heavy metal dangling below his crotch—another PA. Was Raf pierced down there as well?

"What did Raf do to my—to Theo?"

Hender sat down. "Raf wants an American wife." Then Hender grinned broadly. Flickering light gleamed unhealthily on his teeth. "Well, actually, of course, he would prefer an American husband but the laws in your country mostly do not recognize that relationship and a husband could not help him emigrate. You aren't concerned about what he did to you?"

"Why? Why not me? I was a girl…before."

"He likes to complicate matters. You were too young. He felt you would enjoy being a boy."

"I do!" The response came without thought but thinking only reinforced it. "I don't want to go back. But Theo never wanted to be a girl. Or a gay boy, any man's husband."

"Are you certain?"

She wasn't.

"It's true that Theo was more effort to…persuade." Leaning forward—now the fluttering light made the design at his temple resemble blood, drawn in intricate patterns like the henna on an Indian bride's hands—Hender shrugged. A billow in the shadow behind him made Emmanuel think of great black wings flexing with his shrug. "In any case, Raf's altruism is erratic. He wasn't attracted to you. To your brother, yes."

"What *are* you? The two of you?"

"Three."

"Thijs too?" she blurted, dismayed.

"We have been here so long," murmured Hender, leaning back again. "But Thijs and I are relatively content. Of course, Thijs has no imagination. He lives in the moment—the future is an impossible destination for him. It would not have occurred to Thijs to take advantage of your possibilities before Raf manifested them. Raf—discontent defines him. It always has, longer than you can imagine. You see, we may not leave this place without a sincere invitation."

"It wouldn't be sincere!"

"Are you certain?" Hender asked again. "Raf has gone away before, several times. When the invitation expires, he must return. Not to America however. America interests him. He will be disappointed, of course, for all the world is an outskirt of America in this era, but one can't reason with him. Come."

When Hender rose to his feet the shadowy wings rose with him, pinions glittering like black knives. Emmanuel shrank back but he reached for her hand. His touch was chill, not like ice, colder, and she found herself upright, enfolded in his arms, his dank, oppressive wings that smelled like incense. "You make a handsome boy," he murmured in her ear.

They stood in the doorway of Raf's bedroom. Raf and Teddy lay on white sheets. Emmanuel looked away from her naked sister, looked back. Raf's arm, crooked over Teddy's rib cage as he spooned the young woman, lifted the breasts on Teddy's chest, made them look larger, misshapen. Matched cherry-blossom tattoos seemed to grow together, one plant joining two bodies. Teddy began to stir and Raf, in sleep, tightened his grasp and pressed his lips to Teddy's nape.

"It is not the time, Raf," Hender said. The regret in his low, shuddering voice caused the world to flinch. "This is not the person."

Shrugging off Raf's arm with less effort than he'd taken to toss Emmanuel into the canal, Theo sat upright. He threw his legs over the side of the bed and planted his feet on the carpet, set wide. Emmanuel looked away again: her little brother's dick, at rest, was bigger than hers.

"You were right," Theo said, his voice foggy. "It hurt. But it was interesting."

Behind him, Raf made a noise like ice breaking. Indigo wings thick as snowdrifts clapped, disturbing the air, lifted him. For just an eyeblink, Teddy became a girl again.

"Not now," said Hender.

"Theo?"

Ignoring or unaware of angelic perturbation, Theo scratched sleepily at the flame-eyed skull inscribed on his left biceps. "Not really interesting enough, though. No offense, Emmanuel, but I think I really am straight." He yawned, shuddering.

"I…I don't need the competition."

"Hah." Theo blinked. "Where's my clothes? We should go home. 'Rents probably shitting themselves with worry. Grounded for life," he grumbled, blinked again, looked up at his brother and, as if properly comprehending her nakedness, glanced his eyes away. "Where's *your* clothes? Did you have fun with wotzisname?"

Raf made another noise, like air collapsing, and settled back onto the bed. Theo shifted his seat unconsciously as the mattress settled. Great blue-black wings cloaked crouching Raf, abstracting him from sight. A fierce itch flared under the skin inside Emmanuel's arm, but then was gone.

"But I *liked* Emmanuel!" protested Thijs.

So did I, Emma wanted to say. Her throat was frozen with disappointment and relief. She felt uncomfortable naked in a way she hadn't a moment before.

Thijs's wings were dull scarlet, not as impressive as Hender's or Raf's. His erection had been impressive but it wilted, dragged down by the weight of its metal, as he glared fiercely at the girl who had been Emmanuel. "He was handsome. And an excellent fuck."

Emma felt another intolerable itch, but this erupted between her legs and when she reached to scratch it, horribly, trivially embarrassed, Emmanuel discovered his own proper prick hanging where it should. He clutched it in his hand. The heavy surgical-steel Prince Albert was chill, but warmed against his fingers.

It wasn't nearly as late as they'd thought. Light hung in the west. As they walked the towpath back to the dentist's and professor's house, Theo asked, his voice merely curious, "Are you going to see him again?"

"Thijs?" Emmanuel shrugged, amused. "Probably. We're here another four weeks. Not a professional visit, though, it's not like I want him piercing anything else."

"Yikes."

Theo wanted not to sound appalled by his brother's adventure in body modification, Emmanuel thought without being fooled. He'd *offered* to show the pretty thing to Theo.

"What about you? Going back to Hender?"

"Of course!" Craning his neck, Theo tried to look at his own arm. His shirtsleeve hid the ink, though, and he stumbled. "It's not done yet! But *I'm* not interested in fooling around with him."

"He wouldn't mind, probably."

"No." Great sincerity thrummed in Theo's voice. "I mean, I've had moments of curiosity since…since you told me you were gay, but it's just not my thing."

Emmanuel scratched at his jaw. His stubble wasn't novel anymore but it still felt good. "Just as well," he said. "More boys for me."

"Seriously?" Theo was outraged. "You seriously think any guy wants into my shorts is going to be interested in a big hairy dude like you?" He threw a punch at his brother's arm that made basically no impression. "Manny, bro, even I know better than that."

Manny? As they scuffled, Emmanuel decided this new nickname was acceptable. "Fine, whatever." Grappling Theo around the neck, he knuckled his brother's bristly scalp.

"Besides, you've already got a summer fling goin' on. Now you need to help me find a girl. That's what gay big brothers are for, evolutionarily speaking."

Laughing, Manny pushed Theo away. "You're on." He relished a challenge.

A few minutes later, Theo said, "You know, I've been thinking. About how Simon wanted so much to impress me with his stupid kanji."

"*Happiness puppies.*"

Theo barked a laugh. "Of course, I wouldn't have got my act together to decide what I really wanted if Simon wasn't such a dick about the pain,

TATTOOED LOVE BOYS

the *horrifying pain*, and how brave he was. But it wasn't me he was really trying to impress."

"Don't say it," said Manny. He tried to remember what Simon looked like, if he was as tiresome as Theo.

My family had sent me to see the shrink because they worried about me. In fact I lived by a couple of simple rules. One was that if I always took money for sex with guys and never took the passive role, then I was straight. Another rule was never to tell anyone, especially not the shrink, what I did after school and Saturdays. My Shadow had taught me all this, whispered it in my ear without anyone seeing him.

GRIERSON AT THE PAIN CLINIC
Richard Bowes

"Yes," the lady said, "you were underage. But I was the innocent one. I didn't understand boys like you with semi-invisible friends, boys who saw themselves as tragic prostitutes in their own personal Bette Davis movies."

The lady in question and I go way back, more than fifty years, to a time of legends and wonders. We first met in the waiting room of a psychiatrist in Boston in 1960. I was sixteen and she was twenty-one. She introduced me to amphetamine and straight sex. I gave her a glimpse into prostitution and my doppelgänger—pretty much an even exchange I'd say.

We met again late this spring in Physical Therapy, an appropriate rendezvous for those in our age range. Some years ago when my arthritic left knee first acted up, the place was called the Greenwich Village Pain Clinic, giving it an enticing hint of medical S&M games.

Now it's called Physical Dynamics but it's still right on a corner of Twelfth Street near Union Square and I still think of it as the Pain Clinic. The machinery is like something out of a well-run gym. Lots of the therapists, especially the guys, are young and cute. Eleven years ago arthritis was my first hint of aging. Late this spring the knee began aching again, stairs started to be a barrier and I came back to be taught new exercises and ways of walking.

Lots of the patients are older and in far worse condition than I. On my third or fourth therapy session I was riding a stationary bike, focused on the pain, knowing I had to eradicate the limp that would destroy my mobility.

If I didn't have this to concentrate on I'd have been obsessing about my problems with a publisher who wouldn't let go of an out-of-print novel of mine, *Minions of the Moon*, which a gay press wanted to reprint. Just that morning I'd had an email encounter with a non-cooperative underling at the publishing house.

Minions came out in the late nineties and won a couple of awards. Its themes are addiction and recovery, booze, drugs and gay teenage hustling. Back then it was a bit controversial. These days it would probably be marketed as YA.

Suddenly a lady's voice distracted me. She had just been given a massage in a small side room and spoke in the clear voice of the old Wasp establishment. "You know," she told her therapist, "I've never lived in a building that had a street number. They always just had names, 'The Riverside,' 'The Dakota.' In England it was 'Payson Manor at Abbot's Gate, Helford.'"

The voice, the conversation, suddenly brought the novel back to the front of my brain. I turned and was amazed. The woman's hair was white like mine but somehow had a hint of gold, like the sun rising on snow. She had that luminous skin only the very rich know how to achieve. "Stacey Hale!" I said. Stacey Hale was her character's name when I'd used her thinly disguised in *Minions*.

She glanced around. "That was many years ago and I should have sued..." she started to say, and then looked more closely, focused on me. "Kevin Grierson," she said which is the name I'd given the narrator in the book. She looked mildly annoyed, though I also saw a flash of calculation in her eyes. "You have a gift for the inappropriate moment."

"I can recall a time when you were happy, anxious even, to see me," I said. Her expression indicated that she had trouble remembering any such an occasion.

So I shrugged and turned my attention back to the Exercycle. When I looked up Stacey Hale was out of sight and I was kind of disappointed.

GRIERSON AT THE PAIN CLINIC

I'd thought she'd have stuck around and we'd have more to say to each other after fifty-plus years.

It's my belief that if one has reached his late sixties and an arthritic knee is the biggest medical problem, one is lucky. Especially since in my case I have reason to suspect my condition may be my own fault.

The veins on the back of my knee were very nice and easy to hit. In my early twenties, a not very auspicious time in my life, I'd shot methedrine into them on the advice of someone who was more than a close friend: my Shadow. Knowing that made me even more determined to triumph now. The idea of a future in a walker and then a wheelchair because of youthful stupidity does not appeal to me.

But as I worked my leg muscles, tried to keep my balance on unstable surfaces, practiced new ways of striding, I kept thinking of Stacey back when we were much younger and she needed me. What I remembered most about that time was a tension between me and the world.

My family had sent me to see the shrink because they worried about me. In fact I lived by a couple of simple rules. One was that if I always took money for sex with guys and never took the passive role, then I was straight. Another rule was never to tell anyone, especially not the shrink, what I did after school and Saturdays. My Shadow had taught me all this, whispered it in my ear without anyone seeing him.

To a weird and weirdly innocent sixteen year old, Stacey was tall and elegant and right out of a movie. Obviously she saw something in me, maybe caught a glimpse of my Shadow. Stacey was acute in some ways.

She introduced me to Doctor X, a speed cult leader who'd taken up residence in her mother's house. The mother and stepfather were in Europe and Stacey as I discovered later was his mistress.

I was in public high school and Boston was a small city. Stories about me had begun floating among my classmates. Members of my family had some idea of what was going on.

I was planning to run away from home. One morning I went to school intending to pick up stuff from my locker and split at the end of the day. Suddenly I was called out of class and told a family member needed to see me.

It was Stacey and she'd appeared at the principal's office saying she was my cousin and that there was a family emergency. She got me sprung and I remember us going through the dark and rainy November Boston streets, taking a streetcar out to the nice suburb where she lived.

Stacey was in desperate crisis. Doctor X had stolen her car, a red MG, and her mother and stepfather were suddenly due back from Europe.

My book bag was stuffed with clothes for my great escape. In the inside pocket of my overcoat was a service revolver stolen from a closet in my grandmother's house.

Stacey knew none of this but she definitely thought I was capable of great things. In her moment of desperation she turned to a kid so baby-faced that no one would sell him cigarettes and whose looks appealed only to pederasts.

In retrospect I knew Stacey saw this kid as a contact with the Shadow, the doppelgänger she could glimpse in and around me. Even fifty-plus years later it wasn't wise for me to think about him.

I remembered all this as I walked with elastic ropes around my ankles, practiced stepping off and onto wooden blocks. In the background, sugary cover versions of eighties songs played softly. Over that and the whirl of machines, I heard a familiar voice say, "No, dear, I do not feel like bending down today."

With my session over and on my way out the door I was a bit surprised to find Stacey waiting for me, asking, "Shall we indulge in a coffee?"

And we did. As we made our way across University Place to a café called the Grey Dog or something, she said, "Understand that I no longer have patience with men whose main interest in me is finding out how to get their hair to look like mine."

"Now that you mention it…"

"It's a subtle tint. But you couldn't get it to work, yours is too thin." We sat, not outdoors but just inside. I ordered iced tea. I've been off booze and hard drugs for decades. Stacey ordered a mimosa.

As we waited for our drinks, I said, "So you've had it with guys like me. Been married much?"

"Three times."

"Any of them gay?"

She was a tiny bit amused. "No one who was adorable in childhood or youth ever fully recovers from the experience. You imagine my life has been a long, lonely attempt to find someone like you. I couldn't imagine

GRIERSON AT THE PAIN CLINIC

there being anyone quite like you and had no desire to find him if there was."

The drinks arrived. I sipped my tea. She drank through a straw and put a very nice dent in the mimosa.

"Actually," I told her, "I recall our brief time between the sheets as your payment to me for dirty deeds you wanted me to do."

"Well, you and your special friend," she said with a wise and knowing smile. "I don't see him with you, today."

"We don't hang around together anymore. I've got no idea where he is." Not quite true, but then again I don't trust her.

Years ago on the Shadow's advice I had taken our payment—a tumble in bed with Stacey—in advance. He and I were curious as to what straight sex was like.

From Stacey I'd found out Doctor X was a college psych instructor with ideas above his station. When he showed up, my Shadow was both beside me and part of me.

I produced the .38 and fired it close enough to his head to part his hair. When he left in defeat, Stacey had no more use for us and sent me and my Shadow on our way.

Decades later she gave no indication of remembering any of this. "Have there been other women?" she asked. "I know there were in that ridiculous book."

"Sure," I said, "1960 was the heyday of 'The Tea and Sympathy Syndrome'. Every woman wanted to straighten out some sensitive boy before he got taken down the Hershey Highway."

"It never works," Stacey said looking me over. Something about my clothes made her smile. She sucked in another draught of mimosa. "You're still in shorts," she said.

"At my age and in my physical shape," I told her, "I consider wearing clothes to be an act of philanthropy, a way of hiding unpleasant truths and making the world a little lovelier. But I don't overdo the charity. It's summer and I had to do exercises."

"The last time we met, you did nothing but whine and beg me to buy you longs."

Right then I had no idea what she was talking about. Stacey saw this and was even more amused, like she knew I'd remember when I thought about it. We parted a little later, saying we'd run into each other in PT.

But what she'd said stayed in the back of my mind. Falling asleep that night an image of me seen in a mirror more than fifty years ago came back. I'm crewcut and dressed in a short-sleeved white shirt, striped tie, black oxfords, white socks and khaki shorts.

Somehow I always manage to forget that I spent the summer of my seventeenth year depantsed. For a teenage boy in 1961, wearing shorts in public was one step away from running home in your jockeys after your chinos had been flung over a telephone wire by a gang of bullies.

But this was the summer uniform of St. Sebastian Soldier and Martyr in New Hampshire. During the regular semesters Sebastian's was a military school with uniforms, drill and saluting. In summer it was a place for academic hard cases—problem kids like me. I'd lost a few months of school when I ran away to New York.

During the academic year the Brothers of the Holy Cross threatened us with summer school. No need for them to worry about runaways. There were maybe forty boys age fourteen to eighteen and none of us wanted to be seen in the outside world. Rumor had it that any kid in shorts caught hitching rides anywhere in New Hampshire was automatically brought in handcuffs to St Sebastian's by the state cops.

When we were taken into town little kids sang "Who wears short shorts?" Guys and even girls our age taunted us. The brothers regarded us as an ad for their teen-taming talents.

My life had been coming apart well before the night at Stacey's house. Running away, which my Shadow and I did after leaving her, made things much worse. Sex without any choices or options is brutal. Coming off booze and speed cold turkey is a horrible thing. My Shadow and I split up and I returned home in disgrace with fortune and men's eyes.

St Sebastian's S&M was where they sent me. Life as a Catholic cadet was hell but I was too numb to notice. My Shadow invaded my dreams. In cool hair and clothes he lived in the demimonde of some city that wasn't New York or Boston.

I'd wake up and stay awake to avoid him.

Summer at Sebastian's, though, seemed ok. It felt at first like I'd been freed from the world and from being seventeen. An early childhood that had been taken away was restored.

There were all these boys plus some novice brothers not a lot older than we were. Within a few weeks that summer I had a crush on one of my roommates, Greg, a kid a year younger than me. Brother Allan, a young guy who taught French and Latin and swam in the lake with us, gave me looks that said he knew a bit about the life I'd led. I thought about each of them a lot.

Over the weeks I did a little dance of desire and distance. Into this world one Sunday morning came news. "Grierson, one of your cousins is driving up to take you out for the afternoon. Stay in your church clothes."

My family didn't want to see me. I knew it was Stacey; was torn between curiosity and a desire to avoid her. Greg changed out of his clothes and into swimming trunks right in front of me, caught my eye and grinned while doing it. Then I was being called.

The main building was an old mansion. Visitors waited in a kind of reception room. I entered and saw my reflection in a mirror at the same moment Stacey saw me. She did not look happy.

The brother at the door reminded her to have me back by eight p.m. I was surprised by what I saw in the look he gave her. "The creepiest guys in earth!" she said as we went down the stairs and towards her little red MG. "And what the hell did they do to you, Kevin? You look like you're twelve years old. And just…ordinary." No trace of my Shadow remained.

In the car she had a flask full of brandy, some ups and some downs. I hadn't had access to booze in many months. I hadn't had speed for even longer. Stacey's voice floated to me as we drove down a New Hampshire back road. "Pictures they took without my knowing…have to get back whatever they have…no telling what they'll reveal," she said. "… need you to go in there and…"

This sounded like a variation on the Dr X crisis. "I don't have the gun," I said. The brandy and the pills made a little rhythm in my head. "And I can't do it dressed like this. You need to buy me long pants."

"There's no place in New Hampshire open on Sundays to sell pants and even with them they'd still laugh at you. Where's your secret friend?" Stacey had parked under some trees. "Your aura is gone. It used to be you and then sometimes I could see the outline of your Shadow around you. Do you know where he is, your doppelgänger?"

"I sent him away when he fucked everything up in New York. He's living in a city somewhere. I see him sometimes in dreams. I believe he dreams about me too."

"Summon him!"

"I don't know how." Of course, I did know that dreaming about him, thinking about him intently did the trick. It was just that I didn't want him back. But high and with her hounding me I couldn't think about anything else.

As evening began, we were riding in the two-seater when suddenly it felt as if I was sitting on a lap. 'Hey, Kev, you look like something out of a priest's wet dream,' my Shadow said in a voice that was half inside my head and half out.

Then it was twilight and we were back at St. Sebastian's. "You go right inside and go to bed and nobody will notice how screwed up you are," Stacey said.

She'd just given me another pill, a down this time. I got out of the car and looked at my Shadow with his nice hair, his ankle boots, a turtleneck and tight, black chinos—a hip hustler.

He said, 'See you when you grow up and get out of this hellhole.' He was smiling. In fact he laughed at me and rubbed his hand on my crewcut. Then, like he suddenly remembered something, he pulled back, jumped into the seat and said, 'Let's split before I turn into him.'

Eventually I must have done what Stacey told me because I woke up in bed. But a big chunk of the prior evening was a blank hole in my memory.

If there was ever any magic at St. Sebastian's S&M it must have been in my mind. Because the remainder of the summer was Catholicism at its meanest: dozens of frustrated teenage boys and a bunch of "celibate" older males all together and afraid of the thoughts even the straightest had to have.

Getting awakened at the usual seven in the morning after my adventure with Stacey and the Shadow wasn't so bad at first. Stacey hadn't given me much and I was very young.

Greg was the first problem. He opened his eyes and stared at me with this look of guilt and fear, held his pillow in front of him so I couldn't see his undershorts, for Christ's sake. Something had happened between us last night but I didn't remember what.

For the rest of the day, in fact for the rest of the summer, he avoided me. After dinner Brother Allan fell in step next to me. It was getting to the time in August that you notice evening coming early.

GRIERSON AT THE PAIN CLINIC

"Certain behaviors are so repugnant to God and man that they don't get discussed, let alone acted on, Grierson," he said. "You understand? We'll keep an eye on you for the rest of the semester. Stay away from young Gregory. And first thing tomorrow morning go to Brother Otto and get your hair cut."

Looking in a mirror I realized it had grown an inch overnight. Being touched by my Shadow had done that. I got a new roommate, a big, dumb guy who never spoke to me. He pushed me out of his way every chance he got and punched me a few times. No one in the school spoke to me. Many stared.

I understood the ritual and kept quiet. Only a couple of weeks of summer semester remained. The school wasn't going to tell my family about my behavior or ask them about the "cousin" who'd visited me. It would reflect badly on them.

That fall I was in college and me and my Shadow got together again. Once, I asked him what Stacey had wanted and he said, 'Old photos of her screwing two or three guys and stuff, nothing interesting to me. And stupid things she wrote about doing drugs. She didn't want her family to find out and have her locked up.

'These Weirdos who live in a place in the woods were going to blackmail her. I appeared in front of them like some kind of specter, said I'd haunt them forever. They gave the stuff up with no problem. Stacey wanted us to get it on as her payment but I wanted money and pills.'

Five decades later at the PT clinic, I didn't run into Stacey for a little while. I wondered if her appointments were now at a different time but couldn't find out. The clinic had some younger patients. But mostly it was people my age and older. We reminded me of the fallen angels in Michael Swanwick's story "North of Diddy-Wah-Diddy." Like them we were mostly a displeasure to view but we each still possessed one, maybe two aspects—a lovely arm, a dancer's grace—left over from the paradise of youth.

I didn't quite forget about Stacey or my Shadow. But I was making progress, toughening muscles, learning stretch exercises and a different stride. The arthritis pain had receded and that had most of my attention.

Then one day as I got taught a way of rising from a chair and sitting back down that didn't involve pressure on my knee, I heard the voice.

Stacey emerged from a side room with a young woman therapist saying, "Darling, there's no such thing as a cute old man. Old men are either rich and thus fascinating or poor and tiresome."

Stacey nodded in my direction to illustrate the second kind. She walked past a gaunt senior citizen with a walker and healthcare worker close at hand. "Calvin!" she said, "I never expected to see you here!" He looked up from the simple exercise he was doing and slowly focused. He said her name and tried to straighten his bent back.

"Easy, you could kill him," I said when she came close to me. "But, rich and thus fascinating?"

"C.L. Dickerson? Yes and yes. But it's you I wanted to see. Coffee? Later?" I said yes and knew something was up.

There is enormous satisfaction to be had in looking back over a long and misspent life! So often when I was very young I was tempted to do the right thing. And each time I refused! In my thirties, of course, I reformed, came off drugs and booze, became semi-respectable, found a partner and took care of him when he died of AIDS. But how boring it would be if I'd always been good.

This I thought about as Stacey and I sat in a café. It wasn't the one we'd been in before but the differences were minimal. Again we sat just inside.

I'd caught the hint of tension about her and pretty much guessed what she wanted from me but watching her tale unfold was part of the fascination.

"There was that friend of yours," she said, sipping alcohol through a straw. Stacey was one of the few people on earth who knew about my Shadow. She looked a bit thinner this time, and was prepared to be a lot more direct. "You and he were so close."

"I don't see him anymore," I said. "Don't much even think of him. He and I are kind of like you and me. If we hadn't met at the clinic, would we be on each other's minds?"

"But you can summon him. I've seen you do it." Stacey had a bright intensity. "Not as good as nine lives" she said. "But you do have two."

"However, they run concurrently," I said, "and will probably end at about the same moment. Mostly I try not to dwell on my Shadow. Thinking about him brings him closer."

There was and is more to it. The Shadow is part of me and I'm part of him. He's the bad habits I manage to keep at bay and me taking care of

GRIERSON AT THE PAIN CLINIC

myself keeps us both alive. None of that was any of Stacey's business. To her the Shadow and I were a couple of magic servants she could hire and dismiss at will.

"Your doppelgänger will know I want to see him," she said. I didn't reply but she knew she was right. Remembering the incident at St. Sebastian's had given me a couple of dreams about my Shadow. After that conversation with Stacey, I had them again.

He's old and sick and shabby now. There was one dream, confused and half remembered, in which my Shadow and Stacey talked. I don't remember what happened or what was said but she looked determined, even desperate, and he looked disturbed.

The next time I saw Stacey I was coming out of the PT clinic as she was arriving. "I'm having difficulties with your Shadow," she said like she was complaining about bad service. But she looked pale and unhappy. I was curious but the hint of despair I detected made me wary of her.

A week or two later was my last day of PT. The therapists said I'd done great. Stacey was nowhere to be seen. But I'd had a disturbing dream, almost a nightmare, in which she looked scared, begged for help, and I caught a glimpse of a figure with red eyes.

After that last PT session I was walking home in the first blazing hot day of summer when I saw my Shadow. More than a bit translucent, he leaned against a fence in Washington Square Park looking needy, threadbare. When he moved he had the limp I'd just managed to lose.

"Stacey says you've been goofing off," I told him.

'That crazy lady wanted to get me dragged down to hell.' His voice was kind of wispy. 'She got in touch with me, wanted a job done. I figured it was the same trip as Doctor X or the Weirdos in the Woods.

'But this time she wants me to go to this place out West, wants me go into a cave to tell someone who calls himself the King of Death to lay off her. Instead of having stolen her car or having a bunch of photos of her, this one has her soul.

'I told her no, I wasn't messing with anyone who calls himself the King of Death. She was pissed! Under all her talk Stacey was afraid she was dying.'

"Oh?" I'd seen no trace of that.

'She had all kinds of stuff wrong inside.'

"Had?" I knew passersby saw a senior citizen seemingly holding one side of a conversation with an empty stretch of fence.

My Shadow said, 'I know she treated us like hired help, put me at risk. But she was more like us than anybody else I've met.'

"Was? You think she's gone?"

'Unless she's got someone she knows who's stronger than me. Not that I'm so strong now.' Then, after a pause, he said, 'Let's get back together.'

Encountering him is like running into an old boyfriend with whom you share lots of memories but whom you never want to have near you again.

"Here's the paradox, honey," I replied. "If we're together I'll get so fucked up I won't take care of myself and I'll die. And I'm pretty sure that then you'll die too."

'Why, if I'm so evil, aren't you really good?' He wanted to know.

"We're both doing our best," I said. I send him money, a couple of hundred a month, mailed to a post-office box in Vancouver. But I took out my wallet and gave him all the money in there—twenty-five bucks, maybe thirty. Who carries actual money these days?

'I know where you live,' he told me.

"Good for you! So do I and at our age being able to remember things like that means we're still ahead of the curve." I walked away with almost no effort. The therapy and exercises have pretty much taken care of the knee for now. My Shadow, though, couldn't keep up.

Glancing back as I passed the fountain, I saw him flicker in the sunlight. I looked again and he was gone. But we each know how to find the other in our dreams.

At my door, I looked back up MacDougal Street to see if I was followed. As far as I could tell I wasn't. As usual these days there was nothing of interest in my mailbox.

The idea of us and Stacey as three of a kind, the feeling that we existed somewhere outside the human sphere, alien and alone, wouldn't go away. The thought of her being dead, of losing an acquaintance after not having thought about her for so long, made me sadder than I would have believed possible.

But I climbed the stairs easily now. And I reminded myself that I needed to talk to someone at the publisher about getting back the rights to *Minions*. Which was a nice distraction.

Every clan has their sails tied up and oars stowed but the sun is getting high so they're putting up their shade cloths. Lots of green. Lots of blue. Some gots paintings on their shade cloths, big hawks, octos, many fish in nets. Some gots paintings to read that shout colors about how they think they the best.

WAVE BOYS
Vincent Kovar

Item Catalog #0455-A
Translations made with omniligua.3.1

---fragment begins---

The boats and barges, junks, single-sails, skiffs and catamarans tied up on nine-night, making the third city of the big moon. This city is smaller than the second and third 'cause man o'man the Rooskies are poor losers after a fight. Poor losers until it comes time to sell their stinky Voka or fuck-trade.

This city-time was fighting too. Wattabee and Tat-Tat, his skin all painted over with blue paintings nobody can read, are wrestling on the deck of our boat. Wrestling and punching and sometimes biting so as you'd never know they loved each other like brothers and sometimes something more too. Doobie made a necklace of a pearl drilled through and strung on whale leather that he said he'd tie on the Wave Boy who won.

We's all Wave Boys. Most of us anyway except the oldsters but they keep mostly to the barges and slow-movers anyway. The eight of us, me, Doobie, Tat-Tat, Wattabee, Gem and Ki (they's the green-eyed twins; the only real brothers), plus Sparks and blind-Zef—we's the Tunder-

Boys. We's called that on account of the drumps Tat-Tat's pa taught us to make. He was a thin-eye like Tat-Tat and painted the blue on his skin. He painted some of us too but only pictures of real stuff. Only pictures that we can read. I got a kraken-eye on each ass cheek. Zef's got stars all over his low belly. Most of the other guys have stuff too.

It's part of what makes us the Tunder-Boys though most people don't know that as we usually make clothes to cover our pictures when the cities get made. People see them of course, during Oyo when nobody wears clothes and during market if we want to fuck-trade but that's not the…

---Section damaged/illegible---

…like me an…

…sacred to all Wave Boys…

Tat-Tat throws a good punch and Wattabee spits blood. Not on the deck of course. He spits into the sea, so as to maybe draw the fish. Wattabee has Tat-Tat by the hair see and pulls him in too close. Should have put him face down but didn't. So Tat-Tat throws two, right into Wattabee's lip. Gem and Ki and Sparks all let out a big whup and I'm laughing. While Doobie and Zef pound the drumps as hard and fast as they can.

We's always having fun like that. The other Wave Boy clans know we's at city. They hear our drumps drumpin and want to play and maybe they will but not now. Now is when we just drump and cheer and fight and let 'em all know the Tunder-Boys are here and we's the best.

Three of the Sea Feather boys come up to the rail to watch the fight. I can't tell if they want to fight or trade or if they just can't pay the pass fee to walk across out boat to the next in city. But I know Sparks has his bow up in the rigging and everybody can see the bone knives the twins got strapped to each arm. Then I see the lead Sea Feather boy giving me the eye and so I give him the eye back.

He's a tall, lean one with a gandy face and black hair spiked up on his head but none on the rest of him. He smiles at me. A big wide smile. I can see one of his front teeth has a little chip out of it and under his left eye is a bit of purple-brown so I know he likes to fight. All three of them are slicked up with oil so I know they're out looking to be looked.

I don't smile back. Not yet, though my eye likes him. Instead, I look over the other two, real obvious so I show him I'm looking to look. The other two is neither so tall but they're both hard. The oil and sun makes bright-shine all the grooves in their muscles. Only the lead boy is wearing a loiny. Oily lines carve diagonal down each hip and duck beneath the hide, making a secret. Yeah, he's definitely looking to look 'cause most Wave Boys only cover when they don't want to show their true feeling.

Even over the drumps I can hear Wattabee and Tat-Tat chumping each other. I stare down the Sea Feathers then turn my back. I'm not afraid see 'cause my boys is watching and Sparks has his bow.

When I turn to look Tat-Tat is lying on the deck has Wattabee's head on his chest. There's blood in Wattabee's blond hair. His head is bouncing 'cause Tat-Tat's breathing so hard. Wattabee has Tat-Tat half in a hold, one arm around the neck, one arm going between his legs but he's given up trying to lock his hands. They're all worn out now.

Doobie and Zef stop drumping.

"So who won?" I look up at Doobie who has the necklace and his face is all tight with thought. Gem and Ki and Sparks all start shouting their votes but they keep changing their minds and don't make no sense.

From behind me I hear one of the Sea Feathers say, "the yellow-haired one is the winner. He's on top and has the most blood on him."

I didn't have to turn to know it was the smiley one. I know 'cause I got eyes painted on each ass-cheek and it's like they can see even from under my loiny. That's what I like to tell boys anyway. Gem and Ki and Sparks all start to argue but they's just making noise. So, like always, Blind Zef comes down from the roof of the deck house and makes the decide.

"How's he gonna decide?" I know it's the smiley one talking again, trying to get me to turn around so he can look to look. I talk back without moving.

"Zef's the best wrestler. Watch."

Sparks makes some jokes about Zef being a better archer than Sea Feathers too and that makes us all laugh. Blind-Zef though, real serious, runs his hands all over knot of Tat-Tat and Wattabee, seeing with his fingers where our boys touch and where they don't. He feels the blood too, in Wattabee's hair and running out of Tat-Tat's nose.

His fingers are so light that the blood barely leaves a mark on em. Sometimes his touch is so light he can walk on the waves without sinking. That's what we tell the other clans anyway. Blind-Zef also cops some good feels and that makes Tat-Tat and Wattabee giggle a little. Because his light fingers tickle and 'cause he looks to look with his fingers. He knows 'em already. Both of them. He's hammocked with both apart and both together and his fingers remember every inch of skin that's ever been at any Oyo. He probably would know the boys behind me if he touched them. Maybe even if the wind turned and he caught their smell.

Zef says they should share Doobie's necklace and everybody gets real serious then. I know without looking that even the smiley one behind me isn't smiling no more. Sharing a thing somebody made with their hands makes **---word untranslatable---** like Oyo only a little bit at a time.

The Sea Feathers respect that and pay their toll to walk over. They pay in feathers that we'll make into stuff or maybe we'll trade on. Who knows?

As he walks past me I snatch one side-glimpse of the smiley lead boy. He feels it and looks over. He smiles again. This time I smile back. I tell him my name.

"I'm White Cloud," he says and tells me it's because he was born with white hair. I look real close and yeah, all up and down him. I can see his hair is colored black because down deep in the depths it's coming out of his head white.

He says, "It's one of our totem-ways. We all make it black with octo-ink."

He lets me touch it and it feels very soft. His skin gets red under the brown when I do.

His boys don't like me touching him though. It ain't Oyo and my own are starting to whistle so I take my hand away and the Sea Feathers pass over to the next ship. I wonder if he's got his own eyes painted under his loiny 'cause though he doesn't turn around, I can still feel him looking.

A few more pass-over and pay up. Some oldsters drop a couple reed mats. One brings a net from some Wave Boys who wear them like clothes. We also get three shar tooth-tip arrows for Sparks from the Hawkers. They's always good with the sharp things like the blades they made from blackrock to shave the sides of their heads. They leave a strip down the middle that stands up like a shar fin. The oldsters call that hair a Mohawk.

Pretty soon we got enough that we can pass-over ourselves. It pays to make city early.

WAVE BOYS

Sparks stays back to watch our ship. Wattabee too. But the rest of us is itching to look and be looked so we gather up strings of shells with holes carved in 'em for trade and head to center.

City always catches my wind but I never let it show. All the masts gathered together like a crowd of skinny giants makes me think there's never been anything so gandy in all the world. There are four junks in a line out from center that the skinny-eyes like to use so they don't have to pay pass-trade. Sweating, big-bearded Vice-Kings, all wearing their fight-shirts of whale bone, are pouring weed-wine for cheap on their single sail oar-ships. We see a dozen jangada and there and here some skip jacks.

I even pay our pass-fare to walk over one of the big clippers—the Spana Boys boat—even though it's not on our way. As we pass, they sing down from the rigging and everybody around stops to listen. Their songs don't make words we Tunder-Boys know but the sound rolls down in loops and dances in my head.

"We shoulda brought some little drumps," Doobie sounds frustrated 'cause nobody is looking him. Everybody is looking the Spana Boys.

Tat-Tat is walking Blind-Zef, they each got one arm around each other's waist to make Zef look like he can see. Ki and Gem walk that way too. It makes Wave Boys talk. Sometimes they say we all got a twin or sometimes they think one of us is blind that ain't. We keep 'em guessing and talking. I try to put my arm around Doobie's waist but he is cranked about the drumps.

He snaps, "I'm going off to get some weed wine."

"We'll come too. Wait." Says either Ki or Gem, nobody is sure. They talk sneaky like that. Sometimes they talk together or finish what the other started.

"No."

"Not a Wave Boy without your clan Doobie." Blind-Zef says it and even if it wasn't the totem-way they'd respect him. Part of me is thinking that maybe I'll see White Cloud again and maybe my boys won't be around when I do. Maybe his won't either.

"Yeah take 'em with you. Bring back some star fish before Oyo." I say knowing they will even if they swear about it. They will because I'm the Tunder-Boys bull see?

Doobie stomps off. Walking a gangplank over to an Ice-Bear barge and then on to the next boat.

Kovar

Ki and Gem walk after him, not too close, 'cause they know he'll be fighting soon. The Tunder-boys never fight alone and they don't want to miss out.

Every clan has their sails tied up and oars stowed but the sun is getting high so they're putting up their shade cloths. Lots of green. Lots of blue. Some gots paintings on their shade cloths, big hawks, octos, many fish in nets. Some gots paintings to read that shout colors about how they think they the best.

I know back at our boat. Sparks and Wattabee are putting up our own shade cloths. Ours is green with a big drump painted over a cloud. It means the sound when the clouds drump and make lightning.

We pay to cross over three more boats. We see Tooney and Fat Bru on one of the Ice-Bear barges in a big cloud of smoke. They's always cook up good food. So I trade out some shells to so we all can gobble up three sticks of their fry. I have the shells 'cause I am the bull. Ki and Gem and Doobie only got pass-trade. Too bad for them.

Fat Bru ask, "you boys finding Oyo yet?" Fat Bru loves Oyo even more than most. You always find him at the center of the pile and even when he does try to leave he always has Wave Boys holding on like barnacles.

We don't know about Oyo yet but we talk with Tooney and Bru while we eat our fry sticks. The Ice Bears is one of the friendliest clans but they don't playfight like us. When it does come to a fight-fight you always want Tooney and Fat Bru on your side. Just ask the Rooskies.

Us three keep going to center. Over Hawker boats, other Ice-Bear barges and skinny ships of the Vice-Kings. With the Rooskies gone, the Afro-Chan boats are closer to center: the Barbars swinging clubs, the Gold-Teeth and the Zulu-Zannies in their drift-wood hats.

Now that Doobie is off soaking in weed-wine I can spend the drilled shells without hims moaning. I want to get the Zannies to carve us a big-tittie for the front of the boat.

They say they got plenty made up so I can get one now.

Tat-Tat shakes his head no.

"What you shaking no at me for?" I say and I breathe in deep to make my chest big. "I'm the bull I say when we spend it."

The Zulu-Zannies just stare. Their eyes are like pearls hammered into wood man o'man and their bodies is big fish strong. I don't want to look weak in front of them so I tell him to get down so Blind-Zef can sit. He drops on all fours and Zef sits on Tat-Tat's back. That'll keep him quiet for a while.

I'm looking over the big-titties they got. They got three and trying to haggle it out. They all looking to look Tat-Tat so we might be able to fuck-trade and save the shells but they playin' coy. It's hard to haggle in hand-sign. The Zulu-Zannies all cut their tongues out though. Story says that they hate the lie so much they cut out the tongues of all their new boys to keep always the truth. Also, if you lie to them in hand-sign of if they lie to you, they'll cut off the hand that told it.

The lead Zannie is got gold rings in his ears and they bounce as he taps his hand in the air twice. I think he means two shells but when I start to pull them off the string, they all laugh. They laugh with a gargling blowhole sound as they got no tongues. He taps again to say, two strings. I tap and flip my hand upside down to say two is too much but the Zannie keeps tappin two, two, two.

Tat-Tat lifts his head and shows off his lip which is all nice and swollen by now but they know Oyo is close so I guess they figure they'll wait. I wished Wattabee had come with his bloody hair. Zannies like blond boys.

We close on two 'cause he knows how much I want the big-tittie. A big-tittie on your boat sees the wander logs that smash open the hull. It sees the sun when you sail east and when you sail west. You got a big tittie and you never go down. Never get lost.

The Zannie and me shake. His hand is bigger than mine and dry. Mine gets surrounded by his, like they is hammocked up. I am sweating a little. While our right hands are locked I use my left to slide the two strings of shells down my arm and up onto his, up to his big, big bicep. He rolls it the rest of the way up, to the diagonals between his shoulder and arm. Those diagonals make me think of White Cloud's belly. Some Wave Boys would try to reach for another string but not the Zannies. They bargain hard but they honest like the sun.

The big-tittie is the best. She's got hair carved real nice down over the tops of her shoulders and it's stained dark brown. The rest of the wood has gone to a real nice fade and makes her skin parts lighter. Her eyes are painted blue and when I bend down to look I can see there's little chips of shell in the paint that makes 'em sparkle like they wet. She also has beautiful big lips like an Afro-Chan boy.

Zef stands up to finger-see the big-tittie. He says good things which I like because he is the

---shaman? priest? Literal translation is: holy-boy-voice-of-the-sea---

With Zef off his back, Tat-Tat stands up and starts touching the big-tittie's lips like they real. Reluctantly, he goes, "yeah okay. She's a gandy one," but I don't need him to say so.

And the titties are big. Man o'man. That's the power of the big-tittie. They gotta be big to keep away the shars, and cross waves and kraken. They make the rain come too if you rub the nips with fight-blood. She's the pretty best of all of 'em and I would have paid three strings just to get her.

I feel good about the Zannie boy and I think to look to look for him at Oyo but then I remember White Cloud and decide maybe I'll do with him instead.

The Zannies sign that they will keep our big tittie for us until we come back from center but after Oyo we'll be tired, drunk on weed-wine and walking funny so I decide we'll carry her back now. Passing home never costs. I figure we can wait on our boat until everyone has gone center for Oyo and then pass-over again for free.

"You boys strong?" I ask. It's a taunt.

"Stronger than you." Blind-Zef is probably right. He's as big as Doobie in the chest only not so soft and he's got bigger arms too. At clan Oyo he's wrestled us all down and I think sometimes if he weren't blind he'd be bull and not me.

Tat-Tat gets insulted. Probably because he's feeling snubbed by the Zannies so he spits on my feet. I look down and he punches my nose hard enough to stagger me. Before you knows it we's wrestling and all the Zannies are looking. I know Tat-Tat is just showing off. So I give him an elbow in his fat lip to make it fatter. He sweeps my feet out and I fall to the deck but kick up fast so as to make his eggs sick in his stomach. We fight for a while and make it a good fight but I also want to get the big-tittie home and don't have all day to give the Zannies a show.

Zef is hot and tired of standing around so he follows our noise and starts kicking. This sets the Zannies up making hoots in the back of their throats and pretty soon the Gold-Teeth are watching too. Yeah, city is a lot of fun boy.

WAVE BOYS

He may be blind but Zef lands plenty of kicks on us both. He don't care which he hits he just wants to move us on. I get his toes in the ribs twice and Tat-Tat gets it in the big part of the thigh.

After a while, we're all fighted out so we decide to leave 'em wanting and stop. Zef struggles up the big-tittie on his own but he don't know where from where at city and is as like to fall into the water as get home. I don't want to have to pay Afro-Chans flotsam flee for losing the big-tittie in the sea so Tat-Tat and I get up and help.

Tat-Tat's limping and I am breathing rough. Man o' man. Everyone waves us bye and though we didn't bring our drumps, everyone knows the Tunder-Boys are at city for sure!

The big-tittie is heavier than I thought. It's good wood too. We's so pleased that Tat-Tat signs to the Zannies to come by our boat and we'll give 'em a drump and make ally. They don't sign yes or no. The Bull taps his headdress twice. I can tell he's the bull because hat is woven in with red and blue reeds. The tap means he needs to think about it. Two times means how long he's gonna be thinking.

I'm not mad at Tat-Tat. I'm the Tunder-Boy bull but his pa is what taught us the making of drumps so it's like that.

Though Blind-Zef can lift the big-tittie all by himself, it takes two of us to carry it as it's so big and awkward. That and Zef can't see where he's going. We lift it over the rails between the Zulu-Zannies and back toward the Vice-Kings.

I think again maybe to send my boys away so if I meet White Cloud they won't be around to hoot and whistle. I think maybe to send Tat-Tat home with Blind-Zef but don't want to leave my new big-tittie. Than and nobody's a Wave Boy without you're their clan. Even so, I keep looking for White Cloud.

Lifting is thirsty so we trade Tooney and Fat Bru six shells for three hits of weed wine and they tell us a story about how they stole their own big-tittie from the Shellies in a fair fight. I lean out over the prow and look down. Their big-tittie is good but theirs don't have the blue shell paint in the eyes and one tittie looks bigger than the other. Even looking upside-down I know ours is better.

After a while I can see Fat Bru's beady little eyes starting to stick too long on our big-tittie and he's wiping the fry on his hands into his beard like he's thinking so we lift off.

Kovar

It's when we walking along the barge of the Ice-Bears, who wear their white furs even when it's hot like today, that I hear the conch horns of the King's parade. So we all fall down on our knees and faces. Everyone one of us on all the boats grouped around in city. Even the big Vice-Kings, the hair-proud Hawkers and the Gold-Teeth put their faces right down to deck.

As we hear 'em coming close, Tat-Tat and me and Zef all try to block the big-tittie with our bodies so the king don't see it and decide to take it as his Oyo gift.

I peek up and see-tell by the marchers' ink-stained hair that it's the Sea Feather Boys who's won the election. The clans is parading to Oyo. They's all painted the big kraken eye chests in bloody red and the oil they put on their bodies is mixed with fish-scales so their skin sparkles in the sun. The king is up on his fancy chair, carried by reps of all the Wave Boys. The mantle of shiny fish-skin and shell is around his shoulders and the crown of feathers is on his head. In between, there's the smile of White Cloud.

Nobody told me he won the election and it's not good to wish it on any other boys except your own but somehow I'm happy. He looks down from the carved and painted chair and I can tell he's looking at me not our big-tittie and I am thinking man o'man this is gonna be a good Oyo.

I look for Gem and Ki or even Wattabee but don't see 'em. Then my face gets all hot with shame man because none of the Tunder-Boys is helping carry the King's Chair. I'm the bull but Doobie is the one who usually remembers that kind of stuff and he's off drunk on weed wine and fighting.

White Cloud don't seem to be minding none though. He's still smiling and the carrier boys is waiting. I can't look him in the eye though so I look him over, respecting the knife scars and bruises that say why he's king today. I want to touch them scars. I want to follow them with my fingers and see-touch him like I'm Blind-Zef.

Then comes a thrump, a big thrump, bigger than our tunder and a Afro-Chan junk jumps up in the air before flying to pieces. The boys that been flung up in the air flop around and even from across city you can sense their faces is all confused like, why we flyin' in the air and the boat coming all apart?

WAVE BOYS

The waves makes city ripple, masts and rigging popping up and down like somebody is shaking the rag of the ocean. He is though. We all know who. It's a kraken, come to claim his due from city.

Sunna, everybody is hooting and hollering, running for their homeboats. The King's Chair goes down as every Wave Boy but the Sea Feathers drop it. White Cloud's boys turn, kraken eyes all turning with their chests and looking as he goes down. They none fast enough so I spring up and he crashes into me and we both go down a tangle of skin and crown and noise.

"Take the big-tittie home!" I shout at Tat-Tat and Blind Zef but the next boat, an oldster barge, has a kraken tentacle wrapped around its middle. It don't move so much as it just gets smaller all quick-like and it folds the boat in half with a sound like the time Doobie broke my nose. Only this time everybody hears it and it hurts my ears it's so loud.

Ki and Gem come over a pile of nets carrying Doobie between 'em. He looks like he was drinking then fighting rather than the other way around. There's blood all over his chest and his head is lolling forward. Every time it bobs up I can see he his face is all red-wet too. I'd be real proud only now's not the time.

The barge we're on pitches port-ward real fast then back and everybody goes flying down in a pile like me and White Cloud. They're on the other side of the King's Chair and as it slides it scoops a bunch of them off the deck, smashes them through the rail and into the gap between us and a boat of Gold-Teeth that's untied and trying to pull out.

White Cloud and me is pulled out of our knot as we slide down on top of the whole mess then we fall downwards as the boat pitches the other way. The chair and the nets is above us now but goes flying over. White Cloud grabs a ring in the deck and I grab his leg and for a second we's floating over the water watching the King's Chair splash into the foam.

The deck bucks and leaps, trying to get away from the Kraken, trying to get away like the Gold-Teeth boat that tried but didn't make it. Then the two boats clap together like wood hands man. They clap and every Wave Boy who's holding onto the port side is crunched between the barge and the Gold-Teeth boat. They're not hooting anymore. They're screaming like gulls over and over. Some ain't moving anymore at all.

A mast comes down from behind us, thrumping onto the deck and more boards fold in half, their ends fly up like the hands of Zulu-Zannies signing. The deck swings out toward the water again, not so much this time, not so much the mast comes down on White Cloud and me but enough we can see.

In the waves I can see Sheller Boys face down. They's no friends of the Tunder-Boys, except during Oyo, but some of them is handsome and it's all us against the kraken right?

Now we're not Tunder-Boys anymore, not Sea Feathers or Afro-Chans or Vice-Kings or nothing. We's all just Wave Boys fighting the kraken that's come to city.

There's fire climbing up the masts North Northwest and I can tell that Tooney and Fat Bru's fry has spilled and is making their boat go to char.

City is broken and boats are heading out to all the compass. I see some Wave Boys pull Ki out of the water by his long hair. Some others got Gem too but they see his right leg is torn off leaving insides dangling like red weed. So they drop him back into the water. Ki is screaming because he and Gem is real brothers, twins but there's nothing to be done. The Hawkers is got Ki now. He's flotsam and I know they'll do him like they do. If I ever see him again he won't be a Tunder-Boy no more but a Hawker. Outside Oyo that's what make a Wave Boy part of his clan, the other boys doing to him like they do.

There's still a bit of city left. The boat we're on and fish skeleton of others branching off the main line. Blind-Zef is three boats down now and holding up bloody Doobie by the chest. Doobie's feet are dragging and his knees are bent. I yell again at Tat-Tat to take the big-tittie home.

"I'll go give Blind-Zef some eyes." I say and I start to clamber-climb over toward them when there's sharp in my thigh. I look down and see White Cloud has stuck me with his knife. Not all the way in, not so as to hurt but to mark me. I's pissed off as I'm the Tunder-Boys bull and nobody marks a bull except in a fair fight. As I am looking down at my body though I see a smear of fight-paint from where the kraken eye painted on White Cloud's chest has rubbed off on mine and I know how he's thinking.

Fast like, I rub my hand in the blood on my thigh and put a hand-print of it on White Cloud's face. Now he's black hair, white smile and red print of me—his brown eyes shining between the bloody fingers I've left. Yeah man. Now I am sure sad there's no Oyo as city is all breaking up.

That's when the big bastard lifts his head out of the ocean and gives us a look at his face. It's not just a kraken, it's big Dagon himself. I swear boy. Dagon himself.

His face is like the back of your hand, tentacles hanging down like your fingers only bending every which way. And he's big. Man o'man is he big. He's his own island of greeny suckers and wet fish belly. That's when another junk flies clean over city. Clean over. Scattering screaming handsome boys like a shitting bird dropping its gunk on your deck.

Then I mark White Cloud one more time. I grab the hair on the back of his head. I do it as hard as his black hair is soft and plant a kiss on him. Our teeth crack together and one of us is bleeding. We both taste it I know. It's not a fuck-trade kiss. It's a mark that says nobody is his or mine until we fight at Oyo and decide if who gets the claim. Maybe we both do.

Dagon makes his rattling tunder and everyone is clamping their hands over their ears because it's the loudest racket ever. The sound makes your brains bleed into the back of your throat. The sound smells like sea weed left too long on still water. The sound smells like fish guts when you cut em open and throw 'em at your mate. It's everywhere and Dagon's not just chewing fish, he's chewing up Wave Boys. Then he dives back into the deep-deep and a wave slaps us down.

After that White Cloud goes with his boys. Back to find their own home-ship. There's only four of them left so they gots to move before they get claimed as flotsam or their boat does. I get back to the Tunder-Boy boat right as the last branch of city cuts its lines behind me.

Tentacles are springing up like flying fish and splashing back down. Bits of boats is flying behind. Bits of boys. A foot flying naked of its leg. A bit of rib leaving shiny strings of red air behind it.

In between the tentacles shooting up and down is the horizon of sails. To all the compass, until next city. I think, bye-o Ki. Bye-o. The next time I see you, you'll be walking funny and wearing Hawk-hair. Tat-Tat is there with the big-tittie. She's sitting on the deck and her shiny eyes are looking back at the churn we're leaving behind. I'm at the wheel and am wrestling it west. The sails is up and we've got wind but we aren't going too fast. Not yet.

Wattabee is yelling and pissing off the bow to show we're not afraid, not even of Dagon. The boat is pitching and yawing and he's using his hands to hold onto the boat rather than to his thing so the piss goes as much on him as on the ocean. But he don't care and we don't care 'cause after the churn, at the next city, we'll tell 'em all that Wattabee pissed right on the head, right on the very head of Dagon because Tunder-Boys aren't afraid of nothing. I turn around, bend over and yank up my loiny to show Dagon I got kraken eyes just like him. I show him my ass-eyes to say he's nothing and that I ain't scared of him behind me.

Behind us, the sea makes three big thrumps and masts of water spurt up after each one. Some oldsters are dropping their tanks of sod-yum, the water lightning that they make we don't know how. It's all cloud powder that wants to get back to the sky if you try to drown it. Man o' man does it thrump big.

Two Narrow-Eye boys climb on board. They're scrubbed by the sea. Nothing to mark 'em so when we get clear we'll fight 'em and do them like we do and then they'll be Tunder-Boys. They wrap themselves in each other and stay real quiet on the deck against the rail.

Over the side, I hear somebody yelling for help.

Wattabee yells back to us, "I see the beard of a Vice-King and he's crying."

And though everybody is dying all around we laugh 'cause no Wave-Boy should cry in battle.

"What's he say?" I shout back.

"He say nothing. He sink real fast is all."

We know that a tentacle took him from below. Tat-Tat starts to drump on the big drump, the one with our Tunder-drump and cloud painted on it. The passing ships look at us like we're crazy for drumping while death is up from under but we shame 'em all. Far away, a Narrow-Eye boat gets the brave and blows its horns back to us. I turn to the two on our boat, the flotsam boys and tell them to get up and drump and drumble. Pretty soon we's all making a racket and hooting our Tunder-Boy cry out as we head to horizon.

I look around and take a count. I see four Tunder-Boys and two flotsam. "Zef?" I shout out. "Where's Blind-Zef?"

"He's with you." Wattabee says and his words are sharp. I see he's wearing the pearl Doobie drilled. The one he now shares with Tat-Tat.

The other Tunder-Boys stop drumping and are quiet. The flotsam boys stop drumping. They're not made yet and they don't know our rules so they're smart to go still. There's just the waves and the creak and, farther and farther away the horns of the other ship. Tat-Tat looks storm clouds at me. His face says he remembers me saying to haul the big-tittie when we should have been giving eyes to Blind-Zef. And they all remember me hanging on with White Cloud instead of my own boys.

Spark says it also. "He's with you," and I know the vote's being taken. I lost our holy-boy-voice-of-the-sea. When we clear the churn they'll elect the Wave Boy who'll knife fight me to be bull of the Tunder-Boys.

"Where's Doobie?" Wattabee asks and touches the string around his neck.

I know what I have to say but I don't want to. "He was with me, but now he's not."

"Where's Gem?" It's Sparks this time, from up in the rigging. I look up. The sun is behind Sparks and he is a shadow with edges of fire. I can't see it but I know his bow is out. I know a bone-tipped arrow is pointed down at the smear of White Cloud left on my chest.

"He's with Dagon." I shout this, as though it makes it better. Though it don't.

"And where is Ki?" Tat-Tat keeps the ritual going.

"Ki is not with us."

"Who is he with?"

"The Hawkers." This is maybe the worst thing I got to say besides losing Blind-Zef. Dagon taking a Wave Boy is one thing. Another clan doing what they do to one of yours and making him theirs is crime man o'man.

Doobie, Ki, Blind-Zef all dead. Gem is flotsam, so dead to us. Just like the flotsam boys we salvaged is dead to whatever clan that lost 'em.

Wattabee knows the way of things. So does Tat-Tat. So does Sparks is up in the rigging with his bow, honest as the sun. The flotsam are watching us. Their narrow-eyes real wide now. I can see they're not scared of us doing what we do and making them ours. They's scared for me.

I spit at their feet to show them I'm the bull and I ain't feared, though I am.

The challenge is gonna come from Wattabee or Tat-Tat, Sparks don't like to come down from his rigging and he often only fight with a bow. The challenge comes by knives. I make my face grey clouds and look between them. Wattabee is brave and fast but not so good. Tat-Tat is deadly, man o'man. They vote.

Wattabee say, "Tat-Tat."

Sparks calls down, "Tat-Tat."

Then the boy bends at the waist with his legs straight. He shows me the top of his head and then lifts back up.

I figure I got a half-chance of living and a half-chance of dying today.

Hand to hand they pass the long, bone knife. Each Tunder-Boy but me touches the challenge knife. It's as long as Tat-Tat's forearm. It's spotty with tan where the blood of past challenges has sunk into the blade and turned brown and pale. That's the knife I used to beat Chandro, who was bull before me and tough as a kraken. That's the knife my brother Ivan tried, and my brother Otumbe tried, and my brother Brogan tried to stick into me and make them bull instead. I beat all three and fed their blood to that thirsty knife. Then I pushed what was left into the water to chum the fish.

Now my brother Tat-Tat comes for me and even if I beat him I know I'll face that knife again in Wattabee's hand. Because they're sharing the necklace Doobie made and Blind-Zef tied between them.

Sparks asks, "who will take your stories?"

We argue about this for a while. Sparks can't make the word pictures. Wattabee can but he's not very good so Tat-Tat and I decide we'll take each other's stories. That's the right way of it.

When we hammock up together, we realize how cold we are. We got deep water in us so we put the heat back into each other first to show we have no hard feelings. I stroke my hands over him and he rubs up on me. We wait until we're good and warm then he goes first. I listen to the maybe last story I ever hear and watch his face.

He's older now than when I proved him two years ago. He's got a proud scar from below his starboard ear to his chin that wasn't there in the beginning. Others too. The marks is all good ones though, fight lines. No oldster folds and wrinkly-wrinkles. I run my fingers through Tat-Tat's hair and look for strands like White Cloud but they's all still dark as dark can be. He's a good Wave Boy. Beautiful and wild and strange and keen to fight or hammock equally. His plumpy lip gives his story an extra whisper as it don't always go where he tells it.

He tells me about his pa and making drumps. He tells me the best ways to stretch the skin over the circle and how to make each drump have a voice different from the others. He tells me about all the great cities we been to and how we dreamed about making city ourselves one day. About the Tunder-Boys at center and how all the pass-fares would flow into our boat. He tells me about fights he had with our boys and fights we all had with other Wave Boys. The time we sailed up to a Shellie boat at dark moon and threw fish guts all over them as they hammocked on their deck. The time the Hawkers set our main-sail on fire trying to make us to jetsam but we put it out and we set them paddling away bloody.

He tells me about the fuck-trades he made and times we all got drunk on weed wine and voka. It's gandy to hear it from his eyes. It's like living it twice man o'man. I hear how he dreamed of being elected King of Oyo and being bull of the Tunder-Boys too.

"But not like this." He says soft.

He tells me his story of how I brought him in and how we the Tunder-Boys did what we do to him until he was us.

"I was scared at first," he whispers, so the others can't hear and I know he don't mean the knife fighting but the other thing.

We each take a turn telling it all. We each listen. Then we each write. I look over and see his pictures for reading dance like knife points and I see the ink of my death. I'm not as good at writing it as he is but I do like Tunder-Boys do everything, the best. I'm the bull man. I'm the bull until I die.

Tat-Tat waters out his eyes a little bit and there's not shame in that. Not when you're telling your story and letting the words out all at once. Not when I drink up his story into my bones and he breathes up mine into his. I put my lips on his tears and taste the salt of his water.

Our stories both are almost written when the moon is all the way up. We hammock a couple times, quietly, not to wake the others. This is not like Oyo. This is quiet. Then we took a rest from writing and get up to walk a circle around the deck. Him with arm around my waist. Me with arm around his shoulders.

The other boys are asleep. Blond Wattabee is curled up on top of the pile of nets, the flotsam boys cuddled up on either side of him. Sparks is still up in his sky, in a lump like stowed sails. It looks lonely with just him and his bow but he likes it that way.

For a while, Tat-Tat and me stood at the wheel together and put our hands together on the wood circle, talking. I look at our hands on the wheel. In the dim, our skin is just two colors of dark. Him the dark of storm clouds. Me, shadows on a wave.

I sunna know how much I am gonna miss him. Miss him like I miss Zef, Doobie, and Ki and Gem. I am the bull of the Tunder-Boys so tomorrow I am gonna open Tat-Tat's skin and slash up the blue writing nobody can read.

We come back from steering together to finish our stories. I'm sitting at the table in the deck house with the paints. My fingers is still making what I see into words when I hear Tat-Tat behind me, strapping the challenge knife to his thigh. He makes the words faster than me.

Tomorrow, when I beat him, I'll read his pictures and eat his story just like I ate Chandro's and Brogan's and Ivan's and Otumbe's. The bull is the strongest 'cause he's fed full of the story of all the Wave Boys who came before him.

I can't really see behind me with the kraken eyes painted onto my asscheeks, though I like to tell the other Wave Boys I can. My other eyes just tell everybody, when I show 'em, that I am always watching. It's all the stories in me looking out, watching, even if I can't see.

We'll probably do the challenge at sunrise. I think maybe I should keep my back to the sun when we do. Maybe putting the morning in Tat-Tat's eyes will—

---fragment ends---

```
The above fragment (#0455-A) was found at 41.29°
North, 118.84° West by the surface oceanographic
anthropology expedition that took place circa
5208. The script was hand-written on a scroll of
cured whale hide and sealed inside artifact #0455
(see appendices).

Expedition leaders theorize that the shape of
the artifact indicates it may have been crudely
carved to resemble the bust of a female form,
perhaps for use as a fetish, masthead (see
glossary) or other nautical decoration.
```

WAVE BOYS

Bone fragments found nailed to the artifact (#0455-D and #0455-E) were scheduled for further analysis but were subsequently lost during a renewal of native hostilities.

At some point, he summoned a devil. I'm not sure why. Maybe for knowledge, or maybe to prove his power. It's one of those things magicians do all the time in old stories.

RENFREW'S COURSE

John Langan

"So this is the wizard," Neil said.

"Supposedly," Jim said.

Six feet tall, the statue had been carved from wood that retained most of its whiteness, even though the date cut into its base read 2005, seven years ago. Jim thought the color might be due to its not having been finished—splinters stood from the wood's uneven surface—but didn't know enough about carpentry to be certain.

"Looks kind of Gandalf," Neil said.

He was right. The wide-brimmed hat, long beard, staff and robe, all suggested Tolkien's character, an impression the squirrel at the figure's left foot, fox behind its right, owl on its shoulder did little to argue.

"I know," Jim said. "It's like that statue of William Wallace—did I tell you about that? They wanted to put up a new statue of Wallace—somewhere out near Stirling, I think—so what did the artist come up with? Mel Gibson in *Braveheart*."

"No wonder there're so few Jews in Scotland."

"Apparently, the real guy was much stranger."

"Gibson? I know," Neil said, starting up the hill towards the dirt path that would take them into the nature preserve.

"No, the wizard." Once he had caught up to Neil and they were walking under the tall pine and oak, Jim continued, "In one story, the King of

France was causing some kind of difficulty for the local merchants—an embargo, I think. Michael Renfrew mounted his iron horse and in a single bound crossed the distance from Kirkcaldy to Paris. When he showed up at the French palace, its doors flew open for him. The King's guards found their swords red hot in their hands. Needless to say, Louis-the-whatever changed his mind, and quickly, at that."

"An iron horse, huh?"

"Legend says you can still see its hoofprint on the cliff it leapt off."

To their right, separated from them by dense rows of pine, a stone tower raised its crenellated head above the tree line. "See?" Jim said, pointing to it. "Over there—that's Renfrew's keep."

"Which has seen better days."

"It's like seven hundred years old."

"So's Edinburgh Castle, isn't it?"

"Anyhoo," Jim said, "Renfew only stayed there part of the time. He was the court astrologer for the Holy Roman Emperor."

Neil grunted. No longer angry about the Rose incident, neither was he all the way over it. Had he been familiar with Scotland, he might have gone off for a few days on his own, left Jim to worry about what he was up to, whom he was having long, heartfelt conversations with over steaming mugs of chai. The trip, however, had been Jim's baby, a chance to share with Neil the place in which he'd passed the summers of his childhood while also promoting his surprisingly successful book. Neil could not make sense of the timetables for the trains or buses, and as for driving on the other side of the road, forget it. He had no choice but to remain with Jim and his revelation about his *affaire de coeur* with Rose Carlton, which he had dealt with from inside a roiling cloud first of anger, then pique. Jim met this change in their personal weather the way he always did, the way he always had, by talking too much, filling the charged air with endless facts, opinion, speculation.

Not for the first time, the irony of his book's title, *The Still Warrior*, struck him. How often had he urged his students at the dojo not to be afraid of their own quiet, of remaining in place, controlling their sparring bouts by forcing their opponents into committing to action first? It was a perspective he'd spent one hundred and forty-eight pages applying to a wide range of activities and situation, and based on the early sales figures, it was a viewpoint in which a significant portion of the reading

RENFREW'S COURSE

public was interested. Look at his life off the dojo's polished hardwood, though, and he might as well have been writing fiction, fantasy rooted in the deepest wish-fulfillment. Especially when it came to Neil, he was almost pathologically unable to leave things be, let the kinks and snarls in their relationship work themselves out, as the vast majority of them likely would. Instead, he had to plan excursions like this one, a walk along a nature path that was supposed to bring them...what? Closer? "You can't make a scar heal any faster," Neil had said, which Jim wasn't sure he believed but which Neil certainly did.

Ahead, the path was intersected by a secondary trail slanting up from the right. The new trail was little more than a disturbance in the forest's carpet of needles, but Neil turned onto it. "Hey," Jim said.

"I want to see where this goes."

Neil knew he wouldn't argue. *Prick.* Jim followed him off the main path and was seized by a vertigo so extreme he might have been standing at the edge of a sheer cliff, rather than a not-especially steep trail. He leaned forward, and it was as if he were on the verge of a great abyss, an emptiness that was coaxing him forward, just one more step...

A hand gripped his arm. "Hey—you all right?" The voice was high, familiar.

Vision swimming, Jim said, "I don't," and heard the words uttered in a different—in what sounded like the voice on his and Neil's videos of their old vacations, his voice of ten years ago.

The hand steadying him belonged to a young man—to Neil, he saw, Neil as he had been when Jim had met him at a mutual friend's Y2K party. His hair was down to his shoulders and, as was the case when he let it grow, both more curly and a shade closer to strawberry blond. The lines on his face were not cut as deep, and his skin was pale from a life lived in front of the computer. Mouth tucked into the smirk that had first caught Jim's notice, he said, "Steady," and released Jim's arm.

Jim raised his right hand and brushed the half-dozen earrings that climbed his ear. He could feel his own hair ponytailed along the back of his neck. "Oh my God," he said.

"What is it?" Neil said.

"I—don't you—"

"Maybe the mushrooms weren't such a good idea."

"Mushrooms?" Jim said, even as he was thinking, *Yes, mushrooms, because that's the kind of shit you do now, at twenty-five, psilocybin and pot and occasionally hash and once in a great while a little E, because you're still five years away from the ambush of turning thirty, when you'll throw away all this stuff and more besides—soda, fast food, desserts—in favor of Shotokan karate seven days a week, fifty-two weeks a year. That's the future: right now, you're pursuing your private version of the systematic derangement of the senses.*

"Man," Neil said, "I guess those things were strong. I've never seen you like this before. Wish they would do something for me." He waved his hand in front of his eyes. "Nada."

"We—how did we get here?"

"We walked."

"No, I mean Kirkcaldy—Scotland."

"Wow."

"How did we get here?"

"Easy, there, easy," Neil said. "Work exchange, remember? I'm over here six weeks, that guy—Doug Moore, right?—is enjoying life in NYC. You tagged along because—well, because you're cute and I like you. Okay?"

Of course that was the case. The moment Jim heard Neil's explanation, he realized he already knew it. Cheeks burning, he said, "Okay. I'm sorry, it's just—those were some strong mushrooms."

"Yeah?"

"Yeah. I was having this whole fantasy that you and I were here, only, in the future."

"The future, huh? What were we like?"

"I had written this really popular book. We were here promoting it. You were…still programming, I think."

"Oh, so you're the famous writer and I'm just some computer nerd. Very nice."

"Hey, you were my computer nerd."

"Flattery."

"It's gotten me everywhere."

"You're feeling better."

"I guess."

"Good." The expression on Neil's face looked as if it might portend sex, a quickie amidst the trees, but he turned and continued down the sec-

RENFREW'S COURSE

ondary path. As Jim followed, he said, "Before you went all freaky, you were talking about the wizard, old Michael Renfrew."

"I was? Yeah, I suppose I was. Look to your right, ahead and you'll see Renfrew's keep."

"Where? Oh, yeah. What part is that?"

"Must be near the base. That's—I think that's a doorway. Hard to tell through the trees."

"So what about Renfrew?"

"Did I tell you about the iron horse?"

"And the King of France, yeah."

"There's a story about him and the Devil."

"Oh?"

"Or a devil: I can't remember which. At some point, he summoned a devil. I'm not sure why. Maybe for knowledge, or maybe to prove his power. It's one of those things magicians do all the time in old stories. Anyway, dealing with this guy was more dangerous than your run-of-the-mill evil spirit. If Renfrew could name a single task the devil could not perform, then he could make whatever use of him he wished for a year and a day. If not, the devil would pull him down to hell."

"And?"

"Renfrew took him to the beach, and commanded him to weave a rope out of sand."

"Not bad. What did he have the devil do for him?"

"The story doesn't say. It's more concerned with him outsmarting the devil than with Renfrew using him for his personal gain."

"Maybe that was how he got the iron horse."

"Could be."

"Anything else?"

"Not really. He's supposed to have had something to do with this book, *Les mystères du ver*, but I'm not sure what."

"*Les*—what?"

"*Les mystères du ver*: The Mysteries of the Worm. It's some kind of evil book, Satanic Bible, witch's spell list, that sort of thing."

"*The Mysteries of the Worm*, huh? No wonder you're interested in this guy."

"Worm? Try snake."

"Somebody's overcompensating."

"Merely stating the facts."

Neil did not answer, and Jim could not think of a way to extend their banter that did not sound forced, banal. *It's all right*, he told himself. *Silence is all right. You don't always have to be talking.* Wasn't that one of the things that had attracted him to Neil in the first place, his ability to be comfortable in his own quiet? Even in the length of time they'd been together, hadn't he learned that Neil's sometimes prolonged periods of silence rarely had anything to do with them, that he was usually turning over some work-related problem? He didn't feel the need to fill the air with words, and if that made Jim anxious, that wasn't Neil's fault, was it?

Plus, the sex is fantastic.

Maybe fifteen feet in front of Neil, the path leveled off and was met by another, slanting down from the right to join theirs at an acute angle. When Neil turned at the junction and started up it, Jim said, "Hey."

"Come on," Neil said. "This should take us back to the main trail."

No arguing with that. This track appeared clearer than the one they'd just descended, more sharply-defined. He followed onto it and it was as if he'd tried to walk up a wall. The path rose above him, impossibly high; he staggered backwards, dropped onto his ass. The path loomed overhead, a dark strip of ground about to fall on him, and—

A silhouette leaned in front of him. "What happened?" The voice was flat, familiar.

Struggling against the urge to throw his hands in front of his face, protect himself from the collapse of dirt and rock, Jim said, "I don't," and was shocked to hear the fragment delivered in a voice whose underlying tones were his but which had been roughened, broadened.

The outline before him resolved into Neil, but a different Neil, a Neil whose face might have received the attentions of a makeup artist instructed to advance his age by twenty, twenty-five years. His hair was crewcut short. His skin was grooved across the forehead, beneath the eyes, to either side of the mouth. Under the open collar of his shirt, a faded line of green ink scaled the left side of his neck, the edge of a tattoo, Jim knew—remembered. Were he to look into a mirror, he would see its twin on the left side of his neck, a memento of the aftermath of the Rose Carlton incident, when he and Neil had sought a way to reaffirm their bond. The eclipse had been Jim's idea, a symbol that, whatever events might darken their relationship, they would pass.

(Except that he'd developed a staph infection, which the tattooist, a mutual acquaintance, had spent days insisting could not be happening, he ran a clean shop, until Jim had wound up in the hospital, tethered to an IV antibiotic drip for a week. Nor had Neil moved past Rose, not really: every time an argument escalated to a certain pitch, he reached for her like a favorite weapon.)

"You all right?" Neil asked, the words tinted with something resembling concern.

He's worried about my heart, Jim thought. *The infection affected my heart, weakened it. (What the hell is happening to me?)* "Fine," he said, climbing to his feet. "I'm fine, just…a little lightheaded." *(Is this some kind of long-term after-effect of being sick? Did it mess with my head?)* He gestured at the path. "Go on."

"You're sure?"

"Go."

"Take it easy," Neil said. "This isn't a race." Nonetheless, he hurried to keep in front. "Okay?" he called over his shoulder.

"Great."

After a minute of trudging up the thick, rocky earth, Neil said, "Do you feel like continuing the story?"

"Story?"

"Story, chapter, whatever you want to call it. 'Renfrew and the Giant.'"

Almost before he knew he was speaking them, Jim found the words at his lips. "Having endured Renfrew's displays of power, the Giant was less than impressed by his offer of an alliance between them. He said, 'Little man, you have already shown me that I have nothing to fear from you. Why should I cast my lot in with yours?'

"Although obviously exhausted, Renfrew stood straighter and answered, 'Because you have everything to benefit if you do, and everything to lose if you do not.'

"At this, the Giant laughed, and it was the sound of an avalanche, of boulders crashing into one another. 'Little man,' he said, 'your boldness does you credit. I will eat you quickly.' He reached one enormous hand toward the wizard.

"Renfrew did not flinch. He said, 'I know your name—your true name.'

"The Giant's hand halted, inches from Renfrew. His vast brow lowered. 'Impossible,' he said. 'I hid that where no man—no one might find it, ever.'

"'Yes,' Renfrew said, 'in a cavern under a lake watched over by three mountains, locked inside a brass casket guarded by a basilisk. I have been there.'

"The Giant's hand retreated. He said, 'You read of this in one of your wizard's books.'

"Renfrew said, 'The sole means to open the casket is the tooth of a hydra, which is in the basilisk's stomach. The casket contains a pale blue egg resting on a white pillow. To touch the egg is like touching a furnace; to hear its shell crack is like hearing your own death. Within the egg, there is a stone into which has been carved a single word.'

"The Giant's hand had retreated all the way to his great mouth.

"Renfrew said, 'That word is *Mise*.'"

Neil said, "Meesh?"

"I think that's how it's pronounced. It's Gaelic, means, 'I am.'"

"I am?"

"Yeah. The original story doesn't say what the Giant's true name was, only that Renfrew had discovered it and used it against him. I thought about making it something like 'stone' or 'mountain,' but that seemed too obvious."

"Why?"

"Well, giants are big, you know; if you were going to associate them with anything, it would be a mountain."

"I guess."

"Anyway, it made sense to me that the Giant's name would be his life, so, 'I am.'"

"If you say so. Just as long as this one brings another big advance."

Jim said, "Karen's pretty optimistic. Post-Harry Potter, wizards and magic are big business in kids' publishing," even as he was thinking, *Karen Lowatchee, your agent, who repped you on* The Still Warrior *and, when the heart thing made you scale back karate, suggested you try fiction. She'd liked the chapters on karate for kids, said they showed a real grasp of tween psychology. She was the one who came up with the Jenny Ninja series title, and got you the big advances for the last two. Neil calls her Glenda the Good Bitch; she calls him Microsoft.*

"What happens next?" Neil said.

"In the chapter? Renfrew turns the Giant into his keep."

"That's it?"

"That's what happens in the original legend."

"Yeah, but—couldn't he have used the Giant, first?"

"Invaded England with him?" Jim said.

"Something."

"I don't know. I kind of like the idea of Renfrew living inside the Giant, wandering around him, listening to the echo of his thoughts, his dreams."

"Sounds pretty creepy, if you ask me."

"And what's wrong with that?"

"Isn't this book supposed to be for kids?"

"It's YA," Jim said, "Young Adult. Older kids."

Over the tops of the pines to their right, Renfrew's keep raised its ragged crown. "See," Jim said, pointing at it, "the windows look like eyes."

"What has eyes like that?"

"It's supposed to be a monster."

"Aren't giants big people?"

"Not all of them. The ancient Greeks described giants with a hundred arms."

"Where do you get this stuff?"

"Depends. The ancient Greek stuff's available all over the place. Information on Renfrew is harder to come by. Mostly, I use that website, Blackguide.com."

"The one that crashed the computer?"

"I told you, it wasn't that: it was all the porn you'd been looking at."

"Very funny."

Neil's pace slowed. In front of him, their path intersected another sloping steeply down from the right. As he stepped onto it, Jim said, "Hey."

"I'm pretty sure this'll lead back to the beginning of the trail," Neil said.

This place isn't that big. I'm sure if I kept on a straight line, I'd come out on a side street, eventually. However discouraging the prospect of an even more strenuous climb was, though, the inevitable spat that would result from him not following Neil, not to mention, the two or three days after that before the situation returned to normal, prompted him up the new path. As he did, his vision went dark. He had the impression of something huge in front of him, something vast hanging over him, like a wave, only solid, ready to crash down on him. He wanted to cry out, but his tongue was dead in his mouth; his heart lurched like a racehorse stumbling mid-stride.

Somewhere close by, an old man's voice said, "What is it? What's the matter with you?" The words vibrated with rage, barely-controlled.

What's Neil's father doing here? Jim thought. He tried to speak. "Mr. Marshall—"

"Don't Mr. Marshall me. I know who I am. I'm still lucid."

The host of the questions the outburst raised were silenced by the clearing of Jim's sight, which revealed Neil's face inches from his. Its angry expression was almost parodic: eyes wide and staring under lowered brows, top lip arched, teeth visible, chin jutting forward. It was also the face of a man in his mid-seventies. Neil's hair was white, as were his eyebrows; both hair and brows were thick, bushy. The lines across his forehead, to either side of his mouth, appeared cut right down to the bone, while his skin looked loose, its grip on his skull slipping. His gaze was fierce yet unfocused, as if he were unable to pinpoint the source of his rage; already, his lips were retreating from their snarl into the tremors that shook them incessantly.

The Alzheimer's, Jim thought. *That was the first symptom: before the memory loss, the mood swings, that spasm was telling us what was on the way.*

"What happened to you?" Neil said. "Is it your heart? Are you having another heart attack?" The emotion under his words was sliding into panic.

"I'm fine," Jim said. "Just caught up in..." *What? What do I call whatever's happening to me? (And, by the way, what the hell is happening to me? Is this some kind of stroke?)* "In a rather vivid day dream, I suppose—a memory, really, of one of our past visits here."

"Oh? Was that before or after you fucked Rose?"

"I didn't—"

"Yes, yes, that's what you always say; what you've always said."

"But you've never believed me, have you?"

RENFREW'S COURSE

"I don't know what I believe. I'm the one whose brain is disintegrating, remember?"

"It isn't," Jim started, then stopped. Technically speaking, Neil's brain wasn't disintegrating, but there were worse ways to describe what was happening to his personality, to the aggregate of memories and attitudes that composed Neil. Anyway, Neil already had turned his back on him and was striding up the path. The disease might be wrecking his mind, but so far, his vitality was undiminished. Jim labored not to fall too far behind.

Neil said, "Do you remember the end of Renfrew's story?"

"Do you mean my book, or the legend?"

"Which was which?"

"My book ends with Renfrew entering the cave at Wemyss in search of the path to the Graveyard of the Old Gods. He leaves Thomas, his apprentice, in charge until his return, which doesn't take place during Thomas's very long life, or that of his apprentice, or that of any of the men and women who have come since. However, the book says, that doesn't mean that, one day, the old wizard won't emerge from the mouth of the cave, squinting at the light, and begin the long walk back to his old home."

"That wasn't it."

"You want the legend, then. That ends with a group of the Covenanters coming armed to Renfrew's keep in order to arrest him on charges of sorcery. When they arrived, though, they found the place deserted, as if no one had lived there for decades, or longer."

"That isn't it, either."

"I don't—there's a tradition, a kind of afterword to the legend proper, that if you follow a certain course through the woods around Renfrew's keep—and if certain conditions are right: the stars are in alignment, that sort of thing; I think an eclipse is supposed to figure into the equation, somehow—then Renfrew himself will appear to you and offer to teach you what he knows. Is that what you were thinking of?"

"Yes," Neil said.

Jim waited for Neil to add something more; when he did not, he said, "What makes you ask?"

"Ask what?"

"About Renfrew's course?"

"What about it?"

"You just asked me to tell you about it."

"I did." Neil shrugged. "I don't remember that."

There was no point in anger; though buttressed by his meds, Neil's short-term memory was far from perfect. Jim said, "You know what I was thinking?"

"How much longer you have to wait before you can put me in a home?"

"What? No, I told you, I'm not going to put you in a home."

"That's what you say now."

"That's what I have said—what I've been saying ever since you were diagnosed."

For a change, he hoped the silence that greeted his reassurance meant the subject of their debate had slipped through the sieve of Neil's immediate recollection. His quiet seemed to imply that it had, another moment caught in the plaque crusting his neurons, then he said, "I hope you and Rose will have the decency to wait until all my things have been moved out for her to move in."

"Neil—"

"It would be nice if you could wait until I'm in the ground, but I'm guessing I could hang on for a while, and you certainly aren't getting any younger. Neither is she; although she isn't as old as we are, is she? Maybe she'll be inclined to do the decent thing, but you won't, will you?"

"I'm sorry: I can't talk to you when you're like this."

Neil lengthened his stride, mountain-goating up the path. Jim didn't bother chasing after. Better to hang back and hope that, by the time he caught up, Neil's thunderstorm of emotions would have passed; though he wasn't sure what he rated the chances of that as. It had been years, almost a full decade, since he and Rose had seen one another, and that had been by accident, a chance encounter at the Union Square Barnes and Noble that had led to nothing more than the occasional e-mail. If he hadn't told Neil about the meeting, or the correspondence, it was because, long after his whatever-you-wanted-to-call-it with her had receded in his memory, in Neil's mind, it was a flame only recently and poorly extinguished, whose smoldering embers might yet ignite again. He would have made too much of the e-mails in which Jim told Rose about his visit to the set of the Renfrew film, Rose told him about her recent trip to Paris with her ninety-two year old mother, mountained the molehills

RENFREW'S COURSE

into a secret, ongoing affair. In the wake of Neil's illness, he supposed he had been writing to her more frequently, but his correspondence with all his friends and family had increased as his communication with Neil had grown more erratic.

He was almost at the top of the path. He had climbed higher than he'd realized; to his right and over his shoulder, he could look down on the roofless top of Renfrew's keep. To his relief, Neil was standing waiting for him. "There you are," Jim said—panted, really.

"Here I am," Neil said. His expression was almost kindly. "Need a minute?"

"Half a minute," Jim said, leaning forward. "Neil—"

At Neil's feet, their path formed an acute angle with another climbing up from the right. As he started down it, Jim said, "Hey."

"I can see the place where we started," Neil said, pointing.

Jim squinted. Was that the white of the wizard's statue? They would have to descend from here somehow, he supposed, and this new path, crossed by tree roots that formed an irregular staircase, was probably the best option he could expect. He stepped down and it was like dropping into a well. There was the sensation of falling straight down, and the impression of everything flying up all around him, and the sound of roaring filling his ears. Terror swept through his chest, his head, made them sickeningly light. He flailed his arms. There was nothing under his feet; he was falling.

Something crashed into him from the front. He heard an, "Oof!" felt his direction change. Now he was moving forward, his arms and legs caught with someone else's, tangled, the pair of them thudding and scraping against rock and dirt. He rolled over and under, over and under his companion, then landed hard on his back, his right kidney shouting at the rock it came down on. Above him, the sky was a blue bowl someone had set spinning. He closed his eyes, and when he opened them, Neil was leaning over him. There was a cut high on his forehead leaking blood onto his brow, but aside from that and some dirt, his face was the same as it had been at the start of this strange walk, thirty-nine and looking it. "You klutz," he said. "Karate master, my ass."

Jim flung his arm around him, flinching as his back complained. "I'm sorry," he said into Neil's shoulder. "Are you okay?"

"You mean, aside from the gaping wound in my head? Yeah, I'm peachy."

Jim released him. "I am so sorry," he said as he struggled to his feet. "I just…I slipped."

"And you couldn't miss me on the way?"

"I didn't want you to feel left out."

Fighting it, Neil smirked. "You are such an asshole."

"But I'm your asshole."

"Enough shit comes out of you, anyway."

"Ah, I'm sure a little single malt will help."

"First sensible thing you've said all day."

They had rolled almost halfway down the path; no surprise, given the bruises Jim could feel ripening under his shirt, his jeans, the scrapes visible on Neil's arms, his neck. He supposed he should be grateful neither of them had broken a limb, or been concussed. At least Neil had been right about this path returning them to the entrance to the nature preserve: through the trees, the wizard's statue stood a pale beacon. As Neil stepped from tree root step to tree root step, Jim weighed telling him about his…what would he call them? Hallucinations? Visions? Waking dreams? Maybe "experiences" was the best word for them. Whatever: it was on the tip of his tongue to say that he had just relived their life together when they'd first met, then seen them at points another twenty and forty or so years in the future. *When I'm the author of a series of successful children's books and he's in mid-stage Alzheimer's, not to mention, still obsessing over Rose Carlton: yes, that would go over splendidly.*

Neil was drawing away from him. Strangest of all was that, now that the two of them were their proper selves, he was not more upset by what he had just been through, his experiences. (That still wasn't the right word, but it would do for the moment.) While he had been at each of those other times, the moment had been as real as anything—that he had been wrenched from this specific point in his life had seemed as odd, as disorienting, as any other detail. Returned to the age at which he had entered the nature preserve—the age he was supposed to be—Jim found his and Neil's alternate selves suddenly distant, novels he'd read years ago, their plots dim weights resting in the depths of his memory.

So what was all that? Some kind of projection? Easy enough to trace the roots of at least some of it to the current state of his and Neil's relationship. Future Neil's fixation on the Rose business arose from Jim's anxiety that, as time went on, he wouldn't be able to relinquish it. Jim's continued success as a writer was simple wish-fulfillment (although his agent had praised the sections of his book dealing with kids). Neil's grandfather had suffered from Alzheimer's, which his father was showing early symptoms of; from there, it was a short jump to imagining Neil eventually overtaken by it.

The vividness of everything, though, he could not account for. He had indulged in enough hallucinogens in his younger years; could this have been a delayed consequence of that? It seemed unlikely, but what was more likely? The place was the site of a ley-line that produced brief time-distortions? *Funny how all the tourist info fails to mention that.*

To his right, the lower stretch of Renfrew's keep was visible through the trees. Ahead, Neil was already at the statue. Legs protesting, Jim picked up his pace. Neil had stopped in front of the sculpture, and appeared to be speaking to it. *That can't be good. Did I say neither of us was concussed?*

Jim did not see the man with whom Neil was talking until he was next to him. Standing on the other side of the statue, the man had been obscured from Jim's view by it. A head shorter than either of them, he wore his reddish hair short and a dark suit over an open-collared white shirt. Jim wasn't much for estimating the cost of things, but even he could recognize the quality of the man's clothes, which made the stains on his jacket cuffs, his shirt, all the more conspicuous. The man raised his eyes to Jim, and their green notice was a physical thing, a heaviness passing over him. "You're Jim," he said in a voice that was soft, accentless.

"Yes," Jim said, extending his hand. "You are…?"

The man's hands were in his trouser pockets; he kept them there. "Renfrew."

"Like—" Jim gestured at the sculpture.

"The very same," the man said, "though the likeness is a poor one."

"Wait—what?" Jim glanced at Neil, who was watching the man intently. "I'm sorry: I thought you were saying—"

"I was." The man withdrew his hands from his pockets. Blue flames licked the unburned skin of the left; while a slender emerald snake coiled around the right.

"Jesus!" Jim leapt back.

"Not quite."

"What is this?"

Neil said, "We completed the course."

"You did." The man—Renfrew?—nodded. "Per the terms of a contract that is older than any of us, I am here to offer one of you my tutelage."

"One of us," Jim said. "What about the other?"

"The price of tuition," Renfrew said. "A gesture of commitment."

"Okay, that's enough," Jim said.

"Take me," Neil said.

"What?"

"Very interesting," Renfrew said.

"Neil, what are you saying?"

"The Alzheimer's: that's a sure thing?" Neil said.

"Sure enough," Renfrew answered.

"And you can cure it?"

"I have been this age for a very long time," Renfrew said. "You need never meet that old man in the mirror."

"Are you kidding me?" Jim said. "Are you listening to yourself?"

"And there's no other way?" Neil said.

"There are many other ways, if you know where and how to find them. This is my way."

"I'm sorry," Neil started, but Jim cut him off: "This is insane."

"There was a link," Neil said, "on the Blackguide site. I clicked on it, and it led to an account by a guy who had walked this course in the 1930s with his brothers. With each new turn of the path, the three of them were at a different point in their lives: younger, then older, then much older. When they arrived back at the beginning, Renfrew was waiting for them."

"So all that was real?" Jim said.

"Real enough," Renfrew said.

"I thought if we could follow the course, then I could see how things would turn out—if we'd still be together; if we'd be happy; if Rose would still be around. I didn't expect—oh, Christ," Neil said. "Do you have any idea what it's like—no, you don't; how could you? Everything—you're aware that something is wrong, deeply wrong—you can feel it in everything around you—and you're sure you know what it is, what's the matter, but you can't remember it. And then you can remember, and you realize that the problem isn't with what's outside, it's with what's inside, and

RENFREW'S COURSE

you know it's only a matter of time until you forget again and the whole process starts over." His eyes swam with tears.

"Neil, honey, it's okay," Jim said. "I'll be there for you."

"No," Neil said. "Don't you get it? I can't—I won't go through that. Now that I know—now that you know, how could you ask me to?"

"So instead you're going to…how does that story end, the one about the guy and his brothers?"

"The younger brother accepted Renfrew's offer. He and Renfrew disappeared, and when the older brother returned home, it was as if his brother had never existed. He was the only one who had any memory of him."

"Weren't there three of them? What happened to the other brother?"

"He vanished, too. No one remembered him, either."

Jim's mouth went dry. "The price of tuition."

"Speaking of which," Renfrew said, "we really need to move this along."

"You aren't going to do this," Jim said.

"What choice do I have?"

"You could choose me—choose us."

"Are you sure you don't want to make me an offer?" Renfrew said.

"Me?" Jim said. "I thought Neil—"

"Was here first, yes, but that's more a recommendation than a rule. I'm curious to learn how your convictions fare when the situation is reversed."

Neil's mouth moved, but no sound issued from it.

"Well?" Renfrew said.

His fear seemed outside him, an acrid saturation pressing on him from all sides at once; nonetheless, Jim was able to say, "Fuck you." The frown that darkened Renfrew's face was a small pleasure. Jim looked at Neil, who was staring at the ground. "What I had with Rose—it was never as bad as you thought it was, and when I said it was over, it was."

"For you, maybe."

Renfrew swept his left arm up and down, blue fire trailing from his fingertips, tracing a seam in the air that opened into something like a door. He nodded at Neil, who crossed to and stepped through it without another word. Jim was as astonished by his lack of a parting remark as anything.

"Now," Renfrew said, extending his right hand at Jim. The serpent wrapped around it raised its wedge-shaped head and regarded him lazily. The space behind the wizard darkened, full of an enormous shape. Jim thought, *How did the keep*—and realized that what had stepped closer was not the keep, or, not anymore. It arched towards him, impossible mouth open to consume him, all of him, not only the flesh and bones it would grind between teeth like boulders, but his past, his present, his future, his very place in the world. He wished his fear would leave him, but he supposed it was better than the serrated edge of Neil's betrayal waiting beneath it. At least he could keep his eyes open; at least he would not turn away from the emptiness, the silence, descending on him.

For Fiona

You figured because I'm a squid, I'm different. Look, you take away the scaly skin, oily complexion, vestigial tentacles, preternatural strength, and innate sex appeal and squids aren't all that different from pinks. Even FBI pinks.

WETSIDE STORY

Steve Vernon

1

There is nothing more beautiful than a dead fish under moonlight. There's just something in the way that their scales catch the dance of lunar beams and streetlight and shard it back into your eyes like a perfect cod liver oil slick.

Bucky threw the mackerel high over the deep water and Big Stinky rose up and caught it.

"Damn, that's pretty," I said.

Bucky grinned me back a picket fence full of pleasure. The toxic waste that riddled his cavities gave them a wonderfully fluorescent neon gleam. His scales glittered as prettily as those of the dead mackerel had.

My heart went thump.

Bucky and I had been lovers for damn near ever, since about three minutes after we'd first met. Not that it's all that much of a deal, mind you. Cross-current sexual practices aren't nearly as commotion-worthy for us Wetsiders as it is for you intercity pinks. This was our sixth summer together. I hadn't realized I was a sea-fag until I met Bucky. Things can happen awfully fast, here in Darktown.

"You want me to throw another?" Bucky asked.

Vernon

I shook my head. "No. I just took a swim and I wouldn't want Big Stinky going all Technicolor in the mouth on us."

Darktown was where the monsters lived. It had been built back in the 1930s when Senator McCarthy had decided that in addition to blacklisting authors, actors and directors that filmed monsters also needed to be attacked. His campaign against the film monsters had proven to be so successful that a congressional committee came up with a plan to segregate all of the monsters from proper society.

"Shh, Finn, she's sensitive."

"She's a two-hundred-foot bulimic sea monster who weighs about as much as a half-dozen fully loaded super tankers and that's talking postbarf. The word sensitive just doesn't come into it."

"Finn!"

What can I tell you?

I'm just not one of those sensitive kinds of squids. They call me Finn and I'm the war leader and head bullyboy of the Dread Darktown Cephalopodic chapter of squids. We're the original squids, the primal spawn and I don't care what anyone else tells you. We don't claim to be descended from any dubiously tentacled elder god. A bunch of freaking name droppers I call them. Hell, half of them couldn't even pronounce the elder god's true name.

I knew better. Forget about all of this guppy-swallop about in-the-elder-god's-image. No sir, we're just a handful of bottom-sludge, social-climbing mollusks that have crawled up from the mud and made good.

"Don't you remember last year when Big Stinky swallowed that school of killer whales and then power-hurled them up onto the beach? The damned deadheads frenzied into the freshly spewed mess and we were cleaning up zomboid orca fish-chunks for two full moons!"

"Even deadheads have got to eat," Bucky said philosophically. "Besides, some of that zomboid orca was pretty good eating, not that I would know."

"Right," I tactfully agreed. As much as I loved Bucky there was just so far I could expect his gustatory predilections to expand. Basically, Bucky was a goddamn eating machine. "Just save the fish for later. We got business to do. Are you packing?"

"Loaded with bear," he said, pointing at his extra-caliber, double-barreled blunderbuss.

WETSIDE STORY

"Don't you mean loaded for bear?" I asked.

"I generally say what I mean, Finn. I've got this sucker loaded with gunpowder, tomb dust, rusty nails, broken glass and a string of medicine bear teeth that I won in a Texas Hold 'em poker game with the Manitou Man. Like I said, loaded with bear."

What can I tell you? Wetside is a little like Texas. Everything has to run to the larger side of big. What you need to realize is that Wetside is home to a significant portion of Darktown's heavy-hitting giant lizards. Like Bogart said, they come here for the waters. When you weigh as much as a small sumo planetoid, the flotational qualities of the deep Atlantic are not to be sneered at. So, naturally, we have to be ready for the occasional Tyrannosaurus temper tantrum, when Gwangi goes orang-outang-o-rango.

We're talking a need for maximum firepower.

"Right," I said. "Loaded with bear. I got you."

"How about yourself?" Bucky asked.

"I got Betsy."

"Durn it, Finn, when are you going to trade that popgun in for something with a little more kick?"

I patted Betsy's butt. Betsy was my gun, only calling her a gun was a little like calling King Kong a spider monkey. Betsy was a hatchet-handled, semi-auto shotgun with a graveyard frame and a full clip of modified tombstone load self-preaching bone-stoppers.

"I got kick enough, right here." I assured him "And if Betsy ever lets me down I've got a half-dozen backup guns hidden up in my sleeves."

I flexed all six of my biceps hard enough to give me a walking cerebral hemorrhage, and not in a good way. I could bench press a fully-grown zomboid killer whale without breaking a single bead of sweat, not that I'm trying to brag.

"Cave fish," Bucky called me.

"Bottom feeder," I returned. "You know we're not supposed to be here to shoot anyone."

Bucky sighted down the barrels of his blunderbuss. "I'll try and keep that in mind," he said. "But has anyone told the Nazi Zomboids Uberbottoms that?"

I looked out onto the water. There was no sign of the Zomboid Uberbottom Death Sub, but I could see the mermaids singing in the distance, capering out their long fishnet tails and hungry-toothed veils, patiently seining the churning surf for whatever bit of meat they could find. Our petty politics and playground fistfights didn't concern them one bit.

Maybe they had the right idea.

"If those Nazi zomboids don't know that we're on a peace-keeping mission," I said. "I reckon we'll have to remind them of that particular fact."

"You figure he'll hold up?" Bucky asked, pointing towards the FBI agent, who was hunkered behind a barrel of diesel oil, probably the last piece of cover you'd want to hide behind in a firefight, looking as officially well-hoovered as he could manage.

"You can never tell with pinks," I answered. "But he'd better learn fast."

I figured we were going to need everything we had, going head to head against the Auf Wiedersehen Oom-pa-pa Zomboid Nazi Uberbottom Unterseeboot Deathclan.

2

It started with love.

Now there's a four-letter word if I ever heard one. There has been more trouble generated by that particular noun/verb than any other crossbred term found in the history of verbal and nonverbal communication.

Don't believe me?

Ask Helen of Troy.

Or Goldie.

Goldie was the son-spawn of Kahuna Ghul, one of the prime leaders of our little waterside clan. It seems Goldie had fallen head over heels in love with an Auf Wiedersehen Nazi Zomboid unter-Kapitan. Kahuna Ghul had sent for me to tell me about it. I guess I must just have that kind of face.

"It happened during a river raid," Kahuna Ghul explained. "As near as I can tell that kid, Goldie, took one look at that Nazi zomboid unter-Kapitan and started getting unnatural kind of ideas. The next thing I knew he'd run off and was trying to cross over."

"Have you tried talking with him?"

"I sent him a message."

"And?"

Wetside Story

"He mailed me back his left ear."

"I guess that's his way of telling you he isn't listening," I observed. "You've got to love those Van Gogh moments."

"It'll grow back," Kahuna Ghul pointed out.

"Doesn't mean he'll listen any better," I remarked.

"It's damned unnatural," Kahuna Ghul said. "But what the hell can I do?"

I looked at him, trying to be gentle in my irritation. "He fell in love with another fella. Is that what you call unnatural?"

He threw me a dirty look but I refused to catch it.

"I know about you and Bucky. That's different. At least you're both squids. Zomboids and squids shouldn't mess with each other," Kahuna Ghul said. "The sooner they illegalize inter-special cross-breeding the better, I say."

"Uh-huh," I said right back.

I didn't want to get into any discussions involving politics, genetics, race or religion. Conversations involving those four apoplectic horsemen just have the damndest knack for running downhill at a full tilt gallop.

"You got something to say on that?" Kahuna Ghul asked.

"I figure love is an ambivalent son of a bitch who'll bite anybody he takes a fancy to," I said. "Who am I to tell you how to go about suturing that particular open wound?"

Diplomacy has ever been the better part of my valor.

"Like needs to stay with like," Kahuna Ghul maintained. "Zombies and squids ought to stay on opposite sides of the water."

"Uh-huh," I said.

"It's against nature. I mean, how are they going to spawn?"

"Uh-huh," I repeated.

Who says squids don't have rhythm?

"Is that all you've got to say?" Kahuna Ghul asked. "Uh-huh?"

"Uh-huh," I clarified. "So why'd you name him Goldie?"

Bull's-eye.

Kahuna Ghul spent a half a moment studying the seaweed and jetsam grain on his clam-top desk.

I had clearly embarrassed the man.

"It was his mother's idea," Kahuna Ghul finally allowed. "She named him after a fish."

"His mother slept with the fishes?"

Kahuna Ghul said nothing but his silence spoke volumes. I guess a fellow can pick at a scab for an awfully long time.

Finally I let him off the hook.

"Look, your wife isn't the first squid to go ga-ga over a guppy," I said. "And Goldie isn't the first squid bastard to cross over to the zomboids and this isn't any of this sea-fag's business. I'm going back home and me and Bucky are going to get down over some hot-buttered sea bass and deep-fried prawns. There's no telling what unnatural activities might follow such a gustatory fiesta. Meanwhile, you ought to learn how to deal with all of that water you got running under your bridge."

Kahuna Ghul didn't have anything else to say to me, so I left. Bucky was waiting outside of the big man's office.

So was the FBI.

3

"Finn?" the FBI pink said to me.

When pinks start calling me by my first name I generally start reaching for my gun. I had Betsy out and pointing at the pink's head when three more pinks stepped out with their own guns pointed right at my face. The fourth pink ignored Betsy and drew his own pistol. I just stood there and let him get away with it.

For now.

"Four pinks against one unarmed squid," I said. "I call this a Mexican stand-off."

"What do you mean one squid?" Bucky asked, drawing a bead with his blunderbuss.

I knew I could always count on Bucky. He was kind of like a seventh arm to me. I gave him a grin of appreciation.

"This is a matter of Darktown security," the pink G-man officiously said.

Yeah right.

"Blow me," I replied. "Whatever was stolen, I didn't take it."

"Finn is a pretty secure guy," Bucky added.

"You were talking to Kahuna Ghul," the pink said.

"I was exiting his office. That implies that I entered it. I generally talk to someone when I enter their office, unless they're not there at the time of entry."

"He was," Bucky added.

"You were talking about Goldie Ghul," the pink ignored my finely tuned logic. "We're interested in what you had to say."

"I wasn't," I explained. "I don't mess with family disputes. I suggested he call Dr. Phil. You four might do the same, right after you untangle yourself from the Maltese Monkey Love-knot that I'm about to tie you into."

I flexed, hard.

The pink that was doing all of the talking didn't blink but the three other gun-packers flinched.

I figure my honor was satisfied.

"Goldie Ghul is the spawn of Kahuna Ghul," the head pink went on, ignoring his compatriot's collective flinch. "And Kahuna Ghul runs anything that moves, swims or crawls up from the Wetside waterfront."

"And you must be the man who states the blatantly obvious," Bucky said. "Can we have your autograph?"

"If Goldie Ghul continues to fraternize with the unter-Kapitan of the Nazi Death Clan, there might be a breach in Darktown security."

Fraternize.

It was a good word.

I filed it away for future use.

"Pillow talk is a bitch," I said. "I'm sure that Goldie and his Nazi latex love toy will be too busy breaching other social bastions before they ever get around to discussing Darktown security. Now if you'll excuse me, I'm late for a hot-buttered sea bass."

The head pink cocked his pistol.

I expected he was getting ready to make a point.

"Crossroad Studios," he said.

"Am I supposed to recognize that particular trademark infringement?" I asked.

"Crossroad Studios has an interest in retrieving an assortment of Wermacht World War II paraphernalia that was made off from their Hollyweird studio lot."

"Meaning the Nazi zomboid's death sub?"

"Exactly."

"And that means?"

"There may have been a reward mentioned."

"Aha."

"If you can manage to retrieve this paraphernalia there might be some financial compensation involved."

"A reward."

"Exactly."

"Aha."

Which is how Bucky and I and the FBI came to be involved in shooting it out with the Auf Wiedersehen Oom-pa-pa Zomboid Nazi Uberbottom Unterseeboot Deathclan.

4

"Can you see them out there?" the head FBI pink asked.

"It's about as pitch black as a slow crawl up the wrong end of King Kong's fundament. How in the hell do you think I can see anything more than you can?"

The pink shrugged. He didn't have much in the way of shoulders, but I didn't want to rub it in.

"I thought all of you Darktown types had some kind of see-in-the-dark night vision."

Bucky laughed.

I let him laugh.

"The words 'think' and 'you' just don't go together," I commented.

"I just figured…"

"You figured because I'm a squid, I'm different. Look, you take away the scaly skin, oily complexion, vestigial tentacles, preternatural strength, and innate sex appeal and squids aren't all that different from pinks. Even FBI pinks."

"You've got a point," the pink admitted.

"Which he sharpens every chance he gets," Bucky added.

"Sweet talker," I said.

Then I looked back at the pink.

"Does it bother you?" I asked. "Bucky and me? We ought to know this before we get into a firefight situation."

"Whoop, whoop," Bucky shouted. "Homophobe in the house."

Wetside Story

"I'm not homophobic, damn it," the pink said.

"What are you then?" I asked. "Presbyterian?"

"Existentialist?" Bucky chimed in.

"Crustaceaphobe?" I added, showing off some of my inner Latin.

"They told me about your delusions of stand-up comedy," the pink said. "It's good to know that my channels of information run deep and true."

I gave him that but wouldn't let up.

"You're still dodging the question," I said. "Does it bother you to be out here with a couple of cephalopods who have a habit of sleeping with each other?"

"Any chance we get," Bucky added with a cheeky fluorescent grin.

"I was told you could handle this sort of work," the pink said. "How you two spend your free time is no concern of mine."

"So you say," Bucky said.

A little puddle of silence seeped in around the three of us. It was the pink that finally broke it.

I guess he just had to ask.

"So what's it like being gay?" he asked.

Bucky laughed.

I couldn't blame him.

"It's not so bad as being pink," I said. "Can we end this encounter session now?"

"I knew he was a homophobe," Bucky said. "I knew it."

"You started it," the pink said.

"Sure I did, but my mother can beat your father with three arms tied behind her back. Besides, that death sub out there is heading straight at us."

The two of them looked.

Sure enough, the Nazi Zomboid Death Sub was coming our way. I could it see it out there in the deep water, pointed straight at us. I caught the glint of binoculars being turned our way. Maybe Zomboid Nazis saw better in the dark than squids did.

They loaded up an armored landing sloop, and were sailing it straight towards us. There were an awful lot of Auf Wiedersehens on board.

"This would be a good time to come up with a plan," I suggested.

"What, we don't have one yet?" Bucky asked.

"Don't look at me," I said. "I packed the plan last time. Tonight was supposed to be your turn."

The pink kept looking at the two of us and staring out at the death sub like a rabbit in the headlights. He was going to give his eyeballs a hernia if he wasn't careful.

"That's not how I remember it," Bucky argued. "I'm certain it's your turn."

"That sloop is coming our way," the pink said, trying his best to remain federally calm.

"I hope so," I said.

"Shouldn't we do something about it?"

"I already did do something. I invited them. I sent a message this morning telling them that we'd be out here tonight waiting for them. I told them that a handful of three-fingered, half-blind Boy Scouts could sink their rusty little tub with a potato gun and a corkscrew. Then I told them that I had a corkscrew. They took the whole thing very personally."

Both Bucky and the pink stared at me in a simultaneous display of mutual and unnatural disbelief.

It was so worth it.

"So what do we do?" Bucky said, hunkering down and aiming his blunderbuss in the general direction of the death sub. We were way out of range, you understand, but the aim was just something more like principle.

"Put away the guns, for starters," I said. "It isn't seemly for prisoners of war to put up much of a firefight, and we're about to surrender."

"We're shooting it out with them, aren't we?" the pink asked, pointing a pistol that looked as if it had delusions of future cannonization.

"You can shoot if you want to," I said, holding all six of my arms up in the air. "I'll be busy surrendering."

Bucky grinned, poking his own arms up into the air. He knew what I was up to and I loved him for it.

The pink still didn't get it.

"We work best close up," I patiently explained. "By surrendering I'm guaranteeing a shot at proximity."

"Proximity means close," Bucky explained. "First we get them to take us on board and then we take their Death Sub from them. Easy."

WETSIDE STORY

It sounded good when he said it fast. Bucky was with me and the pink seemed to be almost convinced. I looked up at the night sky. The stars didn't look all that confident and neither was I, but it was the only plan in sight.

5

Damn, but he was a big one. The unter-Kapitan of the death sub was tall enough to give me a kink in the neck, even when I wasn't looking straight at him.

"You will tell me what you were doing on the waterfront?" he asked.

What, were you expecting a gunfight?

You've been watching too damn many pink movies. I had a lot more hair than Bruce Willis ever did, which is saying a lot given my kraken ancestry. I tried to think Buddha-thoughts rather than thinking with my budda-budda-budda burp gun. I was out here to resolve an issue, not start a war.

Guns have their time and place but right now they were strictly props.

We were standing on the deck of the death-sub, surrounded by more Zomboid Nazis than you could healthily shake a stick at. As near as I could tell they outnumbered us by about thirteen to one.

I tried to appear confident.

"Seashell hunting," I suggested. "I've spent my life searching for the rare bivalve tricockled honey-dipper."

Strangely enough, he didn't buy my cover story.

"You will tell me," the unter-Kapitan repeated, only he didn't use a question mark this time.

I smiled. It never hurt to say nothing.

I practiced my mysterious grin daily.

"We're out beyond the city limits out here," the unter-Kapitan pointed out. "Out here you're not the Squid Warlord. Out here you're just a passenger, cargo, or maybe even dead weight. The best you lot can aspire to is a possible collective anchordom. Let me ask you, have you ever seen an anchor swim?"

It was a pretty good question as rhetoricals went.

Vernon

"I think if we were standing on the surface of Jupiter's farthest hemorrhoid, there's just no way that Finn would ever be 'just' anything," Bucky said.

"Sweet talker," I said.

I could see Goldie standing behind the unter-Kapitan, leaning against his back, looking mildly interested in what was going on.

"Hey Goldie," I called over the unter-Kapitan's shoulder. "Are you happy?"

It took a minute for him to figure out what I was talking about. I guess when your daddy is king of all Darktown, you don't really have to grow much in the way of cognitive capabilities; either that or maybe his ear still hadn't grown back.

Goldie grinned and nodded, squeezing the unter-Kapitan's undead torso, so I guessed he was happy.

"Well that's all that counts, isn't it?" I said.

And then I hit the unter-Kapitan with three simultaneous right crosses.

It's good to be a squid.

"This is between the unter-Kapitan and me," I shouted.

The next thing I knew, there were about twelve guns pointed directly at my face and I could feel a thirteenth behind me, committing some sort of unmentionable proctological examination. If I farted it could be a damned unlucky moment in the history of unexpected fire-fight gas-passing.

I should have known better. That "between you and me" shtick only works in the movies, I guess, and I didn't look a thing like Bruce Willis.

"Throw it Bucky," I said.

You see, while everybody was watching me getting busy handing the bad end of rowdy to the uberbottom unter-Kapitan, everybody forgot to watch as Bucky pulled a second dead mackerel out from his pants and lobbed it straight up over his head so that it fell back squarely onto the deck of the death sub, right next to where we were standing. He didn't throw it high enough or hard enough for me to miss noticing the Bucky-sized teeth marks in the belly of the dead mackerel, but I decided to not mention it. Especially after Big Stinky rose up and grabbed the mackerel, death sub and all.

Who said I forgot to bring the plan?

6

It took a Los Alamos team of international scientists and engineers several years to construct the world's first nuclear weapon.

It had taken me and Bucky about five minutes to come up with our brilliant plan of action, which in hindsight might not have been that amazing at all.

In fact hindsight was about all we had going for us. It was goddamn dark in the belly of Big Stinky.

"Bucky," I said. "Smile."

Bucky grinned, and shed a little neon fluorescence on the situation.

It helped a little bit.

"What in the hell did you do to my boat?" I heard the unter-Kapitan ask.

I stomped down hard on the deck.

"The boat's still here," I said, "Right where we left it. I planned it this way."

"You planned it?" Bucky said pointedly.

"Well, we planned it," I admitted.

"Planned it?" the FBI pink said. "You planned to get us swallowed by a goddamn sea monster?"

I shrugged.

The motion was lost in the darkness, but I felt it was important to get the gesture across.

"We work best close up," I explained.

"Well you don't get any closer than this," the FBI pink said. "Now how in the hell am I supposed to get those zomboids back to Hollyweird?"

"The zomboids? I thought you wanted the death sub?"

"That old prop? To hell with that. I came here for the zomboids."

"What do you need a bunch of back-from-the-dead Auf Wiedersehens for?"

"Extras."

"Huh?"

"Stunt doubles. You can shoot a lot more realistically if you can shoot real bullets without worrying about killing your actors. These aren't really Nazis. They're just a band of renegade extras escaped from the remake director's cut of *Das Boot part XIII—Rambo Grows Gills*. The geeks at Hollyweird hired Uncle Sam to bring the zomboids back."

"And you hired us."

The pink nodded.

"Now you've got it. Only you went and fucked it up. Who in the hell told you that you were supposed to feed our zomboid extras to a goddamn sea monster, you goddamn, fucked-up homosexual squid?"

His voice went up at least twelve octaves in mid-rant. It was beautiful to listen to, but I decided it was time to shut him up.

"I'm not homosexual," I said.

That did it. I felt both the FBI pink's and Bucky's silence, just as loud as a moonless asphyxiation.

"You're saying you're heterosexual?" the FBI pink said.

"I used to think that," I said.

"Huh," the FBI pink said.

"I used to think I was heterosexual. Then I met Bucky and things kind of fell together."

"You figured out you were homosexual."

"Too damn many syllables."

"Huh?"

"I figured out I was sexual. And sexually speaking, I figured I was attracted to Bucky. There's really no need to make any bigger deal of that than what's there to begin with—simple animal attraction."

Bucky grinned even harder raising the illumination just enough to silhouette the entire death sub crew.

"It was my natural sea-blue eyes, wasn't it?" Bucky asked.

"That and the fine tight curving arc of your dorsal fin."

"Please," the FBI pink said. "I don't want to go to my grave with that kind of an image."

"Holy shit. An FBI agent who doesn't want too much information. That's a first for you. Why don't you take a look around you? Take a look at every face you see here. You're an FBI agent, isn't suspect identification a prerequisite?"

"I can't see a damn thing," the pink said. "It's too dark."

"That's right," I said. "We all look the same in the dark. Just warm bodies to hang to."

I gave Bucky a cuddle.

WETSIDE STORY

"I'm hanging onto my best friend, and I expect the unter-Kapitan is hanging onto his right now. Who are you hanging onto, pink? Your gun?"

Nobody spoke.

The sound of silence sung about us sweetly.

Simon and Garfunkel couldn't have said it any better.

"Besides, who said anything about dying?"

"Huh?"

"Wait for it," Bucky and I harmonized.

Which was right about the moment that Big Stinky went tsunami.

7

Holy mother of Regan, the Zomboid Death Sub chudded on out of that sea monster's hurling gullet like an armor plate unter-chunk of upchuck uberbottomed projectile expulsed out and over the ocean water like a vomitous albatross of glory.

Bucky grabbed onto me and the unter-Kapitan grabbed onto Goldie, and Goldie grabbed onto the FBI pink who was hanging onto me.

And we kept on soaring.

For just a half an instant I could see all of Darktown spread out below me. It was like a shot of pure god, smacked hard into my eyeballs. I could see a multitude of lives being lived out below me in the dirty concrete entrails of my city, and each of those lives were hanging onto other lives.

It was beautiful and then it was over.

We hit the beach, death sub and all, smacking hard against a sand castle. The belly of the sub crumpled up against the sand, accordioning itself. I felt my knees buckle and I grabbed onto the FBI pink harder than ever.

"You see," I shouted. "In the end all we've got to hang onto is each other."

And then I sat on him.

"And just in case he hasn't quite seen the light," I said to the unter-Kapitan. "Why don't you and your people make yourself scarce, while I sit here on this fellow, allowing him to contemplate my fine fog-hornish farts. I imagine you folks can lose yourselves quite nicely in the muddle of Middle Darktown."

"Just that easy?" the unter-Kapitan said. "What about our sub?"

Vernon

I shrugged.

I had a magnificent shrug and it was good to share it with others in plain daylight.

"It's just so much beachfront property for now," I said. "Maybe Bucky and I will move in. You definitely have to move out."

"It's a big old target," Bucky added. "You folks were nothing but sitting ducks out there in this ironclad dory. They sank the Bismark, they could easily sink you."

Now it was the unter-Kapitan's turn to shrug.

Amateur.

"We've got each other," Goldie said, hanging onto the unter-Kapitan like he was the biggest undead life preserver in the middle of a lonely ocean. "Anything else is tinsel."

"God bless us every one," Bucky said.

And so they drifted away, which is what things on the ocean generally do. I sat there, feeling the FBI pink squirming beneath my butt like a pimple with ambition.

"Be still and try not to breathe," I told him. "You're tickling my prostate something fierce."

After a few minutes the Zomboid Nazis had fully pulled their tents. By this evening I expected they would be successfully co-mingling with the darker denizens of the Wetside Darktown underkingdom. You get far enough down into the underkingdom and nobody's going to get you up out of there.

I stood up, and Bucky peeled the FBI pink off my butt. The pink lay there on the beach like a bit of flotsammed bubble wrap.

I didn't think he'd be making any trouble too soon.

"Come on," I said to Bucky. "Let's you and me go on home and get ourselves next to some hot buttered sea bass and get down to some good old fashioned fraternizing."

I heard the mermaids singing out on the deep ocean water and I damn well knew they were singing for me.

They hopped the fence and landed in a silent park. Unblinking strangers peddled lazily on bikes that steered themselves. Some tapped on invisible keyboards as they rode. No one looked at Victor and Aakash.

NEXT DOOR

Rahul Kanakia

At three AM, the itching got so bad that Aakash rolled off his mattress and crawled across the garage floor to the bug-free patch of concrete where Chandresh and Rishi were sleeping. But after a shivering hour next to his restless brothers, he got up and trudged to the bed. He was just crawling in when he spotted a black speck on his pillow. Shuddering, he flung the bedding away and huddled atop the bare plastic with which he'd shrinkwrapped the mattress.

At first, he kept the light on, but then Chandresh started rustling around on the floor, so he switched it off. In the dark, he felt the featherlight touches all over his skin, running up his legs and across his chest, pausing on the tip of his nose and then jumping into his hair. He knew that most of the sensations were probably just imaginary bugs, conjured up by his anxiety. He needed to relax. They'd only had the bugs for a few weeks. His boyfriend, Victor, had lived in a bug-ridden squat for two years, but he'd gotten used to them after a few months. "They're no worse than mosquito bites," Victor had said.

But Aakash couldn't stop feeling them. Finally, he gave in, and raked his nails over his neck, arms, legs, chest, stomach, armpits, and groin. But, the scratching brought no relief. The points of itchiness multiplied, until he didn't have enough fingers to deal with them. He screamed silently, and beat on the mattress, but then his mother, Deepa, sleepily murmured, "What? Who?" so Aakash clenched his hands together. There was no sense in waking her up, too.

Fighting tears of frustration, he got off the mattress and went to the far corner of the garage. He crossed his legs and sat down next to the spigot that provided their water. He was surrounded by junk: skis, a lawnmower, three bicycles, boxes of christmas ornaments, books, and old clothes. It all belonged to the family of strangers that owned this garage. Whenever Aakash tried to move any of it, little bots would sizzle out of the junk and sound a warning beep until Aakash moved away.

Chemicals couldn't get rid of the bedbugs—modern bugs were immune to most all pesticides—but those tiny little bots could run through the garage and zap them all in an instant. Aakash looked upwards and mouthed a silent prayer to the owners of the garage. He was right on the verge of cranking open that garage door and walking up to the big house and knocking on the door and begging the owners to make that tiny adjustment to the bots and set Aakash's family free from this menace. But Aakash stepped back from the edge. He was a squatter. He didn't have any rights.

In most squats, the strangers were so zonked out that their squatters could make them do anything, but Aakash's strangers were a little more awake than most. They seemed to understand and accept that there were people living in their garage, but they'd also set firm boundaries; whenever Aakash tried to move into their house, he found that everything was firmly locked and secured. Aakash couldn't risk what would happen if they decided to withdraw their unspoken invitation. No, the answer was the same as always. He had to move out. He had to find a new squat: a bug-free squat.

So he called Victor.

Victor always kept late hours. He answered the call immediately, "Hey there."

"I can't take another day with these bugs," Aakash whispered.

"Stay strong. We'll have our own squat soon enough."

"How? When? We've been looking for a year."

"It'll happen."

"The new place will probably get the bug too. Every place has them, nowadays."

"Not our place. I'll make sure of it. I got a surprise for you."

NEXT DOOR

Aakash smiled. "What?"

"I'll show you tomorrow. Go to sleep. Make sure you rest up."

"I can't sleep for shit. Come on, what is it?"

"What, you really want me to ruin the surprise?"

As they whispered back-and-forth, Aakash grew drowsy, and, finally, fell asleep.

He awoke when the garage door rolled up and let in a stream of morning light. A stranger—the man who owned the house—stood in the doorway, saying to himself, "Hold on. Hold on. I think I put it in the bin marked 'radical self-expression in grossly materialist contexts.'"

Aakash glanced at his phone. It was eight AM. Victor's last text said, "Hope you're finally asleep. I love you."

Aakash's mother ran forward and pulled sleepy Chandresh and Rishi out of the way as the stranger stepped into the garage. The stranger was walking blindly, using his fingers to manipulate keyboards and windows and graphical elements that no one else could see. Their visual implants allowed the strangers to see much more than was actually there, but it also meant they mostly ignored the real world.

Bots—tiny tangles of wire—wriggled out of the stranger's hair and radiated across the concrete floor, emitting low-powered zaps. One of the bots zapped a speck of dust. Aakash pulled out his phone, and it identified the speck as a bed bug.

The stranger clattered through the junk in the back corner. Finally, he said, "Found it!" and pulled out a large machine.

The bots wouldn't go farther than three feet from the man, but, when he passed Aakash's bed, hundreds of them crawled into it. Aakash's heart leapt.

Aakash sucked in his stomach and tiptoed behind the man, trying to get within the bots' range. The bug-killing bots leapt directly from the stranger's hair onto Aakash. They crawled all over his body. Each time he felt a tiny static shock, Aakash sighed with relief.

As the man left, Aakash tiptoed behind him. He was close enough to kiss the man. His mom and brothers were looking at him with shocked expressions. A half-dozen would-be squatters were gathered around the garage-door with bedrolls and bags. They were clearly hoping the garage would empty out, so they could snake the squat for themselves. A few of them laughed at Aakash's absurd dog-step.

"What the hell are you doing?"

The interjection came from another stranger: a teenager with the wispy hint of a beard.

"Be patient, Joel!" the man said. "I *just* found the laser-saw."

"I wasn't talking to you, Dad," Joel said. "Can't you see this guy riding your ass?"

The man glanced back. His face was just a foot from Aakash's. Aakash smiled, but didn't pull back. The bots were still working.

"Oh, it's just a street person," The dad handed over the laser-saw. "All right...are you ready to reclaim your cultural heritage?"

The son pulled Aakash back by the arm. "Jesus, give my dad some room," Joel said. Aakash could hear the powered-up hum of the personal defense system embedded in the son's shirt. He was probably getting ready to unleash an arc of electricity that would shock Aakash into unconsciousness.

"Don't worry about him," the father said. "The street people are harmless."

The father snapped his fingers and the garage door started closing. Aakash shouted to his mother, "I'm coming in. I'll stay today."

"No, no," his mother yelled. "Victor will be waiting for you! You need to keep searching!"

Aakash ran in and grabbed his bag from the high shelf, then rolled out and under the door. When he got up, the father and son were walking away.

One of the would-be squatters standing by the garage-door said, "I hate that kid. I can't wait until he finally goes to sleep."

"At least he doesn't ignore us," another said.

"Man...if they didn't ignore us, how could we live with them?"

Aakash looked at the pair. He'd seen them around, but he didn't know their names. Aakash said, "Cmon guys, what're you waiting around for? Didn't you hear? Our squat has the bug."

One of them said, "So what? My bedroll has the bug, too. At least you've got a roof."

Aakash shook his head. Someone had to stay behind to stop these guys from stealing the squat, but why did he always let his mom do it? His mom never got a break from being eaten alive in there. He knew he ought to slap on the door of that garage and make her hoist it up from the inside using the manual override. He needed to pull his weight and do his time. But then he felt the phantom touch of a bug crawling across his neck. He texted Victor, "I'll be there in an hour."

As he trudged towards the bus stop, Aakash fell in with the tens of thousands of other homeless people who were wandering the streets of LA County. Every streetcorner was a marketplace. Street stalls sold crude handicrafts to the few passersby who looked as if they had any money. People delved into collapsed buildings, pulling out copper wire, aluminum coils, rags, and paper and piled their goods into shopping carts for resale at some distant recycling center. At red lights, children ran into the crowds of sleek, self-driven cars, begging the occupants for dollars until the lights turned green and they were stranded in the middle of the lane by the zooming rivers of cars.

And every few blocks, crowds of hundreds of people surrounded the dispensaries. With the bots, manufacturing was cheap and easy. Many strangers—acting singly or as part of organizations—had set up points of distribution to give away clothes, canned goods, shoes, prepaid cellphones, or whatever else they could program their bots to churn out. Aakash spent most days waiting in long, slow lines, so he could accumulate something to take back to his family.

Not today, though. Today, they had enough food stockpiled back in the squat. Today, Aakash was going to engage in the other major pastime of the streets. He was going to head up into the hills to look for a new squat.

With their visual implants, the strangers spent more and more time in their own realities, so they didn't much care what happened to their houses. Most of them weren't as awake as the one who owned Aakash's squat. Usually, a house's owner was just a wired-up body lying in a bed, dreaming for twenty-three hours a day. So it wasn't hard for a squatter to just move right into the spare rooms. Sometimes the owner even got carried down to a cellar or something, if the squatters needed more space.

But the owners were starting to die. And an ownerless house soon shut off; the electricity, the water—even the doors—stopped working. Eventually, ownerless squats fell apart, and their occupants had to look for another place.

Kanakia

And there weren't many places left. In this part of the Hollywood Hills, there were more rubble-filled lots than upright houses.

Aakash knew that his odds of finding his own place were pretty bad. Hell, some people would say that he was a fool for wanting to leave the garage. But he couldn't stop searching for something better. Something clean and spacious and graceful: a place fit for a human being.

Victor and Aakash never went to each other's squats. Instead, they began their daily search by meeting in an abandoned steam pipe nexus underneath Griffith Observatory. To get there, Aakash passed through a long corridor whose wall was covered in frescoes of the exploding universe and whose floor was cluttered with food wrappers, broken bottles, and used condoms.

The dark corridor was a popular meeting place. In one corner, two voices were whispering.

One said: "We're evaluating your kid today, aren't we? You excited?"

The other voice said: "I just hope he does his duty. Sometimes he seems a little…careless."

"I'm sure he'll be fine." A moment of silence, then, "Should we clear out the street-people before your kid arrives?"

"No…he needs to learn how to deal with them."

Aakash kept walking. Lingering over someone else's secret rendezvous was against the corridor's etiquette.

The temperature in the steampipe room was over a hundred degrees. Victor, stripped to his shorts, sat cross-legged on their mattress and gulped water from a plastic bottle. He rose and leaned forward to kiss Aakash, only to be pushed back.

"No," Aakash said. "I'm probably *covered* in bugs."

Victor's smile threw strange shadows in the shaky light they'd dangled from an exposed wire. "So what? Now we both have it," Victor said.

Aakash said, "What if, in a few hours, we crack open a door and come up in an abandoned mansion! A place with running water and electricity and three thousand square feet of space. And what if, with our first footsteps, we infect it?"

Aakash hung his clothes from a blisteringly hot steam pipe. Then he gingerly reached for the steam valve. The jet of steam had burned him once, but that'd been six months ago. He was more careful now. They had to heat the room to over 120 degrees and then stand here for an hour to make sure the bugs died.

"Wait!" Victor grabbed him by the waist and pulled him back. "You haven't asked about your surprise yet!"

Victor pressed an aluminum canister into his hand. Aakash held it up to the light. The aerosol can was covered in Chinese characters.

"Pesticide? We've already tried *everything*. We have the chemical-resistant bugs."

"They're not resistant to *this*," Victor said. "It's never been used in the U.S. It's illegal here."

"Shit, then it'll kill us."

"No, it's just illegal because it kills birds or something. One treatment shouldn't hurt us. In China, they spray this on kids to kill lice."

"Where did you get this?"

Victor kissed Aakash. "I started looking for it on the day when you first told me your place had gotten the bug. You never blamed me, but…I felt so guilty."

"But you could use this on your own place…to help your own family…"

"No. This is for our new life. We'll find a place, spray it up, close the door, and lock our troubles on the other side."

Aakash hugged Victor, but he couldn't stop thinking about the closed door that his mom was locked up behind.

A light momentarily blinded them. A stranger had entered, holding a powerful lantern. He glanced at the nearly-naked pair and rolled his eyes. The stranger dragged in a chair from the hall. Aakash and Victor stepped to the side of the room. The stranger flipped their mattress up into a corner, then he hopped up onto the chair and examined the ceiling.

"Hey," Aakash said. "I think that's the son of the stranger who owns my squat."

"What?"

"Yeah, I see him all the time. His name is Joel."

The teen looked down and said, "Can't you guys swish it up somewhere else?" He pulled a machine from his bag and held it up to the ceiling.

"Is that a laser-saw?" Victor whispered.

"Keep it down!" Joel said. "This is hella dangerous."

"Umm….what are you doing?" Aakash ventured. He'd lived under the boy for years, but he'd never said a word to him before.

"None of your damn business," Joel said.

Aakash whispered, "I think he's trying to break into the observatory."

"Really?" Victor said. "By lasering through the floor? Seems like someone would notice. This guy's going to go to jail."

"It's Sunday. The place is closed and empty," Joel said.

"But there are guards," Aakash said.

"There's one guard," Joel said. "I've had cameras in there, watching him, for the past two weeks. We're under the atrium right now. There's an hour-long window when he doesn't ever look into it."

Victor said, "Couldn't this kid just—" but Aakash shushed him.

"I bet I can get in there before you do," Aakash said.

"Sure…right. When the guard arrests you guys, that'll be a great distraction. Now can you leave me alone?"

"If I get there first, you need to program your bots to zap your entire garage for bedbugs."

"What? You're bug-infested? That's disgusting."

"Is it a bet?"

"No. Of course not. What would be in it for me?"

"I'm not some random punk. I know who you are. I know where you live."

"Sure," Joel said. "My shirt is a Shield S400. It'll shoot an arc that can lay you out before you—"

"I think that the cops might be pretty interested in what you're doing."

"You wouldn't. You'd lose your nice little squat."

"I don't care. Those bugs are…I don't care."

Joel's face reddened and contorted. "Fine. Whatever. It's a bet."

They hastily donned their steam-pressed clothes. In the corridor, Aakash bounced up and down, and whispered, "Mom will be so happy! We'll be bug free forever!"

"Wow, that kid was a straight-up fool," Victor said. "I guess strangers aren't too used to having to think."

The hallway's exit emerged from a fenced-off hill. They hopped the fence and landed in a silent park. Unblinking strangers peddled lazily on bikes that steered themselves. Some tapped on invisible keyboards as they rode. No one looked at Victor and Aakash.

Strangers didn't usually spend much time outside, but Griffith Observatory was a popular enough LA landmark that it managed to attract a few dozen visitors every day. A few strangers were sunning themselves on the grass. Some were walking virtual dogs that only they could see. Others were jogging or throwing balls. But all of them were seeing far more than Aakash and Victor could see. Their data displays were so dense and information-rich that the world of grass and concrete and flesh was only a minor part of their visual field.

When Aakash took a running start and leaped up onto the lip of the observatory's first story, no one looked up. He gave a hand to Victor. They shimmied around to the front of the observatory and—in full view of almost fifty people—clambered up to the open slit of the dome. Then Aakash stepped onto the thin mezzanine that was just inside the dome. Below them, the guard was walking his rounds, but he never looked up.

"This is nice," Victor said. "I could def live here. Why did we strike this place off the list?"

"It's only two feet wide."

"Oh. Right."

When the guard moved away, they dropped down.

A floor tile rose and a head poked up. Joel stood up, then pulled out three gadgets. Aakash and Victor crouched down next to him. "Is that to, like, identify laser tripwires?" Victor said.

Joel opened his mouth, closed it, and then nodded.

Aakash laughed, "This place doesn't have any laser tripwires."

"Well, it's got them installed," Victor said. "But I think the guard deactivated them. Too many false positives."

Joel pulled himself out, then handed his camera to Aakash. "Fine, you win. Just take some pictures of me, All right? I gotta prove I was here."

By the time they'd dropped back into the steam-pipe room, Joel was laughing. "Wow, you guys really schooled me," he said.

"No!" Aakash stepped forward. "Actually...you...umm, definitely have skills. We just...well, it could've gone either way."

"My dad mostly taught me computer stuff," Joel said. "I guess he kind of overlooked the basic skills. Or maybe I was supposed to know them already..."

"Your dad?" Victor said.

"Yeah, this is kind of a family business for us," Joel said. "After I pass my evaluation, he and I are gonna set up shop down here and pop up at night to secretly restore the telescope. It's a great early twentieth century piece, but when the lens broke, the curators just hung up a "Do Not Touch" sign and let it fall to pieces."

"Why?" Victor said.

"Money. They don't care whether it—"

"No...why do *you* care?"

"That's what we do. We keep things preserved after the sleepers abandon them. We're doing it for you...so you'll have some kind of history left."

"Look," Aakash said. "About those bugs. It's just a little thing. It won't be a problem to reprogram the bots, right?"

Joel's phone buzzed. He looked at it, then grimaced.

"What? Is it the next task?" Victor said.

The kid looked up at them with moisture-filled eyes; it was like he'd never seen them before in his life. "My dad saw me with you in the atrium," Joel said. "He says that my carelessness could've compromised the mission."

Aakash cranked his mind. How could he convince this kid to pay up on the damned bet?

Joel's eyes widened. He tapped at his phone for a long while.

Then Aakash got a call. His mom was shouting, "The lights turned off! And I tried to pull open the doorway, but the rope snapped! You need to come home. I don't know what's happened. Oh God, I knew it was wrong to stay in this country; I knew we didn't belong here; I knew..."

As Aakash talked his mom through her panic, Joel's face became more grim. When Aakash hung up, the stranger said, "It will be awhile before my dad notices that power is out in the garage. Your family might be trapped for days."

"What did you do?" Aakash said.

"I'm sorry that I had to do that," Joel said. "My dad says that I'm not adaptable enough for front-line work...but I'm gonna show him. And if you want your mom to get out safely, then you're gonna help me."

Joel wanted to hack the Observatory's computers and insert himself into their HR database. With his finger-, voice-, and retinal-prints on file, he'd be able to go in and out whenever he wanted. Then his dad would *have* to come around. Joel promised that once the operation was successful, he'd restore power to the garage.

As they walked around the building, Joel outlined a long plan that involved knocking out the lights and executing a lightning-fast, perfectly timed run. They'd memorize the floorplan, descend on wires from the ceiling, run inside in total darkness, switch the lights back on, hack the computers, and then hide until morning and leave—just like any other tourist—after the observatory opened to the public.

Aakash's stomach was churning. His mom was trapped…in the dark… with the bugs. "Fucking Christ!" he interjected. "Why bother with all that spy-shit? The reason there's only one guard is because no one gives a damn whether we break in or not."

Aakash pulled three sticks of gum out of his bag and started chewing. Then he spit out the wad, took a deep breath and ran up to the front gate of the museum. He pressed buttons and pummeled the door with his fist. Five long minutes passed before the guard opened the door.

Aakash held up his bag. "Hey, I'm sorry to bother you, but I was wondering if you could let me pick through your bins."

The guard said, "We got a guy who takes out the cans. He's a big, bald fella."

"Yeah, I know." Aakash lied. "But he only does cans. He spotted some copper coils in there, though, and tipped me off about them."

"Jeez, I don't think…"

"Please…I need this. My tooth's been killing me for months." Aakash opened his mouth and touched the blackened incisor he hadn't thought about since the bugs had come. "I need a big score to pay for pulling it."

The guard rubbed his own jaw. "Well, all right, but I gotta watch you." As he entered, Aakash stuck the wad of gum against the door's locking mechanism.

Aakash followed the guard down a set of stairs. His phone buzzed. A text from an unknown number: *We're in.*

As they walked down a corridor, Aakash's practiced eyes could see the patch where the door that led to the exploding galaxy hallway had been sealed off entirely. Steel chains secured by a big combination lock barred a set of doors that said *James McKeever Memorial IMAX Theater.*

"You ever catch a movie?" Aakash said.

"No," the guard said. "That was already locked up when I started working here. Makes sense. What we've got is way better than IMAX." The guard laughed and tapped at the visual implant pasted to his temple, but then he looked at Aakash's bare brow and said, "Well, the implants also have downsides. After you've got them for awhile, the ordinary world starts to seem a little…dull."

It was hard to stay impassive while rooting around in the dumpster at the loading dock. The theater was all that Aakash could think about. The theater probably still had electricity. And they wouldn't have to stay inside it 24-7 to keep it from getting snaked by someone else. The guard would keep everyone else out!

The guard's phone rang. Red lights flashed. A raucous alarm echoed from wall-mounted speakers. Aakash tensed up.

But the guard just waved his hand. "Oh man, this happens all the time," the guard said. "Some bird probably hit a window and now I gotta go disable the alarm." The guard looked over Aakash's shoulder. "Damn…you haven't found the coils yet, have you?"

Aakash winced and rubbed the side of his face. "No…I…I guess I'll go," he said. "Thanks for everything you've done. He said it was pretty far down at the bottom…but if you've gotta…"

The guard said, "Look. You don't mind if I lock you down here, do you? I'll be back in just a second."

When the guard left, the electronic lock clicked behind him. And why shouldn't the guard feel safe? There was no way that some streetkid could break a top of the line cryptographic lock.

But Aakash wasn't going in through that door. Instead, he took a slab of plywood from the dumpster and manually levered up the vehicle gate a few inches, so he could reach inside with a stretched-out wire-hanger and hit the button to open the gate.

The lock barring the theater was idiotically simple. It must've been put in before they replaced everything with electronic locks. He pulled down on the lock to put pressure on the internal mechanism and slowly rotated the numbers until the tumblers clicked into place.

The theater was a paradise. A tall ceiling. A long silver screen. Hundreds of padded chairs. The lone glow of an emergency light meant readily available power. The dust was thick and undisturbed. Aakash was the first person to step inside here in years. And no people meant no bugs.

NEXT DOOR

Footsteps echoed outside. Aakash gasped. The alarms had just gone silent. Was he going to be trapped in here? He forced himself to calm down. He listened. There were two sets of footsteps. He opened the door. Joel and Victor were running down the corridor.

"In here, you idiots."

"Alarms, cops, caught," Joel gasped.

Victor pulled Joel inside. Aakash stepped out, closed the doors, slapped the padlock back on, and forced himself to walk, briskly but quietly, back to the loading dock.

When the guard returned, he said, "Yeah…some kind of bird or something. Oh…you haven't gotten the coils yet? Look, I'm sorry, but…I think I gotta take you back."

As they passed the theater door, Aakash smiled. He and Victor had finally found their new home.

Over the next day, Joel sent him a stream of increasingly frantic texts: "What the FUCK are you waiting for?"; "Get me out of here, or your mom's fucking going to jail!"; "Don't THINK about ratting me out. My dad knows people. He can get me off, no prob."

Aakash's mother called a few times, too, and he had to soothe her as well. He was being torn in a dozen directions. Even after he saved Joel, how could he leave his family under the teen's thumb? How was he going to placate that kid?

But he wasn't going to screw this up by acting rashly. He texted with Victor, and they both agreed to wait. Night fell and still Aakash waited. He felt guilty when he lined up at a dispensary for his meal. Victor and Joel…had to be getting pretty hungry right now. He knew he could probably run inside and rescue them, but he'd looked for that place for years…for his whole life. He couldn't risk setting off the alarm again and making the guard suspicious.

When morning came, he was cold, damp, and hungry. But he was the first person in the ticket line. The guard had changed, so no one recognized him. He sauntered down that corridor, and picked the padlock unhurriedly.

Victor embraced him and Joel clawed for the door. Aakash restrained Joel. "Wait a second. I saved your ass here. You gotta admit that you owe—"

Kanakia

The doors reopened. Two strangers—Joel's father and some woman—walked in.

"Congratulations," the father said. "This will be a fine base of operations."

"We'll be moving in our equipment throughout the day," said the woman.

Joel was shaking. "Then…I passed?"

The father said, "Your method of handling these street-people was unorthodox, but it got results. I've never been prouder." He embraced his son.

"I…I also put you and me into the staff database," Joel said. "We can come and go whenever we want."

"What the fuck?" Victor said. "You guys can have the telescope, but this theater is ours."

"You can stay in the garage," Joel said. "I'll reprogram the bots. It's no problem."

Aakash groaned. He'd known this was gonna fall apart, somehow.

"No!" Victor said. "We *need* this place. We want to live here, do you understand? We're not just pulling some kind of guerrilla art stunt… we're talking about staying alive."

His father glanced at Joel. Aakash wondered if that hug could be taken back.

"No, wait!" Joel said. "These two, they're good. They want to join us."

"Fuck you guys," Victor said. "You're *really* going to snake this from us? We have nothing at all and you're really gonna…"

"Calm down," Aakash said. "Let's just get out of here."

Joel said, "Come on. What's wrong with letting them live here and help us? Aren't they the ones who'll inherit all our work?"

His father said, "You don't need to placate them. They're probably illegal. I'll arrange to have them deported."

Joel's mouth opened. "Cmon, Dad…that's not funny."

"You know that I'm in favor of helping the street-people whenever we can, but these two have already proven themselves to be dangerous and untrustworthy," his father said. "From the beginning, they threatened to compromise you. Finally, you had to extort them into helping you. If we let them go, they'll sell us out for a quick payday."

"No, I'm *not* backing down," Victor said. He held up the can of Chinese pesticide. "You can all eat bug-spray." He pulled the tab and gas billowed from the top of the can. The strangers' eyes got big and their shirts flashed and bots swarmed out of their hair. What were their informational overlays telling them about this gas? The smoke enveloped Victor.

"Crazy bastards, that stuff is—" Joel's father said.

"We need to go!" the woman said.

Joel took one last backwards look before he followed them. The doors slammed behind them and the padlock clicked. Joel's father probably thought he was locking them in to face a fatal poison. Aakash fell to his knees, took off his shirt, wetted it with a water bottle, and shoved it against the door to stop the smoke from seeping out and setting off god-knows-what alarms.

From within the smoke cloud, Victor laughed. "What a bunch of posers," he said.

The smoke reached Aakash. He tried not to breathe it in, but it was everywhere. He reached for Victor. "Is this really happening?" Aakash said. "Have we really done it?"

"They won't bother us again. I'll send out a few messages and tie them up in knots, thinking we got killed by this stuff. They won't want to come within five miles of this place."

"But…what about…"

"That kid isn't going to mess with your family…not after what he's already done to you."

"But he won't help them either. The bugs…"

"We could be alone: here, together, forever. No one would ever bother us. If we bring our families, we'll be in danger every day. Who knows who might try to take it from us? Or whether someone would attract the guards? Are your brothers really gonna be quiet for weeks, months, years? We'll have to think about their food and their water. We'll have to make dispensary trips every day; each trip means another chance of getting caught. And we'll have to—"

Victor's speech was broken up by a long fit of coughing. Aakash's throat and lungs were also feeling ill-used by the pesticide, but hopefully the pain would fade soon enough.

Victor continued, "We'll have to build toilets and find some way to get running water. And what if they bring more bugs? Do you really think we can live like that? Do you really think that'll work?"

"Not really," Aakash said. "But...we have to try. I can't be happy here, knowing Rishi and Chandresh are growing up in that place."

Victor was silent for a long moment. Aakash could feel his boyfriend giving up that old dream, and trying to orient himself to the new one. Could he do it? Or would he leave?

"Fine," Victor said. "We'll open this place up to everyone and your mother."

After they kissed, Aakash turned and spit out the toxic dust he'd picked up from Victor's lips.

"You're amazing," Aakash said. "I'll text my mom and—"

"Wait," Victor said. "Do it tomorrow. Can't we have it to ourselves for at least one day?"

The ceiling was so high and dark that it looked like the night sky. The pesticidal dust on the carpet was so white that it looked like frost. And the two lovers lay down next to each other so tenderly that, for a moment, they looked carefree.

The guard frowned. Instinct warned him to make the kid shut his trap. Some things weren't meant to be spoken aloud and the pucker of his balls suggested that this was such a one.

A STRANGE FORM OF LIFE
Laird Barron

Wind screamed along the rooftops of the prison, scattering night birds and bats.

Station 3 lay near the edge of the Hanford Nuclear Reservation. The prison was huge and decrepit. Built in the 1930s, allegedly atop Indian burial grounds, there'd been murders and fires, rapes and riots, and haunting aplenty, so much so that even the diocese loathed sending in clergy to take confessions or spread the faith. The aura of corruption emanating from the prison's very walls was too much and the word from Rome was fuck it, more or less.

Now, despite the state's perennial problem with overcrowding at correctional facilities, the vast rusting blight sat mostly uninhabited, a high plains Alcatraz. Two hundred inmates and a skeleton crew of guards and support staff called a wing of the prison and the surrounding miles of prairie home. Scuttlebutt had it that come next year's election the complex would be bulldozed and the land sectioned into commercial office space, staff and occupants displaced to the Devil knew where. The Devil. Everyone at Station 3 thought about Old Poger quite often, for one reason or another.

The guard and the convict went into a remote section, long shut down and abandoned, and fucked, exactly as they had done twice a week for the past three months since the convict transferred in from Walla Walla.

Usually they rendezvoused in the library after hours, or the machine shop. Tonight, the convict had insisted on more privacy, claimed he had something important to share. The guard humored the lad; he didn't have much else to do.

Here the darkness was almost complete except for the distant glow of a lamp at the intersection. Water dripped from corroded pipes that carried the moans of the wind. Rats scuttled among fallen masonry. A heavy odor of dankness and rot clung to concrete and stone and the impression was that the lovers had strayed from the workings of man into a deep cavern of the earth.

The convict gripped the bars of the defunct block gate, his stance wide. The old guard thrust so forcefully the convict's forehead bounced against the steel. The convict always chatted while the guard worked, though his nervousness seemed acute. The kid was in the middle of narrating the story of his life, the chapter about how he almost got away. —We took down the bank at the end of the shift, y'know. Coulda made a clean getaway, except for some cops who ran along the sidewalk after us. Russ crashed the car in a field. I think one of the pigs shot our tire. We booked outta the car, every man for himself. I stuffed money into my pockets and down my pants and beat feet.

The guard rolled his eyes and snorted. His breathing was heavy as a horse that'd been flogged down the home stretch; sparks whirled as his brain began to ignite. He gripped the convict's hips and made a final, agonized lunge and had a vision of the con's head getting wedged between the bars. That would be tricky to explain to the other screws, although Whitey and Reggie would just laugh. The guard wiped himself and zipped his fly. He slumped against the arch of the tunnel and lighted a cigarette. The sharp flame spun shadows across the walls, momentarily revealing blocks of satanic graffiti and water stains curdled with mold. Then he flipped the lighter shut and brought back the dark. He smoked, free hand resting on his gut that sagged over his belt like a cannonball. Twenty-seven years on the job had given him a drinking problem, a bad back, flat feet, flattened nose, three missing teeth, and contempt for humanity, himself included. Nonetheless, as he gasped for air to smoke his cigarette, another vice picked up in the line of duty, a sense of grudging affection for the convict mellowed his habitual resentment toward the universe.

A STRANGE FORM OF LIFE

The kid became quiet, sort of hanging with his arms stuck through the bars, pants around his ankles. He wasn't really a kid, probably in his late twenties, the bloom off the rose and all that, but still taut and smooth and irrepressible. His skin gleamed in the darkness. The silence didn't last. Without glancing backward, he said, —I hauled ass through the field and come to a bumpy old road. Getting set to cross it when a car rolls by. Real slow. Cruisin' like a shark. Dunno why, but something was off about it. Spooked me bad. I had a premonition. An omen. Whatever you wanna call it. Goose run over my grave.

—Fix your britches and I'll give you a smoke, the guard said.

The convict pulled up his pants. He accepted a cigarette and let it dangle from the corner of his mouth, striking a pose like a tough from *Westside Story*. He smirked and winked until the guard's composure cracked and he chuckled. The convict said, —Then the dude riding shotgun looked back at me. I was so freaked, man. I ran into the tall grass and hid for like six hours. Damned dogs found me. I got a scar from the hole the fucker tore in my belly.

—A guy spots you in the ditch and that scares you?

—I was already scared. That made it worse. That was the icing, chief.

—You lost me.

—It was dark as a well digger's asshole. *No way* he could see me hidin' in the Tooley weeds.

—But he *did*. Looked right at you.

—Like he could see in the dark. Stared into my soul.

Wind moaned somewhere deeper in the tunnel. The guard was surprised to feel the hairs on his arm prickle. He imagined the kid crouched in that country ditch, body hidden, face camouflaged in dirt and grease, behind a lattice of grass and leaves. Then the car, long and sleek, dome light on so the driver and passenger were illuminated like figures in a shadowbox. The figures were wrong, though. Too large for the compartment, oversized and vaguely monstrous as caricatures in a fairytale book, or misshapen puppets in some horror show. He took another drag and expelled the bad spirits to float among their fellows in the gallery beyond the wall of bars.

—That's not all, neither. There's more, the convict said.

Of course there was more. The guard frowned. Instinct warned him to make the kid shut his trap. Some things weren't meant to be spoken aloud and the pucker of his balls suggested that this was such a one. Any inclination to heed this primal instinct had been burned out by his recent exertions and he simply glanced into the metaphorical abyss and took another long drag on the cigarette. —Tell, it punk.

The convict pouted. —Hey. I'm no punk. I ain't no bitch.

—Sorry, the guard said. And he was sorry; a little. It felt like the first crack in the back of a shelf of Antarctic ice.

—Be nice to me. Be nice to me, man.

—See, there's your problem. Appealing to the Man. He's not nice. Shut up or I'll beat you with my Billy club.

—What, again? But, fine. I'm not gonna tell you why I was scared shitless. You blew it. Blew your chance.

—Blew my chance? Like you can stop your gob for five seconds. I hang around long enough, I'll hear all about your tale of woe from the cradle onward, want to or not.

—No, you blew it and it was a good story, too.

—Come on, kid. I've been on the job since Hoover was trying on his mama's heels. I heard every story there is. The guard was conflicted. Part of him really wanted to hear that story the way one is compelled to peel the scab from an itchy wound. The other part of him knew better. —Want another cig? Don't be mad. I brought you some coffee, too. Two baggies of Colombian dark. Coffee was the gold standard in prison. He took the younger man's hand in his own scarred paw. He kissed the convict's fingers and sighed. —Go ahead. What else happened? You figure out who those guys in the car were?

The convict sulked for several moments. He relented and let the guard give him another cigarette. He smoked, and in the black and blue haze he seemed far too young and fragile for this prison. —They were demons. The Great Dark's bootlickin' servants on the loose in the world. My uncle was a minister. He showed us how to recognize 'em when we were kids. Ain't hard if you got the knack. The flesh of humanity don't fit quite right.

—You bring the hellfire AND the brimstone, huh, boy? Doesn't seem Christian, knocking off banks, blasting women and children and folks. The guard smiled bitterly. Oh, how they all gave it up for the Lord once that steel gate clanged shut. Practicing their choirboy arpeggios for the day they'd sing before a parole board.

A STRANGE FORM OF LIFE

—*My uncle* was a minister. Mom and Pop weren't anything special. Went to church on Easter for the potluck. And I never shot anybody. That was Russ smoked the girl in the bank. He's a stone cold motherfucker.

—You find Jesus here in the pen? Get right with the Sky Warden?

—I don't believe in God.

—Don't believe in God. Don't. Believe. In. God. Demons, though. Demons you can get behind as a concept.

—Every culture's got its demons, the convict said. —Monsters don't need no brand of religion to do what they do. Christians believe in possession. Indians got skin walkers. People from other places call 'em whatever, but I expect they're all the same.

—Well, hell, that makes sense, the guard said. —Good for you, sonny. You've got depth. A country philosopher. Too bad you never blasted anybody, though. Kinda turned me on when I thought you was dangerous. A young Charlie Bronson. Mm, mm, mm. He extended his hand through the gloom and pinched the convict's baby-smooth cheek. —Enjoy it while it lasts. I was a lean mean screwing machine in my heyday. The spitting image of Lee Van Cleef is what all the girlies said.

—You look mean enough.

—I *am* mean enough.

—And you got his beady eyes.

—But not the fame, money, or cars to go along with them, more is the pity.

—You got the big ol' ring of keys, though. Man with the keys got everything.

The guard didn't answer. He squinted and cocked his head, sure he'd heard something down the ruined tunnel; a noise, distinct from the wind, that lasted only a moment, then subsided, and mutated in his consciousness, echoed there just as an aftershock of brilliance imprints upon the inner eyelid. He unholstered the heavy Maglite and clicked the rubber toggle. The bulb brightened and died. Click, click, click.

There were rats in the walls; armies of them. Legions of cockroaches, too. The guard didn't think rats accounted for the new sound. Gone now, lost in the regular creaks and groans and whistles. He should've been gone by now too; gone from the prison, retired, sipping rum and coke on a beach while the steel drums played. He'd come to the profession late and now he had a sneaking hunch it was *too* late. That thought usually visited him for an instant upon waking prior to his morning shift, weighing upon his chest, a succubus straight from images of hell in a medieval tapestry. But it was here now, wasn't it? He glanced toward the intersection where the far off light dimmed slightly.

—Lemme ask you something, the convict said.

—All right.

—I can't stay here.

—That a question? The guard tried smacking the Maglite with his cupped palm. Nothing and more nothing. He whistled through his teeth just as his father had done when nervous. Whistling past the graveyard, the old-timers called it.

—No, man. What I mean is, I can't stay here at the Station no more. I ain't safe.

—Who is?

—I been thinking of making a run at the wall. The convict wiggled two fingers, pantomiming legs on the move.

Me too, the guard thought, and chuckled to mask a sob. He said, —Dawson's boys will cut you down before you get ten yards. They enjoy snuffing cons. A few years ago, some of them, the real twisted fellers, ran a game. A con on the cons, you'd say. They'd pretend to be on the take, conspire with the desperate cons about breaking out for a little payoff. Agreed to look the other way when the cons snuck by with their knotted bed sheets, or what-have-you. Then, when the poor suckers made a move…Pow! A thirty-ought-six hollow point through the back of the skull and the Dobermans ripping apart the carcass. Bastards would sit around and laugh their asses off. Word got around, so there haven't been any turkey shoots lately. Don't think about it. I like you, boy.

—You got it right; nobody's safe in the Station. Bad juju, chief. Peeps are getting' weird. Fucked in the brain. They was actin' the same way in Walla Walla. The shit is spreading. Now it's here. It's among us.

The guard nodded, one eye still focused on the shadows. It wasn't the entire staff…nonetheless, some of the screws *were* behaving oddly. Odder than usual, at least. Secret conversations held in whispers and knowing smirks, the humming of off-key ditties, the cracking of knuckles. He'd seen Big Dan twitching like a headless chicken in the locker room that very afternoon. Three or four seconds of Grand Mal action. Big Dan

A STRANGE FORM OF LIFE

snapped out of it and smiled a creepy, evil smile and went down to the yard and beat the Harris brothers to a pulp over a trifle. And yesterday, Harley Koschek had walked right into the cafeteria wall, full speed, and busted his nose. The crazy sonofabitch had tilted his head back and gulped all the gushing blood. Nobody said anything, not a fucking thing, and so the guard had concentrated upon his ham on rye and chewed and thought dark thoughts.

The convict kept talking, naturally. —Maybe something in the water. Man, I read about a radioactive cloud movin' underground from Hanford toward the Columbia. One teaspoon of that shit will light up the river and kill a half million whitebread assholes in the 'burbs.

—We're upstream. Snug as bugs in a rug.

—I know. What I'm sayin' is, people are off their feed. Last few nights, those Mexicans in the next cell been whisperin'. Don't make no kinda sense, neither. Sergeant Sheckley come down and visited them. Psss, psss, psss! Just whisperin'. Afterward, he stood by my door for ten minutes. Didn't say nothin'. Stared at me and smiled. Man, last time I saw a grin like that it was cut into a pumpkin.

—Maybe he's one of those demons your uncle told you about.

—Somethin' was livin' in Sheckley's eyes. Not *him*, though. He was long gone.

—This was the second part of your story, huh? You bring me here to make a dire prediction? The Aztec Calendar roll over a year early? Tonight is the last night on Earth? Mankind going out with a whimper?

—There's a whatchamacallit…an eclipse…

—A lunar eclipse. I forgot, yeah. What time is that happening? Three quarter moon. We wouldn't see anything even if we could go outside in the yard. Too much cloud cover.

—Can I bum another smoke?

The guard lighted his last two cigarettes, briefly extending the lighter between the bars, a Dark Ages explorer trying to survey the depths of a strange cave, in vain. The darkness shrank a few inches, but that was all. The metal at the lighter's crown heated and blackened and the flame doubled and licked his thumbnail. The yellow core transfixed him.

He lived three miles down the road in a doublewide in a shabby court. The court was owned by his aunt on his mother's side and she cut him a deal. He ate microwave dinners, except for Friday nights down at the Rattler Saloon. Those nights he bought a t-bone steak and a pitcher of draft and watched the game on the plasma hanging over the bar and pretended to give a shit. He usually slept on an antique La-Z-Boy by the dying light of a box television. His dog, a Boerboel named Zilla, had passed away the week before Christmas last year, so now he talked to himself while watching *Masterpiece Theater* presentations of Agatha Christie mysteries, muttered his hypotheses regarding whodunit into empty air. None of the guys knew he watched *MPT* and *Nova*, and he was careful not to let on. Crassness and insensitivity were armor and shield at the Station. More importantly, these traits were camouflage. They thought he brutalized the inmates he took a shine to, that he coerced his lovers. Romance, sentimentality; those were traits his colleagues would sneer at. Contempt was dangerous at the Station.

The guard blinked and snapped the lighter shut. He said, —I watched a special about ants on *Nova* the other night. Well, I saw two things, related though. One on the ants, these mega-colonies that are spreading all over the planet. Trillions upon trillions of them. Foreign tribes don't make war when they meet. Scientists brought a few over from a colony in Japan and exposed them to a colony that's taking over California. The ants shook pincers, made love, assimilated. The white-coats didn't say it in so many words, but the bugs are planning something. Probably a *coup d'état*.

—Saw the movie, the convict said, taking a disaffected drag on his cigarette. —When I was a kid. Goddamn gigantic ants taking over the Earth. In black and white. I hear lotsa bad shit about ants on the news. A lady at an old folks home in Arizona got eaten alive by a bunch a red fire ants. She had dementia and some other stuff and couldn't move. Ants came tricklin' through a hole in the wall. Started with her eyes and nose, I guess. True story.

—Jesus H., the guard said. He imagined the old lady as a husk wrapped in flannel, and the black train of ants traveling through the wall and across the shiny floor of a night desert. The moon clouded and blackened as the metal of his lighter had clouded and blackened. The music of the stars was a faint shriek. —The other story on *Nova* was about zombie ants.

—What the fuck? Zombie ants. That's some crazy shit.

—There's a prehistoric fungus that was recently discovered in the jungle. Very rare. It releases spores that infect ants. Consumes them from the inside and controls their behavior. Tries to send them back to the main colony to spread the joy. When the victims die, tendrils sprout from their corpses and eject more spores. The pictures are gruesome. Sure, it's just ants, but holy shit.

The convict chuckled and his voice changed, became softer, androgynous. —Oh, I saw that episode too. Frightfully macabre, how the fungus causes its prey species to fruit. That's what it's called, the horror of the ants bursting apart with fungal blooms. Fruiting. Cue the jokes. Or not. The convict tossed his cigarette butt away in a trail of tiny sparks. He straightened and drew himself to intimidating height with a prolonged crackle of his spine. —It's called Cordyceps and it doesn't devour ants exclusively. There are thousands of variations on the progenitor, each adapting to a diet of a specific species. I'm here to tell you that Cordyceps is a relatively new organism, an adolescent scion. The mother genus is much older. Much older and, as of these past months, much more aggressive.

The guard smiled reflexively and turned his head slightly away before lurching forward and smashing the convict across the jaw with the Maglite. The flashlight made an odd, hollow clink, and its plastic bits flew apart as its metal crumpled and the guard's arm went dead as if he'd struck a cement pillar. The convict slapped the broken weapon away and pushed him onto the damp floor as one might flatten a toddler. The guard lay in an inverted crucifix position, and he saw the light at the intersection go out. Then he saw nothing but the blackness that encased the world.

The convict said, —There, there, lover. You're all right. You're with me. I won't let the bogeymen get you.

—You *are* the bogeyman, the guard said.

—I'm a pet. We're all pets, servitors of the gods. I was infected that night in the field. That's why the powers-that-be transferred me and a few of my fellow initiates here. As you said, to spread the joy to the entire colony. The insane part of this? You aren't even talking to me. I retrograded nine nights ago. You've been copulating with a fruiting corpse these past several trysts. This conversation is stimulated by pheromones that render prey compliant through hallucination. The geography cone squirts something similar at fish. The fish enters quasi-paralysis, swims in place, confused and disoriented. Then the cone slides over and does its dirty business.

—I'm talking to myself. I'm talking to myself. I'm talking to myself.

—No, you're speaking to the gloriously transmogrified hulk of a former human being who will soon add your quiescent flesh and screaming brain to the mother of all mushroom beds. Like any man who has ever spoken to his god, you're also answering your own questions. Those spores attack the mind, cause it to compartmentalize, to create a multiplicity of simulated consciousnesses.

The guard traced the wall of memory in search of a crack, a flaw, a blackout, that might signal the demarcation of dream and reality, the place he'd swerved from the road. He found, with a feeble pang, that everything prior to this terrifying moment in the dark, was rapidly crumbling and sliding into an abyss. What he'd eaten for breakfast, listened to on the radio while commuting to work, his home phone number, his mother's maiden name, gone. All of it siphoned away. He caught a glimpse of himself driving across a landscape crawling with white cotton candy, the dark bulk of the prison enmeshed in it like a tumor eating its way through a lung. He glimpsed bloated half-corpses of men in cells, quietly rupturing, birthing pallid tendrils and tubers. He said, —Please, no. Let me go.

—Go where? It's all over but the crying out there. The Rapture you all waited for hath come at last. Be at ease. I'm going to kiss you. The convict's breath was ripe and cool and very close. —Welcome to the garden of our lords. And his tepid mouth closed over the guard's. It tasted of sweet, black earth, raw with ferment. The guard struggled, imagining a billion spores shooting down his throat, crocheting a murderous skein through his internal organs. He felt his blood reversing up the esophageal passage, engorging the parasite mounted atop him. Everything brightened, became white incandescence. He screamed into the mouth suctioning his own.

The guard shuddered and opened his eyes and nearly fell as vertigo assailed him. He was still leaning against the wall; the cigarette still smoldered in his hand; the convict watched him, features obscured in shadow. The light at the intersection dimmed and flickered, then was steady. —My god. My god.

—You okay? the convict said. He sounded concerned, sounded himself again.

A STRANGE FORM OF LIFE

—What were we talking about?

—How I almost got away, but ended up in this shithole? Gonna be a movie of my life story. Starring you and me.

—Before that. Before that.

—There's nothin' before that, man. Nothin' important, anyhow.

—We've been away too long. Better get back to the block, see you to your bunk. The guard said this without conviction, his thoughts turned inward, a snow flurry accelerating away from his grasping fingers.

—I got an idea, the convict said. —Nobody's missin' us. C'mere. Let's rest a while, here in the dark. He opened his arms.

The guard smoked his cigarette to the filter, vaguely troubled. The vertigo dissipated, replaced by contentment, a diluted sensation of euphoria he hadn't experienced in an age and almost didn't recognize. He crushed the butt under his shoe. He slouched over to the convict and pressed into the circle of his arm and closed his eyes. His heart began to speed. —Ah, I know what this is, he said.

—Yeah, what?

—Love, the guard said. —This is what falling in love feels like.

The convict laughed and kissed him softly, first on the neck, then the mouth. It went on forever.

The Pacific is the largest body of water in the world. Its name means peace, but Terrence wondered how many had actually found any in its depths. How many would he have to fish from the water only to have them beckon him later to find more?

Night Fishing

Ray Cluley

Terrence leaned the throttle forward and the *Siren Cisco* lurched over a swell, coming down in the trough with a bump that did little to shake the feeling of dread that had settled like bilge in his heart. He knew what he would find today and there'd be no setting his nets until he'd hauled it aboard.

The moon was full; he'd see it easily enough. He'd see it as clearly as he could see the bridge spanning the bay ahead, though perhaps that wouldn't be for long; a low fog was coming in. It always did on nights like these.

Glancing behind, he saw that Laura had joined him at last. She was always the first and she always came in at the stern. Stern Laura, with the sky in her eyes and seaweed in her hair. She was staring past him and he wondered, as he always did, if she stared at the bridge or into the darkness of the waves that had failed to claim her.

Three hours earlier, Terrence had been pushing his shopping cart down one aisle and up another, filling it with his usual fare. An easy catch: crackers, gherkins, spaghetti in tomato sauce, cheese, beer. Some meat, maybe. Never fish.

"Tertle," came a voice from behind, then—*clisch!*—her cart had rammed into his.

"Hey, Jill."

Jill's cart was filled with various soon-to-expire goods. "How's you?"

"Oh, you know," said Terrence, "Slick as an oil spill—"

"—and twice as dark."

They smiled awkwardly at each other for a moment, remembering the poem.

"The tiramisù's good for another day," Jill said eventually, reaching into her cart. "You ever had tiramisù?"

Terrence shook his head. He may have been the wild man of Castro, but Bobby was the adventurous one when it came to food. Jill took out the dessert. "You'll like it," she said, and put it in his cart. She eyed the rest of his shopping. "Wanna come over for dinner tonight? Suzie misses you. Way she carries on, sometimes I wonder if she's really gay."

Terrence smiled.

"Well? Come on, we haven't seen you in ages."

He wasn't able to answer; the sea had found its way in. It surged ankle-deep from the top of the aisle down to the checkout and washed up in a sudden wave that splashed the tills. The operators swiped grocery after grocery—*bleep! bleep!*—and the water receded without them knowing it was there, leaving lines of sand and pebbles in its wake. A crab scuttled beneath the shelves of cereal.

"You know, most men would love a home-cooked dinner with two women all to themselves, but if it's the company,"—her voice became cautious—"then there's this guy I know…"

Terrence closed his eyes but he could still smell the brine of the wet floor and somewhere he could hear a fish as it flopped for breath. Or maybe it was his own struggle to breathe as he tried to wake up. Jill's voice had faded entirely. He knew, if he were to open his eyes, he'd find she was gone. The aisle would be empty. Or Laura would be there instead.

"This is a customer announcement," the speakers began. The voice bubbled and choked as if the throat was filling with water. "Terrence Shelby to the Golden Gate Bridge. That's Terrence Shelby to the Golden Gate Bridge."

He opened his eyes. Laura stood broken and limp at the foot of his bed, pointing.

"What time is it?" Terrence asked, rubbing the sleep from his eyes. He knew she couldn't answer.

Night Fishing

Laura spoke a dribble of ocean, all she ever spoke, and went from the room on legs that folded too much, twisting at the hips as if her spine were made of shingle.

Terrence followed her out, the carpet squelching beneath his feet whenever he found the wet prints she'd left behind.

He eased off the speed when he caught sight of something pale bobbing port-side. His seemed the only boat out this late at night, but it wouldn't be long before others were leaving the bay to trawl for the day's specials. His catch of the day would be of a different sort, though.

The water rose and fell slowly, a welcome relief to the steepness of the city streets. "You're a city fish," Bobby had said once, "But you wish it was on the water instead of next to it." He'd been right about that, as he'd been right about so many things. They'd been on Telegraph Hill, watching the fishermen come and go. The "city fish" line, and much of the view they were admiring, found its way into Bobby's "Night Fishing." Sometimes Terrence still went to the hill and watched the ferry come in and he'd think of Bobby, entering the city in the same way as his hero, Thom Gunn. Bobby, who would wonder at a snail's fury and peer at the world through the keyholes of hotel rooms. But as good a view as the hill offered, Terrence preferred to be on the bay itself. His favourite days were when the sea was an open flatness spoiled only by the churning engines of other boats.

The pale bobbing thing in the water was nothing.

Nothing, the wanton name that nightly I rehearse till led away to a dark sleep.

He wasn't sure he remembered it right—was it supposed to be present tense? He didn't read poetry much anymore, Gunn or anyone else. He didn't want the patterns they promised; he was already living in a rhythm he didn't like.

In the water, the pale pages of an open city map rose and fell. Rose and fell.

"You lost?" Terrence had asked, more right than he knew. And Bobby, fresh from the ferry, had smiled and said, "Not anymore." His poise had hooked Terrence but the smile brought him up out of the water, gasping for air. Bobby was looking for Castro on a map that forced his arms to full length. Terrence had pointed it out gladly, said he went there a lot himself. Testing the waters.

Closer, Terrence saw it wasn't a map at all in the water but the open spread of a newspaper page that sank away with his memory. Thoughts of Bobby had fooled him, forced a reminiscence that was still as sharp as a fishhook.

Something else in the water caught his eye. It was another nothing: a sea-filled plastic bag, fat as a jellyfish. He took down a boathook to scoop it aboard; it wouldn't do to keep seeing it, wasting time wondering who it could be.

The bag came up easily, dripping.

A bloated pink face came right up after it.

Terrence fumbled the boathook as he stumbled backwards. He managed to juggle it back into his grasp as the rest of the body surfaced, the skin puckered and fish-nibbled. He stared, getting his breath back, merely startled, then calmly hooked the folds of an "I heart San Francisco" shirt and pulled the body closer.

"Hello, Matthew."

He wasn't startled when the eyes opened and the man smiled the frothy smile of the drowned. Blood-tinged bubbles spilled from his lips in a careless vomit of foam, just as they had the first time Terrence found him.

"You coming aboard too?" Terrence asked, knowing the answer.

Instead of bumping against the boat's hull, the man passed through, disappearing into the vessel.

By the time Terrence had thrown out the tattered plastic bag, the drowned man was standing with Laura. His chin rested on his chest at an angle that had him forever looking down, but his waist had folded backwards on impact with the water, straightening his gaze a little. Matthew was an engineering student, stressed with his studies and finances and the certainty that he'd fail.

"How many more are coming?"

But of course, they didn't answer him.

Night Fishing

"Come on," Terrence said, "I can take it."

Terrence and Bobby were in bed, naked, eating Japanese food from boxes and talking about why Bobby's family disapproved of his recent life choice.

Bobby tangled some squid with noodles and gave the reasons. "Your age, your colour, and your 'inclination.'"

"You have the same inclination."

"Yeah. But it wasn't real to them until you."

Bobby did not play the gay scene. He went to the clubs, made a lot of friends, but resisted the casual sex with a strength Terrence only had because he'd been there and done that. Terrence used to worry they'd met too soon upon Bobby's arrival. Taking him to Castro, fresh from the ferry, he'd thought that Bobby would want to experiment, live a little, like he had at Bobby's age. But Bobby didn't want to live a little. Falling hook, line and sinker for Terrence, Bobby had written him a copy of Gunn's "Tamer and Hawk" to prove as much, sticking it on the fridge with an alphabet letter the morning after they'd sealed their love (omitting the final stanza, Terrence learnt later). Not long after, Bobby had moved in.

His family did not approve.

Terrence scooped noodles to his mouth, then speared a prawn for Bobby.

"So they don't mind that I'm just a lowly fisherman."

"Nah, Christ was a fisherman so they're good with that. Your lack of religion, though…" Bobby tut-tut-tutted.

Terrence had grinned, chewing his food. "Means you're the only one going to Hell."

Looking up at the bridge, buffeted by a chill wind and rocked in the chop of an irritable sea, Terrence hoped there was no such place, but he knew there was because he was in it most days. Those gathering at the prow only proved it. Laura, Matt, and now the shin-splintered Lee holding himself up by the gunwales; Terrence had pulled all of them from the water over the last year, pulled others out after, and none of them would leave him alone.

The three stood, as best as they could, looking out at the bridge they had jumped from.

The Golden Gate Bridge was once the world's longest suspension bridge and was declared a modern wonder. With the exception of London's Tower Bridge, it was the most-photographed bridge in the world. It was also the world's most popular suicide spot. "From the golden gates to the pearly ones," Bobby had joked once, back before his own dive from its heights. "People come from all over to do it. A permanent solution to their temporary problems."

Statistics varied. One jumped every two weeks or thirty jumped per year, and Terrence had read somewhere else that every month saw as many as five people drop to their deaths. The only thing that didn't vary was the fact that from that height, three hundred feet or so, hitting the water was like hitting concrete. Some survived, but not many. And usually not for long.

Terrence only ever found the dead ones.

Except Bobby.

"You should write something that's more you."

Bobby was struggling with a new poem. A new poem about one of Thom Gunn's poems.

"Like 'Fisherman,' you mean?" He screwed up the piece of paper he'd been scratching away at and threw it behind him. It landed nowhere near the trash can, rolling to a stop among brothers of balled-up paper sitting in crumpled crowds around the lamp stand.

"Fisherman" had been a flop, according to Bobby, which only meant his buddies at the open mike didn't like it. They didn't like it because it offered them no familiar landmark to comment on, no reference to another poet with which to expound their knowledge, display their intellect like birds spreading feathers to attract a mate. They'd loved "In Praise of Our City" because of how it played with Gunn's poem, personifying the city into the masculine without losing any of the eroticism and altering the sense of entrapment. "Fisherman," on the other hand, had been all Bobby and it was beautiful. Perhaps it was too personal for critical appreciation, but Bobby had told him poetry was all about sound, and "Fisherman" had turned his words into music.

Terrence loved it.

It would be useless to say as much with Bobby in one of his moods so he only watched as Bobby mouthed words quietly to himself, testing their shape and texture, tasting them without quite swallowing like an expert judging wine.

Night Fishing

"Which one are you using this time?" he asked eventually. He knew it would be another Gunn.

"'On the Move,'" said Bobby, confirming it. "Problem is it isn't going anywhere."

Terrence laughed. Bobby scowled, deciding whether to be hurt or not, then leaned back in his chair and laughed with him.

"Let's go out for some dinner," Terrence suggested when the laughter subsided.

Bobby's laugh became a smile which became an apology. "I can't. I need something for tomorrow night."

He reached for the book in his pocket, a collected volume of poems that was always there, though surely he knew it by heart. Terrence said that he carried the book like it was both his shield and his sword at once, something to hide behind while making his own poetic jabs. Bobby's eyes had glittered with a smile, and then he'd sulked, claiming later after some make-up sex that he'd been jealous. "You're poetic without even trying," he'd explained. Then he stole the line for "Night Fishing".

"Night Fishing" was Bobby's poem about the gay scene, his family, his poetry. It was about how hard he found it to fit in; about how he'd looked for lovers and failed; about the hooks his family had in him; about how he'd deliver his rhyming lines fishing for compliments, hoping for applause that was more than polite, and getting it only if he stole from someone else. He was Gunn's wayward bullet (a metaphor Terrence had never liked), casting his lines blindly in the dark.

"I want to go out," Terrence said.

"Okay."

For a moment Terrence thought he'd agreed but realized quickly he'd only offered permission, already lost in bastardized rhythm and rhyme.

Terrence went out, with no idea where he was going.

His ghastly crew pointed as one. Nine of them now had been drawn to the boat, stretching their arms as best they could to direct his gaze, gargling salt water and their own frothed mucus to get his attention.

Not a bag this time.

He gunned the engine just enough to turn, then cut it, drifting to where the woman rose and fell with the tide beneath the bridge. As he neared, the dead he carried with him left one by one. Some disappeared into moonlight. Others wavered like reflections on water and were gone. One or two threw themselves overboard, replaying their own end. They were gone before any splash could mark their absence.

Terrence was left with the woman in the water, the skirts of her dress billowing around her like a lily pad, she the grotesque flower. Her stomach was large and round, and he felt his usual horror that she might have been pregnant, but it would be gas. He hoped it was gas. It built up in the intestines, bringing a body to the surface after about two weeks. He'd come to know a lot about it. He knew her skin would be puckered like a washerwoman's hands. Her eyes would be missing and the softest of her flesh eaten away, but otherwise she'd be remarkably well preserved thanks to the temperature of the water. Bones would be broken from the impact. Sometimes the impact didn't kill a person, though, and they'd drown. Their violent attempts to breathe would whip the water and mucus in their lungs to a foamy froth, tinged with blood from ruptured vessels. Sometimes the sudden shock of impact and cold gave them a heart attack. Sometimes, paralyzed, they lived long enough to die from hypothermia. If they managed to do it at night, with no one watching.

This one was mottled and bloated, grinning a lipless smile at the bridge above them. In the shadows of its structure her teeth shone bright in a grimace of bitter triumph.

Terrence radioed it in.

There was the usual poor joke about his alibi but they let him haul her out of the water. They knew him well enough now.

He hooked her under the right arm and dragged her close, then leaned over to grab a handful of sodden dress, polka-dotted and clammy as flannel. She was Japanese, or Vietnamese, or Asian anyway. It was hard to tell now. It made him think of Aokigahara. With a grunt of effort he hauled her up over the gunwales. There was a wet ripping and a button flew free, ricocheting with a sharp *ping!* off something behind him, and the dead woman toppled to the deck with a heavy soft sound that was only partly water.

He didn't want to look at her, but he did.

She lay with her broken legs splayed open at unnatural angles, a gesture all the more obscene for the exposure of her breasts. What were once her breasts. They'd maybe suckled a child at some point, perhaps pleased a number of lovers, but most recently only fish had nuzzled there. If you were imaginative, it was where Death had laid his lingering kisses.

Terrence bent to pull the torn dress closed over them.

A plastic envelope, the kind designed to protect papers in a binder, was folded over and taped to her waist, Scotch tape looped around her body. The tape no longer adhered to her skin but it wrapped her like a belt and the swelling of her flesh had kept it there, something she was unlikely to have considered. Her suicide note was clearly visible inside.

He took it without thinking about what he was doing, shuddering at the feel of how her chilled skin moved under his fingers. It loosened in the water, which was why he always grabbed for clothing. Once, in wrestling one of the first bodies aboard by the hand and wrist, he had felt the skin shift under his grip, trying to come away like a glove.

This woman had written only a single page, but she had filled it. The top was little more than a blurry smudge of ink despite the plastic but the rest of it told of heartbreak and dependency and despair. Yet it was spotted with drawings of stars and hearts and had been signed off incongruously with a sun and a smiley face.

Terrence withdrew a notepad and pencil from inside his jacket and copied it down, drawings and all.

The note Bobby had left was written on the same paper as his poems and lay folded among them on the desk. Terrence hadn't noticed it for two days and even then he didn't recognize it for what it was. He had been looking for a note addressed to him, something explaining where Bobby had gone, why he hadn't called and wouldn't answer when Terrence tried. They'd been drifting apart, Bobby growing melancholy and Terrence trying to help but only making things worse. The first day he was gone, Terrence assumed he was in a moody sulk and staying with a friend, but the second day he became worried. Jill and Suzie had put a few calls around with no results. So Terrence looked for a note but found only pieces of Bobby's poetry, including *My Sad Captain*. *I used to think that obstacles to love were out of date. Much that is natural, to the will must yield, but I'll resist by embracing nothingness. I regret nothing.*

Only when he'd seen his name on the reverse did Terrence realize it was intended for him; the folded crease that was supposed to allow it to stand had failed in its duty, or Terrence himself had knocked it in his hasty search through the papers. Yet even when he realized it was for him he thought it was a break-up letter, a Dear John, thank you for fucking me but I'm leaving you. He didn't know it was a suicide note until an awful angry phone call from Bobby's father, who had identified the body. Terrence wasn't allowed to see it, nor was he invited to the funeral. He was never able to say goodbye.

My Sad Captain. I used to think that obstacles to love were out of date. Much that is natural, to the will must yield, but I'll resist by embracing nothingness. I regret nothing.

None of the words had been Bobby's, and in this new context they didn't even make much sense. Terrence had raged about it in a drunken fury to Jill and Suzie. All the fucking quoting and paraphrasing. The sad truth of it was, Bobby's poetic homage, his frequent tributes, were derivative and often misunderstood the original work. Terrence hated Bobby trying to write like someone else and Bobby's family hated him trying to live like someone else. "Bobby was only Bobby when he jumped," Terrence had said, back when he used to visit Jill and Suzie, before he realized how unfair those visits had become, how selfish. "Couldn't he just be Bobby? Couldn't they just let him fucking be Bobby?" And he had barked a harsh laugh because *fucking be Bobby* sounded fucking stupid, like an old rock 'n' roll number, and then he had sobbed. Jill had held him all the while, knowing about the churned waters of death and how there were no set tides, only a draining away that gurgled and spluttered and never really emptied.

There was no reason for it that anyone could fathom. Bobby never got on well with his family, his poetry didn't take off as much as he'd hoped, and his relationship with an older black man was under some strain (mostly because of those other factors) but none of this seemed enough, not when you knew Bobby. It wasn't enough to make him both the hurler and the hurled.

Temporary problems, Bobby. Temporary. Remember?

Terrence looked at the woman on his boat. Her reasons didn't seem all that different from Bobby's. It wasn't enough, not to Terrence. Hell, in that case he had plenty of reasons of his own.

He copied her note and replaced it. He would add his copy to the others he had collected. Soon he'd have enough to make a small book of them, *Words of the Dying*. Like that guy who made a film of them jumping to their deaths. Terrence had seen a part of it on YouTube, *The Bridge*, and it had been enough. He had been shocked and angered and compelled to watch, which Bobby said was the point. It was supposed to raise awareness, apparently, a grim visual proposal to build a suicide barrier. But such a precaution was deemed too expensive and too difficult, too much of a risk to the integrity of the bridge. Plus it would spoil the aesthetic, not to mention the view, and that would upset the tourists. "Not all of them are people 'who have come to go,'" was how Bobby put it.

All the bridge needed was a net. There'd been one when it was being built, saving the lives of steelworkers who fell (the Halfway to Hell Club they called themselves) but there would never be a net now that it was complete. The only nets they found themselves in, other than whatever tangled one led them to jump in the first place, belonged to Terrence as he dredged their carcasses from the sea.

He wouldn't make a book, of course. They weren't his words to use, and the notes were private. They were the explanations and goodbyes he'd never had.

Terrence shook out a large blue section of tarp and draped it over the body, weighting it with coils of rope. She looked cocooned, ready to change into something else, though he had no idea what. Maybe something with more hope than she'd been allowed in this life.

The tarp moved. Terrence thought he'd imagined it. Thought his brain was still playing with the cocoon image. When the arm flopped out from beneath, banging hard against a rail then resting out over the water, he told himself a sudden move of the boat must have done it, one of the moves he was used to and hadn't noticed. But as he watched, her fingers curled until only one was left pointing. And she sat up.

There was a sequence of clicking sounds, a slow crackling as she rose in an effortless sit-up. She lurched to the right. Maybe to aid the pointing gesture, maybe because of the shape her spine was in. The sockets of her slackened face turned his way and he saw a darkness in them not very different to the one he saw each day in the mirror.

She opened her mouth and seawater came instead of a voice, draining from her skull in a slobbering splash against the tarpaulin, a brief loud sound in the quiet morning. A string of something dark was caught in her teeth. They came together with a sharp clack sound when her head lolled suddenly down to her chest, unsupported.

"I'm not going home yet, am I?" Terrence said.

The woman brought her arm in close and broken bone slid from the flesh of her elbow, disappearing back inside when she straightened the arm again to point.

"All right. Okay. I'm going."

As if exhausted, the woman slumped back down, her head knocking hard on the deck. Her arm remained outstretched, moving like the needle of a compass as Terrence steered their course. He wondered if this time he had a suicide pact and he turned the boat around, feeling like the boatman on the river Styx as he steered into the mist creeping across the sea.

The Pacific is the largest body of water in the world. Its name means peace, but Terrence wondered how many had actually found any in its depths. How many would he have to fish from the water only to have them beckon him later to find more?

He had escaped the ebb and flow of its tides only once, and then not for long. He had gone to Aokigahara. There had been mist then, too, low and clinging, clutching the trunks of trees but torn to tatters by his moving feet. Before then, the closest he had been to Japan was the Japanese Tea Garden. He had been there with Bobby lots of times. When he went to Aokigahara, though, he went alone. Bobby was dead, and Terrence was seeing others like him. After the fourth, and the tests, and the fuss, he had gone to Japan to see if he saw them anywhere else; the Golden Gate Bridge was number one, but Aokigahara was the second most popular place in the world for suicide. It was a forest at the west base of Mount Fuji, also known as the Sea of Trees. Terrence had simply swapped one ocean of death for another.

There hadn't been much to see. The forest was famously absent of wildlife and the wind-blocking of the tall trees meant there was nothing more than shadows, an eerie quiet that had scared the crap out of him. Not like the sea which, even quiet, had an abundance of background noises. Terrence would never walk among those silent boughs again. There had been no sound, and no bodies. No rock-scraped corpse walked the woodland. Nothing dripped its blood from the branches, pointing with a tangle of intestines the path it had travelled down to get there. Considering *ubasute* was once practised in the woods of Aokigahara—the abandonment of the weak, the old, the infirm—Terrence had expected the forest to be a stumbling ground for aged Hansels and Gretels, frail with cold or starvation, looking for a way back to the community that had given them up. He saw none of this.

All he saw to tell him it was a popular suicide spot were the signs. Written in English and in Japanese, they urged people not to kill themselves, to seek help. They were probably no more effective than the help lines situated at points across San Francisco's bridge, the phones only there so people had someone to say goodbye to.

He stayed as long as he could before the city and its bridge called him home.

The mist that enveloped him was the outer edge of a full fog bank, but the sun would be up soon to burn it away into vaporous shreds. Besides, Terrence suspected he'd be going little further than the bridge he was under. The lady he'd retrieved was pointing along the length of its span, not beyond it, so he took the *Siren Cisco* north.

The bridge was the city's only route north. Before it, people had crossed to Marin County by boat, historical trivia Terrence found difficult to believe even though he'd seen the pictures. To him, the bridge had always been. It was a constant presence, reassuring in its solid construction and gaudy colour. To Terrence it was a symbol, albeit one he found difficult to define. A reminder of what could be achieved in life.

It was an altogether different symbol to those who jumped from it.

"From the golden gates to the pearly ones," Terrence muttered, trying to believe it. He didn't hold with the notion that suicides went to Hell, figuring it was exactly the place they thought they were escaping. Religious or not, those who jumped could only go straight down.

He looked out into the fog and saw nothing. Out there somewhere in nature's shroud was the famous Alcatraz, but Terrence knew that there were stronger prisons. He was in one. Laura, Matthew, Lee, Samantha, Jess, Dan, Stuart, Elisabeth, Catherine, Sun…they'd all been in one, escaping the only way they knew how—with a sudden, sharp splash.

It came so suddenly on the tail of his thought that Terrence wondered if he'd conjured the sound. Less of a splash, more a crashing explosion of water—and to starboard a group of ever-expanding circles pushed outward. There was a sequence of smaller splashes as someone rose from the centre. Somewhere above was the screech of tires but it sounded to Terrence like his own internal scream, one he voiced by crying—

"Bobby!"

He knew it was stupid, that it couldn't be, but he called anyway. He'd have said the recently dead pointing him to new corpses was impossible, yet that's what they did, and he did as they told him so maybe this was his reward, Bobby brought back to him. A chance to save him.

Terrence surged forward, looking for the man to reappear, speeding to where he'd last seen him.

"I'm coming, Bobby!"

There, splashing, sucking up breath.

He cut the engine. "I'm coming!"

Oh Jesus, oh Bobby, why did you leave me? Why didn't you make me listen? I could have helped.

"Here!"

Terrence was leaning over so far he was nearly in the water himself. He was leaning too early as the boat drifted closer. Bobby was too far away, out of reach. His head was back, his long fringe a darkness over his face, mouth gaping, sucking up air with loud "huh-huh-huh" noises. One hand came out of the water occasionally and swept an arc that had him turning.

He grabbed the boathook and knocked it to the deck in his haste. Picked it up and lunged it over the side, Bobby's hand coming down on the pole quite by chance. He clutched at it and Terrence pulled him in.

The water washed across the man's fringe, plastered it across his forehead, out of his face.

It wasn't Bobby.

Terrence growled, cheated, angry with himself for ever thinking such a thing. Of course it wasn't Bobby. He nearly wrenched the hook from the man's grasp. Nearly withdrew to lunge and spear him with it instead.

"Leemee."

Terrence was close enough to grab some sleeve. He released the boathook, let it sink into the bay.

"Come on, I'm here. Come on. Grab my arm."

Night Fishing

He leaned back and heaved the man to the boat. The man gave a shrieking cry of pain, but Terrence was able to get his hands under the man's armpits. He heaved again, sickened at how easily his upper body moved as if separate to the limp legs that came up after. The man's chest went in instead of out, each ragged breath pushing it close to the shape it was supposed to be.

Twisting his own body around, Terrence leaned to bring the man up and over the rail. He struck the deck feet first with another shrill cry and Terrence saw the man had a length of bone sticking out from the bottom of his shoe, a jagged white shard pushing out from under the heel.

"You're going to be all right."

He stripped off his sweaters and draped them over the man. More of a boy, barely mid-twenties. Bobby's age. Bobby's build.

The man coughed up some of the Pacific. It dribbled down his cheeks in thin lines of bloody water. "Leave me."

"I'm going to get you to a hospital."

"Please."

Terrence saw the word on the man's lips but didn't hear it. It was too soft. He knelt closer and took the man's hand. It felt strange to Terrence, not because of how the wrist was angled but because it had been so long since he'd held hands with another man.

"Hurts."

"Yeah," said Terrence. "But you've got to fight it. Grit your teeth, come on."

"You," said the man, pausing to swallow a wheezy breath. "You don't understand."

He could no more understand than a net could hold water, but he realized then that he didn't need to. What needed to be understood was that he never would.

It wasn't Bobby, but it was. He said, "Let me go."

Terrence turned the boat and brought the engine to life with a throaty roar. His speed did not matter, for the man on the deck had already died, but even if Terrence had known he'd have leaned on the throttle all the same, speeding away from the bridge that haunted him.

Ahead, the lights of the city outlined the reasons he would never follow Bobby, or any of those he pulled from the bay. He didn't enjoy life, not anymore, but he clung to it as a drowning sailor might clutch at the wreckage of his ship. He'd clutch the wreckage and kick, toward, toward, and maybe sometimes he'd even scream for help, but he'd never let the dark waves take him.

He wanted to, but he didn't know how.

I pull the wolfskin on over the tee. With the leather pants too, it's gonna be hot as hell, but it's a necessary part of the whole kit and kaboodle. Besides, the ensemble has a rockstar-cum-hustler bad boy chic that tickles my fancy. It doesn't do me any favours with the PETA-loving emo kids, but it's just *awesome* for starting fights with small town dickwads who think *queer* is an insult.

SIC HIM, HELLHOUND! KILL! KILL!

Hal Duncan

1.

I wake curled up at the foot of the bed again, back snugged tight into the crook of my boy's legs—tight enough to be on top of them really. He groans, slaps the alarm clock off, tries to pull the quilt over his head. Doesn't work with me weighing it down, clambering up to lick his face.

—Get up, I say. Get up get up get up.

He shoves me away.

—Get *down*, he says.

I roll off the bed, grab whiffy boxers from the floor.

—I'm *hungry*.

He groans.

A boy and his werewolf. Truest love there is.

Breathe. Then eat, he says. Or eat, then breathe. You know you can't do the two together.

I raise my head from the bowl of cornflakes, give another cough as I lick milk from my lips then dive back in. I don't have to look to know he's shaking his head, smiling wryly. Hey, he knows it's all part of the method anyway. Guzzling food, snuffling crotches, rolling in things he

Duncan

has to hose off. And that's his part of the deal—to deal with that shit, to handle it, handle *me*.

Every agent has a handler, don't you know?

They tried it without handlers, I hear. Like, back in my alpha's day, back before he became a recruiter, some bright spark figured they should try letting us off the leash. A lone hellhound on the road—he'd just be one more drifter, right? Like *Kung Fu*. Or maybe *The Littlest Hobo*. Things got kinda messy though, it seems; there were a few incidents; cops got eaten and, *yes*, they were fascist pigs, but it *just wasn't on*.

Don't know why they were worried about the handlers in the first place. Like I'd ever let anything happen to my boy.

He sits on the edge of the bed, flicking through the file, glancing up now and then as I run the water in the shower.
—You're actually using the shower gel this time, yes? he calls.
—Absolutely, I shout.
I stand behind the half-open door, peeking at him through the crack. After ten minutes, I duck my head under the water, turn it off and come out towelling my hair. He puts the file down, open at the photograph, the missing kid. *Dead* kid.
—I know you didn't actually wash, he says. My sense of smell isn't that bad.

2.

You got your cover story down, right?
I pick up a sleeveless tee, give it a sniff to make sure it's good and stinky, then pull it on.
—Yes, boss, I say.
It's the same story as ever, just different monickers: we're poor orphaned brothers, just moved to town to be near an aged aunt. I got ADHD and other issues. Impulse control. Drugs. He's the older bro sworn to raise me on his own, put me through school and all.
With the regeneration that comes with the shifts, you'd never know I've got…well, a few years on him.

Sic Him, Hellhound! Kill! Kill!

I got bitten as a pup, see—bitten in the metaphorical sense, that is. I mean, forget what you think you know about werewolves. Silver bullets? Came in with the silver screen, dude. Wolfsbane? Man, that's poisonous to *everyone*. And all that contagion crap? Not how it works. No, how it works is ritual and magic—a wolfskin coat, a hipflask of dirty water drawn from lupine pawprints, and a bit of blood and dancing under the full moon. Being bitten might help, but it's all in the mindset. Shifting is a fucking skill, motherfucker. Not something you can catch.

When *exactly* I got bitten—in the metaphorical sense—that's a hard question though. Cause I remember a dream I had, age nine or so, of running across an old viaduct, a wolf pack at my heels. But I wasn't being chased, dig; I was at the head of them, *one* of them. When I woke up sweating, it wasn't with fear but with excitement. Was that when I got bit? *Maybe* it was years later, when my alpha took me in off the streets, turned this teenage stray into an initiate. But even at nine I had…that dream.

Reckon we're born this way, my alpha used to say. It was important to him, the gruff old fuck, and I can kinda understand, what with every movie at the drive-in painting us as cursed abominations, beasts with monstrous appetites. *Fuckin unnatural?* he'd growl as he scratched his chest tat through the leather vest. *This is who I fuckin am.*

Me, I'm sort of a bolshie bastard about it. No quarter. Ask me if it's nature or nurture, and I'll tell you it's a choice. I'll tell you it's my fucking choice to make, right? So deal with it.

3.

I pull the wolfskin on over the tee. With the leather pants too, it's gonna be hot as hell, but it's a necessary part of the whole kit and kaboodle. Besides, the ensemble has a rockstar-cum-hustler bad boy chic that tickles my fancy. It doesn't do me any favours with the PETA-loving emo kids, but it's just *awesome* for starting fights with small town dickwads who think *queer* is an insult.

Duncan

My boy scruffles fingers through my hair, scratches my ear. I wonder what those dickwads would make of our rough-and-tumble play-fights. Or sleeping arrangements.

I grab the car-keys from the coffee table and bring them to him, hold them out, take a step back as he reaches.
—Give, he says.
—Take them, I say.
—We don't have time for this.
He makes a grab and I snatch the keys away, turning so he has to reach round me, try and prise them from my hand.
—*Give.*
I give them up. He's the best handler *ever*, my boy, swear to God. There's no way what happened to the Louisiana team will happen to us. That was a *bad* werewolf, a weak handler. *We're* invincible.

I knew it from the first day he came to the Pound, the way the truth didn't even faze him. I mean whatever run-ins they've had with the nasties we track, the handler candidates always come out of it with a fucking iron will, else they'd wouldn't be joining the cause; but usually the whole secret agency thing leaves them at least a little *what the fuck?* But he just strolled down the line of pups and returnees till he came to me. I saw it in his eyes.
—What's your name? he said.
—You decide, I told him.

~ You ready?
As he pulls the car up at the gates of the school, I bring my head back in from the window, grin at him and throw my hands in the air.
—Rub my tummy!
—Behave, he says.
I give him my best puppy eyes.
—Not. Now. You have a job to do, so go on. Git.
I climb out of the car, bathtime slow. When he drives away, he'll be abandoning me, like, *forever.* He sighs, knowing what I need.
—*Where's the vampire?* he says. *Go find the vampire, boy!*
And suddenly I'm as keen as his voice.

SIC HIM, HELLHOUND! KILL! KILL!

4.

One hundred million hours later—one bazillion trillion hours of History and French, or Maths and Geography, or fucking whatever later—I'm sitting in the school cafeteria, on my own at a table in a corner, eating burgers out of the buns and trying my best to be human about it. Not standing out is a lost cause—I'm the new kid, and a weird one at that—but we're still in the avoidance stage; the freaks and geeks aren't sure if I'm one of them yet, and the alpha jock's still working up to his challenge.

Then *they* arrive.

I take a furtive sip from my hipflask, not enough to spark a shift, but enough to boost my sense of smell. Because she's all flowers and soap and chocolate and Bibles and *need*—so much need, so deep an aroma of insatiable yearning that it almost masks his stench. The smell of her longing fills the room, fills the *school*; shit, I've been smelling it all day, that perfume of victimhood. Without it I wouldn't have to go through this bullshit to catch his trail, so I don't think it's too harsh to give a little growl, is it?

So, OK, hers is a scent of sickness, not in a twisted-and-malicious way but in a patient-in-a-hospice way. I should pity her. But she's got… that classic Mary Sue look—that's what my boy calls them—all nice and normal, a little plain, a little plump. A cross round her neck, or a crucifix maybe; I can't tell from here. She's not pretty enough to be popular, not strange enough to be an outcast, just a mannequin of mediocrity, blandness and banality, desperate to be made more by her Ghoul Boyfriend Forever.

As fucking ever.

As for him? Yeah, he's got the boyband looks…if you trust your eyes. Which ain't a good idea.

Truth is, ticks got a sexy rep these days, all that Byronic bullshit, teen girls swooning over brooding tortured souls, but if you think vampires are *hawt*, you ought to read the motherfucking lore. *These are corpses, fuckhead*, my alpha told me way back. Rotted, stinking, fetid corpses that walk as men. Shit, it takes them years of feeding to even get to *that*.

So this tick sure looks like some pale poetic catwalk cutie, but I can smell his soil.

5.

Here's how this vampire started. It started with some manipulative leeching bastard dead in a grave, some kiddy-fiddler or wife-beater, some Ponzi scheme merchant—or, worse, politician. It started with someone so deep into using people they couldn't stop even six feet down with maggots eating their tongue. It started with their ghost haunting the people they'd abused, feeding on them even from the grave, sucking this…energy—chi, my alpha called it, or kundalini.

It was just a spectre at first, dig? No fangs, no frilly fucking cuffs on flouncy shirts. Just a mindless parasitic poisonous miasma.

There's a stink of the pulpit on this one, oak and ink, sermons scribbled by lamplight. It's old; shit, the victim probably wasn't even born when this fucker came seeping up from its silk-lined coffin to carry on its spiritual vocation, polluting the living with dreams of death, fears of the flesh and all its sordid passions. It's the smell of chickenshit, that stench, of something so gutless in the face of life and death it can't face either, has to deny them both. There's nothing uglier than the mockery of a human being you end up with then.

Fuck, let me tell you how much of a heartthrob the first tick I tracked was. Baby, my alpha took me to a cemetery, and I could smell the fucker from the gates, smell the stench of misery, even before this reanimated rotting corpse—this ghoulish, mummified, zombie *thing*—came digging its way up out of the earth with the bones of its fingers. It was more filth than flesh, blood-sodden graveyard dirt packed round bones, and the first thing it did was make a bee-line for a nearby field, to feed on a fucking cow.

Real romantic.

SIC HIM, HELLHOUND! KILL! KILL!

Stage two, said my alpha. If your vampire can feed enough as a spectre—suck juice from some debt-ridden fuck till he blows his own brains out in the depths of depression, or drive some insomniac mother to drown herself and the sick child she doesn't have the strength to care for—if the tick can bleed just enough vitality from the vulnerable, it can dance its own corpse like a fucking muppet.

—Only ticks look even half-human are stage threes plus, the ones who find some sad bastard, eat their insides out, wear them as a motherfucking skinsuit.

6.

The tick and the Mary Sue sit down at a table over near the door, holding hands, gazing into each other's eyes. They're the centre of their own little world—scratch that; they're the centre of everyone's world. You can smell the delusion wafting from them, the psychic smokescreen that lets a tick like this walk into a high school without a single question. Me, I got fake transfer papers, but all a tick needs is confusion and conviction. The glamour that makes everyone buy his new kid bullshit. Give him time and he'll have the whole town believing it.

You see…fuck, the reason most ticks don't come out in the daytime is cause you can see the skinsuit's stitches even *with* the glamour. Yanno why ticks and mirrors don't mix? Really? Because even stage threes puke at the sight of themselves.

But then there's these stage fours.

—A tick *can* pass, my alpha told me, if they can just find some human sick enough to swallow that glamour so commitedly they put every ounce of their own energy into bolstering it.

An amp for the signal, dig? With a Mary Sue beside them, that tick can fucking *dazzle*.

So he looks just like our missing kid, just like the victim, but creepily… "better." Ice-blue eyes and blond hair, cherry lips, skin smooth and spotless as an angel's ass. Fingernails manicured to metrosexual perfection. Every girl in the cafeteria, or near enough, is either gazing at him with wonder or looking daggers at Mary Sue. Some of the guys too, though they're shiftier about it; one of the indie kids over at the till is outright obsessed, the poor fuck, stinking of adolescent lust. No shame in his spicy scent, at least, but he's way out of luck.

Another high school job, a few years back, just before the…accident that sent me back to the Pound and a new handler, to my boy—which was totally a great thing in the end, really, cause there's no way that sort of thing would happen with *him*—I got into a beef with these football fuckwits. They were yacking on about how their girls were all into tick-lit.
 —Vampires are totally gay, one of them said.
 So, yeah, I kicked the crap out of him.
 These days, for most ticks, there should be an *ex-* in that sentence.

7.

Jared Swift. That was the kid's name. Not the tick's name, mind. You think I give a fuck about this motherfucker's name? No, I'm talking about the kid in the photo, grabbed by the tick some night, in some dark place the boy wasn't meant to be, dragged off into the woods to be devoured. And worn.
 Quiet kid, the report said, sorta *sensitive*. No girlfriend. Journals and sketchbooks found after his disappearance indicate suicidal thoughts.
 Jared Swift. That's the only name that matters here. Not the tick's or the Mary Sue's, not mine or my boy's. Just Jared Swift.

What monicker the tick's going by here isn't worth shit; he'll have snatched it from Mary Sue's dreams while she was sleeping anyway, as he lurked outside her window, jonesing over her emptiness, or crawled in to crouch by her bed, whispering bitter nothings in her ear, watching himself glow radiant with glamour in the mirror of her dresser. If he did it over enough nights, he probably fucking glittered by the time he showed up as a late transfer in school to take her breath away. She, of course, being the only girl this gorgeous hunk had eyes for.

I can smell what little of Jared Swift is left in the skin worn by this ghoul. I can smell the shreds of soul in it, the despair and desire the tick has strung together into a semblance of self—behaviours born of terrified restraint, habits of shame—the salt of tears and spunk that tinges the tick's own bloody stink. I can smell a fucking moment, the words *oh, Jared's not really interested in girls yet* echoing as Jared casts his eye across a different cafeteria, fixes it on a different girl. Someone unattainable enough he'll never need to...

This would be the point where I realise I'm snarling, top lip curled back, teeth bared. Not that it matters in a blowing-my-cover sorta way; ticks don't have the wits to even know there might be hellhounds on their trail, and if the Mary Sue notices, all caught up in the glamour of her Ghoul Boyfriend Forever, she'll likely just write me into her self-centred story as another possessive potential, out to own her like her beloved does, jealous of the competition.

It does finally spur the dickwads into action though.

—Freak.

—Faggot.

Fuck yeah. At last!

8.

I ignore the detention because, well, you know, the principal's *bad puppy* voice just doesn't carry the tone my boy's does; like I'm gonna play cowed to some yapping cur thinks he's top dog. Besides, we'll be out of here tomorrow if we get the job done tonight. So, out by the parking lot, skulking out of sight behind a dumpster, I watch them climb into a car that reeks of her—him in the driving seat though, naturally. And as they pull away, I take a deep slug from my hipflask. Strip the t-shirt off. Unbuckle my belt.

They always play it as painful in the movies, like some hideous Jekyll and Hyde transformation, man being remade as beast in wrenching agony. Shit, it's more ecstasy than agony, and I mean that in the chemical sense, a fucking *buzz*. Skin-tingling shudders running up and down your spine, every inch of you alive with sensitivity. It's not so visual, natch, but if you can imagine a psychedelia of smell, that's how it rushes in on you when you turn wolf. When my alpha took me through my first shift, man, I thought he'd spiked the punch with acid.

Bones crunch into new shapes, muscles shift, and wolfskin furls tight to my form, binds to my naked skin, *becomes* it. No doubt my boy'll bitch about me leaving the leathers in a dumpster yet again, but it's the handiest hiding-place, boss, and it's either that or a halfway wolfman look that's bound to sparks some stares loping down the streets and through the woods after the car. Whereas I *might* get away, in this form, with just a few confused souls wondering if they really did see that motherfucking massive…husky? Cause it couldn't *really* be…could it?

I run like that car's a supercharged stag but I got a turbodrive in my adrenal glands and a hankering for venison. I run like I have a whole pack at my heels, betas splitting off to flank the quarry. I pound the tarmac with paws that move so fast, so light, they barely make a sound. I leap walls to cut through yards, crash through bushes and fences, pace never slowing, gaze cold and keen as steel on my prey as long as it's in my sight, flared nostrils directing me when it's not.

I fucking *love* chasing cars.

9.

I'm kinda disappointed when he parks the thing at her place—he opens the door for her; hugs her but baulks when she moves in to kiss him; spins her a spiel about how he's scared he'll hurt her; strokes her cheek—then sets off on foot for his hidey-hole. I'm kinda disappointed cause ticks move slow as humans, mostly—slower even, sorta floaty—which is just plain boring. Stalking is OK, but it's nowhere near as much fun as chasing.

If it wouldn't lead to a seriously stern *bad werewolf!* scolding, I'd take him down here and now.

But no. I got my part of the job, and my boy got his. If the ticks are a fuckload less impressive than some would have you believe—if they're feeders not fighters, if they don't tend to offer *that* much in the way of struggle once you've torn their limbs off, decapitated them with your

SIC HIM, HELLHOUND! KILL! KILL!

teeth, and spat their head across the room—well, there's putting them back in the grave and *keeping* them there. So there's all that clean-up afterwards, with the garlic and salt. And quicklime. Handler stuff.

And there's the whole…loyalty thing. I suppose.

So I prowl through the brush behind gnatboy, hanging back in the shadows of early evening, following him to a fancy house out past the edge of town, all clean-lined concrete and glass…real modern. Swimming pool out back, and an SUV out front. I can smell rotting bodies inside, but not so's I can make out how many. More than two, I reckon. He spider-crawls up the side of the house and in a window.

After a quick sniff and a piss-tag on a tree, I turn, lope off.

Lassie come home, motherfucker. It's chow time.

~ Hello hello hello hello! I love you!
—Yes, I know. I love you too.
—But I *really* love you! I missed you so much!
—And I missed you too. *Yes, I did! Oh, yes I did!* Now, down you go.
—But I *missed* you!
—I know, but we have work to do. Did you find the lair?
—It was *easy!* Come on. Grab the gear and let's get this tick squished.
—OK, hang on.
—Hurry up!
—You know, maybe you should put some pants on.
—Don't need them. Hurry up! Come on!
—I'm coming.
—Come faster! Hurry up!
—Stop. Pulling.

10.

The last guttural purr of the engine as we pull into the driveway; soft clicks and thuds of doors opening and closing; crunch of gravel underfoot; snick of the trunk unlocking: my ears pricked even in human form, all of it's acute, carved in the quiet like radio play sound effects.

Duncan

He pulls my spare hipflask from his pocket, hands it over, starts loading up with his own kit—crucifix, holy water, carbon-quarreled crossbow, gun with silver bullets. None of it actually means shit, we figure, but every tick's so convinced of their damnation these empty symbols mostly work.

Ready? I say.
He nods, closes the trunk on the canisters full of disposal substances, and we look into each other's eyes for a moment, saying something that can't be put into words. Somewhere in there is the story of how he signed up for this gig, how he got sucked into this weird world, how he came close enough to living death to spit in its face. But you don't have to hear that story. All you have to know is that it's maybe something like Jared Swift's, but not.

I'll fucking *never* let it be that story.

Soft and easy, padding on feet half-human, half-wolf, I take point, leading my boy in through the splintered front door, muzzle twitching, senses taut. I can hear the flies buzzing, count the corpses by scent, even before we hit the dining room. I can even tell that the tick isn't in there; but we go in anyway, to remind ourselves why we do this.

Rippling with maggots, Mom and Dad and three kids sit at the table, the family dog an autopsy or feast upon it. Both.

Sanity is the first thing a tick takes from its victims.

The Zoroastrians have this ritual, you know; when someone dies they bring a dog to the corpse, and no matter what the doctor says, no matter how it looks, the person is only declared truly dead when the dog treats it as such. Way I hear it, it used to be one of us. Way I hear it, that might even be how the agency started—werewolves and their handlers brought in to make sure the dead will stay that way—but no one really knows the grand story of the origin. Or cares much.

We care about the corpses.

SIC HIM, HELLHOUND! KILL! KILL!

11.

I follow the stench into the basement, my boy at my back all the way. I know he's thinking about Jared Swift, about the thing that's wearing his skin now, the ghost become a ghoul become a glittering glamour of humanity, cold and dead inside, empty as the not-so-pretty head and hollow heart of a Mary Sue who can't read between the lines. Can't see what's under this sketchy fantasy of self-denial and overwrought passion.

In the broken concrete of the floor, a dirt mound marks where the tick has burrowed, its grave.

I piss on it.

~Softening the earth? says my boy, but I'm already snarling, ripples of the shift running up my spine as I hit the dirt with furious claws, in a shape barely hominid, scrabbling, tearing, rending the earth. You could call it *digging*, but that would be like calling a hurricane *breezy*. The scent of vampire rot is so rich it thickens the air, turns my stomach. I want to tear this fucker up from his sleep, rip him apart, and roll in the filth of what's left so I will *stink* of his ending.

A white hand bursts from the muck.

The rest of him follows in an explosion of dirt, an eruption of flailing inhumanity, leaping for the walls, the rafters, a corner of the ceiling, to cling there, hissing and hollow-eyed. Still glamoured to fuck, it's every inch the smooth Adonis, skin of white marble and blue veins, lithe and limber as a fucking cat but its twisted perching a mockery of a true predator. This is a fucking parasite, a tapeworm from the bowels of humanity, a leech with limbs and a face. Spitting, thoughtless, ravenous loathing.

—I will eat you and shit you out, I say.

~Really, no, says my boy. I'm not cleaning up that— And in the second I turn, it's fired itself at him, over my head, not baseball-fast, but fast enough; and his quarrel goes wild, but at least the holy water doesn't, like acid in its face, stripping glamour to raw horror. And by then, I'm launched, hitting the tick just as its jaw opens like a snake's. A glimpse of ragged shards, broken bone for teeth. I slam into its side,

Duncan

slam it the fuck off my boy and into a concrete wall. There's a sick thud, splattering gore.

12.

The fucker's already broken though, been broken since before it was dead, and it rolls away, scuttles back and whirls. Its lolling head snaps back into place, for all that its brains are oozing down its back. Fuck, it's a tick; whatever brains it has it likely scavenged from sewer rats, just so's it could ape the life it fucked up when it had the chance. Its eyes lock on my boy again, and I'm thinking, fuck, I hope it didn't get a taste of him there—at the exact same moment I scent his blood on the air.

No.

Then the smell of him is rich in its scent. I can hear him fumbling, cursing, losing the trust in himself to handle this, handle *anything*; I can smell the fear of failure, smell it in the tick's breath as it sucks it in, shrieks it at me, a searing mockery, cause if he can't handle this, he can't handle *me*, he's just a boy, not a boss, just a boy, not *my* boy and—-

I snarl as we leap, the tick and I, my claws ripping through the air, rending its belly, swatting the fucker clear across the basement.

I come down hard, something stolen from me in the touch. Shit, the smell of panic is so fucking physical, I stumble. I shake my head but I can't get rid of it, look to my boy but that's where the fucking problem is. He's choking, collapsing, and if he's weak, I-I don't know what to do. I want to snarl in his fucking face. I need you, you fucking fuck, need you to fight for. A boy and his werewolf, motherfucker. Loyalty. I need your fucking purpose, need you and fucking hate you for it.

Fucking bitch ass…

And then the tick is on my back, clamped tight; and it's not fangs or a feeding tube—it's not physical at all—but I can feel the bite at the back my neck, at the base of my skull, feel it reaching in to shred my thoughts and suck them out. Loyalty? I'm a fucking freak of a beast of base desires kept in line by a lie. There's no love here, only need, the need

SIC HIM, HELLHOUND! KILL! KILL!

to follow, to fawn, to be favoured with treats and scraps of attention, the need to be needed, to be needed to need—

13.

And I'm turning, growling at this fucking wretch of a weak handler on the ground in front of me, this fucking faggot kid on his back, his throat exposed like the craven whelp he is, just some backwoods bottom boy who opened himself up to a tick once before, no fucking wonder he let it happen again. All I can smell now, as I crouch to leap, is his fear and my anger, his weakness and my power.

I don't know how he manages it, the roll to one side as I jump. The crossbow smashing down on my nose.

—Don't you fucking dare, he says.
I'm still growling.
—Off! he shouts.

And he's bringing the gun up even as I go back and down, firing it once, twice. The bullets don't hit my skull, but it feels like they might as well have as the tick is blasted off me. There's a scream of pure despair that hits my boy hard. I see the gun barrel turning, pointing up, towards his chin, but he's my boy again now, and—I'll apologise later for nearly biting his hand off.

I whirl to spit twisted steel at the tick. And howl.

I howl as it scrambles upright, limbs clicking back from ragdoll dislocations to roughly human placements. I howl as it backs away, scuttles to this side and that, looking for a point of attack. I howl at the tick from all fours, standing over my boy, guarding him as he hauls himself back and up. I howl like Cerberus at the gates of Hell as he stumbles to his feet beside me, lays a hand on my back, a hand that steadies as I howl, as purposed as the one that's raised now, pointing.

—Sic him, boy, he says. *Kill!*

I hit the tick as a berserker, slashing chest and belly, tearing through one leg's hamstring as it spins, wrenching the other leg off at the knee. I catch it by the wrists as it flails, raise it in a cruciform and tear its jaw from its face with my teeth, spit it into the grave. Half its head follows in a crunch of bone. Then the rest. With a foot on its chest, the fucker's arms pop from their sockets like chicken wings.

When I'm done shaking it in my teeth like a stuffed toy, there's not much left.

14.

Still, there's *something* left. Fingers twitch and grapple at air. Toes curl. Wherever there are joints intact, they jerk and spasm. This is the creature in its natural state, I reckon—a set of clutching convulsions, twitches and shudders, driven by a brainless impetus to play out its travesty of existence. I crack open its ribcage, chew out the brown lump that passes for a heart and drop it in front of my boy, like a ball. He empties a full chamber of silver bullets into it and dissolves what's left in homeopathically-diluted holy water. Eventually, everything is still.

My boy stands there with the empty gun still dangling in one hand, looking down at the mess of the creature that ate Jared Swift. The scent of a moment of crisis is still on him, and for all the grim determination summoned by a bloody-minded howl of defiance, there's a hint of shame too. He's not happy, and it's my fault, I know. Don't know why, but I know it's my fault.

Then he looks at me, and something changes in his eyes, and he says two words and everything changes.

—Good boy!

And I am motherfucking *magnificent*.

I shift back to humanity, feeling slick and shiny, and I don't just mean with the viscerae. I feel *fierce*. Every shift is a remaking, after all, and if the transformation to wolfman unleashes a beast in me, well, so does the return to this human form. Like humans aren't beasts too? I grab his hand as he moves toward the stairs, towards disposal chemicals and rubber gloves and all that jazz, pull him in to lick his face, exuberantly. Hey, it's cleaning, sorta. He stops me, wipes a sleeve across my mouth.

—Like people, he says.

And we kiss.

SIC HIM, HELLHOUND! KILL! KILL!

So maybe I get a bit carried away as we're washing the gore off each other with holy water. Maybe it's the wolf in me that ignores the protest of *not here*. Or maybe it's the human in me that says, *especially here*. So you think we're both monsters? A hellhound and a human so offay with carnage we don't see how fucked-up it is to let the passion loose here and now?

I say it's life, to fuck as humans in the ruins of death.

As living, breathing, eating, shitting, *fucking* human beings in the ruin of death.

And that was the battle, more or less: how His Majesty's frigate *Milford* fell to a pirate queen, with never a shot fired in anger. And how I found myself eye to eye with her, shortly afterwards; and, "Will you spare the boys?" I asked.

KEEP THE ASPIDOCHELONE FLOATING

Chaz Brenchley

"Well, then," she said softly, menacingly. "Give me one good reason—one—not to kill you. Here and now."

I don't take prisoners, she was saying, *I don't collect ransoms. The living are too much trouble.* There were heavy splashes from astern, as the captain—the *former* captain—and his officers went overboard. No trouble at all.

I said, "There's only one ocean. One. All the waters of the world, all intermingled, all *talking* to each other, and they're under us right here, right now. Listening to you. Weighing you, weighing me. Is that good enough? Big enough?"

"It should be," she said. High sun glinted off the pocked blade of her cutlass. Another splash came from aft; I didn't look around. Down below, someone screamed: thin and hoarse, I thought it was a man. Or had been. Her eyes didn't flicker, her blade didn't twitch. I was counting on that.

She was solid: sure of herself, sure of her crew. Nothing to prove.

"It really should be," she said again. "Enough. But—you don't buccaneer. No one ever called you Pirate Martin. Did they?"

"No," I said. "No, they never did."

"No. And I don't carry passengers. So…"

The blade was like liquid sunshine in her hand, hot and ready. She'd do this herself if she had to; God knew, she must have had practice enough.

She really didn't want to, but she thought she'd do it anyway. She'd be famous, maybe: the one who put Sailor Martin down, the one who sent him to the bottom at last.

That's why she didn't want to. It's not the kind of fame a person looks to carry, even on land. Out here, on the attentive waters—well. If she was hesitating, that was why.

Unhurriedly, I said, "I can cook, though."

Now I'd surprised her. She blinked, took her time, said, "You can?"

"Yes, actually. I can cook for you." Not buccaneer, but feed her and her crew: that, yes. Nothing in that to sear my conscience or darken my long story more than it was dark already. I wouldn't be feeding prisoners, conniving at their capture. What my new shipmates did to those they took—a swift blade and a splash astern—would be on their souls, not mine. I was comfortable with that.

I'd be hanged regardless, if we were taken.

I was tolerably comfortable with that, too.

"Good, then." Her cutlass slammed back into its sheath, and she turned towards the poop. "Help my people get this mess cleared away, I want to round Dog Point before sunset. You're ship's cook, but I carry no idlers; you're starboard watch, and you'll scrub and stow and haul like any of them."

"Aye aye," I said, "cap'n."

For once in my life I was aboard a naval frigate, rather than a merchantman; for once in my life, I was on the passengers' manifest, rather than the crew's roster. I'd come aboard at Port Herivel, seabag on my shoulder and my name like a whisper rolling up the gangplank and across the deck before me: *Sailor Martin, that's Sailor Martin; he'll be luck for us, good luck in tricky waters...*

The captain welcomed me to his poop deck and his table, would perhaps have given me his cabin too if I hadn't insisted on bunking in the gunroom with his junior officers.

"Those pipsqueaks? Unbreeched boys, I warn you, they'll keep you up half the night demanding stories."

"That's my intention," I said cheerfully. "Perhaps I can teach them something. Youngsters listen to me."

KEEP THE ASPIDOCHELONE FLOATING

He grunted and didn't argue, for whatever brief good that did him. Not half an hour later, I was followed up the gangplank by a woman in black veils and her two servants, one a dusky matron and the other a boy. I stood by the taffrail and watched while the captain and his first lieutenant went to greet her. After a minute, the captain called for his steward and there went his cabin after all, gifted necessarily to the lady. He took her through to view her accommodations; her servants followed with the baggage; the first lieutenant came thoughtfully up from the afterdeck to join me.

"Who is she, Number One?"

"Florence, Lady Hope. Says she's sister-in-law to Sir Terence Digby, king's man at Port St Meriot. That's barely out of our way, and we're only running cargo anyway; the old man said we'd take her. Between you and me, I don't believe he likes the idea, but…" A shrug said the rest of it: that even the navy bowed to politics, and a wise captain did nothing to aggravate the civilian power.

For a little time, I thought of reclaiming my seabag and treading spry down to the quay again, seeking another ship. I knew Sir Terence, by more than reputation; I knew why the king had sent him to Port St Meriot, and why he'd gone. I knew he had no family, in or out of law.

But I was ever curious, it's my besetting sin and why I can never quit the sea. I held my tongue and settled into the gunroom, amused the lads and tried not to interfere too badly with ship's discipline while I kept a weather-eye on the lady and her people.

She herself kept her cabin, didn't join us for dinner, rarely showed abovedecks and never without her veil. She was in strict mourning, seemingly. Gunroom gossip said it was for her husband, or else her lover: either way, the man who had brought her from England and then had the discourtesy to die of yellow fever, leaving her with no alternative but to fling herself on the charity of an unfortunate but obliging relative.

Her boy had little enough to do, and was apparently glad—at first—to have the freedom of the ship. I found him everywhere, from the lower hold to the higher rigging, gambling with the idlers or racing the midshipmen from deck to masthead and down the shrouds again.

After our second day at sea, though, I saw him mostly in the company of the boatswain. Who was a bully, as are so many of his calling; and the boy looked less than happy now, red of eye and bruised of spirit, bruised of body I suspected as he slunk about, obedient at the big man's heels. Well. No doubt that would be a lesson learned. No doubt he'd find it useful. Myself, I spent my time in pursuit of the abigail as she laundered smallclothes in a barrel of fresh water, stood over the cook in his galley, sat to her needlework high on the foredeck in the late of the day. Her name, she said, was Delia. Tall and broad-shouldered as her mistress was—convenient, she said, for fitting dresses—she was goodnatured and open with it. Firm of purpose, knowing her own mind, finding her own course in life and cleaving to it. Free to do that, serving her mistress because she chose to: "I was never slave. I wouldn't have stood that. A person should be free. If she ain't born to it, she should take it." As she spoke, her eyes roved the ship, the crew, the set of the sails, the horizon. I didn't need to keep watch myself; I could depend on her to do it for me.

No surprise, then, when the look-out hailed the deck: "A ship! Hull-up, two points off the starboard bow!"

Really he should have seen her sooner. I rather thought Delia had, though from the foredeck we could make out only the scratch of her masts on the skyline. She was adrift under bare poles, so the man had some excuse, but even so I thought he'd probably face a whipping come Sunday, when his officers would have time to attend to it. A warship with a skeleton crew such as ours, reduced by disease and desertion, too few to work the ship and man the guns at once: she needed fair warning above all, to close with friends and keep her distance from any threat.

I should probably have said something to the captain, that first day. Too late now. Captain and first lieutenant both were halfway up the shrouds, telescopes in hand, to see for themselves. Before their polished boots hit the deck again, I could see the first smoke rising from the other ship, a greasy smudge against the sky.

"She looks to be a whaler," the first lieutenant confided, while his captain paced the windward side of the poop alone, considering. "A derelict, in trouble. We'll go to help. It's our duty."

Duty could bring a rich reward, salvage-fees on a vessel full of sperm-oil and ambergris. I held my tongue. Nothing about this captain impressed me, from his own indecision to the quality of his officers to the manners of his crew. I wouldn't interfere now. I distrusted even his ability to run away.

KEEP THE ASPIDOCHELONE FLOATING

Even the wind was a conspirator, lying handsome off our aft quarter; in less than an hour we were drawing alongside. Even in his cupidity, the captain wasn't entirely stupid. He'd had the guns loaded and run out, so that we had at least the appearance of a wary warlike vessel in His Majesty's vigilant navy. Every officer bore a loaded pistol, every man went armed.

Even so, that was just routine. The ship was really not expecting trouble. Even so, I was still exploiting my privilege, lingering on the poop with the officers of the watch, just to see what happened. What happened first was that Delia swung up the companionway to join us. There was no sign of her mistress, nor their boy. Delia might be free but she was a woman, a passenger, a servant. The captain merely stared; the first lieutenant moved to evict her as swiftly as he might, as rudely as need be.

"Madam, by all that's holy, you may not—!"

She forestalled him, with a swift nod of her turban'd head towards the other ship. Where a plain red flag had broken out astern, and a boil of men erupted from below.

"My God, sir, they're pirates! Hard aport! All hands, bring us about!"

Delia said, "I'm afraid you'll find that my man has cut your steering chains." Her man, she said, not her boy. I pictured her supposed mistress, as tall and broad of shoulder as she was herself, veiled in solitude. And wondered, a little, what the boy was up to.

The man at the wheel cursed, as it spun freely in his hands.

"Belay that order! All hands to the guns! Fire as they bear!"

"Unfortunately," Delia said, "I don't believe your guns will fire. I'm afraid my boy has been fooling about in your magazine since we boarded, mixing powdered glass into all your gunpowder. He's a skittish lad, so you may be lucky; but if he's done his work properly…"

The first lieutenant tested that, jerking the pistol from his belt and levelling it straight at her face at no more than two yards' distance. She simply stood there, waiting.

He pulled the trigger. There was a flash in the pan, a sullen smoke, no more.

He flung the pistol furiously at her head. She ducked, and when she straightened she had a cutlass in her hand, drawn through some cunning slit in her skirts.

She was just in time to meet his blade with her own. She was a big woman, but even so: a hanger with a man's weight behind it should have been enough to finish her quickly. Somehow, it was not. They fought from leeward to windward, and when they came bloodily apart at last it was she who stepped back and he who slumped boneless to the deck.

That the captain and his other officers had only stood and watched, transfixed—that said all that was necessary about the ship's command.

By the time they saw their brother officer fall dead, it was too late to recover. A man in skirts came bulling up from the afterdeck, with his veils thrown back and pistols in each hand; grapnels were already flying across the rail to drag the doomed frigate closer, while the pirate crew came swinging aboard on ropes.

There was fighting down on the quarterdeck, but none up here now. Everyone waited for the captain; what they saw at last was his sword-belt hitting the deck as he let all slip.

And that was the battle, more or less: how His Majesty's frigate *Milford* fell to a pirate queen, with never a shot fired in anger. And how I found myself eye to eye with her, shortly afterwards; and, "Will you spare the boys?" I asked.

"Perhaps. If they swear to follow me, and if I believe them. Boys can be taught. Don't waste your time pleading for the men. You might be better served by pleading for yourself."

"Perhaps, but I don't plead. Ever. You know my value, you know what I am. You choose to keep me, or you don't."

"Well, then…"

And so I found myself ship's cook and standing a watch, everything next worst to a pirate true. I saw the boys I'd slept with herded over onto the bait-ship, where no doubt they'd be tested and tested. I watched, and wished them luck, and hoped that some at least might survive, for a while at least.

One boy remained, as Delia took possession of her new flagship: the lad she'd brought aboard. I saw him come up from below, scrupulously cleaning his knife. A little later, I saw men carry up the bloodied ruin of what had been the boatswain.

Well, small blame to the boy for that. I remembered the screaming, and still blamed him not at all; I had a fair view of what he'd done, as the men swung the body overboard, and still not. I never did like bullies. The boy came up and glanced at me, and seemed surprised; turned to his captain with a questioning glance, "Why's he—?" and won the only proper response, a quick cuff to the ear.

"He's our new cook. And you're his galley slave, till I say otherwise. Get below, the pair of you, and see to the crew's dinner."

His name was Sebastian, he said. That was the most of what he said for a while, caught in a fit of the sullens as we scrubbed and chopped. He held our captain too much in awe to disobey even my commands, let alone hers, but he was bitterly resentful. He really didn't understand why I was still alive, let alone why he should be set under me.

Matters eased between us when I contrived to let him think that he was really there to watch me, to stand by with that good knife of his in case I tried to poison his captain or set the whole cursed ship aflame.

After that, it was easy enough to get him talking. He was barely twenty yet and mightily pleased with himself and the wild tangle of his life, bubbling over with it, spilling stories. He'd been a stable boy in Jamaica and then tiger on his lady's curricle, until he was snatched in a tavern and pressed into service on a buccaneer. Twelve years old, stolen for his pretty face and given the same choice that faced those boys on the bait-ship today: swear fealty to a pirate and knuckle under, or die.

Sebastian had sworn, smart boy, and survived. Longer already than most pirates did; and somewhere in that lucky life, he'd fallen in love with it. Like any boy he could be vicious and fearful, passionate and sentimental by turns, hungry for adventure and hungry to sleep in the sun.

Playing cabin boy to a pirate crew had fed each of those urges and more; serving Delia had brought him to the point of worship, her total devotee. I could have found no simpler way to win his heart myself, than to let him talk about her.

I hadn't planned to win his heart at all, I hadn't planned to stay—one cruise, one port, I'd be away—but even after so long at sea, the sea can still surprise me.

So can a boy. Even after so long, so many boys. I had him stir the porridge for loblolly, not to let him ruin his precious knife hacking at the navy's salt beef, harder than the barrels it was kept in. In the end I fetched a mallet and a sharpened caulking-iron. Between my pounding and his giggling, we agreed that it was wondrous condescension on her part, that she would eat this with her men; and that let me ask, "How does she come to lead a crew of men, white men, in any case?" There had been women freebooters, there had been black freebooters; probably there had been black women; but not as captain. I was sure of that.

"We elected her, of course. It's the tradition." Then he pulled a rueful face and went on, "I think it was a joke. Our last captain was no use, he lost us too many prizes and sailed us into trouble, time and again. We were hiding out, hungry and afraid with the navy at our heels and hunting. Delia had been the captain's doxy, that's why she was aboard. She was sensible, someone to listen to. Even so, it was a joke. We wanted rid of the captain before he got us all hanged, but you never call for a vote unless you know who's going to win it, and there were too many men who wanted to. That's dangerous. Nobody dared stick his neck out until Double Johnny got drunk enough. He called the vote, the captain asked who stood against him—and Johnny named Delia. Because he thought it was funny, or because it was a measure of how much we despised the captain, or because he was so drunk and the rum so bad hers was the only name he could remember, hers the only face he could make out. I don't know. I think it was a joke.

"But he named her, and when the captain had quit laughing, he asked if she would stand. And she said she would. He already had his hand on his cutlass, he knew just how this would go: of course he'd win the vote, and then he'd kill her, and then Johnny, and that would be that.

"Only he lost the vote. We all hated him that much, and we all loved Delia. So we voted her in. And then he tried to kill her anyway, but she was ready for him. She had a loaded pistol in her skirts, and she blew his head away.

"I think we thought she'd stand down after, and let us have a proper election for a real captain. Only she didn't do that. She took it on herself to be a real captain. She found us safe harbour and led us to a prize; and then we wouldn't have let her stand down if she'd wanted to. She's hard on us, but she's kept us alive all this time; and now we have a warship," unthinkable bounty. And he might want to give all credit to his captain, but he still did keep a little for himself, how clever he'd been, playing servant all those days while he quietly sabotaged the gunpowder and never gave himself or his companions away.

KEEP THE ASPIDOCHELONE FLOATING

He wanted my applause, so I gave it him; then I traded stories with him. Soon enough his eyes were bugging out, as he finally understood just who I was. Or thought he did. He'd have known it sooner if he'd listened to the crew of the *Milford*, but he was a boy: full of himself and his own daring, listening at first to nothing and nobody but his captain.

And then to nothing and nobody but his own sorrows, once the boatswain had him. I had apparently entirely passed him by. I might have been wounded, if I didn't understand him all too well.

Still, he made up now for that neglect. I was famous, all around his limited little ocean. He'd heard the common stories about Sailor Martin and wanted to test them, to hear them again from the source. *Did you really...? Is it true that...?*

He was a boy, he could readily be squashed at need. For now I talked more than I ordinarily do, I told him more than I was entirely comfortable with. I wanted an ally, perhaps a spy, certainly a bunkmate. He was still pretty; he'd do.

Pretty and willing and trained, as it turned out. Better than willing, awed and grateful. I had worried that the boatswain might have killed his pleasure in the act, but one night's careful negotiation took us past that. Gentleness was a revelation to him; so was anything that didn't directly marry my cock with his arse. Soon enough he was melting-hot under my hand, far past caring how roughly I handled him. He was rough himself, with the unexplored strength of the young; making me grunt was a triumph, apparently. Even if it cost him extra chores in the morning.

I took cheerful advantage of his body, day and night, this way and that: any excuse to fuck him at any opportunity, any excuse to heap work onto his wiry shoulders. The more I left to Sebastian, the more I could sprawl at my ease on the foc'sle on a bed of coiled rope in the sun. The captain didn't mind, so long as she and the crew ate three times a day; and she'd been light on crew even before she had to divide it between two ships. Really, feeding those she'd kept on the *Milford* was no burden. Not to me, at least. Sebastian grumbled, but even he didn't seem too outraged.

Our consort, the *Nymph Ann*, showed herself to be a true old whaler by her lines, when she wasn't pretending. She'd probably never been much of a pirate, but she'd made a good bait-ship. Now she offered a good shakedown to new crew, those navy boys. From my rope throne I could watch them being put through their paces, up in the rigging and around the deck, swabbing and holystoning and hauling sail. I saw one of them flogged on a grating, two dozen strokes of the cat; next day I saw a rope slung from the yard-arm and thought I was about to see one hanged.

And so I did, nearly—except that they hung the boy up by his heels and just let him dangle, for punishment or amusement or I know not what. For a while he writhed and begged shrilly, loud enough to carry across the water, while the old hands laughed at him. Soon enough he fell quiet and only hung there, and they grew bored and left him.

They might have left him too long, he might have died, if a boy can die of a blood-flood to his brain; but he saved himself at last, pointing and squealing, trying to cry out as a good boy should.

Someone looked, and called a proper warning to the ship's master at the wheel. He responded with a bellow that sent hands swarming up aloft; I suppose one of them must have taken the time to cut the boy down, if only because he was in the way of the fore course's falling.

The *Nymph Ann* veered close on our starboard, within hailing distance.

"Whale, cap'n! The boy saw her blow!"

"Where away?"

"North and two points east. If he could see her, the boats can reach her."

The captain hesitated, but only for a moment. Then she nodded, yelled her approval, started yelling orders to our own crew.

A simple cruise makes a decent shakedown—but hard sudden work, the chance of danger and the chance of profit makes a better. Pirates and whalers are close kin, half of them have been the other thing at some time; we had enough experience between the two vessels, maybe enough boats too.

What boats there were went overboard, and collected crews to row them. Harpoons came from the *Nymph Ann*, cables from our own locker, courtesy of His Majesty.

"Sailor Martin: do you whale, if you won't buccaneer?"

"I've served," I said, "on a whaler."

"Take a seat in the gig, then. Pull an oar, if you can't throw a harpoon."

KEEP THE ASPIDOCHELONE FLOATING

I could, but not as well—I was sure—as the lean tattooed creature crouching in the bows of the gig as we pulled away. The whale must have shown again, because voices called down to us: directions, exhortations, blessings on the day. Nothing excites a crew like first sight of a blow. Nothing is harder than to catch sight of your whale from a little boat on the swell. We rowed to where we thought she had been seen; our ships were no help, having to work up against the wind, soon left behind. We rowed and craned our necks around, seeking and seeking. We were a fleet of three, the ocean is desert-vast, and whales can swim far and far underwater; I thought we were safe to lose her. I thought we had lost her already. It was almost a relief. Our crews were learning their work, whaling or pirating or both together; and Sebastian was in *Milford*'s other boat, and if we found no whale then he was at no risk. That sat more easily in my mind and on my stomach. I hadn't expected to worry for him, but—

"There! There she is! She's logging!"

She was; and she was a cruel unlucky fish, that we should find her adrift, asleep in the water, almost impossible to spot from a boat unless you came right on her, as we had.

Once spotted, a logging whale is easy to spear. We coordinated by voice and eye, gathered all three boats together, hit her with three harpoons at once.

She dived straight down, our cables whipping out hard and hot, fit to take a man's arm if he tried to grip one. But she couldn't stay down long, she couldn't go deep, she'd had no chance to breathe; soon enough the cables slacked as she rose and breached.

Rose and breached and dived again, and now she was dragging us, and what could three cockleshell boats, two dozen men do against such a monster? This was the perilous time, when a boat can swamp or turn turtle, when a whale can turn against a crew, a fluke can splinter planking, men can die.

We hauled on the oars, legs braced: backing water until the shafts bent and our shoulders popped, until we had to yield or something broke. Then we let her pull us, until we'd recovered enough to strain again.

We worked her and worked her, each boat in turn or all together; she hauled us hard, worse when she stopped diving and only swam because she needed the air. Our little boats sheared through the swell, flew off the peaks and slammed back into the troughs, again and again. I never thought they'd survive; I never thought we would. It's always a surprise after a Nantucket sleigh ride, to find yourself and your mates intact.

If you do.

I watched Sebastian's dory when I could, when spray wasn't cutting at my face like knives, when the gig wasn't flying or smashing down into the whale's wake or tossing so hard that we could do nothing but hold on.

We lost oars, we lost sight of anything outside that eggshell, we lost hope; we never lost the whale though I thought we must at any moment, the rope would break or the boat would break or the harpoon's barbs would tear free of her blubber and strand us in mid-ocean.

None of that. She slowed, the world lost its madness, the sea settled back beneath us; we recovered what oars we could and backed water one more time.

You can brace and look about you, both at once. Heaving, I turned my head and looked and looked. There was a dory, there were men in it, braced as we were, bending their oars against the whale's pull. Salt spray blinded me and I had no hand free to wipe my eyes; sun was setting, and I had no good light; I had no breath to bellow his name. Nothing to do but haul and wait, haul and wait until that fish at last stopped fighting.

Then, when she lay floating, as still as we had found her, wheezing in great bubbling salt-stink gasps; then we could call from boat to boat. I held my tongue, having nothing useful to say, but youth is loud; I heard Sebastian exult at finding himself alive yet, nothing worse than wet and sore.

I heard him call my name across the water. I heard him hushed peremptorily, hoarsely: "Quiet, lad, no chatter now. You'll start her again. Who has a lance?"

From beyond the dory, no answer. I wasn't sure if there was still a boat.

Our own harpooner fumbled in the shadow of the bow, found a lanyard, pulled it in. Blessedly, it hadn't snapped in the fury of the whale's wake or any of the impacts of the boat on water. At the end of that rope rose a long iron shaft, cruelly bladed. Once that had been in the gig with us; I hadn't noticed it go, being too busy keeping myself aboard. Lucky it hadn't taken one of us with it, or at least an arm or so. A whaler's lance is wicked sharp; it needs to be.

KEEP THE ASPIDOCHELONE FLOATING

The dory had apparently lost its own. Poor whale. The harpooner stood in the bows as we rowed slowly in beside the floating monster. She was aware, I think, that we were coming; her fins stirred, but feebly. No danger of Sebastian's voice starting her now. I thought she was utterly overdone, we'd exhausted her beyond recovery. Even so, she had sent one boat, eight or nine men to the bottom; and all whales are female, like ships, but this one truly was. A bull would have been half as long again, maybe twice the weight. More spermaceti in its head, more ambergris in its belly, more oil in its blubber—but twice the power too, many times the temper. Never mind boats, full-grown bulls had sunk ships in their time, in their fury. I doubt we would have survived a bull, any of us.

The dory pulled up beside us at the whale's flank. Sebastian didn't risk his voice again, so recently scolded, this close to the monster's shadow. He didn't risk standing, either, let alone the leap I was half dreading: from one boat to the other, his to mine. I saw an arm wave wildly, that was all, and knew him in the murk—and, God save me, I did wave back. And then very suddenly needed both hands for holding on again, because the harpooner plunged that vicious lance in through the hide of the whale, deep in, probing for lungs or heart or anything that mattered. The great beast spasmed, though she lacked the strength to surge beneath the water. Perhaps she only shrugged in pain; perhaps she meant to swamp us. One small eye caught the last of the sun, gleaming in the vast dark bulk of her head, making her seem more intelligent than she was. Perhaps.

That little movement raised a wave that forced us from her side. Our harpooner left his lance jutting from her flank, preferring to let go than dangle, ridiculous and at risk. By the time we'd baled and caught the oars and pulled ourselves back in, the dory had our place and a man there had the lance.

A man? No—a boy. Sebastian, of course: on his feet and taking a man's task, wanting to impress me. Pulling the lance free of her flesh's suck with one swift draw, that sweet unsuspected strength resolved into grace in shadow; letting the dory's drift carry him a yard down her flank before he drove it in again, power and spring and determination, knowing himself under my eye, coiled at the heart of my anxiety.

Again she flung herself about in the water as that vicious needle struck deep into her innards. Again, her wash forced the boats away. Sebastian was too slow to let go, too young to understand the need or else too focused on twisting the blade, probing for her heart, wanting to be the one who slew her cleanly. He found his platform suddenly gone altogether from beneath him; I saw him hang by both arms from the dipping lance's shaft, and then I saw her roll him underwater.

And then me, me too, as though her one movement had carried us both down. I swear, I never chose to dive. There I was, though, swimming through the dark in quest of him. Something on her hide glowed phosphorescent, like moonlight trapped in water; weed or living creature, I couldn't tell, but by that faint illumination I found his shadow as he sank.

Of couse he couldn't swim, what sailor can? Apart from me, of course.

Rumour says that I could log like a whale and drift like a derelict and never need to shift a finger in effort, that the sea would bear me up. Rumour is an ass. In this and many things. I swim because I learned to swim, the way I learned to handle boats: with work and time and practice.

I swim for the same reason that I sail, because I love the sea, not it loves me. Because it is dark, because it is salt, because it is deadly. Because it is bitter, and because it is my heart. Dark, but not obsidian; deadly, but not mortal. Not necessarily mortal. Bitter, but not unbearable. I saw Sebastian, by the grace-light of the whale's hide. I struck down and reached him, found him still clinging to the shaft of the lance. Desperation or good sense, whichever, I had cause to bless it now. If he'd let go, he'd have sunk; if he'd sunk far from that gentle light, I never would have found him.

He wasn't about to let go now, even though I'd found him. I wasn't about to allow him. If he ceased to clutch at the lance, he would clutch at me instead; then we'd both sink. I have seen men drowned by their friends, and I didn't mean to join them.

The whale meant for both of us to join them, but I too can be dark and salt and deadly. The beast had rolled deliberately, I thought, to hold Sebastian under the water. His eyes were screwed tight shut, so he was no trouble to me, if no help. If he'd been looking, if he'd seen me, he'd have lunged, I think. I didn't even touch him. I only laid my own hands beside his, and twisted that lance as sharply as I might.

KEEP THE ASPIDOCHELONE FLOATING

Poor thing, she'd been trying to shake the boy loose and shed the pain. Now here it was again, worse than before; what could she do but roll up to the air again, and breathe, and suffer?

Sebastian's death-grip was tight enough to fetch him out, no chance of shaking loose. I hung on by grim purpose, through the wrenching tug of that roll; and there we were, breaking back into the world, gasping and coughing and holding on, still holding on as we dangled and kicked above the surface of the ocean.

And there was the dory, seeing us, pulling back to the whale's side: giving us something to drop into, if Sebastian would only let go. At least his eyes were open now. He stared at me, wild, frantic—and then twined his legs around my waist, a death-grip too late to do harm, and swung us both back and forth.

Working that lance-head in the whale's innards, back and forth…

Finding something, I know not what, but something that mattered. Slicing into it. Bringing one last brutal spasm from the beast, and then a groaning stillness.

The dory came back for us again, and this time I let go, this time it was my turn to practise my death-grip on the boy, wrapping my arms around his shoulders so that all my weight hung from his determined hands.

He laughed in my face, and held on that one last second, long enough to kiss me. Then he let go, and we fell.

Bruisingly, into the crowded boat: oar-handles and benches and other men contributed all their share of bruises, but mostly mine came from Sebastian. He seemed all elbows in my grip, and all deliberate, and all delight. Wet lithe muscled boy, once again exultant and alive; I had to cuff him hard to make him let go, and then again just to calm him. He spat blood and grinned dizzily up at me, settled between my legs there on the boat's boards in the awkward cramping space between the rowing benches and other men's feet, and said, "What now?"

Said it to me as though I were captain, as though the decisions were mine. It ought not to have been true—but the dory fell silent, as though all the men there were waiting on my answer. Across the water I could hear the silence in the gig too, matching.

Into that delicate moment, dying or dead, the whale let rip an abrupt and tremendous fart. Which shattered the tension nicely, throwing us all into gales of laughter; and in the subsiding cheerful chatter that followed, I took an easy charge.

Got a rope around the whale's tail, not to lose her in the encompassing night; joined both boats together with another, for the same reason; said, "We'll just sit out the darkness, lads, and wait for the captain to find us in the morning. She'll come. She'll have to: can't hardly handle one ship without us, let alone two."

"How's she going to come, then, if she can't—ow!"

I suppressed my boy handily, amid another ripple of laughter, and asked who had rum or hard tack in their pockets, tobacco still dry in a pouch, anything to share around to see us through the waiting.

Later, we sang; later still, we slept, those who could, sparing only those on watch. Sebastian could most likely sleep through a hurricane; I hoped to have the chance to prove it, another day, another voyage. For now I cradled the slumped weight of him, felt the slow seize of stiffness in my joints, learned that it is possible for a man's parts to be both numb and excruciatingly painful, both at once.

When he woke, he was youthfully, outrageously limber. Also he was youthfully and outrageously heedless, teasing me and disturbing everyone, knocking men out of their slumbers as he mocked and stretched, making the whole boat rock as he scrambled to his feet to peer into the dawnlight for his beloved captain. In the end I pitched him overboard, left him to squawk and splash for a minute before I let a man thrust out an oar for him to snatch at. As we hauled him in dripping over the gunwale, he was still squawking, but not in protest now. He'd swallowed too much water to be coherent, or else he was just too angry—but he was a good boy, he kept pointing and making noise until we turned, until we looked, until we understood. The sky was pearling to the east, the other way, the way I'd pushed him. Westward was still dark, but it was too dark. Not sky-dark, not even storm-dark: a rising arc of shadow split the night, cut away the stars. Now, in the hush of experience, I could even hear the sounds of surf breaking against rock.

I had not thought we were that close to land, but the whale had hauled us far and far, out of all reckoning. "Good, then," I cried, pounding Sebastian between the shoulder-blades as though it were his achievement, as

KEEP THE ASPIDOCHELONE FLOATING

though I didn't just enjoy pounding the lad. "Landfall will make our wait more comfortable; there'll be water, sure, and green timber to raise smoke, to tell the captain where we are. Out oars, lads, and haul away. We'll haul our catch to dry land, and be dry ourselves…"

Sometimes I am wrong and wrong. Even now, even still: wrong and wrong and wrong. We came ashore in the false dawn, with our false hopes high; and found ourselves cast on a hard rock, hard and bare and empty. No trees, no habitation and no water. One of the hands talked of an island he'd seen rise overnight, a seething volcano building itself in fury from below; but that had been far to the east, half a world away. There were no such stories here, save the ones he told. In the end I sent him to the high bleak peak of this rock, to keep watch for the captain. He'd have no way to signal her, but she should come in any case, as soon as she sighted land. If she were anywhere on our trail, anywhere near, she'd come. Even if she knew what little comfort this place offered, she'd still come. Any sailor would. We love the sea, and turn to land like a needle to the north.

She'd know to find us here, sure as storm.

Meantime—well. There was no fresh water, and no timber for a fire except what we'd brought with us; and no sailor would ever burn a boat. Even so, more than one hand sat on the ridge-rock shore and dangled bare hook-and-line into the tugging sea. Hope springs eternal, and you can always eat fish raw; and it was always possible that the captain wouldn't come.

That was a possibility we didn't talk about. Every man held it private, in the back of his own skull, with all that that implied. To one boy, it didn't occur at all. Sebastian was full of excitement, empty of doubts. As full as he needed of rum, perhaps, that too: I thought the men had been topping him up, for his reward for being first to cry land or just for their amusement.

He was a happy drunk, happy and confident and trusting, almost impossibly pleased with himself. He couldn't keep still, but he didn't want to walk. The rock felt rocky under sea-legs, and his triumph floated large and alluring just off shore; he wanted to row around the whale's corpse and relive the whole adventure, show me the jutting lance and tell me how clever he'd been, how kind I'd been to come after him, how wonderfully we'd worked together.

I didn't mind, so long as he did the rowing. One lean lad shifting a heavy gig: the work of it would burn the rum out of his bones and maybe even still his restless tongue. Also, we'd find a privacy on the water that I hoped to celebrate, in the whale's shadow and down between the benches, doubly out of sight from shore. The men would speculate wildly and mock cruelly when we came back to them, I hoped with every justification in the world…

Sitting in the stern, manning the tiller, I got to watch his face as he pulled: all strain and anxiety until he had her moving, until his confidence came back. Then concentration, the determination to do the thing well, not to catch a crab, above all not to splash me more than he could help; then awe at the simple size of the thing, his achievement, the tales he could tell as we came into the windshadow of the whale. A more simple smile, when he looked at me.

An unreadable expression, when he looked over my shoulder at the island at my back. He had no breath spare, but his eyes were speaking for him. I twisted around, and saw a sea-cave rising broad and high, just a little way along the coast from where we'd come to land.

"That," I said, turning back to the boy, "looks big enough to shelter the *Milford* and the *Nymph Ann* too. You may have found our new hideaway, lad."

"Oh, I didn't…"

The protest was breathless and instinctive and utterly meaningless; he thought he did, I could read that all through him. The mighty adventurer, slaying beasts and leading us to treasures. He was almost unutterably pleased with himself.

"You were the first to see it," I said, feeding his imagination happily. "We'll call it Sebastian's Cave—"

"—Sebby's Cave, they'll call it, only you call me Sebastian. You and the cap'n—"

"—All right, Sebby's Cave, but we still won't go in there till we have torches. It's dark, and anything could be hiding out already."

"I want to go now." A dead whale, a tale told had lost all its attraction suddenly, in the face of an adventure not yet lived. It would be the same with me, I thought: right now I was all the world he lived in, as the captain had been before me; sooner or later, I would be a tale told.

It was a boy's life, that was all. Sooner or later, perhaps he'd be a man. I felt unutterably old, and played that hand as I had to: "I know you do, but we'll still wait. You don't want them calling it Seb's Folly, because it's where you went to die. It looks like a mouth, half-open, ready. Just pretend you can see teeth hanging down, and wait till we have lights. Now row me round to the other side of this fish."

He pulled a face, but then he pulled the oars. Still a good boy.

Still a boy: he sulked, and complained about the stench of it. I laughed, and said, "You should be used to that, sleeping down below. You should get used to it. Wait till we flense this fish, before you worry about smells."

Then wait till we fry it, but I didn't say that. One step at a time. Little by little, let him learn. "Now ship those oars, and come here."

Time and tide, the movement of small vessels on great waters. Sex in the scuppers. It's all one.

While I had his clothes off, I gave him his first swimming lesson. Unless the whale had done that, and all I had to do was reinforce it. All I wanted him to learn was not to panic—which made it really a lesson in trust, which started as it had to, with trusting me. "Let go of the gunnel, Sebastian. Just let go. It's perfectly safe. I'm here, and I won't let you sink…"

Eventually I had him with his arms hooked over a floating oar, kicking furiously for shore. Soon enough, I thought he'd trust himself; sometime after that, he'd learn to trust the water. And probably start calling himself Sailor Sebastian, thinking himself immortal, *the sea will hold me up*.

At the moment he was all effort, more splash than surge, and that good oar was all that held him up. I paced him in the gig, one slow stroke and then another, easy work. I was ready to pluck him out if he exhausted himself entirely, but I thought the whole crew ought to thank me if I brought him back weary to the bone. He could sit in the sun with his good knife and make himself useful as well as decorative, pick limpets from the rocks, give us all something to chew on while we waited for the captain.

We couldn't make smoke to guide her, but oh, she was good. Not four bells in the afternoon watch, and there was a bellow from the peak, a wildly waving figure, our watchman running and slipping and sliding down the long slope, risking bones and softer parts to bring us news.

"I'd have sent the boy up to you," I murmured, once we had him safely gathered in, "if you'd only waited."

Sebastian just looked at me, and went on sharpening his knife. I grinned. "Go on, then. What did you see?"

"She's coming, she's there, she'll be with us by sundown…"

"No. What did you *see*?" There were other ships in these waters, and few of them were friends to us.

He saw the point, nodded, stuck to his guns despite: "Two ships, mast-high. One warship and one whaler, I rate 'em—and don't tell me I don't know the *Nymph Ann*, for I do."

"She might have been gathered in by a king's ship. Which might have sunk the *Milford*, if the captain made a fight of it. If she could. Or the king's men might have taken both, hanged everyone, might be coming now to hang the rest of us."

If they were, there was little enough that we could do about it. Still, we all trooped to the peak to watch the ships' approach. Of course they were the *Milford* and the *Nymph Ann*, that was clear soon enough; we had to wait to see the scarlet shock of the captain's flag, to be as certain of her.

We had her gig; we had to row out to fetch her.

Sebastian insisted on pulling an oar, only so that he could lay claim both to the whale and his cave, before any other hand got the jump on him. Cap'n Delia could manage him, better than any of us. Better than me. She gave him everything he deserved, in due order: praise and encouragement; mockery; a stinging slap to the head when he wouldn't subside.

Finally, after she'd seen all that we had to show her, after we'd brought her to land, she said, "Well, then. There's work to do. Food and grog for all you marooned lads and the lads who came to save you; Martin, see to that. Use the galley on the *Milford*; people will be busy on the *Nymph*. She still has all her try-works from her whaling days, but they're down in the ballast, largely. Someone wriggly needs to haul them out. Sebastian, that's you, and those boys we took from the navy. You'll be in charge down there, but that's not an excuse to slack. I want everything out and set up tonight; you don't get your grog until it is. Don't drink the bilge-

KEEP THE ASPIDOCHELONE FLOATING

water meantime. Sorry, Martin, but we need to boil down that fish before it starts going bad. You'll be on your own today."

That was nonsense, of course, and she knew it. You're never alone in a ship's galley. Even with half the crew on another ship and half the remainder ashore, with the watch reduced to a bare skeleton few, there's always someone with time on their hands and oil on their tongue, hoping to wheedle a jot of rum, or else a handful of soft tack and a dip of it in the slush.

I had company, then, and I could put them to work, but I did still miss my boy. Which was unexpected and curious, interesting to watch in myself, not easy to understand. Not easy to shrug off. Boys are like deep ocean swell; they come, they go, there's always another on the way. This one—well. Apparently I wanted to ride the wave awhile.

I could do that. I could afford the time. That's something I've never been short of.

A hasty dinner for all, then, as each mess of men was relieved in turn. No time for the salt meat to soften, so I gave them hasty pudding. When every mess had been fed, I watered rum for the grog and took that up on deck to serve it out. Last in line, as ordered, came the boys: sodden and stinking, exhausted, elated. Arms around one another's shoulders, leaning into each other even before the rum hit them. Last of all was Sebastian, proud of his command and proud of their work, determined to show me. I'd seen it all before, but still: for his contentment, I let him row me ashore one more time, a lamp in the gig and fires on the shore to guide us. Not till after I'd dunked him in the sea one more time, though, in the tropical sunset glow. I called it a swimming lesson, and forbore to fetch the scrubbing-brushes.

The men had roamed all over this rock-bubble island while I was busy, and found no beach. Some way down the coast from Sebby's Cave, though, the rock shelved out almost level, like a lip. Here they'd hauled the whale ashore already, secured her carcase with rocks and ropes, drained the spermaceti out of her skull and begun to flense her carcase. Come morning, they'd open her belly for the ambergris; in the meantime, no reason not to start rendering the oil out of her blubber.

The *Nymph Ann* was too old to have try-works built into her deck, all bricked about for safety, as the modern whalers did; so the great iron pots had been set up ashore on tripods, with empty barrels stacked behind and slow fires already lit below them. Those would burn night and day now, until we ran out of either blubber or barrels, depending.

"See, these are the blanket pieces, these long strips we cut straight off the fish. I did one myself, this one I think," nice boy, honestly laying claim to the least of the stacked strips, the shortest and most ragged, "till Twice Tom took the flensing-knife off me. Then we cut 'em into blocks, the horse pieces, I don't know why they're called that; and then they're sliced down for the pot. Bible leaves, Tom says these sheets are called. He wouldn't let me cut those, he says I'll take my hand off..."

He was likely right. I was grateful to Twice Tom, and impatient to quiet my boy, to stop him bubbling over with what I already knew. I knew too well what the bubbling pots would smell like, all too soon; I'd sooner be back aboard before then, or at least on the other side of this island. Besides, the reek of rendered whale-oil clings to clothes and hair even worse than the smoke of a smudge-fire, and I'd only just washed him.

I kissed Sebastian, then, to silence him, and guided him away uphill. He was too tired for the long haul back to the ship, it'd only make him quarrelsome if I tried to take him far from his triumphs; too tired to sleep, he could yet be charming company if I only flattered him a little and taught him a little. The island offered no softness, but we'd contrive.

"Sailor Martin." Hers was the one voice I couldn't ignore. She was sitting alone in a blaze of starlight, halfway up the slope; I swallowed my sigh, settled on a rock below—the perfect courtier, attentive and obedient and not threatening her status—and tugged Sebastian down at my feet, let him settle against my legs, played with the damp straggles of his hair while I waited to hear what was on her mind.

"I had a look inside that cave," she said, "after the men's dinner, before my own." I knew it; her lamps had been lit from my galley fire. "It's not as deep as I've seen them, but it's even higher inside than it is at the mouth. It'll take both ships with ease, even at the height of the tide, and not a sign to see outside. I wouldn't want to be caught in there in a storm, mind, but if we need to duck a king's ship, that's the place. Hell, I don't think this rock is even on their maps; it's not on mine." And hers, of course, had been the king's before. She'd have nothing more recent or more reliable than the *Milford*'s charts.

"That's good news," I said, which was true, but irrelevant: good news for her, of little interest to me, not what she meant to tell me.

"Yes. Somewhere to run to. All we need now is a reason to run." Here it came. "The *Nymph Ann* doubles very nicely as a whaler, and now we have an honest cargo to prove it. We don't need to take it to Port Royal and let those thieves bilk us for a tenth its value; we can head for Port St Meriot and deal openly for once. Only, not with me on the bridge."

Well, no. News of a black woman pirate captain might have spread through the islands already; even if it hadn't, news of a black woman whaler captain would still raise too many questions. It wouldn't be believed.

"The master can stand in for you," I said.

"He can—but so can you. Everybody knows you, everybody trusts you—and you know Sir Terence Digby. I thought we might pay a call. Word on the water is he's giving a ball."

Likely he was. Everything in its season, and this was dancing weather. Light muslins damped with sweat, candlelight on gold brocade, military boots and dainty slippers, scents of jacaranda and musk in the fevered air.

I understood her perfectly. I said, "I still don't buccaneer."

"You don't need to. You only need to be there, in port, visible. Master of a whaler with her holds full to bursting. Of course he'll invite you to his dance. Of course you'll ask to bring your chosen men: your mate and the surgeon, the specktioneer and the skeeman. A couple of likely boys you think the navy might like to look over. That's your part, all I'm asking. We'll do the rest."

I could imagine the rest. She'd be in the kitchens, with a few more men: fresh fish from the harbour, perhaps, or vegetables from the market, rum and sugar syrup from the hills, something. And all Sir Terence's guests in all their glitter, the finest jewels for a thousand miles—and no prisoners, no hostages. She wouldn't change her customs on dry land. The cream of the navy would be at that ball, all the senior officers and most of the young hopefuls; why would she ever leave them living behind her, knowing her face now and hot for revenge? They'd scour the ocean till they ran her to ground. Better to hew a hundred heads at a stroke, leave the navy and its government rudderless and adrift, leave no one to come after her.

"That's not what I signed up for," I said mildly. "I'm the cook."

"You are. And, for the moment, a man of mine." If that was a warning, it was pleasingly oblique: no threat, simply an observation of what was owed and owing. "Think about it. We'll be days here, salting that fish down."

She rose and left. I'd have stood to see her off, but Sebastian had fallen asleep with his head in my lap. For a long time once she'd gone I only sat there thinking, watching the stars wheel slowly around the sky while the moon dallied with the horizon.

Whalemeat for breakfast—of course!—with biscuit-crumbs fried in the grease. The crew gorged, men and boys together; the only one not groaning as he rose was Sebastian, and only because I'd rationed him.

"Oh, why?"

"Swimming lesson later, and I don't want you seizing up with cramps. You've eaten enough. The cap'n wants to move the *Nymph Ann* into your sea-cave first, then the *Milford* after, see if they both fit. Go climb the mainmast, see if you can touch the roof as she ducks under."

He went off happily enough, knowing that if he went up aloft on either vessel he'd be raising sails rather than fooling with the cave roof. The master was a disciplinarian with a ready rod, and the captain was probably worse; and half the men were ashore wrestling with the whale, so it'd be a lean crew managing some tricky sailwork. In honesty I thought it'd be easier to put the men in boats and tow the ships in, but there was pride at stake all around.

Pride has never been my problem. I cleaned up in the galley and then went on deck to watch the *Nymph Ann* through the cavemouth. Looked for my boy but couldn't spot him: not high in the cross-trees, he was probably hauling ropes down below. No matter. Even a vigorous swell couldn't lift the whaler anywhere near the roof; the master kept her on a perfect line and she headed slowly into ship-swallowing darkness. The *Milford* would be next, but not me. I've headed often enough into damp uncertain nights, I didn't need another. The little boats were all busy, ferrying the working crew from the *Nymph Ann* back to the *Milford*; I gave

KEEP THE ASPIDOCHELONE FLOATING

Sebastian—and everyone else, but I did hope that Sebastian at least was looking—an object lesson in the confident swimmer's entry to the water. One neat dive, down and down into the measureless ocean; I could almost see the island from its underside before the water threw me up again, up and out like a breasting dolphin, vigorous and free. I swam ashore and dried off in the sun, walking over rocks. First to the try-works just to see how the men there were coming along: to stand upwind of the seething pots and counsel care with the ladle there, count the barrels filled and sealed, count the exposed ribs of the flatulent giant carcase.

And then away, up the rising curve of the hill that was the rock that was the island; and soon enough down again, to a high cliff-edge that I sat on with my feet hanging over. And leaned down to look and no, not a cliff after all, the mouth of another great sea-cave. And I thought about that, and the stars in their slow shift last night, and the way the moon had seemed to drift on the horizon; and I was almost expecting Sebastian's hail when it came, in that way that lovers do anticipate each other. I was almost commanding it, indeed, that way that lovers can reach out in extremis.

I said, "The captain let you go, then?"

He sat contentedly at my side, swinging his bare heels above nothing: utterly trusting, utterly vulnerable, soon to be utterly betrayed. "She said the men at the try-works don't want me and nor does she, and there's no point leaving more than a watchman on an empty ship, so she sent me to find you."

"Uh-huh." He was, I guessed, my bribe or my persuader, a little of both; she held him in her gift, and offered him to me. He was ignorant but willing, sweet and savage and desirable. I was something close to desperate, even this close to the sea. Normally, properly, that's all that matters; but nothing was quite normal now.

"Go back," I said, holding my voice steady with an effort that I could only hope he was too young to hear. "Go to the captain and say I sent you, tell her this: that Sailor Martin says there's a storm in the offing and a king's ship nearby. Tell her to bring back all the men she can, and stand by. She may need to move both our vessels out to open water, but she shouldn't do it yet. Just be ready. Tell her that. You take an oar and help to ferry, get everyone aboard if you can. Tell her that we'll watch the try-works, keep the fires going, feed the pots. Just the two of us, we can manage that between us. Leave the gig with the *Milford* once you've got them all aboard, and come back with the bumboat. Then we can get to the cave when we need to, to bring word of the storm or the king's men. Tell her that."

He stood, straight and slender at my side; he stared around the long horizon; he said, "I don't see a storm. Or a ship."

I said, "Sebastian. Which of us is a green brat, and which of us has been at sea forever?"

He grinned. I waited, and soon enough I saw that smile slip as the weight of what I'd said, the reality of it sunk into his head.

I nodded. "Tell her nothing is immediate, but it'll blow up fast when it comes. She needs to be ready now. She should fetch the look-out down, if she doesn't want to maroon him. I'll keep watch. Go."

This time he went, urgent and easy, trusting me as he trusted the rock beneath his feet, as he trusted his captain too.

There was a look-out high on the mound of the hill, watching all the wide ocean. He too would have seen nothing, neither storm nor ship. That didn't worry me. He didn't have my name. The captain might flog him just on my word, that something was coming. It wouldn't be just, but no pirate looks for justice. Besides, I didn't think he stood in too much danger of her whip. I sat brooding on the brow above that sea-cave, waiting for something to show. Too long, I thought I'd waited, before at last the sea seethed and surged below me to speak Her coming. She was late, She was slow on Her own behalf. I guess it takes time, all night and half the day, for the heat of slow fires to scorch through a shell as thick as rock, as hard. Her head was as massive as a ship itself, thrusting forward like the ram of some unimaginable galley before it rose clear of the water on a neck too long, too monstrous. Her eye might have stood for the rose window of a cathedral, if those were ever glassed in black, a single untraced lens. She looked right at me; I could see myself reflected in that glossy horror, just as a diver sees his own self rising in the stillness of a pool before he breaks it.

I thought She didn't even need to eat me; Her eye would swallow me down.

KEEP THE ASPIDOCHELONE FLOATING

She'd need to be faster than this. I was already running, while She deliberated. Over the rise of Her unthinkable shell and then down, down to where smoke smudged the air, where the bumboat rocked in the water, where nobody yet knew anything. Where a figure stood waiting—and a second, rising to stand beside him. Two men, two: and neither one slim as a willow, neither one rushing to meet me…

I was coldly, painfully breathless; it took time even to gasp, "Where's Sebastian?"

"Cap'n took him. She said he's your boy, and you're cook; it's his duty to polish the ship's bell, she said, and he could do that while we all waited for you. Is it coming, then, that storm o' yourn?"

She knew, then. Not the facts or she'd have one ship out by now and be working for the other; but she knew something, not to trust me, something. She was changing her habits after all, using long-established custom to hold one boy hostage. For now, for this little time I had…

Not long enough to take the boat and row that little way, to find any useful truth to tell her. Not long enough to do anything but get there, whichever way I had.

I turned my back on the bewildered men, left them to their smoky fires and seething pots—not long!—and ran again.

Along that flange at the water's edge and up the shoulder of Her shell, to the high edge above what we had taken for a sea-cave: where our two ships lay in companionable stillness, where their crews had gathered in secrecy and darkness. Where I had sent them, to a cold destruction. Where the captain held Sebastian, but would not hold him long. One way or the other.

Straight to that high edge, and straight over.

I have dived into water so still I could see myself come at me. I have dived into the steady swell of the deep ocean, where nothing but myself disturbed the water for a thousand miles all around.

This was…not like that. Even as I went, I could see how the sea's surface bent and stretched below me like a mill-race at a sluice, as great things shifted out of sight.

Down and down I went, purposeful as a hurled knife. As I plunged through the broken surface, I felt the water's familiar grip, tight as a sleeve closing about me; but I could feel the first slow tug of dreadful currents too.

Too fast to be seized, I went down and down, as far below as I had been above; and further yet, far enough that I really could see Her underside this time, the plastron of Her shell. Clad in barnacles and weed but unmistakably floating, more like a vessel Herself than an island; and here came Her flippers, ponderously unfolding to pull Her down below the surface, to cool that fierce hot spot on Her back.

Unfolding from behind those great arches we had taken for cave-mouths, that I'd only understood late and slow, and too late now. What must it be like within the shell there, on board ship and still not understanding, knowing only that the great cliff of the cave-wall was moving, lurching forward, crushing one ship against the other and both against the inside of Her shell, heedless as a man crushing snail-shells underfoot?

What must it be like in the captain's head, thinking *he knew; Sailor Martin saw something, knew something, sent us all into the ships exactly for this, because he knew...?*

Never mind the captain; I was looking for my boy.

Either one of the ships might have been lucky, might have been popped out like a bottle from a cork—but I'd have seen the shadow of her overhead if she was, parting company from the vastness of the turtle, bobbing away. I did look, up into the brightness of the sea-sky.

No ships, no. The great broad blade of Her flipper, undelayed by whatever ruin She had wreaked on its way—and here came the first fringes of that ruin, splintered timbers and twisted ironworks, heading for the bottom. Timbers and ironwork and a boy, floundering, frantic. Sebastian, with the ship's bell on a rope around his neck, a terrible brass weight to drag him down, sounding his knell for him as he went.

The captain hadn't even bound his hands or feet: just belled him and thrown him overboard, as soon as she felt the trap close about her. Let him struggle as he would, the bell would bear him all the way, irresistible. That was a cruel touch, one last vengeful fling at me, though I ought never to have known it.

Except that I was here, and down he came towards me; and she had taken his good knife, of course, but I had mine. I caught the bell first, and severed that rope with a slashing cut; then I caught my boy.

KEEP THE ASPIDOCHELONE FLOATING

And shook him hard, and held him until he remembered his lessons, not to panic, not to flail about; and then held him and kicked for us both, kicked for the surface.

We were too deep, too short of air. Even I don't have gills, to breathe salt water; and I couldn't breathe for him. His mouth was closed yet, but his eyes were bulging; he couldn't last. And there were men in the water all around us, not all of them broken or dying yet, dead yet; and those jagged plunging timbers, those were a danger too, though the men were worse; and—

Men in the water and a woman too. Of course she'd never learned to swim, the captain; of course she had weights of her own beneath her skirts, weaponry and harness and whatever else she chose to carry against ill-chance, gold and more. Here she came, easy to know in the chaotic waters with her skirts puffed out around her like a jellyfish, like a ship's bell...

Like a bell, yes. Yes.

Easy to know, easy to reach. Poor Sebastian was dragged by his neck again, though this time it was my arm curled about him; and I dragged him below the margin of his captain's skirts and thrust him upward, past her kicking legs to where the billowing fabric still trapped a bubble of air.

Just a bubble, but enough: enough for him, for now. I held him by the body, and felt it as he gasped, as he breathed and breathed.

Then pulled him free of those entangling skirts, and didn't let him see her as she fell below us: faster now, with that last buoyancy stolen from her, dwindling into the dark. He didn't need that face in his memory, those mute curses on his mind. He barely knew what I had done there, only that I'd found him air from somewhere. Air for him. None for me, and I can't breathe water—but I can hold my breath longer than most, and think while I do it.

And look around, and see the vast bulk of the ancient turtle sliding by, and act against all obvious good sense. Tow my boy *towards* that surging shadow, not away. Perhaps he thought that I was mad at last, mad for lack of air perhaps; he tried to kick against me, to pull me back.

He had no chance of that. I took a tougher grip and towed him on, into the currents of Her passage. Turtles use their front flippers to drive them forward. Their back feet do quieter work, acting as vanes against the water. I wouldn't have risked this if She was coming at us, but that lethal front flipper was past already. Besides, we were committed now, caught in the turbulent suck of the water She threw back. Rolled over and tossed about, I clung and kicked and maybe prayed a little; and saw what I was looking for, a break in a mighty wall, a gateway not quite blocked by the massive limb protruding through it...

You can trap air in a skirt, until it leaks out in a thousand streams of bubbles. You can trap air in a bell, and it won't leak; make a bell big enough, you can lower a man to the sea-bed and have him breathing all the way. How much air can you trap in a cave, if your island takes a dive? Enough, there'll be enough.

I hauled Sebastian in, and the water flung us up, and there was air; and even a hint of light, that same phosphorescence that had clung to the whale. Enough to show that we floated in a chamber where half the wall was rigid shell and half was shifting leather, the obscene leg of the thing. It looked like seamed rock, but no rock ever moved with such purpose, this way and that like the rudder of a ship under steerage-weigh.

Everything about Her was slow and mighty; She had no reason to heed us little things. I helped Sebastian pull himself out of the water, up onto a ledge of Her leg, and found just strength enough to follow. Then we lay against each other and only breathed awhile, painfully, gratefully.

When he spoke at last, his voice sounded strange in that strange space, distant and muffled and hollow all three. He said, "We, we're inside it. Aren't we?"

"Her," I said. All ships, all whales. All giant turtles, seemingly. It felt right. "I suppose we are."

"Like Jonah."

"Something like Jonah. Not swallowed, though."

He thought about that, then said, "What happens now?"

I didn't know, but lying's easy in the dark. I said, "She won't stay down long. When She rises, we'll go out and see where we are, who's about. There'll be someone to signal, or land we can reach. We'll be famous, shipwrecked mariners who survived Leviathan, like St Brendan survived Jasconius."

His head was on my thigh, wet and warm and welcome. He sounded sleepy, like a child; he said, "You're famous already."

KEEP THE ASPIDOCHELONE FLOATING

"I am, I suppose. Not for anything particularly praiseworthy. Just for surviving, mostly; and here I am again. Doing that. And here you are, doing it right alongside me."

"I'll be a part of your story." No self-deception there. The fact of it, the act of it, the being with me: that could only ever be temporary, in the nature of the thing. He knew. But the story of it, that goes on for ever.

"You will," I said, toying fondly with his ear. "And you'll tell it yourself, to Sir Terence Digby yet; he'll invite us to his ball, and we'll dress up fine and dance all night," and take no prisoners and do no harm and perhaps Sir Terence could find a berth for him, some other life that he could love, not buccaneering. And perhaps I'd be there with him for a while, be a part of his story, however briefly told. "It'll be a masked ball, naturally. You can go as a pirate boy, you'll like that. Yo ho," I said, "Sebastian."

THE CONTRIBUTORS

LAIRD BARRON is the author of several books, including *The Imago Sequence*, *Occultation*, and *The Croning*. His work has appeared in many magazines and anthologies. An expatriate Alaskan, Barron currently resides in Upstate New York.

RICHARD BOWES has won two World Fantasy, an International Horror Guild and Million Writer Awards. His new novel, *Dust Devil on a Quiet Street*, will appear in July 2013 from Lethe Press, which will also republish his Lambda Award-winning novel *Minions of the Moon*. Recent and forthcoming appearances include: *F&SF*, *Icarus*, *Lightspeed* and the anthologies *After*, *Wilde Stories 2012*, *Bloody Fabulous*, *Ghosts: Recent Hauntings*, *Handsome Devil*, *Hauntings* and *Where Thy Dark Eye Glances*.

CHAZ BRENCHLEY has been making a living as a writer since the age of eighteen. He is the author of nine thrillers and several fantasy series, under the names of Daniel Fox and Ben Macallan as well as his own. Chaz has recently moved from Newcastle to California, with two squabbling cats and a famous teddy bear.

RAY CLULEY has been published several times in the TTA Press publication *Black Static*. One of these stories was selected by Ellen Datlow for *The Best Horror of the Year*, Volume 3, and another was republished as a French translation in the annual anthology *Tènébres 2011*. He has also been published in *Interzone*. His non-fiction has been published in the British Fantasy Society's journal but generally he prefers to make stuff up. You can find out more at probablymonsters.wordpress.com.

Hal Duncan's *Vellum* was nominated for the World Fantasy Award, and won the Spectrum, Kurd Lasswitz and Tähtivaeltaja. Along with the sequel, *Ink*, other publications include a novella, *Escape from Hell!*, a chapbook, *An A-Z of the Fantastic City*, and a poetry collection, *Songs for the Devil and Death*, with a collection of short fiction forthcoming from Lethe Press. He wrote the lyrics for Aereogramme's "If You Love Me, You'd Destroy Me" and the musical *Nowhere Town*. Homophobic hatemail once dubbed him "The.... Sodomite Hal Duncan!!" (sic.) You can find him online at halduncan.com, glorying in that infamy.

K. M. Ferebee has worked as a laundry maid, subway musician, and household assistant. (She also used to play in a Balkan rock band.) Her short fiction has appeared or is forthcoming in *Lady Churchill's Rosebud Wristlet*, *Not One of Us*, and *Shimmer*.

Alex Jeffers (sentenceandparagraph.com) published seven stories in 2012, a personal record, and 2013 is looking pretty good so far. His books are *Safe as Houses*, a full-length novel; *Do You Remember Tulum?* and *The New People*, two short novels; *The Abode of Bliss*, a novel-length story sequence; *You Will Meet a Stranger Far from Home*, a collection of wonder stories; and, this year, *Deprivation; or, Benedetto furioso: an oneiromancy*.

Rahul Kanakia is a science fiction writer who has sold stories to *Clarkesworld*, the *Intergalactic Medicine Show*, *Apex*, *Nature*, and *Lady Churchill's Rosebud Wristlet*. He currently lives in Baltimore, where he is enrolled in the Master of the Fine Arts program in creative writing at Johns Hopkins University. He graduated from Stanford in 2008 with a B.A. in Economics and he used to work as an international development consultant. If you want to know more about him then please visit his blog at blotter-paper.com/ or follow him on Twitter at twitter.com/rahkan.

Vincent Kovar is a writer, teacher and editor living in Seattle, WA. Currently, he is editor and curator of Gay City Anthologies and a college professor at Antioch University Seattle and Everett Community College. His recent work can be found in *The Touch of the Sea* from Lethe Press (ed. Steve Berman) and *Tales of the New Mexico Mythos: Weird Fiction from the Land of Enchantment* (ed. Paul Bustamonte).

John Langan's new collection of stories, *Technicolor and Other Revelations*, is forthcoming from Hippocampus; the title story was in the second *The Best Horror of the Year* (Datlow, ed.), "The City of the Dog" and "The Revel" in the third, "In Paris, in the Month of Kronos" in the fourth, and "The Wide, Carnivorous Sky" in the 2010 *The Year's Best Fantasy and Horror* (Guran, ed.). His first collection, *Mr. Gaunt and Other Uneasy Encounters*, was a Stoker finalist. He has stories appearing recently in *Fungi* (Grey and Moreno-Garcia, eds.), *Black Wings II* (Joshi, ed.), *A Season in Carcosa* (Pulver, ed.), and *Postscripts*. He has written a novel, *House of Windows*; a second, *The Fisherman*, is in progress. With Paul Tremblay, he edited *Creatures: Thirty Years of Monsters*.

L Lark (l-lark.com) is a writer and visual artist currently living in South Florida, a place with its own fair share of monster sightings. Links to her projects, publications, and blog can be found on her website. Her favorite summer activity is watching thunderstorms form over the Everglades.

Steve Vernon is a storyteller-born with a campfire embering at his feet. He's written ghost story collections such as *Haunted Harbours* and *The Lunenburg Werewold*—as well writing close to a hundred short stories that have appeared in such venues as *Cemetery Dance* magazine, the *Hot Blood* series and Tor's *Year's Best Horror*. These days he was working the digital field—writing a continuing serial called *Flash Virus*.

THE EDITOR

Steve Berman writes way too little fiction but does manage to edit at least one anthology every year so his feline companion, Daulton, can be kept content with daily meals of rotisserie chicken. The *Wilde Stories* annual series has twice been a finalist for the Lambda Literary Award, which pleases Steve because he does have a great love for queer speculative fiction. He resides in southern New Jersey, the only state in the Union with an official devil.

FICTION
FIC WILDE
Berman, Steve